D0456436

"Grant, I met you only two days ago. Do you know how jolting it is to be simply—"

"Simply what?"

Her arms were around his neck, and their faces were too close for her to look away. "Simply swept off your feet," she finished softly.

"Why couldn't you tell me?"

"Grant." She laughed. He was so unrelenting in his directness. "What did you want me to do? Fall into your arms?"

"Yes. I'd have caught you," he said, tightening his embrace, as his half-closed eyes held hers.

Oh God, Ashley, what are you doing? she thought as she relaxed in his arms, returning the passion in his gaze . . .

ONLY 'TIL DAWN

by Esther Sager

author of CHASING RAINBOWS

By Esther Sager
from Jove

CHASING RAINBOWS
ONLY 'TIL DAWN

Only 'Til Dawn

ESTHER SAGER

A JOVE BOOK

ONLY 'TIL DAWN

A Jove Book / published by arrangement with
the author

PRINTING HISTORY
Jove edition / June 1982

All rights reserved.
Copyright © 1982 by Esther Sager
This book may not be reproduced in whole or in part,
by mimeograph or any other means, without permission.
For information address: Jove Publications, Inc.,
200 Madison Avenue, New York, N. Y. 10016.

ISBN: 0-515-05850-5

Jove books are published by Jove Publications, Inc.,
200 Madison Avenue, New York, N. Y. 10016. The words
"A JOVE BOOK" and the "J" with sunburst are trademarks
belonging to Jove Publications, Inc.

PRINTED IN THE UNITED STATES OF AMERICA

Only 'Til Dawn

PROLOGUE

THE SINGLE BRASS lamp above the hospital bed threw a cone of light down onto the still figure lying beneath the white sheets, making the look of death about the inert body even starker than it was. Death screamed into the silence of the sterile room, and sliced like a rapier into the heart of Ashley Welles as she sat in a narrow, metal straight chair by the bed, watching her brother die.

It was eight o'clock in the evening, on a Thursday, and the nurse had just left after making the hushed hourly check of her patient. Ashley hadn't left during the nurse's visit but had remained in the chair where she'd been seated for two and a half hours. Ashley was a tall woman, and after sitting for so long in the uncomfortable chair, her long legs crossed at the knees were stiff and her back hurt. Yet she ignored her discomfort. It was so insignificant when compared to the agony of what was happening here, to her brother, to her own life, that it became meaningless. She did change position slightly but never once took her despairing eyes from the bed.

Just then, he made a movement. His fingers shifted against the starched sheet a fraction of an inch, and Ashley sat forward immediately, taking her brother's slender hand in both her own. "Grif?" she said softly.

Griffith Welles was twenty, six years younger than Ashley, but he looked eighty years old to her as he lay on his back with his sunken eyes closed, his disease-ravaged body skeletal, his shock of bright red hair all but gone now after the radiation and chemotherapy treatments. The machines that had kept him miserably alive for so long were useless now, and the only attachment left on him was a tube in his left arm drifting down from a glucose IV hanging on the wall above the bed.

"Can you hear me, Grif?" Ashley asked more loudly, and tears pooled in her violet eyes as she watched her brother's own pain-filled eyes finally open slowly, halfway.

"Mom?" he breathed, turning his head toward her.

"No, honey. It's me. Ashley," she said with a catch in her voice, her tears spilling onto her cheeks at the sight of his faintly hopeful expression. Their parents had been dead for years, and the two of them had been raised by an aunt and uncle. Grif was no longer lucid enough to remember that. "It's Ashley," she repeated.

"Is Mom gone?" he asked plaintively.

"Grif, just rest," she told him tenderly, reaching over to soothe his brow, and as she did so, the sleeve of her sweater brushed against his gaunt cheekbone. She was still dressed from work, in a navy wool kilt, fashionable white silk blouse, and green cardigan; she'd come here to Memorial Sloan-Kettering Cancer Center directly from her office in midtown New York City, as she'd done faithfully every day since Grif had deteriorated to the point of having to be put in the hospital four months ago. She had on her black boots, for the metropolitan area was being lightly dusted with a late March snow, and she glanced briefly to the window; the white flakes were still falling against the glass, visible in the glaring light from the parking lot pole lamps.

"Ashley?"

She quickly looked back to Grif. He was as motionless as always, but his blue eyes had widened, and there was a sudden clearness in them. "I'm here," she assured, giving her warmest smile to his recognition of her; in the last two weeks, he hadn't always known who she was.

"Ashley, help me," he whispered fearfully.

Ashley closed her mouth on the jagged cry his plea brought to her throat, and the tears that had come to be part of her everyday life now quickened, coursing rapidly down her face. She'd spent her life since she was thirteen years old doing everything she could to help him, looking after him, loving him—as sister for brother, mother for son almost—but there was nothing she could do this time. Not for this. There was no way for her to ease the suffering that even morphine could no longer dull or to breathe new life into him so that he could once again be the robust, good-looking, sensitive young man who'd wanted more than anything in the world to be an architect. That dream was lost to him now, but at least he'd had a chance to taste it with one year in college, paid for by Ashley's hard work, before his devastating illness had struck him down. "Grif, I'm here," was all she could answer, her voice breaking.

Griffith's fear of whatever shadows he was seeing was still in his eyes, and he looked up at her. "Hold my hand."

"I am."

"Hold my other one. Please?"

Ashley reached across him and too¹ his right hand, bringing it over his fragile body as she held onto it tightly. "I've got them, Grif," she said softly.

"Promise you won't let go?"

"I promise."

The tension around his colorless lips eased, and Ashley saw that he'd begun to smile all of a sudden, a faraway smile that just slightly curved the corners of his mouth as he looked up toward the ceiling. "Remember how we used to play in the creek?" he asked.

Ashley's whole body went cold. She'd heard it said that clarity sometimes comes back just before death, that in the last moments of life a person often had a clear recollection of long-ago, nearly forgotten events. A sob escaped her but she swallowed the next one, resolutely. She'd been preparing herself for this time for months, and now that it had come, she would do her best to give him what he needed, help him go with whatever peace he could find. "Of course," she answered, forcing herself to tilt her head pertly. "How could I forget? You were always pushing me in."

"There were fish there, minnows. They slithered when they swam. When you tried to catch them, they slid out of your fingers."

"I know, Grif. I know." Ashley's eyes were brimming with tears again as she heard his shallow breathing; she knew by heart every sound he made, and there was a new one, faint, brittle, horrifying. It was a rattle in his respiration. "Do you . . . do you remember the time the foxes got into our barn?" she asked with painful brightness.

He was still watching the ceiling. "They were possums."

So, he did remember; they'd been having this argument for years. Ashley didn't really want to talk about it, because the recollection of all the good times they'd had together hurt now: Ashley the tomboy who'd loved the outdoor life with the same passion her brother did, who'd been able to ride and pitch softballs with the best of them, and who'd even learned to shoot; Grif, the strong, younger brother who'd enjoyed his sister's spirited company, who'd teased her yet always needed her womanly, compassionate presence in his life on the Pennsylvania farm of their aunt and uncle, Brett and Georgia Welles. Someday maybe she would be able to savor the memories, to hold onto them for comfort, but here, in this cold, tiled, barren room, they cut.

"No, they weren't possums," Ashley objected in a gentle voice, summoning up from God knew where the fortitude to smile again and continue the ridiculous argument. "They were foxes, two of them. They hid back in the hay, and you wanted to run them out but I wouldn't let you."

Grif's small rally of strength seemed to be fading. His smile drifted away, and he sighed once. "Foxes don't waddle," he said, as he had so many other times.

"Well, they were fat foxes."

Grif dragged his eyes from the ceiling then, turning his head toward her on the pillow. "You're going to be all alone," he said abruptly.

Ashley felt as if she'd been hit in the chest and couldn't answer directly. "Grif, you should rest," she said, swallowing hard.

"Will you be all right?"

His expression of frail worry for her, the vestiges of his brotherly protectiveness even as he lay dying, were more than Ashley could take, and she had to look away. She stared at the sparse furnishings around the room, at the fresh bouquet of carnations she'd brought to him that evening, and drew several deep breaths.

"Ashley?"

"What?" she asked softly, pressing her lips together as she turned back to him.

"I love you."

Her tears were drawn again instantly, stinging her eyes as they dropped down on her cheeks. "I love you, too, Griffith," she said in a strangled voice.

They looked at each other, and Ashley saw the good-bye that, like the flicker of candlelight, passed fleetingly across Grif's eyes before they widened again, then glazed over. Her own eyes widened as a sob wrenched from her, and she wanted to scream, to get up and run to the door, jerk it open and shout uselessly for the doctor, but she couldn't leave him. She couldn't give up these last few precious moments of his still being with her. But more than that, she had promised she would hold his hands.

And she did until he died.

PART I

Three Years Later

There is no such thing as chance;
And what to us seems merest accident
Springs from the deepest source of destiny

Johann Christoph Friedrich von Schiller

Chapter 1

ASHLEY WAS STUNNED when her car ran off the road.

Up until then, at that point on U.S. 66 just beyond the sign marking the official end of Flagstaff's city limits, she'd been doing fine. The headlights of her silver Datsun had been penetrating the curtain of heavy snow coming at them head-on, allowing her passable visibility to the road ahead, and the narrow tires of the automobile had plowed steadily through the deepening cover of snow on the four-lane road. On the far side of that highway sign, however, the situation changed abruptly. The wheels lost traction at the same time the wind picked up; a powerful gust buffeted them, blowing the snow in a blinding sheet across the windshield. The car went into a skid. It fishtailed once, twice, then went out of control completely, sliding sideways all the way to the right for what seemed an agonizing eternity until it came to a sudden, dead standstill—on the shoulder of the road, she hoped. The engine ran for an instant longer, then sputtered and died.

For a moment, Ashley remained just as she was—rigid in the driver's seat, her hands gripping the steering wheel—then, as relief that she and the small car had managed to land on their feet surged through her, she flopped back against the bucket seat with an audible sigh. She'd left Phoenix several hours before in her friend Margaret Chapman's car, completely unaware of the weather situation farther north. She'd run into the first signs of snow a ways back but, not particularly disturbed by them, had pressed on. If she'd had any idea, however, just how fierce this winter storm was soon going to become, she'd have decided differently with those first snowflakes and pulled off at a motel, leaving until tomorrow the thirty-mile drive remaining to Margaret's cabin in the mountains north of Flagstaff.

"Hindsight, Ashley," she said as she cast a rueful glance at herself in the rearview mirror. "Always so crystal clear."

The brutal cold was beginning to insinuate itself into the warmth of the stalled car, and Ashley reached over to pick up

3

her gloves lying on top of her only traveling companion: the well-worn leather overnight case she'd been carrying on short trips since college days. Fully recovered at this point from the momentary terror of the skid, she began to feel the flutterings of annoyance at her sudden predicament—of all things to have happen! There was nothing for her to do at this point, however, but get out and take stock of the situation. With a resolute sigh, she looked again into the rearview mirror as she settled her ski cap firmly down around her ears, looped her scarf several times around her neck, then pulled on her gloves.

She opened the car door, after battling briefly with it against the wind, and stepped out into a whistling, white oblivion. Holding onto the door handle for balance, she first checked her rented skis, fastened onto the roof rack, then made her way with difficulty around to the back of the car. At the right rear wheel, she stopped but didn't bother to lean down to check the extent of the problem; she didn't have to take a closer look. It was plain that the tire was mired well up past its rim in a bank of snow, and judging by the angle of the car, she knew the front tire was the same. She bit her lip. There was no deluding herself that she could get out of this dilemma by her own devices, and after a moment more of morosely eyeing the snowbound tire, she transferred her gaze out to the distance behind her, looking for some sign of what was now her only hope: another car, another driver. Another *anything* that was living or breathing in the desolation of what was fast developing into blizzard.

There was nothing; all around her there was only the darkness and the curtain of driving snow, pelting her face, singing against the sway of ponderosa pines somewhere off to the right of her and beyond the road. And there was no road really—only the endless white, obliterating any evidence of man's asphalt trespass across this rugged countryside that had gone so momentarily, and effortlessly, back to nature.

She couldn't stay out there any longer; the cold was gnawing at her hands and feet even through gloves and boots. Pulling her scarf up to shield her wind-bitten cheeks, she made her way around to the car door again and got back in. After a moment of trying the key in the ignition, the engine caught, and she switched the heater up to high. There was enough gasoline to last for a little while, if she used it sparingly, she thought as she glanced at the gauge; there might be a blanket in the trunk, but she didn't know. She hadn't thought to look. Her watch read nine thirty, and as she huddled down in the seat, marking time until nine thirty-five when she'd shut off the engine again and check once more to make sure the tailpipe was free of snow, she wondered how long it would be before Margaret would start to worry. How long before Margaret, who was the only one who would realize where she probably was at this moment, would get worried enough to sound an alarm to the rescue patrols that Ashley hoped were being sent out on the roads? How long before the cruel winter on this deserted stretch of highway might just possibly take to itself a solitary human life.

"Pull up over here!" The Arizona State policeman shouted into the wind, clutching his hat with one hand and waving with the other as he motioned the driver of the Bronco jeep to stop at a spot directly under the awning of the Saguaro Motel. The vehicle pulled up, discharging its cargo of passengers: two men, a woman, and a young boy huddled in their overcoats and carrying suitcases. As they made a run for the motel door, the driver shut off the engine, then swung out; he was a tall man wearing faded denims, tan sheepskin coat, Western boots, and a Stetson that nearly got lost to a sudden gust. Catching the brim with one hand, he rounded the front of the jeep and sprinted to where the trooper stood in the partial shelter of the awning.

"That's the last of them on Seventeen, Frank." Grant Copeland also had to shout to be heard over the storm.

In response, the policeman motioned toward the door. They moved inside, and though it seemed relatively silent there after the high wind outside, the noise level was far above normal; stranded travelers were milling around the motel lobby, grouped around the desk signing the register, chattering, trading harrowing tales of their ordeals. The chief of Highway Police, Frank Mehan, glanced briefly around the crowded room, then back to Grant. "We've got two cars left out on Sixty-six East. They've picked up their limit and just radioed that they've spotted a stranded car westbound. A station wagon."

Grant took off his Stetson and ran a hand through his damp hair. "Were they going to go back for it?" he asked.

"No. I guess I'll send Whitford after them."

"I'll go," Grant said immediately. "It's on my way home,

and I can drop them at the Aspen Motel. That's the only other car?"

"Christ, I hope so. Another half hour and everything'll be shut down. Even the trucks won't be able to move." Frank lit a cigarette and flipped the match into an ashcan by the doorway. He peered outside for a moment through the double glass doors. "You know, it's been twenty years since I've seen a storm like this, one that came up so fast and angry. And it's not gonna quit anytime soon, either."

Grant's eyes followed the other man's gaze. "No, you can count on that." He seemed lost in thought as he watched a film of white already beginning to gather again on the hood of his jeep, then abruptly came to and replaced his hat. "Well, I'd better get moving. I'm going back to Coconino after this pickup. Call me there if you need me."

"Okay. And Grant . . ." Frank waited for the other man to turn and look back to him, then smiled tiredly. "Thanks. You don't have to be doing this."

Grant gave him an easy smile of his own. "I know," he said and strode out the door.

Frank watched him go, then searched the motel lobby for his associate, Bill Whitford. When he spied him, he signaled, stubbing out his cigarette just as the younger patrolman joined him. "Come on," Frank said. "We're going to take a last run along the canyon road. That's about all we can do."

"Thought you wanted me to go after that wagon on Sixty-six."

"Grant Copeland is taking care of that," Frank said. "He's gonna drive the folks on up to the Aspen Motel."

Whitford glanced out the door in time to see the taillights of the green Bronco disappearing into the blackness; he cocked an eyebrow. "Funny a man like him coming out on a night like this to help."

"Whitford, you're new around here. You've got a lot to learn." Frank settled his own hat back on his head and pulled up the collar of his thermal windbreaker. "Grant Copeland stands for a lot in this neighborhood."

"Yeah, like money," Bill muttered.

"Like help when you need it. Come on. Let's go."

"Oh, this is so exciting! Just think of it, Dwight, stranded in a blizzard! Did you ever imagine such a thing would happen to us when we left Tucson, that we'd have such an adventure?"

Nora Bonnard brushed at her mousy brown hair and took time from her steady stream of conversation to glance briefly at her husband. His thin face was shadowed in the darkness of the jeep, wire-rims in place on the bridge of his nose, and unlike Nora, he looked ten years older than their age of thirty-five. Overweight had so far spared Nora the onset of any marked age lines, that and her perennial interest in everything that was beyond the limited scope of her own housewife's existence. They were settled in the back seat, she, Dwight, and five suitcases, and she looked back finally at Grant Copeland, barely able to make out the profile of the man who'd been their rescuer. He'd spoken only when he'd had to—though politely enough—since they'd left the Bonnards' family station wagon some distance back on the side of the highway. Her delight with the circumstances made her unconscious of the fact that the treacherous driving required enormous concentration and might be the reason for Grant Copeland's reticence; she tried him one more time.

"Don't you think it's just beautiful outside? I do. I've always loved snow, though we don't get any, of course, in Tucson. We don't get much of anything in Tucson, you know? We have six children, did I tell you that? Skippy would go wild. He's our son, the rest are girls. And all blonds, like their father. He just loves snow, too. Skip, I mean. He went sledding once, when we were up visiting my Aunt Thelma. Well, Skippy isn't really his name. We just call him that. His real name is Russell. Do you live near here, Mr. Kaplan?"

Grant eyed the rearview mirror and stifled a smile. "Copeland."

"Copeland! Oh, *Cope*land, *Cope*land." Nora shook her head in acknowledgement of the correction. "What nationality is that?"

"Just call me Grant." He kept his deep voice even and his eyes on the road, or at least on where the road was supposed to be. Nora Bonnard's persistent drone faded from his hearing as he leveled every sense on keeping the jeep steady in the sudden gusts of wind; he knew these roads well and they were coming to a bad stretch, one that held the ice tenaciously. He continued to keep his attention forward, finally making out the highway sign looming up in the near distance. And something else beyond.

". . . and I'm going to tell her so, too, Dwight." Nora's

petulant voice seeped back into Grant's consciousness. "Just see if I don't. I get tired of her telling me the most exciting thing I've ever done is hang the wash out on the line!"

"Nora . . ." Dwight Bonnard was leaning up against the back door in his tweed coat, which was too thin for this weather.

"Oh, look! There goes Flagstaff." She was pressing her face against the back side window as she squinted into the darkness, and it sounded to Grant as if she were happily counting off properties on a Monopoly board. "We just passed it and something that . . . looks like—"

"A car." Grant brusquely finished the sentence for her; he'd seen the automobile also and was already edging over toward the shoulder of the road. He hadn't been able to distinguish what make of car it was, and when he finally brought the jeep to a standstill, they were some distance beyond the car. He cut the jeep's engine and looked over his shoulder, directly at his passengers for the first time. "Stay here. Dwight, if I need help, I'll signal. Otherwise, don't get out." He looked straight at Nora.

She smiled widely and Grant shifted back around, briefly bracing himself before unlatching the door. He swung it open finally and stepped out into the storm, breaking into a dog-trot as he headed back in the direction they'd come. He'd stopped the jeep farther up the road than he'd realized, and as he made his way through the driving snow, he'd even begun to wonder if there *was* another car—until it finally came into view, and he was able to identify it clearly.

It was a small, silver Datsun, securely wedged into a bank of snow.

Chapter 2

ASHLEY SAT CLOSE to the car door in the front seat of the Bronco beside Grant Copeland. She'd been riding in the jeep for nearly fifteen minutes, and when Nora Bonnard asked for the third time if Ashley hadn't found the fright of being stranded out on the road "absolutely exhilarating," Ashley finally gave in and answered the query directly.

"No, I would hardly call it exhilarating. It was more aggravating than anything else," she said in her clear contralto and turned her gaze toward the side window.

Ashley knew she shouldn't be feeling annoyed. After all, she'd just been rescued from a very unpleasant situation. Grant Copeland, upon hustling her out of her car and back to his jeep, had been quick to reassure her that she'd be able to reclaim her automobile and skis from Selby's Garage in Flagstaff just as soon as the roads were cleared and the vehicles towed in, so she'd dismissed that source of worry. And the interior of the Bronco was infinitely warmer than the inside of the Datsun had become after her hour of waiting in it. Under the circumstances, she had no possible reason for complaint.

Yet, she was feeling aggrieved. Her vexation with the fact that she'd been waylaid from her visit to Margaret's was compounded by Nora Bonnard's nonstop interrogation. Ashley had been doing her best to tactfully deflect the personal inquiries she found to be so intrusive, but at this last inane question, her patience had snapped.

Grant was carefully watching the road ahead, but at Ashley's remark he shot her a look of interest; he'd been doing that each time she sidestepped one of Nora's questions. But her straightforward reply now seemed to spur the woman on even more. "Do you have children?" she persisted.

Ashley frowned sharply but forced herself to resume a pleasant tone. "Children? You and Dwight have six, didn't you say? How do you manage?"

Grant gave Ashley another look as Nora launched into the

effusive response Ashley had hoped for, then he slipped the jeep into a lower gear. Driving had become nearly impossible, and the wind was pulling at the steering wheel under his hands. When a brief lull came in Nora's monologue, he finally voiced what had been on his mind for minutes now. "We can't make it to the motel. It's too far, and the roads are too slick. We're going to stop at my home."

Ashley looked at him quickly, feeling an immediate stab of dismay. "But how much farther is the motel?" she asked worriedly. "The Aspen, you called it?"

"Four miles."

"Four miles isn't all that far," she said, quickly smiling to mask the objection.

"In this kind of weather, one mile is very far." Grant glanced at her briefly. "Coconino is just ahead."

Nora's interested voice filtered up from the back seat. "Coconino?"

"My ranch."

Ashley was still watching Grant. It was difficult to see his face because of the darkness; too, his Stetson was angled down over his forehead, and the woolly collar of his coat was hiked up around his neck, leaving to view only a straight nose and wide-set eyes, the partial plane of a square jaw. She could tell by his set expression that to argue any further about where they would be stopping was futile, and her frown deepened. She thought for a moment, lightly touching a finger to her lip as she contemplated how best to elicit a point of information she very much wanted, and finally settled on commenting, "I hope your wife won't mind having uninvited guests tonight."

They'd left the highway sometime before and had been traveling along a secondary road. Grant maneuvered the jeep into a righthand turnoff, heading them through a break in the pines down what was barely recognizable as a lane. "I don't have a wife," he answered easily. "But if I did, I'd like to think she'd welcome into her home anyone unfortunate enough to have been caught out on the road in bad weather, short notice or not."

Ashley smiled faintly, but her heart sank even more at his disclosure, and she looked away from him and back out the window to where only the curtain of snow was visible. For a time she was lost to her unquiet thoughts, unconscious of Nora's renewed spate of conversation. She came to finally at

the sound of Dwight's voice, at what she suspected was his
usual tone of resigned exasperation.

"Nora . . ."

"Well, I'm only interested." Nora broke off her questioning of Grant to give Dwight a look, then turned back to the
man in the front seat. "I just wish we could *see* something!
The snow is so thick. I've never been on a ranch before.
Have you, Ashley?"

"I—"

Ashley wasn't about to answer that question, but this time
for a reason that went far beyond simple annoyance. She
could come up with no oblique answer off the top of her
head and spoke quickly to Grant instead. "Is it much farther?" she asked, forcing an inquiring smile.

Grant was gearing down as a long porch appeared ahead
out of nowhere. "We're here," he answered.

Nora peered out the window. She could just barely make
out the longish building. The porch was low, columned with
narrow square beams, and she could just see a slatted bench
placed under a window through which a light was shining.
"Do you have horses?" she inquired.

"Quarter horses," Grant replied.

"Is there a bunk house?"

'Nora, for God's sake!'' Dwight rubbed his forehead, leaving his fingertips pressed briefly to the points of his eyebrows
before dropping his hand wearily.

"Yes, as a matter of fact, there is."

Grant brought the jeep to a standstill directly in front of the
house, and as she glanced at him again, Ashley saw that he
was smiling; it had to be because of the pair in the back, she
decided, and couldn't help a fleeting smile of her own at the
Bonnards' interplay. Her humor was short-lived, however, in
the face of her aggravation that circumstances had gone so far
beyond her control, and when one of Nora's five suitcases
grazed the back of her head on its way by, it was the last
straw. She looked out at the desolate expanse of white, at the
ranch house where she would be forced to spend the night,
and her moodiness became more than she could politely
contain. She vented it abruptly on her benefactor. "What are
you anyway, some kind of cowboy?" she asked Grant with a
testy frown.

Grant's hand was on the door handle; as the couple in the

back started to get out, he turned toward Ashley, for the first time giving her a straight look. And then he began to laugh.

Coconino was a compact but spacious ranch house with a main, cathedral-ceilinged living room from which two single-story wings spanned out on either side. An Indian houseman dressed in jeans and Western shirt greeted the group at the door, was introduced as Michael Redchief, and after a word from Grant, immediately led the unanticipated guests through the central room and down the wide corridor to the left.

Ashley's quarters turned out to be the last of three spare rooms; the Bonnards would be next door. Thanking the wiry Indian at her bedroom door, she set down her suitcase just inside and stood for a moment looking around.

The decor of the room, like the rest of the house she'd seen so far, was rustic and warm; the walls were white stucco and the wide-planked floor was strewn with colorful woven rugs of Indian design. Across the simple wooden bed was a thick sheepskin, the heavy drapes at the windows were of some unbleached fabric, and the single bureau and night tables were unvarnished pine. Set up against the foot of the bed was a low dowry chest, and Ashley crossed to it, sat down heavily on one edge, and let out a long sigh.

She just couldn't believe that fate had dropped her into this kind of situation a second time—stranded overnight in the company of an unmarried man—and as she sat with her elbow propped on her leg, forehead in hand, she vividly recalled the earlier incident. It had happened during a sailing trip a year or so ago, with Doris and Everett Penry and their bachelor friend, Blair Phelps. They'd gone out on the Penrys' yacht just for the day—a casual excursion Ashley had agreed to join, just to fill a few of her too many free hours—but the boat had developed engine trouble late in the afternoon; they'd been forced to remain on the bay overnight before the problem could be fixed, and though Blair Phelps had never even hinted at anything improper, for her there'd been a trying aftermath, as if some blatant indiscretion had occurred. She frowned unhappily toward the floor as she remembered and remained sitting disconsolately on the chest for almost fifteen minutes before glancing up and catching sight of herself in the dresser mirror. She still had on her coat, cap, and scarf, and she stared at her reflection in the glass. "Damn!"

"Something is unsatisfactory?"

Michael Redchief stood in the doorway, looking at her questioningly. Ashley was momentarily too taken aback to speak, then shook her head, embarrassed. "No. Of course not," she said with a self-conscious smile.

"Mr. Copeland wishes you to know there will be a late meal, if you're hungry. Marina is serving it now."

Ashley briefly studied the thin man with the high cheekbones and jet black hair, judging him to be near her own age of thirty. "Thank you for relaying the message, but I'm not hungry," she said, not entirely truthfully. The thought of food was appealing, but more of Nora's voluble company was not. "I'll have coffee or something later," she added.

Michael Redchief nodded. "Mr. Copeland also said you should feel free to hang your clothing in the closet," he went on. "It's there." He gestured toward a narrow paneled door at the left of the bureau.

Ashley glanced at the closet, then back to Michael. "Thank Mr. Copeland for me, but that's not necessary," she said, smiling again. "I'm only going to be here one night. I'll be leaving in the morning."

Michael's teeth were a white gleam against his dark skin as he smiled broadly. "No, ma'am. It's coming off the San Franciscos." With that pronouncement, he left.

Ashley stood staring after him, her eyes widened in horror. "No, ma'am," he'd said. What did that mean? She knew, really, exactly what that meant, that he thought she'd be stranded here for longer than simply overnight. Days, possibly? At that prospect, she turned abruptly, shed coat, cap, and scarf, flinging them onto the bed in an unhappy agitation that had suddenly multiplied a hundredfold. She paced the room twice, her brow knit in worried thought, going into, then out of the tile bathroom, and she finally stopped in front of the mirror again. This time, however, she didn't even see the dark-haired, willowy woman dressed in a fashionable silk blouse and black wool pleated trousers that was reflected there, nor did she consciously register the look of decision that passed over her face. She hurriedly ran her fingers through her hair, straightening it, then walked briskly from the room.

Nora Bonnard was talking enthusiastically to Marina in the dining room. The slender Indian woman—Michael's wife— smiled now and then in vague response as she served cold ham, salad, biscuits, and coffee to the couple seated opposite

one another at one end of the long refectory table. Grant
leaned against the doorframe, highball in hand, watching.
He suppressed a smile at Marina's efforts to field the onslaught
of questions with her characteristic silence, and at the sound
of staccato footsteps coming from the main room, he turned.

Ashley had just entered and stopped in the center of the
square room, her determined air dissolving to one of uncertainty as she discovered herself to be alone. Grant straightened away from the doorway to the dining room but didn't
move immediately as he took the opportunity to study her.

A strikingly attractive woman, somewhere in her late twenties, he thought. Her black hair was cut short, brushed casually away from her narrow face, and she had distinct, well-cut
features, but with a certain softness to them and around the
corners of her mouth, though that mouth was set at the
moment in a firm line. Her eyes were expressively large and
outlined with dark lashes. Her looks were arresting, certainly,
but after another moment of appraisal, he decided that it was
her bearing more than anything else that struck him so. She
was very slender, quite tall, with an erect, confident carriage,
and after searching his mind for a word to accurately describe
her figure, Grant came up with one: statuesque.

He stepped into the living room. "May I get you a drink?"
he inquired pleasantly.

Ashley turned at the sound of his voice and was startled
beyond words to see an altogether different man from the
Stetsoned stranger of the jeep. He had changed to a cashmere
turtleneck sweater and navy wool trousers pressed to a sharp
crease. His handsome, clean-shaven face was even more
angular than it had seemed when half-obscured, and his brown
hair was neatly trimmed and parted to one side. He was
standing across the room from her, drink in hand, and it
occurred to her that he might've been any of a hundred Park
Avenue businessmen she used to see nearly every day of her
life, except for one very discernible difference. There was a
healthier look about him, the absence of city pallor. She
recovered from her momentary astonishment and walked straight
to him.

"I'm sorry, but I can't stay here. I'd like to go on to the
motel," she said in what she hoped was a reasonable tone.

He raised his eyebrows slightly at her straightforward
approach, an involuntary smile coming to his face because of
it. She was standing directly before him now, and her shoul-

der was only three inches below his; that made her unusually tall, for he was a big man. "Oh?" he returned mildly.

"Yes," she continued in the same friendly but decisive manner. "Michael seems to feel that there'll be no way out tomorrow," she explained.

"Michael's right." Grant moved around her then and crossed the room toward the stone fireplace. Covering nearly half of the back wall, all the way up to the high ceiling, it was the focal point of the room and roaring with a fire that cast an orange glow on the stucco. He turned his back to the flames. "I doubt very seriously anyone will be leaving here in the morning, or for several days after that. This isn't your average winter snowstorm but something approaching a blizzard. Perhaps you didn't notice," he added dryly. "February is never the most reliable time of year in these parts to be counting on travel plans, and since you don't seem to know that, I have to assume you're from out of town." He smiled again as he threw her the lead-in.

At present, Ashley had no intention of taking it. "Tomorrow or the next day may be impossible," she said, "but tonight the roads are still passable, if we leave right now. And I'd pay you for the trouble," she offered with a hopeful expression.

Grant's smile disappeared instantly. "I'm afraid you don't have much choice but to stay here. I'm not about to go out there again." He ignored her offer of compensation, which he'd taken as an insult. "But even if I were inclined to give it a try, it would be useless. There are at least seven inches on the ground already. Another half hour and it'll be eight. Or more. I think you're going to have to accept the fact that for the time being, you're stuck here."

Ashley's eyes held his a moment longer, then abruptly she turned away, unmistakably upset.

"Tell me, are you always so gracious when someone is kind enough to do you a favor?" Grant's voice, so much closer now, startled her. She turned quickly to see him standing just behind her, watching her with patent disapproval.

Suddenly she flushed crimson; she could no longer ignore the fact that she was not only being unreasonable but was behaving with abominable rudeness. It took a moment for her to collect herself, and when she had, she gave him a conciliatory smile. "I'm sorry. I really am," she said. "I know that you're right about it being foolish to try to leave tonight, and

I didn't mean to seem so ungrateful. I'm not at all. It's just that I'm tired, and . . . well, I have things on my mind, that's all.'' Her shoulder lifted in a slight shrug as she offered another apologetic smile.

''You only had to say the word back there, and I'd have left you to freeze along the side of the road.''

Ashley blinked. ''I . . . said I'm sorry,'' was all she could answer after a minute.

''Yes, so you did.'' He turned and walked away.

Ashley knew she deserved Grant's coldness and stood looking at his broad back across the room from her now. And in the silence that followed the uncomfortable exchange, she made herself take a good hard look at her situation.

Yes, she knew from the previous experience of the sailing outing with the Penrys that her being stranded like this in a bachelor's home for some indefinite length of time could cause a lot of unpleasantness for her, but after all, that would only happen if Ross ever found out she'd been here. He would undoubtedly look upon it as a ''compromising situation,'' a source of great distress, but there was no reason why he had to find out. With the Penrys, she'd been in the company of Ross's close friends, so that Ross had easily learned about the innocent situation. Afterward he had subjected her to an angry upbraiding, entirely undeserved, and though that had been completely humiliating for her, and infuriating, worse had been what she'd suffered later—the so-familiar, demoralizing feelings of guilt for having upset him once more. But here, far away from her own world . . . no, there was really no cause for worry.

Ashley relaxed and was completely chagrined for what now seemed to be her initial overreaction. And she'd been unconscionably ill-mannered to this man who, after all, was only being generous in opening up his home to three strangers. She cleared her throat and tried, a bit awkwardly, to start the conversation moving again. ''Do you always work with the state police?'' she asked.

''When I'm needed, yes.'' Grant was leaning now against the wooden mantle, watching her openly.

His undisguised appraisal made her uncomfortable; that and the lingering, strained atmosphere she herself had precipitated. She traced the back of the sofa briefly, looked up once to give him a smile that felt lame on her face, and decided finally to return to her room. That was just as well, really;

conversation meant trade-offs of information, and although she'd perhaps been paranoid before, she still wanted to be cautious. She needed time to decide how best to handle him, and with that thought in mind, began walking toward the hallway leading to her bedroom.

"Who *are* you, anyway?"

Ashley faltered in her stride, then stopped. When she turned back to Grant, it was with a composure that didn't come easily. "What do you mean?" she inquired with forced lightness.

At that, Grant pushed himself away from the mantle and strolled over, stopping a few feet away from her. "You were plainly annoyed to have been picked up in the first place . . . obviously reluctant to have a few personal inquiries put to you," he reflected. "I grant you that Mrs. Bonnard goes a little past tact on the first date in the things she asks, but it seems odd to me that after being stranded alone like that in a driving snowstorm, with no promise of immediate rescue, one wouldn't welcome at least a little friendly conversation with a fellow human being once it was all over. To release the anxiety, if nothing else. Yet, you didn't. You changed the subject every time something was asked of you and were very unwilling to give out any information about yourself at all, except that your name was Ashley. Simply Ashley. People usually have last names. And now this, your strenuous insistence upon leaving here, a perfectly acceptable refuge under the circumstances. It makes me wonder what it is a motel offers that Coconino doesn't. Solitude, perhaps? Privacy? Anonymity?" he added and paused to study her keenly. Finally, he cocked his head slightly. "All told, your behavior strikes me as that of someone who doesn't want to be seen. Which leads me to a natural curiosity about just exactly who you are."

Ashley hadn't realized she'd been so transparent in her attempts to fend off Nora's nosiness, or was Grant simply more astute than most people? In any case, he clearly believed in speaking exactly what was on his mind. She stalled as she tried to formulate some kind of response. "Do passing strangers always interest you so much?" she asked.

Grant smiled slightly. "No. Unless they act oddly. Or toss my hospitality back in my face when they'd be a damn sight worse off without it."

Touché, Ashley thought, as she heard the echo of her question that had made her sound rude one more time. Having now had a moment to marshal her wits and come up with some answer, she faced him squarely.

"I wasn't annoyed that you'd picked me up but merely annoyed at having gotten stuck in the first place," she explained, a faint dimple appearing in one cheek as she smiled. "It was an inconvenience I hadn't counted on, and I've been eager to see Margaret—the friend I was on my way to visit—for a long time. As for the way I avoided Nora Bonnard"—she tilted her head—"I just don't care for that kind of high-pressure questioning. It makes me shy away from answering much of anything at all. A little perversity in me, I guess," she added with a small laugh. "And my desire to leave here is merely because I don't like to impose upon people. That's all there is to it," she concluded, smiling again.

Grant arched an eyebrow almost imperceptibly. Her explanation had been very reasonable and might've passed if he weren't such a student of people. Even though her manner had been light, her shoulders had been tensed and those extraordinary violet eyes had been ever so slightly shadowed. Perhaps what she'd offered had some truth to it, but it wasn't the full explanation; he felt that instinctively, and his intuitions were more often right than wrong. And yet, none of this really mattered to him, except that puzzles always intrigued him. And that he couldn't remember ever running up against a woman who'd instantly struck him as being so totally *alive*.

"I see," he said at last, and set his glass down on a nearby table. "Well, it's unfortunate that you had to be delayed, but you were and will be for a while, I'm afraid. Now, don't you think it would be thoughtful to give your friend a call and let her know you're all right?"

Ashley was relieved that he'd moved away; his nearness had an unsettling effect on her, oddly making the back of her neck tingle, as if someone had been blowing lightly on it, And, too, there'd been something more to his searching look than just the interest most men displayed in an attractive woman—an intelligence, a knowledge of things and people. Disconcerted, she smiled faintly at him again, and as she deliberated over whether to stay any longer or go ahead and retire for the night, she heard Nora Bonnard's voice growing distinctly louder; the sound of it made up her mind for her.

"I can't get in touch with Margaret," she said truthfully as she began moving toward the hallway again. "She doesn't have a telephone. Her place is only a cabin in the mountains. I'll just have to hope we're not snowed in for too long and that she waits awhile before panicking. And there's no one else I need to contact,'' she felt compelled to add, as much to reassure herself as to stop any further questions. Nora was just about to appear with Dwight no doubt tagging along behind, and Ashley picked up her pace. ''If you'll excuse me now,'' she said, giving him her engaging smile once again. ''I'm going on to bed.''

''You still didn't answer my question.''

She turned around to see Grant watching her from his position near the sectional. ''I thought I'd——'' she began uncertainly.

''Who are you?'' he repeated.

Her hesitation was only for the space of a moment's rapid thought. ''Ashley Welles,'' she answered and walked out of the room.

Chapter 3

IF ASHLEY HAD still harbored any illusions the night before that she might not really be a snowbound prisoner of Coconino, she couldn't doubt her plight any longer as she stood looking out her bedroom window the following morning not long after dawn. There was nearly a foot and a half of snow on the ground, with it still coming down, and in the light of day, something of the surroundings had become mistily visible.

Off in the distance was a towering, snow-covered mountain, Humphrey's Peak—the highest of the San Francisco Peaks, she knew, for that's what Margaret had told her last year, the first time Ashley had traveled to these parts. That time, too, she'd come for a weekend of skiing and much-needed talk. They were old friends from college days, she and Margaret, and Ashley knew she could confide in her frankly. Just now she needed more than ever to talk to her friend about the unhappiness that had sometimes threatened to overwhelm her in the past year. She prayed that Margaret really would wait before getting frantic about her, and not contact Ross in desperation. Well, there was nothing she herself could do about it, Ashley thought once again, and resolutely she directed her full attention back to the view.

To her left was a large, shingled building with a cement extension, then another long structure, and to the right a post-and-rail fence line that, some distance away, switched to strands of barbed wire disappearing into the snow. Beyond that, there was little else for her to see in the heavy snow; this was canyon country, filled with river-carved fissures of staggering proportions, flat-topped mesas and long steppe plains, and though that was all masked from Ashley's sight at the moment, she knew it was out there. Rugged, forbidding, beautiful.

She'd dressed immediately upon rising in a black cowlneck sweater and jeans; it was lucky she'd brought along sturdy boots, she thought. Leaving the window, she paused before the mirror and gave herself a critical glance.

Almost too thin, so many of her good friends often described her. A tall willow, others said. Whatever the reason for her marked slenderness, she'd always been that way and had come to accept it. She turned to the bureau where the few personal things she'd brought were scattered, and picked up the delicate gold ring she always wore on the little finger of her right hand. As she put it on, a tender smile lit her face; the design was a small oval, monogrammed with the initial *A* in fancy script, and Grif had given it to her on her twenty-first birthday. "You always knew just what I'd want," she told him softly as she continued to study the gift he'd given her with such brotherly pride, then shook herself out of the wistful reverie, tucking her thoughts of Grif back into their spot in that special corner of her mind. Glancing back up to the mirror then, she neatened the lock of hair across her high forehead and left the room to search for the kitchen.

It was across the length of the house, past the dining room, and at the far end of the other wing. When she entered, she found a stocky man in boots, green quilted parka, and Stetson standing beside an Indian woman—Marina, Ashley decided—at the counter near the stove. At the sound of her footsteps in the doorway, the man looked over. "You're up early," he remarked.

"I couldn't sleep any longer," Ashley answered truthfully.

He cocked his head. "You're Ashley Welles, right?"

He was fair-haired, with a blond mustache and nice eyes set above the sharp bridge of his nose; he looked to be somewhere near Grant Copeland's own age—thirty-eight or nine, Ashley had guessed her host to be. She wondered who this personable man was who leaned so comfortably against the counter and who had obviously been filled in by Grant on the strangers at Coconino.

"Yes, that's right," she answered with a light smile.

The man turned back to Marina and accepted a thermos she'd been filling with black coffee from a large pot. "Thanks. That'll keep us for awhile." He looked at Ashley again and gestured to a long table in the very center of the big kitchen; there were benches on either side, like a picnic table. "Sit down. Have some breakfast."

Dirty dishes sat at one edge of the table, Ashley noted as she slid down onto the corner of the bench, and she was surprised; she'd anticipated that she'd be the first one up, at this hour. Marina gave her a silent smile and began setting her place, moving back to the stove finally to put slices of bacon on to sizzle.

"Who are you?" Ashley inquired pleasantly when the man continued to look at her.

"Oh. Sorry. Nick Peters. Grant's ranch foreman. Tell Marina to make you one of her omelets. They can't be beat." He winked at the cook, receiving a smile in return. "Well, I gotta get moving," he said. "The guys are waiting for the coffee. Nice meeting you, Ashley." He touched the brim of his hat in salutation, then left by the back door, letting in a blast of cold air that lingered behind him for minutes.

Ashley ate heartily Marina's omelet breakfast, then left the warm kitchen to stroll around the living room. She'd decided the dirty dishes Marina had finally swept off the end of the table belonged to Grant; he was nowhere to be seen, but the wakeful presence of the owner of the house could be felt everywhere. The fire in the stone hearth was already lit, snapping and popping behind the black mesh screen, and the woven shades had been rolled up from the windows, letting in the daylight. The big room was bright and alive, and with the leisure of privacy, Ashley gave it a better scrutiny than she had the evening before.

Back near the fireplace was a natural wood staircase leading up to an enclosed loft; she'd barely noticed it the night before and concluded now that it was Grant Copeland's bedroom. It seemed an obvious assumption, for there was a freshly pressed shirt on a hanger hooked over the banister as if it were waiting to be taken upstairs. The decor of the main room was almost exclusively Indian, except for the long beige sectional sofa. Fringed rugs of earth colors were not only placed around the floor for covering but were hung from the walls as decoration, providing the pattern and color for the beige and white room, and what had first appeared to be tables and cabinet pieces of primitive construction turned out under inspection to be something more: examples of fine hand craftsmanship, unvarnished but painstakingly fashioned. Ashley assessed the rustic room as a whole, liking and feeling comfortable in it, and she thought to herself that Grant Copeland was a man who seemed to know exactly what he preferred; there were no two objects alike, no matched sets of anything, anywhere. It reminded her of her old Manhattan apartment, which she'd decorated with similar selectivity and with an eye to achieving the same relaxed atmosphere. Out of the corner of her eye she then saw the folding doors at the edge of the hallway that last night had been completely closed; now they stood slightly ajar, and after a moment of trying to resist the beckoning open door, she finally gave up and went over, venturing inside a step. And when she'd entered, she stopped dead, stunned.

The room was obviously Grant's library, and it was a complete contrast to the rest of the rustic ranch house. It was a handsome room, darkly masculine and urbane in atmosphere with its mahogany paneling, elaborate bookshelves, paintings, and imposing, beautifully carved desk; there were brown leather wing chairs and brass appointments, masses of reference books and a globe. It suggested the professional chambers of an extremely successful businessman engaged in far more than simply the running of a stable, a financially unreliable enterprise at best, Ashley thought as she glanced around in bemusement. A grouping of charcoal sketches on the wall beside the door caught her attention, and out of habit, she went to them; they were scenes depicting the Old West, and she was further startled when she looked at the signatures. They each read: *G. Copeland*.

And then there were the paintings. She walked over to the nearest one, studying it before moving on slowly to examine the others. They were Remington originals, all of them; Ashley had the training to know that. And they revealed some of the artist's best work: frontiersmen, rearing mustangs fighting the white man's rope, Indian squaws. She stepped back finally from the last one and unconsciously fingered the folds of her collar as she contemplated this newest revelation about her host.

He was not only a connoisseur of Indian and Western traditions but of art as well—art that she had good reason to know was very expensive and that, like the rest of the library, seemed so unexpected in this simple setting. She found herself considering the emerging complexities of this man, Grant Copeland, the inconsistencies about him, then suddenly blanched at the recollection of the remark she'd made to him the night before; no wonder he'd laughed. By all appearances, he wasn't exactly the cowboy she'd so condescendingly called him. She didn't know quite what to think about him, really, but there was one thing she did know: She, herself, had made the worst first impression on record.

Curiosity satisfied, Ashley returned to the living room,

where her movements took on the air of rattling around. Michael appeared once and spoke briefly before passing on through; Marina was nowhere to be seen, nor were the Bonnards. Ashley finally sat down on the couch, tucking her legs up under her as she picked up a copy of *Arizona Highways*. After only a moment of flipping through the pages, however, she laid the magazine back down on the coffee table; sitting quietly inside, idling away her time, was not something Ashley had ever been able to do with ease, and she glanced toward the unshaded window. The falling snow was visible, whispering up against the panes, and after a time, the lure of the fresh outdoors was too much for her. Getting abruptly to her feet, she headed for her bedroom, and in minutes she had on her coat and was on her way with a light gait toward the back door.

Grant swung the bale of hay backwards once for momentum, then heaved it forward, sending it sailing from the loft down toward Nick Peters below. He was standing in the high rafters of the big barn, one booted foot balanced against an open beam for support, and at Nick's signal moments later, Grant picked up another bale. He was already on the forward swing, just before releasing the heavy bundle, when he saw Ashley step into his line of fire below. "What the—get out of the way!" he exclaimed.

It was too late to do anything himself; he was committed to letting go, and his shout of warning came a split second after the wire bale ropes had left his gloved hands. Fifty pounds of dried alfalfa hay went flying toward the floor, and before even Nick could react and shove her out of the way, the bale clipped Ashley on the left shoulder just as she looked up. The blow sent her reeling backwards as the bale went on past; she didn't fall, but she landed up against the side of an idle power mower directly to her right, cracking her arm sharply on it.

Grant was out of the loft and down the narrow ladder instantly. By the time he'd reached Ashley, Nick was already by her side. "Are you hurt?" Grant asked. His face was etched in a deep frown of worry as he stripped off his gloves, and with his hands on her shoulders, he guided her down onto the seat of the mower. She looked pale, he thought, giving her a sharp once-over, and she blinked several times as she put a hand unconsciously to her temple.

"No, I . . . well, stunned a bit," she admitted with a shaky laugh.

"Just sit for a minute. Let your head clear," Grant said quietly.

She managed a smile and began making movements to stand up again. She was thoroughly embarrassed by what had happened and wanted only to get back to her feet and forget it. "I'm fine. Honestly," she assured and grabbed hold of the mower steering wheel to push herself up.

"I said, just sit!" Grant insisted, putting a hand once more on her shoulder.

Ashley eased back down onto the seat, rubbing her sore elbow as she looked at Grant directly for the first time; he was standing over her, and the outdoorsman of the jeep had returned, Stetsoned and in his outfit of jeans and heavy winter coat, though today he'd added a green bandana that was knotted around his muscular throat. He still had his hand on her shoulder, and she finally responded to his stern directive. "All right. I'm sitting," she said mildly.

Color was flushing back into her face, and reassured now that she wasn't greatly harmed, Grant began to frown in earnest. "Now, I'd like to know what the hell you were doing. Didn't you see what was going on?" he asked.

"No," Ashley said honestly. "I came in that way." She pointed toward a pair of high double doors some distance back along the wall, then looked back up at Grant, her expression entirely open. "I came in under the loft. I saw Nick, but it wasn't until I'd come out in the open that I realized——"

"What are you doing out in the first place?" Grant interrupted shortly.

"I felt like getting some air," she explained as she propped a heel on the running board of the mower. "I saw the barn. There were tracks in the snow, and I was just curious——"

"You should've stayed back in the house." He'd interrupted curtly again, and he didn't try to stop her this time as she again made an effort to get up. When she was standing beside the two men, Nick tactfully disappeared into a tool room under the overhang of the loft.

By now Ashley was beginning to bristle at Grant's unfairly harsh attitude; after all, it had only been an accident.

"I didn't *want* to stay back in the house, because I like the outdoors," she said, a small frown coming to her brow.

"Why are you up so early?" he demanded.

A breath of frustration escaped from her. "Please don't grill me this way!" she objected, her frown deepening.

"I could've seriously *hurt* you!" Grant snapped, then spun away and strode over to pick up the bale that had hit her, using the activity as an anodyne to his acute irritation, which was really only a reaction, a release of tension; he'd been appalled to have her—or anyone else—step out of nowhere directly into the target zone. He heaved the bale onto the stack of others in the corner and turned back to look at Ashley. She was standing her ground against his uncalled-for tirade, still frowning with her chin slightly raised. Somehow the very fact that she hadn't backed down made him relent. "All right. Never mind. But why *are* you up so early?" His tone had tone abruptly conversational as his tension dissipated completely, and he passed by her and began climbing back up the ladder.

"I always get up early," she called up to him, annoyed at having to raise her voice. He was already at the top of the ladder, agilely swinging a leg over the rafter beam.

"Thought you couldn't sleep." Nick had reappeared, and offered the comment in a low voice as he passed. He looked up at Grant and called, "Okay!"

Grant had another bale in hand and glanced to Ashley. "Move . . ."

"Out of the way! I know!" She was thoroughly exasperated at this point, piqued at herself for choosing that particular moment to come into the barn and at them for the way they were acting. They obviously thought her out of place here, which was ridiculous; she was as comfortable as they were in this barn. For lack of anything else to do, she turned her back on them and left them to their business, listening to their exchange of amicable shop talk as she wandered on down the length of the drafty barn: The "boys" were somewhere out inspecting a canyon range fence line, a heifer was missing in the storm, two batteries had gone dead on needed equipment, and a line was down out near the road. She tuned out finally, and their voices faded altogether as she passed from the main part of the barn and its stores of grain, hay, and tools to a narrower section that was merely a long cement tunnel with doors lining both sides. Her breath hung in the air before her as she stood looking down it; after a moment the scent of horseflesh reached her, then the sigh of a nicker. She realized then that she'd found Grant Copeland's stable of quarter horses.

There were twelve stalls; three were empty, with the Dutch doors standing ajar. She remained for almost ten minutes at the first door she came to, rubbing the muzzle of a bay. Horses had always helped relieve the stress of life for her; she found them to be such silent, willing friends. Listeners. She thought of her beloved Sharif, the big black thoroughbred hunter she'd had for three years now and whom she rode hard out over cross-country fences, reveling in the challenge of conquering the rough terrain below on the sailing grace of her horse. After awhile she felt better and was even reviewing the hay bale incident with a bit of wry amusement. When she overlooked the blow her pride had taken, she actually laughed at the mental picture of her inopportune entry—right on cue, as in slapstick. She had just laid her forehead down on the muzzle of the bay horse, caught up in a spasm of giggling, when a small voice piped up beside her.

"What's so funny?"

Startled, Ashley's head came up, and she looked across her left shoulder, saw nothing, then glanced down. Standing beside her was a young boy, perhaps seven, maybe eight years old, and his dark Indian face was all but hidden under a colorful knit cap pulled down to his eyebrows, his slight figure just about lost in a gray thermal snowsuit. His eyes were saucer-wide with expectant curiosity, and Ashley smiled at her engaging little companion. "Me," she answered.

"How come?" he inquired, reaching up the full length of his arm to touch the nose of the horse sniffing down toward him over the door of the stall.

"Oh, just because all of us are funny sometimes," she dismissed with a laughing smile, then tilted her head. "And who are you?" she asked, unable after a moment to resist reaching down and pushing the oversized cap up slightly away from his eyes.

"Timothy Redchief," he announced. "My mom and dad work here. I brush the horses sometimes," he advised as he walked jauntily around her. "Mr. Copeland lets me."

"He does?" Ashley said, infusing her voice with the proper amount of awe and respect for the young boy's accomplishment. She began walking with him down the corridor, totally enchanted by his manner. "And what else does he let you do?'' she asked as the two of them stopped again at a black gelding.

Timothy hiked up his snow pants with both hands, stuck for a minute. ''I carry buckets,'' he offered finally, his round little face bright with pride.

Ashley laughed softly at his expression. ''That's terrific.'' She, too, thought briefly, then asked, ''Have you ever hooked a halter?'' He shook his head. ''Well, let's show you how,'' she said comfortably. With just the smallest bit of difficulty, she hoisted him up by the waist and sat him down on the top of the stall door, keeping the curious horse's nose at bay for a moment while the boy steadied himself. ''Okay,'' she said then. ''Here's how it's done.'' Reaching up to the black horse's head, she began unhooking the leather straps of the halter, carefully explaining as she went. When it was off, she slowly slipped it back on, glancing over several times to Timothy's face, which was a study in fascinated concentration. She rehooked the piece of equipment, then said, ''Okay, now you try.'' Gamely, Timothy duplicated the process, with only a little assistance from Ashley here and there, and when he'd gotten the halter off, then back on again, he turned a radiantly hopeful face to her.

''How's that?'' he asked.

''Wonderful,'' Ashley answered, laughing as she helped him hop down from the door. She took his hand, and they strolled on, stopping at an enclosure that was larger than the others she'd seen so far, not rectangular but square, with an iron grate set into the heavy, single panel door. *Dakota* was imprinted on a bronze plaque just below the wire inset, and just as she put her face to the mesh of the grating, she heard bootheels coming down the cement corridor. She looked into the stall anyway, and Grant's voice came to her at the same moment the cold nose of a big buckskin touched hers.

''Look out, he bites,'' Grant warned. ''He's not nearly so gentle as the black.''

Timothy was all smiles as Grant came up to them. ''Guess what!'' he said excitedly. ''I know how to hook a halter!''

Grant grinned down at him. ''I know. I saw you learn.'' His smiling eyes moved up to Ashley's face, and he added, ''Looks like you had a good teacher.''

She blushed and turned her attention back to the buckskin horse. ''Is that why Dakota's behind bars, because he bites?'' she asked.

Grant studied the blue-black lights in her hair as he answered. "One reason," he said. "He kicks, too."

"Yeah, he tried to kick me once, but I was too fast for him!" Timothy bragged.

"No, you were just too short for him," Grant countered with a chuckle and gave the boy's shoulder a light push. "Go on. Nick's waiting for you. You said you were going to help put the tools away." Timothy's eyes lit up at the reminder, and he was off like a shot toward the main barn.

"He's adorable," Ashley commented, her eyes alight with affection as she watched the little stable hand disappear through the doorway, and at Grant's smiling nod of agreement, she glanced again to the buckskin. "Dakota's a stallion, I assume, since he has such bad manners," she said and looked through the grate at the animal who'd sauntered off to one corner of the stall. "He's beautiful," she added with an admiring smile.

"That he is. And difficult. *And* cribs on every available surface. He prefers wood, of course," Grant remarked.

Ashley looked back over to him; she was well acquainted with cribbers, those problem horses with the vice of grasping wood in their teeth then sucking in air. "Put a strap on him" she advised. "Or line the stall edges with aluminum, though that probably won't help," she added with a resigned laugh. "Cribbers are notorious for adapting their preferences to whatever's around."

"I do strap him," Grand answered. "And I don't bother with the metal for the very reason you just gave. It doesn't help." He was looking at her in that thoughtful way he had the night before, and Ashley again felt the need to move away from him. She went to the next stall down, Grant following and stopping beside her. "I apologize for back there. I didn't mean to be so short with you," he said abruptly.

Ashley looked up and smiled warmly. "Oh, that's all right. And I didn't mean to get underfoot," she offered reciprocally. "I just needed to get out of the house."

"So you said. Next time announce yourself."

Ashley's smile faded slightly. "I will, but please stop talking to me as though I were Timothy's age. I don't like it," she said truthfully, "and I didn't deserve it. This time," she was obliged to add.

Grant laughed outright; he liked people who stood up for themselves. "No, you're right," he conceded, and his smile deepened the sharp hollows in his tanned face. "You didn't deserve it. The fact is, you scared the hell out of me. One of those things can snap a neck, you know. I wouldn't have liked it to be yours."

Level ground, Ashley thought; she was glad to finally be on it with him. She glanced away from him to the horse in the stall in front of her. "Who's this?" she asked, by way of offering them a new beginning.

Grant rested both forearms on the stall door. "Remo. She's Dakota's dam. He's the only colt of hers I kept."

"Do you breed purely for pleasure or for profit?" Ashley inquired interestedly.

"Both, although I often have to wonder about the profit." He grinned at her sympathetic look. "It can be a tough business. I do breed mostly for resale, though. I keep only a few of the foals for myself."

He was talking now in the easy manner of someone discoursing on a favorite subject, and as Ashley continued to look at him, she noticed for the first time that there was a scar on his left cheekbone. She turned her attention back to the mare in the stall.

"So, if Dakota's such a problem, why keep him?" she asked. "Some people believe that cribbing is an unsoundness anyway, although I'm not sure I go along with that," she said.

"No, I'm not sure I do either," Grant answered, "but I keep the horse because I like him. He's all right, if you know how to handle him."

Ashley smiled and was about to say something more when Nick interrupted their conversation from the doorway some distance down.

"You can lock up the shed," he told Grant and tossed him a ring of keys. "I'm taking the Bronco to check on the cattle barn again, and then I thought I'd run down by the airstrip and see about things—if I can get there. It's still coming down, and we better do what we can now. Tell Marina to hold lunch. We're all gonna be late." Nick turned to go, then swung back to look at Grant. "Oh, I almost forgot. I owe you ten." He grinned and disappeared.

Ashley walked on, suspicious that Nick's last remark had been at her expense. *Five gets you ten she doesn't make it in one piece down the stable corridor* . . . their wager had probably been something like that, she thought, and was very aware of Grant's presence behind her as she continued to walk down the length of the corridor. She stopped finally by a large, open pen at the end.

"This mare's going to foal any minute," she observed. The sight of the pregnant horse standing in the center of the straw-lined enclosure with her head hung low banished everything else from Ashley's mind, and she went right in. "Grant, really!" she added over her shoulder, worry in her expression as she surveyed the animal with an experienced eye.

"I know." Grant's own voice was concerned as he entered the stall behind her. He ran his hand along the mare's swollen belly. "It's a hellish time to be foaling, in this temperature. And this mare always has trouble," he added.

"Breech?" she asked in alarm.

"Usually."

"What's her name?"

"Kachina."

Ashley's compassion always lay just beneath the surface of her other emotions, and she was taken over completely by it now. She stood by the mare, quietly rubbing her hands along the animal's head as she repeated the name several times in a soothing voice, and when, after a time, the horse nickered, Ashley responded with a gentle touch to the velvety-soft muzzle.

Grant was watching her as he stood with one hand on the back of the mare, and when her preoccupation didn't let up, he tried to rouse her. "Ashley . . ."

"We should stay with her," she said.

"We?" he repeated in surprise. He studied her another moment, then objected mildly. "No, not we, Ashley. Me, Nick, or Hank maybe, but not you."

Ashley remembered his and Nick's earlier attitude toward her and looked up. "I wouldn't be in the way, if that's what you're afraid of," she said calmly. "I can help. I've had a lot of experience with horses."

"So I've noticed," Grant said dryly and came up to join her then by the horse's head. "And I didn't mean to imply that you'd be in the way," he went on. "It's just that it could be a long wait, which I'm sure you must know, and it's freezing in here. There's no reason for you to be subjected to that. And besides," he added with his easy half-smile, "I don't usually make it a practice to put my guests to work in repayment for room and board. You'll be a lot more comfortable back at the house.''

"No, I really wouldn't.'' Her objection came immediately, and she laughed a little sheepishly at Grant's look of surprise. "I'm not much of an indoor person,'' she explained. "When I have free time on my hands, I'd always much prefer to be outside. I'm not a hothouse flower. Grant, I meant what I said,'' she went on. "I *am* experienced in this sort of thing, and I'd like very much to give you a hand, if it's all right with you.''

Grant was smiling appreciatively as his eyes roamed her face; she really didn't mind speaking right up. "It'll be uncomfortable,'' he warned.

She conceded that with a nod of her head. "Then I can stay?'' she pressed.

He studied her for another instant. He was struck again by the uncommon color of her eyes, the sensitivity in them. Finally he said, "Yes, if that's what you want. I have several more things to get done that'll keep me occupied for the rest of the morning, and then you and I can take the first shift.''

Chapter 4

"THE MARE'S DOWN," Nick commented sometime later as he opened the gate to the pen and walked in. Grant was kneeling to one side of the horse, winding leg bandages into rolls, and after setting down the bucket he'd carried in from the barn, Nick went over to help. "Everything looks fairly good on the property, as far as I could see," he said, crouching down beside his boss. "I just got back in. Marina's putting lunch out at the bunk house, and I told the boys to go on. Thought I'd drop in and check on Kachina first. You eat yet?"

"An hour ago," Grant said.

Nick nodded and looked at the horse lying on her left side in a bed of straw. Her labored breath was coming in short blasts that hung in a vapor about her nostrils, but despite the frigid air in the cement building, her neck was glistening with sweat. "How's she doing?"

Grant stood up and walked to the corner of the pen to pick up an army blanket from a pile of them near the wall. "I don't know," he answered. "You'll have to ask Ashley here. She's doing all the work."

Nick too had risen and glanced from Grant to Ashley, kneeling by the horse's head, the collar of her ski coat pulled up, her knit cap covering all but several loose wisps of black hair. He'd seen her when he'd come in, of course, but had thought she was merely watching. "Oh," he murmured.

Grant returned with the blanket and grinned at Nick's expression. "It turns out she's a lady well versed in the science of equine obstetrics," he said. Catching her eye finally, he shared a smile with her, then looked back to Nick. "It's probably going to be awhile yet. Go on and get something to eat. You and Hank can take over later, if Kachina's labor goes that long. We can manage for now."

When Nick was gone, Grant settled the blanket over Kachina's belly and joined Ashley near the horse's head. Crouching down, he ran his eyes sharply over the mare's body. "She doesn't look good," he said quietly.

Ashley shifted her weight back on her heels. "I know," she said, frowning in concern. "It worries me that she's just . . . shut down like this. It shouldn't be. There are no contractions, nothing. And she's heaving as though she can hardly catch her breath. What do you think, Grant?"

He'd been facetious when he'd told Nick she was handling everything; Ashley had known that, letting the comment pass without correction. They'd been at the barn for nearly an hour, ministering together over the distressed animal who'd been down and in pain when they arrived, and she watched Grant with a receptive expression as she waited for his opinion.

"I think there's nothing to do but see what happens," he said. "Now come on. We might as well get established somewhere." He touched her shoulder as he straightened. "Take two of those blankets in the corner. You can sit on one and throw the other one around you."

They made themselves as warm as possible. Then silence fell around them, broken only by the mare's heavy breathing and the whistling wind, as they settled into their vigil. A single light overhead illuminated the enclosure, throwing everything else into shadow, and after a time, Ashley shifted. "God, it's cold in here," she said, her breath a fog before her as she cast Grant a feeling look.

He smiled slightly. "I told you."

"Yes, I know."

"You can always go back in."

"No thanks. I'll be fine," Ashley said firmly and drew the blanket more closely around her. "I was just making conversation."

"Suit yourself," he said quietly. "Not that you wouldn't anyway." He shifted back against the wall as if to appraise her. "You know," he said, "if your behavior up to now is any indication, I'd say you do pretty well for yourself in this life. In making your wishes known to the world around you, at least."

"I . . . well . . ." She struggled to respond, then abruptly burst into ringing laughter at her very speechlessness. Just what had she expected from this man whose business she had walked right into as if it were her own and who'd already proven he believed in plain speaking? She shook her head at herself, finding that she could only answer by telling him exactly what was on her own mind.

"You know," she said when her amusement had subsided,

"all this time I've considered that a sign of strong character, the fact that I speak right up, *do* things. Hearing you comment on it, however, makes me wonder if I shouldn't reconsider." Her laughter rekindled. "Funny, isn't it, how benevolent we are when it's ourselves we're evaluating? Traits that in others might seem less than terrific become absolute virtues when we see them in ourselves!"

Grant grinned, but said nothing right away as he simply watched the laughter on her face; it had an infectious quality to it, and her whole demeanor had begun to sparkle. "I hadn't meant to start you reconsidering," he said at last. "I was merely making an observation. I think it's fine to be so straightforward."

"Noble?" Her eyes danced.

"Well, maybe not noble," he demurred. "Admirable, possibly." He frowned as if he were giving the matter due consideration. "Yes, I think you could take 'admirable' as a pat on the back."

Ashley's laughter dissolved into a smile that lingered comfortably somewhere inside. After a brief moment of studying her hands, she looked up to see him still watching her; it made her conscious abruptly of the ease of their brief exchange; how quickly they had stopped feeling like strangers. She straightened and clasped her hands around her knees.

"I guess I really do owe you an apology," she said quietly, "for being so stubborn about your letting me stay here with Kachina. I think I was a bit overbearing, but you see, I've never been able to sit by and not get involved where I know I can be of some help."

She paused, and as he watched her, Grant found himself thinking for the first time in years of another woman he'd once known, Mara Glynnis; she'd kept her professional modeling name even after they'd gotten married. It suited her, she'd said. Mara had been nearly as tall as Ashley, though not so thin, and of a different character altogether—wispy, a gossamer silhouette of a woman. He recalled a phrase Ashley had used earlier: a hothouse flower. Mara had been that: an orchid, fragile, beautiful. And completely incompatible with everything he was as an individual. His announcement that he'd bought a ranch deep in the heart of the high country of Arizona, which he'd loved since boyhood trips here with his father, had ended their short-lived union, for it would've meant separation for her from the satin sophistication of the high life they'd been living, a life on which she thrived. He saw Ashley pull her booted legs more closely to her chest, and Mara faded from his thoughts, the same way she'd faded from his life over ten years before: with no regrets, except that a venture tried had failed.

His reverie was interrupted by Nick's appearance at the entrance to the enclosure. "I stopped up by the house for a minute," he said, "and while I was there, your uncle from New York City called. I figured you might want to return the call right away, and since I was passing back by here on my way to the bunk house, I thought I'd relay the message. Oh, and I forgot to tell you before," he added, "when I was out earlier, I didn't get a chance to look in on the planes."

Grant smiled. "Thanks for the message about Walter, but it can wait. And the planes should be all right. The hangar's secure." Nick nodded and left again, and Grant turned his full attention back to Ashley. "So, you'd much rather be outdoors," he picked up as he removed his Stetson and laid it on the dirt floor beside him. "What else do you like to do?" he inquired, easing his head back against the wall. "Nora has divulged just about all there is to know about the Bonnards, but I have yet to be told anything much about you."

Ashley didn't answer him immediately. She couldn't. Nick's remarks were still ringing stunningly through her mind—*your uncle from New York City . . . didn't get a chance to look in on the planes*—and anxiety had caught her in its steel grip all over again.

Grant Copeland was no simple rancher whose life and livelihood were confined to the perimeters of this spread here in the Arizona canyons. So many things she'd seen about him screamed wealth and position, and Nick's disclosure of moments before had been like a final, blinding light to her. Grant had private airplanes; that meant extraordinary affluence, easy travel. With that knowledge about him, other bemusing discrepancies suddenly made more sense, and she was now certain that Grant was a very prominent businessman who most likely belonged to the upper echelons of affluent society. New York City society? He unquestionably had ties there, and Nick Peters obviously thought a call from an uncle in New York important enough to warrant a special trip out here to tell him about it. As if those ties Grant had there were very strong? She stared steadily at the toes of her boots. The fact that Grant had just been elevated to a new social and financial status in her mind didn't matter to her particularly, except in one very important regard: It linked him directly with her world. If it were indeed true that Grant traveled in wealthy New York circles, then he might very well know people she knew. Which, in turn, made the possibility that Ross might find out she'd been here—and realize how secretive she'd been—no longer so remote.

"Ashley, is there some reason you don't want to answer me?"

Ashley roused herself from her anxious thoughts and looked into his perceptive eyes. And just then she came to a decision, one she despised from the very depths of her soul, but one she felt had to be; protecting Ross and herself from more discord, at the moment, rose paramount above all else in her mind.

She forced a smile. "No, of course not. What would you like to know?" she asked.

"Oh, who you are, where you come from, how it is you know so much about horses," Grant answered easily. "You've obviously spent a good deal of time around them."

"Yes. I have a thoroughbred hunter that I take out over fences, show a little," Ashley said, feeling the tension tight all across her back. "I'm from . . . Chicago, and I'm a . . . photographer there." She smiled again, flatly she knew. "Freelance."

"I see," Grant said, watching her keenly. "And what kind of work do you do? Magazine layouts? Portraits? Promotional material? Or do you work for newspapers?"

"Oh. Well." Ashley's mind was blank for a moment, and she shifted positions. "I . . . do a little of everything. It—uh—makes it more interesting that way."

"I'll bet it does," Grant said under his breath, then went on clearly, "You didn't bring your camera along. Why not? You could have gotten some spectacular shots around here."

"No, well—no, I didn't." Ashley was holding the edges of the blanket tightly, trying to keep her smile level on her face; it was a difficult thing to do, with her own self-loathing rising steadily with each new falsehood. "I just, well . . . I try not to work and play at the same time," she offered in a low voice.

"I see," Grant said again. His head was cocked thoughtfully to one side; his eyes had never once left her face. He glanced down now at her graceful hands holding the edges of the blanket together at her chest; she'd removed her gloves to work better with the horse, and he noted her jewelry—a watch, a small gold ring on her right hand. No wedding band on her left. He remembered the fact that there'd been no one she'd needed to inform of her whereabouts the night before and smiled slightly. He looked back up to her face then, raising his eyebrows once more in an attitude of attentive interest. "Where exactly do you live in Chicago?" he inquired. "I've been there a number of times. I might recognize the address."

At that moment, Kachina screamed and, kicking, arched her neck up from the floor in a sudden explosion of frantic, birth-pain activity. Ashley's eyes shot to the mare and, gratefully, she threw off the blanket and dove for her.

They did everything they could. Even in the raw air of the cement building, Grant finally got down to his shirt-sleeves, as together they tried to save mare and foal, but their efforts were in vain, for the colt was breech and stillborn, and Kachina's post-partum bleeding turned to hemorrhage. There was nothing for them to do, really, but watch her die, and when the mare's pain-filled eyes finally turned staring, Ashley rose spasmodically and went to lean heavily against the wall. Grant got to his feet slowly and walked over to her.

"Here, come on. Wipe your hands off," he said. "You're covered with blood." He gave her several rags. "Are you all right?" he asked, looking hard at her pale complexion.

Her lips were pressed into a thin line as she cleaned her hands, then threw down the rags, and she averted her eyes from the animals lying in the center of the enclosure. "It was awful," she said in a voice that shook slightly.

"It happens."

"Yes, I know."

Grant was watching her as she stood staring down at the dirt floor. "Look, go on back to the house," he said. "I'll clean up. I can call Nick, and he and the boys will take care of the rest."

Ashley nodded dully. "God, it hurts when it turns out this way," she said in a low voice.

"I know. It hurts me, too," Grant answered quietly. "But you have to take the bad with the good when you breed, and keep your personal hurt out of it. You know that. It's emotional survival, and good business sense." He watched her looking up at him, her empathetic smile tinged with sadness, and he put a hand on her shoulder. "Now go on," he said softly. "You're beat. I'll be up to the house later."

She nodded and trudged off toward the house through knee-high drifts. The falling snow was finally slacking off, she noticed absently. Once inside, she went straight to her room, showered, put on her robe, then wearily crawled under the sheepskin coverlet, falling asleep in a matter of minutes. It was a fitful rest, but she didn't awaken until a knock came at her door sometime later.

"Yes?" she called groggily, sitting up.

Michael Redchief called back through the door that dinner was to be in an hour, and after thanking him, Ashley glanced to the clock. It read seven-thirty. She got up still feeling the lingering drag of the painful afternoon, and put her mind to the business of dressing.

The Bonnards were sitting on the far end of the sectional near the crackling fire when Ashley entered the living room, dressed in the slacks she'd traveled in and a sweater of deep blue. Dwight, she noticed, was wearing a conservative three-piece suit, and Nora too had dressed up for dinner. The table lamps in the room were dimmed in favor of the warmer light from the blazing fire, and the flames softly illuminated the nearby seating area before fading away into shadows. Nora sat forward at the sight of her, brightening with immediate interest.

"There you are," she said. "We thought maybe you were skipping dinner again. You shouldn't do that. It's why you're so thin. I heard Grant Copeland mentioning the horse to someone on the phone in the kitchen earlier, Nick, he called him. And you were *out* there with it. It must've been too gruesome!" She patted the couch. "Come tell me about it."

Dwight gave her a pained look. "Nora, she doesn't want to talk about it."

"No, I really don't," Ashley said gratefully and sat down across from them. She glanced involuntarily to the stairs leading toward the loft, then looked at Nora. "Grant's come in, then?"

"Oh, yes." Nora settled back and smiled in the manner of a self-appointed hostess. "He went right away to change, and I spoke to that little Indian woman about getting some coffee for him. Well, he looked so tired!" She tossed Dwight a defensive look, though he had said nothing. "He came down later and disappeared. He went through there.'' Nora pointed to the folding doors just visible at the edge of the hallway, behind which, Ashley knew, lay his library. ''I can't imagine what he's doing,'' Nora went on, as if she ought to know. ''Well, we could entertain ourselves for the time being. Strange there's no television, don't you think? What do you suppose he *does* at night?''

They were spared Nora's further speculations: Grant's brisk stride could be heard coming to the door of the other room, and in a moment, he appeared. He smiled when he entered the room and saw his guests, and immediately joined them.

''I just got off the phone with Frank Mehan,'' he said. ''Frank's the chief of the highway police in this area, and I thought you all might like to have an update on the situation. The snow has stopped, as you've probably noticed, and they're working on the roads right now. The main highways first, of course, then the secondary roads. Sixty-six should be clear by tomorrow sometime, he thinks, and the others the next day. It's going to take awhile to do something about the stranded cars, but I've asked him to see about your wagon,'' he said to the Bonnards, then to Ashley, ''and the Datsun first.

''At any rate,'' he continued, ''there's nothing we can do until we've been dug out here. Unfortunately, the battery's dead on my own plow. Frank's going to send over one of the trucks, but that can't be done right away. The bottom line to all this is that you're going to have to sit it out here for at least another day, possibly two. I'm sorry.'' He let the news settle, then smiled again. ''And in case you'd like to know, we've gotten twenty-two inches.''

Ashley got up abruptly and went to the fireplace, where she stood silently staring into the flames licking up at the roof of the stone hearth. Grant was aware of her pensiveness as he studied her lithe figure silhouetted against the bright firelight, then shifted his attention to Nora when she spoke up.

''Well, isn't that a kettle of fish! Stranded here for another few days.'' Despite her words, she was looking pleased. ''I've got to call the children and tell them.''

''There's one more thing I wanted to let you know,'' Grant said. ''Tomorrow I've got to be out for most of the day. Nick and I and a few of the other men have to get out on the property to check for damage. If you need anything don't hesitate to speak to Michael or Marina. I should be back by dark, if everything goes well.''

Nora's immediate inquiry about the acreage of the ranch was cut short by Michael's announcement that dinner was being served, and she took hold of Dwight's arm to respond promptly. Grant smilingly ushered them past, watching until they disappeared from the room. He turned to Ashley then. "Are you all right?" he asked. "It was a rough afternoon. And by the way, if I didn't say it before, thank you for everything you did today. You were superb, despite what happened."

His manner now was different from what it had been when the Bonnards were present; he spoke quietly, with a certain familiarity in his tone, and Ashley was very aware of it. The firelight sharply illuminated one half of her face as she looked up at him and smiled. "You're welcome," she said. "And don't worry about me. I'm fine. What happened was shocking at first, but it subsides to just a dull ache."

Grant was standing very close to her, looking down at her face angled away from him; she'd let her attention drift back to the fire, as if she could find an answer there to some troubling thought, and he was absorbed for a moment in watching her soft profile. The scent of her perfume drifted to him, and though he tried to identify it, he couldn't, except to know there was a refreshing lightness to it. He had a sudden, compelling urge to tell her how beautiful he thought she was, but he didn't; he was still trying to come to terms with his strong attraction to her, which was increasing sharply with each moment they spent together. He idly picked up a small Indian arrowhead from the mantle, and when he spoke again it was with a casualness he wasn't certain he really felt.

"I'm sorry for the delay in your departure," he said as he toyed with the object in his hand. "If our own snow plow was running, I probably could've gotten you out tomorrow. As it is, we'll have to wait until Frank can free up something. I didn't want to push him any harder than I did. He's got enough problems as it is."

But you *could* have pushed him? Ashley asked silently. And yet, it wasn't really a question. She was sure now that all her earlier surmises about him had indeed been accurate; only a very influential man could speak so nonchalantly about making requests of the state authorities.

"Ashley?" She'd been silent for nearly a full minute in that pensiveness that Grant read as her eagerness to be on her way. "Don't panic," he said. "You'll be able to get to the mountains to see your friend, and then, before you know it, you'll be on a plane and back in Chicago.''

She looked up at him quickly, but he was smiling with no trace of facetiousness, none that she could divine, anyway. So, he believed everything she'd told him. She relaxed a little, reminding herself that even among the affluent of New York, there were many different social circles. And after all, she'd never met Grant Copeland before, or heard of him.

''You're taking the horses tomorrow, I assume?'' she asked, only partly to change the subject.

''Yes.'' The arrowhead Grant had been absently tossing in the palm of his hand dropped to the floor just then, and he reached down just as Ashley did to retrieve it for him, accidentally brushing her arm with his. They straightened simultaneously, and Grant accepted the stone piece from her with a nod of thanks. ''Yes, we're riding,'' he repeated, replacing the arrowhead on the mantle, and his smile eased into a sly grin as he looked back at her. ''Just think,'' he said, ''you can spend the whole day here at the house tomorrow, thumbing through magazines and chatting over coffee with Nora.''

Ashley looked up into his face. She'd felt a thrill of excitement race through her when his arm had inadvertently touched hers, and in the moment that their eyes had met over the arrowhead, something had been in the look that passed between them—the flash of a certain innate knowledge of one another? A special rapport?

This couldn't be. She could not be drawn to Grant as she suddenly had to acknowledge she was, in a romantic, very sexual way. Her life had set boundaries to it, ones she instinctively respected even though she was unhappy with them, and though it might be the most natural thing in the world, nothing could happen between her and Grant, under any circumstance.

''I'm still waiting for the outcry,'' Grant said, wearing a teasing smile.

''There isn't any outcry,'' she said and smiled faintly back at him.

He gave her a questioning look. ''That's not like you.''

His continued attitude of familiarity did nothing to alleviate the inner turmoil he was creating in her, and she had to end this mood of near intimacy.

"Well, it's like me now," she said and turned around to look at him directly, clasping her hands in front of her.

"Grant, I was very out of line to say what I did this morning in the barn, to impose my wishes on you the way I did. I know I've already apologized for it, but I feel that I should once more. And I just wanted to tell you, it won't happen again. Spending tomorrow here will be fine." She moved away. "We'd better go in now. We're holding up dinner."

"Ashley."

She'd gone several paces and stopped, turning back to see that Grant was still standing where she'd left him. He had an odd half-smile on his face, and she tilted her head quizzically. "Yes?"

Grant's smile lingered a moment longer, then settled in his eyes. "It gets unbelievably cold out on the flat of the plains," he said as he began to walk toward her. "It takes all the socks you own and at least two sweaters. We're leaving at six. Be waiting in the kitchen at five thirty if you're going to come along."

Chapter 5

THEY RODE OUT at six-fifteen the next morning, Grant, Nick, Hank Pearson, and Ashley. The snow was knee-high on the horses, and they waded through it slowly, leaving behind the shelter of the big barn for the rawness of open ground as they struck out along the fence line, heading due west.

The light had just come up along the edge of the horizon behind them. Grant led the way on Dakota, Nick at his side. Ashley was some distance back with Hank, mounted comfortably on a spirited bay gelding, and as the light wind picked up, she turned her collar up against its sting.

"Got stuck out on the highway, huh?" Hank asked conversationally as the horses made their way through the deep snow. He was a husky young man with dark hair and a full beard, and he gave Ashley a friendly smile.

She nodded, then let her gaze sweep across the snow-covered countryside. The peaks of the San Francisco mountains were off in the distance, far beyond the nearer red-rock formations rising abruptly up from the flat range around them. They were pieces of canyon wall, sheer cliffs that jaggedly cut into the skyline, and Ashley studied the snow-edged precipices for a time before turning to Hank curiously. "Does Grant expect to cover the whole property today?" she asked, pulling the reins in on her horse as he began to toss his head.

Hank laughed. "Hardly. That takes some doing in two trips, even with hard riding on clear ground. In snow like this and with the slow going, there's no way. We're just gonna ride the west fence line and check up on the buildings. We'll do the rest tomorrow and the next day."

"How much property does Grant have?" she continued.

"Five thousand acres."

"Oh." Ashley looked away briefly, slightly awed by the figure, yet not surprised by it; it was clear Grant was a wealthy man, and she knew, too, that such huge land holdings weren't extraordinary in this territory where vastness

44

seemed commonplace. Grant's acreage might even be considered fairly modest in these parts, she thought and smiled; everything in life was relative. She glanced up ahead to where Grant and Nick were deep in conversation as they gazed out to some distant point, and she looked back at Hank. "What buildings are you going to check on?"

"The cattle barn. It's a ways up yet. You can't see it from here. Then there's a water shed for the herd on beyond that. And the hangar, of course."

"Yes, I heard Nick talking about an airstrip yesterday," she said. "What kind of planes does Grant have?"

"He's got two," Hank answered readily. "There's the Beechcraft, which is a light twin-engine plane he uses for short trips. What a honey! She really handles. I've been up in her a couple of times with Grant." Hank paused briefly to savor the recollection, and his boyish smile was clear evidence to Ashley that he was an aviation buff. "Wouldn't mind having one like her myself," he added somewhat wistfully. "And then there's the Lear. That's a jet," he added. "Silver Phoenix, Grant calls her, and I've never been up in that one. She's Grant's baby, and he uses her strictly for business."

"You talk as if Grant pilots them himself," Ashley said abruptly.

"He does."

Ashley glanced involuntarily at Grant again. His broad back was to her as he sat easily in his saddle, keeping a tight rein on the buckskin stallion who'd begun to nip at the horse beside him. That one major question that would tell her so much about him lay right at hand, and finally Ashley asked it. "And what *is* Grant's business, professionally, I mean?"

The two men up ahead had stopped their horses by a section of barbed wire fence broken down in the snow, and at Grant's signal, Hank responded immediately. He waved to Grant, then shot a last look at Ashley. "He runs companies," he said, then booted his horse forward toward his waiting employer.

The big cattle barn was bustling with activity when they arrived. It was a square frame building surrounded by nothing but flat plain with the canyon mesas off in the distance behind it, and the remainder of Coconino's ranch hands—eight, in all—were there working with the ninety head of Hereford cattle milling around the open enclosure at one end of the building. Hank joined the other men immediately while Grant and Nick disappeared into a small office with a tall, red-headed man. Left alone, Ashley stood out of the mainstream of things, watching the lowing cattle for a time, then finally went to investigate a narrow corridor opening off at the back of the open cattle pen. It led, she discovered upon following it down its short length, to the other half of the building where the necessary supplies for maintenance of the herd were warehoused: more hay, more feed, more machinery.

They'd come the long way to the barn situated in the westernmost corner of the property. They'd ridden the length of the fence line, stopping often for the men to dismount and make a closer inspection of the barbed wire, repairing it, if necessary, before they'd moved on again. It had taken nearly two hours, and Ashley began to feel the gnawing of hunger. She settled down on a lone bale of hay near the corridor entrance, leaning back comfortably against the wall, removing her cap and loosening her hair with her fingers. They'd brought lunch along in saddle bags, and after another fifteen minutes had gone by, she was just about to decide it was time she got hers when she heard the sound of brisk bootheels coming along the cement floor of the corridor.

It was Grant. He stopped briefly in the doorway to scan the room, then came directly over when he spied her.

"Tired?" He sat down on the opposite end of the bale, laying his hat down between them as he drew open his coat. He had on a blue checked shirt and jeans, and he pulled absently at the white bandana around his throat.

Ashley remained resting back against the wall and laughed slightly. "Why should I be tired? I haven't done anything."

He ran his eyes over her face for a moment, then cocked his head. "We haven't been much company for you, have we?" he said.

"Grant"—Ashley spoke his name in friendly admonishment—"I didn't come along to be entertained. I hope you know that. I was well aware that all of you would be working. I'm enjoying just riding. I always do," she added with a pert tilt of her head.

"I'm glad you did come," he told her. "I thought for a minute after I extended the invitation you were going to decline it. You were awfully quiet," he commented.

Ashley glanced away from him to a branding iron hanging

on the nearby wooden wall; at the end of it was the clear
outline of the rocking *C* she'd seen burned into the hide of
every cow and every horse in Grant's stable. Yes, she had
been going to decline the invitation because she knew so
clearly that staying away from him was the very wisest thing
she could do. She'd *meant* to decline; she'd had it on the tip
of her tongue to say, with a gracious but firm smile, "Thank
you but no, I'll just stay here I think," yet when she'd
opened her mouth to speak, what had come out was a warm,
"I'll be there."

She looked away from the branding iron and studied the
tips of her boots. "Well, I . . . considered staying at the
house, but . . . I decided not to," was all she could say, to
him and to herself.

Grant felt the tension in the air and abruptly shifted forward
to the edge of the bale. "Can you shoot?" he asked.

Ashley's head came up in amazement. "I beg your pardon?" she said.

He smiled at her reaction. "Can you handle a rifle?" he
clarified.

"Well . . ." She laughed slightly. "It's been awhile, but
yes, as a matter of fact I can. I'm not a hunter, but I have
done a lot of skeet shooting." She smiled at his look of
curiosity. "I had an interest in precision shooting," she
explained. "It appealed to my sense of perfectionism, or
something," she said with another laugh. "I like things that
can be definitively mastered, where you can see a distinct
result. There's satisfaction in that."

"What do you prefer, a thirty-thirty or a shotgun?" he
asked.

"The thirty-thirty, I guess. And may I ask at what I'll be
shooting?"

"Nothing, I hope." He dropped the cryptic manner then
and went on to explain. "We've got a heifer missing from the
herd. Nick knew about it yesterday, but there was no way to
look for her then. Several of the boys made a cursory search
of the range this morning but couldn't find her. I think she
probably went up into higher ground where there was more
shelter from the storm. Nick and Hank are going on to finish
checking out the buildings and do whatever needs to be done.
I'm going after the cow, and I'd like you to come along, if
you want to," he invited. He smiled into her eyes. "You ride
like a professional, and besides, if you don't yet know how to

throw a lasso, it's probably about time you learned," he added with a slow grin.

Ashley laughed, her eyes beginning to sparkle as they continued to hold his. "I'd like to go," she responded immediately, "but you still haven't told me why we need rifles."

"It's just a precaution. There are any number of potentially dangerous wild animals up around the canyons—coyotes, cougars. I'm not anticipating any trouble, but I just want to make sure that if we should meet up with something and an argument develops, we're the ones able to cast the deciding vote. Now come on," he said, picking up his hat. "Let's eat first, then get going. We've got a long ride ahead."

It took Grant and Ashley a half hour to cross the open range to the edge of the higher canyon ground at the back boundary of Coconino land. They reached the fence line edging the rocky terrain, then turned and, following it, headed in the direction of where the fence would eventually break from the flat ground and angle up into the hills.

Ashley's rifle, like Grant's, was slipped into a case hooked on the back of her saddle, and Grant had given her a coil of rope to loop around her saddle horn, as he'd done with his own lariat. The day had developed into one that was dreary and overcast, yet the wind had died down, easing the bite in the air. Ashley had left her cap in her pocket when they'd gotten going again, and the light breeze gently picked up strands of her hair as she rode comfortably alongside Grant.

"Grant, what does Coconino mean?" she asked at one point as they made their way along the barbed wire fence.

As she smiled over at him, Grant found himself wondering again what her background was exactly and what she really did for a living. She'd been fabricating the personal information she'd given him; he was sure of it. But he would eventually find out everything he needed to know, including the reason why she was so reluctant to speak openly; he'd already made that decision. "It's a kind of sandstone," he answered finally.

"Does that have some special significance for you?" she asked.

"In certain respects. For one thing, the Coconino sandstone is particular to this region, which is one that I happen to love. For another, it forms one of the most conspicuous and continuous cliffs in the Grand Canyon, reaching great thicknesses at some points. That's representative to me of something that has lasted through the ages and weathered all kinds of storms, if you'll pardon the cliché. I like that. I have great appreciation for things of strength and enduring quality. My home is constructed of Coconino sandstone," he added.

"And your brand?" she continued interestedly. "The rocking *C*? Is that for Coconino or Copeland?"

He laughed. "Both. Either. Fortunate coincidence, wasn't it?"

They rode on in relative silence after that. When they reached the point where the fence turned sharply into the higher ground, Grant brought Dakota to a standstill as he scanned the ground around them. "There. Tracks," he said, inclining his head toward a half-obscured line of animal prints disappearing into the scrub-covered foothills.

Ashley prodded her horse forward, looking carefully at the marks, and she followed them for a short distance. "They bear to the right, up this way." She glanced over her shoulder to see Grant coming up alongside her, and he studied the trail for a moment, then shook his head.

"No. The trail is fresher the other way. Over there." He motioned to a second line of tracks. "And anyway, these tracks turn back on themselves. Come on." He reined Dakota around and moved off.

Ashley was still studying the tracks thoughtfully. "No, Grant. They don't look to me as though they turn back." She eyed the marks again. "They seem to go in just the one direction."

Grant pulled Dakota to a standstill and turned him slightly to face the other horse and rider. "Sure they do, Ashley. Take a good look at them," he said. "The indentations in the snow are wider than if she'd just kept going in one direction. You can even see where she backed up and changed direction. Or where something did. Come on. Let's go," he repeated.

Unsatisfied that they weren't about to go off on a wrong tangent, Ashley shook her head and dismounted. Practically climbing through the snow, she trudged to the edge of the thick copse of shrubbery, scouted around, then stood for a time studying the tracks leading up to it. Finally she looked up to see Grant watching her from astride Dakota, his arms crossed, his hat pushed back away from his forehead, and she smiled in concession. "I think you're right," she said.

"I think I am, too."

Ashley remounted and rode up beside him. "I've got snow in the tops of my boots," she murmured in good-natured disgust, scooping out what she could reach with her fingers.

Grant worked to keep from smiling. "That's what you get for being so opinionated," he said.

Ashley threw the last handful of snow to the ground and straightened. "Well, I just had to make up my own mind," she replied. "And actually, I'm not opinionated. I just have the strength of my convictions."

"Yes, that would be what you'd call it."

Their eyes met, and then abruptly they both burst into laughter. When Ashley's had died down, she tilted her head prettily. "Remind me never to confide my opinion of myself in you again," she complained.

"And remind me never to get into an argument with you over something you really believe in," he countered mildly and, after a slow smile at her, turned Dakota around to head them on up into the canyons.

They followed the tracks all the way up into the heights of the craggy foothills. It was hard going through the deep snow, and the horses strained and stumbled as they sought to negotiate the steep rises and narrow rocky passes leading through the canyons. After an hour, they reached the deepest point of Coconino property, but they found nothing there except more tracks that angled them back toward the low ground in another direction. It took them another half hour to arrive at the lower edges of the canyons, and they saw the blood before they saw the heifer.

"Oh God, Grant, I just can't stand it." Ashley's buoyant mood dropped away from her as she stared at the red stain in the snow. Cold, jewellike beauty surrounded them everywhere, but it seemed to her suddenly as if it held nothing but the specter of death. "That blood is fresh," she observed.

Grant didn't answer right away. He'd already pulled his rifle out of its case, and he cocked it as he eyed their surroundings sharply. A clear view of the open ground of the flat range was hidden from them by a last sheer cliff of canyon wall, and he scanned the ledges over to the left intently. "Ashley, you stay here," he said back across his shoulder. "That blood *is* fresh, and there is more than one set of tracks here. I'm going on around the bend. Wait for me to call for you. And get your gun out," he added.

She was slipping it from its case. "Grant, you can't go by yourself," she objected with a worried frown.

She'd brought her horse to a standstill directly behind Dakota, and Grant shifted around to give her a direct look. "Ashley, I don't know what made that second set of prints, but they're larger than a coyote's. And I don't know if whatever made them is waiting around the corner, but if it is, I'll lay even money on its being a mountain lion. Now, just wait for me to call for you," he repeated firmly.

Ashley had already decided for herself that a cougar was responsible for the blood on the ground, just as she'd already played out in her mind the scene of Grant's lone foray around the edge of the sheer wall: the big cat, its muscles rippling along the length of its silky coat as it sprang from a rocky foothold, down onto his shoulders, pulling him to the ground. She wouldn't have wanted that to happen to anyone, but the fear that it might happen to Grant was like a vise in the pit of her stomach.

"Grant, you can't go alone," she repeated emphatically. "It's foolish. I'll cover you just in case. Or, since you're probably more in practice with a rifle than I am, I'll go first and you cover me. But it's okay either way. I can handle a gun, even when I'm rusty."

"You're not afraid, are you?" he asked slowly.

She was silent for a long moment. "Yes, I'm afraid," she finally admitted in a low voice. "But the point is, this is no time for you to be heroic," she said earnestly. Her worried eyes were on his face, and she expelled a small breath. "Grant, I don't want you to go by yourself. I can't let you. If something really is out there, I'm not sure how much of a chance any lone individual would stand, and I—" She paused, and her anxious eyes entreated him. "Grant, please let me help you," she said at length.

He studied her for an instant longer, then finally nodded. "All right," he said. "Let me go first. And if you see something come flying down from the rocks toward me, for God's sake, make sure you aim for his head and not mine." He winked at her with the jest meant to lighten the possibly grave situation, then shifted back around and prodded Dakota forward.

Ashley's dread was great as they made their way slowly

around the canyon wall, but they cleared the end of the cliff without catching sight of a stalking animal. Relief for their safety swelled over her, and suddenly she and Grant both could see the reason for the blood. Ashley brought her horse up to stand beside Dakota, looking down with Grant toward the dead animal.

It was a jack rabbit, its body torn open and discarded in the snow. Ashley slipped her gun back into its case at the back of her saddle and expelled a long breath. "Well, it's gruesome, but at least it's not the cow. Or us," she added feelingly.

Grant had put his own rifle away. Their horses stood very close, so that Ashley's booted foot in the stirrup was just inches away from his, and after a moment, he reached over and ran a gloved finger across the side of her cheek. "You're one hell of a woman, you know that?" he said softly.

A scarlet flush crept up her neck, and it was a moment before she could answer. "You only say that because you're glad you didn't have to find out if I could aim in the right direction," she remarked at last and was able to manage a weak laugh.

"No, Ashley. I didn't say it for that reason at all," Grant answered in a low tone and let his eyes linger on her face a bit longer before he straightened. "And I don't doubt that you could have aimed in the right direction. If I did, I'd have followed you out. Believe me, if I had to take my choice between a mountain lion and a gun in the hands of an amateur, I'd take the cat every time."

His light remark broke the spell, although Ashley could still feel the lingering sensation of his touch at the side of her face. She laughed, and then Grant motioned with his head toward the flat ground off to their left. "Look out there," he said.

Ashley's eyes followed his gaze, and she saw not very far off in the distance a solitary cow plodding slowly through the snow. It seemed such a rejuvenating sight to her: the lone animal, appearing insignificant against the vastness of white range and jagged rock formations around her, yet somehow a testament to the power of a single life over even the most relentless of odds. "Well, she had better luck than the rabbit, anyway," Ashley said, feeling a light gaiety suddenly envelope her again. She looked back at Grant, unable to keep from eyeing him slyly. "And you know, Grant Copeland," she went on, "if you'd been smart at all, you'd have known all we had to do was stand down here at the bottom of the canyons waiting for her to find her own way out, instead of traipsing all over the steepest rocks in the vicinity.''

''No, if I'd been smart at all, I'd have let you come on out here by yourself, since you seem to know so much about it,'' Grant retorted, then, breaking into a wide grin, said, ''Come on. We've got a cow to catch.''

Chapter 6

IT TOOK GRANT only a short time to rope the cow. He and Dakota were a superb roping team, and though the heavy snow impeded any semblance of smooth progress up to their quarry, who'd broken into a frightened lumbering run at the sight of the two riders coming down out of the canyon foothills, still they worked with precision timing, Grant swinging the rope above his head before letting it fly, Dakota plowing straight in the direction of his target despite Grant's having dropped the reins. Each had his separate job to do and handled it, yet each was in tune with the other throughout the operation.

Grant was on the ground, standing by the heifer's head, when Ashley, who'd reined her horse out of the way while they worked, rode up to them. Dakota was where he belonged—standing a short distance away, keeping the rope between his saddle and the cow stretched taut—and Ashley brought her bay to a standstill directly beside Grant. Dropping her reins across the animal's withers, she smiled down at him in open admiration.

"I'm truly impressed," she said. "Do you and Dakota ever do that in rodeo competition?"

"No."

"You ought to. You're really very good. Both of you."

"Thank you." Grant accepted her compliment unselfconsciously.

Ashley dismounted then, hopping down into the snow beside him. "What now?" she asked.

Grant ducked under the heifer's head and came up on her other side, looking at Ashley over the cow's ears. "The heifer's been trailing blood. I saw a patch of it back there." He motioned behind them with his head. "She might've picked it up from the rabbit or she might be injured. I want to make sure which it is."

"What can I do to assist?" Ashley asked, reaching out to

54

give the young cow a friendly pat as she stood nervously
eyeing the man who was holding her neck firmly.

"Well, we're going to have to throw her down to get a
look at her legs," he answered. "I've already checked her
everywhere else and can't find anything."

Ashley moved her horse a short distance away.

"Okay," she said as she returned to stand by the cow.
"You'll have to be the one to throw her, because I'm sure I
couldn't. You hold her down and I'll check her legs."

"That's what I had in mind," Grant said. "Be sure to
stand behind her back when you examine her legs so that you
don't get kicked. She's going to be flailing."

"I know that," Ashley said mildly.

Grant looked at her abruptly, then broke into an immediate
grin. "Sorry. Of course you know that. Now, stand back a
minute," he instructed, and slipping one arm under the heifer's
head to grab the crest of her neck from the far side, he
took hold of her nostrils with the other hand, getting a good
grip. He braced himself briefly, then moved rapidly to flip
her, throwing his full weight against her at the same time he
jerked her head up and around.

She went down heavily on her side, taking Grant right
along with her as he used his entire upper body to pin her
neck to the ground. Being just a heifer, she was still under
adult height and weight and normally wouldn't have been a
problem for Grant to handle. The snowy ground, however,
was very far from usual, and just as Ashley crouched down
behind the struggling animal and leaned all the way across her
to make a cursory examination of the thrashing legs, Grant's
boot slipped. It caused his weight to shift just enough to allow
the heifer leverage against him, and she took immediate
advantage of the situation. Heaving her whole body upward
in one violent movement, she got her legs under her and
lumbered back to her feet; Ashley and Grant were both sent
flying, one in one direction, one in the other.

Ashley landed in the soft cushion of snow, her body making a perfect spread-eagle impression in it, and she lay there
for a moment. She wasn't hurt at all and barely even winded,
and finally she sat up to look around for Grant. She saw him
not far off, sitting where he'd landed several yards away, his
Stetson in the snow beside him, the woolly collar of his heavy
coat encrusted with snow. He was watching in disgust as the

bellowing cow wandered at rope's length in a wide arc around Dakota.

"Well, that was interesting," Ashley remarked mildly, and eyed Grant. "I thought you knew how to handle these things," she added.

He looked over at her. She had snow both in her hair and all down the front of her ski jacket, and she was having a great deal of difficulty holding back a smile. He was no more hurt than she was, and at her attitude, his irritation slipped away immediately. He nonchalantly balanced a forearm on his knee. "I just wanted to see if you were paying attention, that's all," he returned.

"Oh, I see. You let go on purpose, then?" Ashley inquired.

"Of course. You didn't think for a minute that she got away from me, did you?"

She affected a dismissive frown. "Oh, no. Of course not. I . . ." She tried to go on but couldn't and abruptly burst into laughter. She was picturing it in her mind, the two of them unceremoniously catapulted away from the animal, and she was just able to get out, "If only someone had had a camera to snap the two of us!" before she let herself fall laughingly backwards into the snow.

Her hilarity overcame her completely then; she laughed until tears came to her eyes, and as she lay there convulsed in merriment, snow melting down onto her forehead, she felt suddenly like a teen-ager again, ridiculously irresponsible and giddy. It'd been so long since she'd felt entirely unrestricted, so long since she'd spent time in masculine company of her own age and disposition. In fact, there'd never been any man in her life whose nature matched her own the way Grant's did, and she reveled in the feeling of release that the entire day had given her. She was able to get herself back under control when she realized that Grant was no longer sitting off to her left but had come to stand over her.

"Get up, lady, and quit laughing before you send my ego to the morgue," Grant remarked, and he was grinning broadly as he held his hand down toward her. She took it as she struggled to sit up again.

"Oh, your ego is intact or you wouldn't be standing there grinning at me like that," she dismissed good-naturedly as her laughter subsided.

"That's what you think, huh? Come on. Up you go."

With one strong pull, he brought her up to her feet directly in front of him, and when she was finally standing face to face with him, her amusement evaporated as abruptly as Grant's did. They were suddenly acutely aware of one another, standing so close that Ashley could feel his warm breath on her cheek, and Grant could feel hers on his neck. And it was then that everything finally clicked into place.

For both of them, it was as if the shutter of some inner camera of emotions had been activated, switching a lens plate, removing the old one, inserting the new one—the one that fit, the one that belonged and would be there forever. Grant continued to look down into Ashley's face, and his expression grew faintly quizzical as an innate part of him finally recognized just exactly who she was: the other half of him. Ashley stood looking up at him, her own inner being knowing him in the same moment. They did not think about what was happening but merely felt it, and that chemistry bound them silently in profound emotion for moments before releasing them. They stepped back simultaneously.

"Grant, I—" Ashley felt dazed and pressed a hand across her forehead, giving him another searching look before taking one more step away. She had a physical sensation of being suddenly bereft as she stood out of the field of his presence, and said without conviction, "We'd better get back to the cow. I think with one more try we'll be able to manage it."

Grant was watching her, the sudden seriousness of his emotions enveloping him completely. Almost without realizing what he was doing, he stepped back over to her. "Yes." He answered mechanically as his eyes moved over her face slowly. "You're cold," he went on huskily.

Ashley's breath felt stifled with him near her again. "No, I'm not," she murmured.

"Yes, you are. You're shivering," Grant answered, and he carefully began brushing the snow from around her collar and away from her neck before turning her collar up against her throat. He pressed it there briefly, then finally dropped his arms back to his sides.

Ashley had never once looked away from him, and when he finished, she lifted her own hands and did the same for him, dusting the snow from the shoulders of his jacket as he stood perfectly still. Her eyes met his again, holding them as she let her gloved fingertips remain for a fleeting moment at the sides of his neck once she'd brushed away the wetness there, and then she dropped her own hands and looked down at the ground.

The tension between them was acute, and Grant knew that if he didn't step back from Ashley, he would draw her to him, put his mouth on hers; his desire to do those things—to have her completely—was more insistent and overwhelming than any sexual want he'd ever known. But this was neither the time nor the place to let go completely. He finally moved back a pace.

"Come on, Ashley. Let's get going," he said. "It's getting late."

Ashley was still trying to bring under control her longing to feel his hands on her, to give herself to him, anywhere, any time. She thrust her hands into the pockets of her ski jacket. "What about the heifer?" she asked, hardly caring what his answer was.

"I think that was an exercise in futility," he said. "She doesn't act the least bit lame. I'm more concerned right now about you," he said, his expression growing gentle again. "You're cold and wet. If we stay out here any longer, you'll have pneumonia."

"We both will," she said softly, and when Grant stepped back to her, sliding his arm tightly around her shoulders, she slipped her own around his back and walked with him wordlessly toward the horses.

They arrived back home just after dark and entered the house hand in hand through the kitchen door. Nick was there, talking to Marina as the Indian stood in front of the sink washing dishes, and at the sight of the two people stamping their boots on the mat, he raised his eyebrows.

"Well, I was beginning to wonder if the two of you had gotten lost," he said. "If you'd been much longer, I was going to send out a search party." He grinned and watched Grant shrug out of his damp sheepskin coat, then take Ashley's jacket.

"No, we didn't get lost," Grant said. "We just had a little difficulty with the heifer, that's all."

Ashley looked at Nick with a small light in her eyes. "No, *we* didn't have trouble," she corrected. "Grant did. He couldn't seem to keep a grip on the cow long enough to hold her down so that I could check her and make sure she wasn't hurt. I think you'd better work with him," she added as she looked up at Grant, an impish smile on her face.

His dark eyes were alight with humor. They held hers for a moment, and then he abruptly became all business as he transferred his attention to Nick. "What did you find at the other buildings?" he asked. "Any serious damage?"

Nick shook his head. "Not really," he said. "A few things here and there."

"How about the planes?"

"They're fine. I did put a new padlock on the hangar door. The other one was getting rusty and hard to open. Oh, and Grant," he added, setting down his coffee cup, "about those doors on the hangar. I think we're going to have to reset them in their tracks at some point. I want you to take a look at them and see what you think."

"I don't have to look at them. If you feel it should be done, then do it. You know what's what." Grant turned to Ashley. "You've got to get into some dry clothes," he told her.

"You too," she said softly, her hand momentarily going to his arm in concern.

"I intend to," he said. "Now get going."

Ashley was thinking eagerly of a nice, warm shower as she started across the room; it felt so very familiar now. She'd just reached the threshold of the door when Nick spoke up behind her.

"Oh, I almost forgot," he said. "The state plow was out here today. We've been dug out, you'll all be glad to know."

Ashley stopped dead in the doorway, feeling a wave of cold sweep over her as she slowly turned to look back at Grant. Their eyes locked.

"When did they come?" he asked mechanically.

"Late this afternoon," Nick answered and pushed himself upright. If he was aware of the sudden tension between the two people staring at one another across the length of the kitchen, he didn't show it. "I've already spoken to the Bonnards. Well, actually, Mrs. Bonnard knew the truck was here before I did. That woman's got eyes like a hawk. I told them I'd be happy to drive them on into town tomorrow," he continued. "And Ashley, too, of course." He flashed a smile at her before directing his words back to Grant; but neither Ashley nor Grant had yet looked away from one another. "You said you were anxious to take a look at the east fence line," Nick went on. "You can go on out first thing in the morning, and I'll catch up with you. I don't mind."

"No, I'll take Ashley in," Grant murmured, then, as if shaking himself out of a daze, he said clearly, "No, I'll drive everyone in. Now, what about the cars?"

"They're all at Selby's, ready to be picked up. I gave Frank a call," Nick answered.

"Well. That's very good." Ashley had found her voice at last, but she seemed unable to move from the kitchen doorway and was unaware of her hand gripping the doorframe.

She had awakened also, in so many ways. She didn't belong here after all, as it had seemed for a time she did, but had another life waiting for her somewhere else, other obligations to return to. She'd all but forgotten them after that moment this afternoon, out on the windy range, when she'd felt an overpowering emotion for Grant, a man to whom she could give herself entirely. Love, Ashley. That's what you felt for him, what you feel now, a voice inside her said. For the first time in her life, she loved a man with the most honest of passionate emotions, but she could not share that with him. She could not allow herself to because she was bound elsewhere and had to remember that. The ache of her thoughts went all the way through her, and she pressed her lips together hard as she saw Grant cross the room and stop directly in front of her. He laid a hand on her shoulder.

"Ashley, go on and get out of those things," he said. "We'll eat in about an hour. Michael will let you know. And I want to talk to you later. Alone," he said under his breath.

Ashley looked up into his face, a lump in her throat as she took all the exquisite emotions he stirred in her and locked them tightly away inside her, where they had to stay. She was able, after a moment, to give him some version of a smile, and then before the tears that were welling up inside her could overflow, she turned and left the room.

Chapter 7

"OH, MR. COPELAND, it's been a lovely stay. Lovely. You have such a beautiful home. I mean, *Grant*." Nora sat on the couch, smiling warmly up at her host as he stood before the fireplace, one arm resting against the mantle. Dwight was at her side, thumbing through the pages of a magazine, and at her comments, he looked up.

"Yes, your hospitality was more than generous," he said. "If you're ever in Tucson, please give us a call."

"You're both most welcome," Grant replied, glancing briefly at Ashley, who sat quietly on the couch near Dwight, her eyes downcast.

"What time are we leaving in the morning?" Nora inquired. "I don't want to rush you out of bed. Would ten be too soon?"

Grant checked a smile. "Ten would be just fine. The cars are already at Selby's, so it doesn't matter what time we get there." Once again, he looked over at Ashley, and the shadow of a frown passed across his eyes. She'd been quiet like this—withdrawn, really—ever since she'd reappeared from changing her clothes. All through dinner and then afterward, when they'd left the table and reassembled in the living room for the remainder of the evening, she'd said very little to Dwight and Nora and virtually nothing to him except when she'd had to. And she'd kept her eyes averted from his, smiling—when she'd done so at all—with no communication whatsoever. Confusion and frustrated anger at her sudden, unexplainable attitude of remoteness toward him began working a muscle in his jaw, and he felt a surge of gratitude the next moment when Dwight shifted forward on the couch.

"Well, Nora. It's eleven o'clock," Dwight said. "We've got to get a good night's rest for the trip tomorrow."

"Yes, you're right." She patted his knee. "I was just thinking the same thing myself." She rose, smoothing the pleats of her plaid skirt as she sighed lightly. "It was such a nice change of pace. The children would've enjoyed the

61

excitement. Well, it gives me something to tell them about. And you should get some sleep, too," she added, turning to give Ashley a bright smile.

Ashley returned it as she looked up quickly. "Yes, I will." She stood up immediately, following the Bonnards toward the end of the couch, but when she passed Grant, he reached out and caught her wrist covertly, forcing her to stop as Dwight and Nora went on.

"Good night," he called to the Bonnards, continuing to hold Ashley's arm securely as he smilingly watched his other guests disappear from the room. When they had gone, he looked back at Ashley, his eyes no longer light but shadowed and intent. "Ashley, what's the matter?"

"Nothing," she said, her eyes on the Indian rug underfoot, and she tried to ease her arm out of his hold; his grip merely tightened.

"I don't buy that," he countered. "You haven't spoken two words to me all night."

"Grant, I'm tired. That's all," Ashley begged, and she looked up to give him just a brief smile. Then her gaze slid away again.

Grant's eyes had begun to smolder at her continued distance from him. "Ashley, have a drink with me," he said in a constrained voice.

"No, Grant. Really—"

"Ashley!" His anger flashed out suddenly, but it abruptly evaporated as she looked back at him. Characteristically, he wasn't a man of short temper, but even more than that, the sight of her startled-doe expression and the feel of her just inches away from him aroused a heat in him he wanted to vent only tenderly. He dropped her wrist and gently put his palm against her cheek. "Ashley, have a drink with me," he repeated in a voice that had gone as soft as silk.

Ashley blinked once, then felt her hand rise to his on her face, covering it and pressing it there softly. Her eyes returned the caressing smile that was beginning to seep now into Grant's own, and as he held out his arm, she moved into the circle of it and began walking with him slowly back toward the couch.

They were sitting together on the clay red rug in front of the couch, their backs resting against it. The fire was burning low in the living room hearth, casting a soft glow out onto the

surrounding bricks, and the table lamps had been turned off.
Grant had settled them there several minutes earlier, after
pouring their drinks and flipping off the lights, and as he sat
with one leg raised, his arm holding Ashley warmly against
him, he said into her hair, "I want to know what that was all
about tonight, your complete withdrawal from me. I was
there this afternoon, too, you know, and the way you've
behaved with me all night just doesn't fit."

Ashley's legs were stretched out comfortably before her,
crossed at the ankles, and she studied the glass of brandy
resting in her lap. She shouldn't tell Grant what he wanted to
know; she knew that, yet she was going to anyway. Her need
to express her feelings to him, even if only in words, was
simply too strong for her to keep battling. Slowly she looked
up into his face. "I kept to myself because of the way you
make me feel," she said.

Grant's eyes darkened immediately. "And what way is
that?" he asked in a low voice.

A smile touched her lips, then began to shimmer in her
eyes. "Alive," she whispered. "Very much alive."

"That's no reason to shut yourself away from me," he
objected, his arm keeping her pressed close against him.

She laughed faintly. "Isn't it?" she asked. "Grant, I met
you a mere two days ago. Do you know how jolting it is to be
simply—" She broke off abruptly at a loss for an adequate
description. But, too, she'd suddenly become conscious of
just how far she was about to lead them into their emotions.
She remained silent, uncertain now if she really wanted to go
on.

At her hesitation, Grant leaned across her and took her
brandy snifter, then set both their glasses on the coffee table.
He took her by the shoulders then and gently but insistently
shifted her around, pulling her into his arms and positioning
her so that she lay in his lap, facing him, her back supported
by the leg he kept raised behind her. Now that he had her as
he wanted her, cradled in an embrace and with no space
separating them, he prompted, "Simply what?"

She had her arms around his neck, and as she was forced to
look directly into his handsome face just a breath away from
her own, she could do nothing but go on. "Simply swept off
your feet," she finished softly.

He cocked his head. "Is that what you were?"

"Yes."

"So why couldn't you tell me?"

"Grant." She laughed gently in some exasperation; he was so unrelenting in his directness. She looked at him almost helplessly and said without thinking, "What did you want me to do? Simply fall into your arms?"

"Yes. I'd have caught you," he said at once, tightening his embrace as his half-closed eyes held hers.

Oh God, Ashley, what are you doing? she thought as she lay there in his arms, returning his passionate look. Playing a game you have no right to play. Yet, it wasn't a game; for her, it wasn't, and as her love for Grant overwhelmed her again, she buried her face in his shoulder, feeling the hard muscle of his upper arm lightly brush her forehead as he shifted his hold.

"Don't turn away from me," he murmured near her cheek, his face so close to hers he could've touched it with his lips had he moved another fraction of an inch. He didn't kiss her, however, but smiled slowly instead and drew back a little so he could see her clearly. "Ashley," he said quietly when she looked back at him, "you asked me a moment ago if I knew how jolting it was to be swept off one's feet. Well, two days ago, before you walked into my life, I'd have answered no. Now, however, I have to answer yes, because that's what you've done—very nicely, very completely swept me off mine. I've known a lot of women in my life, but never, ever one like you. You're a hell of a woman. I told you that once today already. I meant it then, and I mean it now."

His words sent a thrill of exultation through her, but she couldn't answer them immediately. She could only lie in the circle of his embrace that had closed around her tightly again. She reached up and softly stroked the side of his face as she said, "Grant, tell me about yourself."

He drew his head back again, studying her face in the soft light of the fire. Her long dark lashes brushed against her eyelids as she looked up at him, and to his mind, hers were the most expressive eyes in the world. He gazed into them and answered. "Only if you tell me all about you," he said.

She dropped her eyes. "I already have," she said in a low voice.

"Ashley," Grant chided fondly, "the inflections of a Chicago accent are very marked and are readily identifiable. I hate to tell you this, but you just haven't got them."

Her eyes flickered back to his, widening at his steady gaze, and then she abruptly sat up. Grant immediately tried to stop her from moving away, but she ducked under the arm he threw across her shoulder and shifted to a spot between the coffee table and couch, just beyond the reach of his hand.

He hadn't believed anything she'd told him after all, or at least had seriously doubted what she could now see had been an incredibly flimsy improvisation. Evidence of how unskilled you are at deceit, Ashley, she thought with an attempt to alleviate the self-contempt gripping her again for her dishonesty with Grant. It was even more abhorrent to her now than it had been at the time she devised the story, yet still she hesitated to be honest with him. It was no longer a matter of worrying about his possible ties with Ross; that fear had been forgotten with the deepening of their emotions, for at this point, Grant would never speak casually of their time together. But if she were to tell him the full truth about herself now, after their having come this far emotionally, how would he feel? She knew exactly how she'd feel in his place, and that was the problem. She wasn't sure she could face his reaction, not when she knew there was nothing she could do to help alleviate it for him. Not when she knew, as she did, that she had no choice but to leave him.

Grant saw her troubled expression, and he guessed that any more discussion about this might push her away from him completely, which was the last thing he wanted right now; it would have to be dealt with tomorrow. Feeling the absence of her weight against him like a nagging emptiness, he sought to repair the situation. "I guess you just haven't lived there all that long," he said offhandedly, then leaned forward and gently took hold of her arm. "Now come back here," he instructed. "I liked you where you were."

Ashley did return to him, but with reserve as she settled herself back against his leg where he guided her. Her head rested on his knee as if it were a pillow, and she kept her gaze steadily away from his. What seemed to her to be a ringing silence stretched out too long, and finally she felt the need to speak into it. "Grant, what companies do you run?" she asked, finally glancing up at him.

Grant's eyes had fallen to give her excellent figure his full masculine attention. The black sweater draping casually from her throat lightly hugged the soft contours of her breasts, flattering their fullness before it went on to lay in loose folds around her slim hips. It took him a moment after she'd spoken to draw her eyes back to her face. "How do you know that I do?" he inquired.

"Hank told me." She felt acutely self-conscious all of a sudden, not only because she realized she'd just admitted she'd been asking about him, but because she'd been fully aware of his admiring appraisal.

Grant reached across her to the coffee table for their drinks, handing her the brandy before settling back against the couch with his bourbon. "So, you've been inquiring about me behind my back, huh?" he said and smiled when he saw her blush. "You can stop being embarrassed now," he went on comfortably. "Actually, I was wondering why you never asked me anything except for those few mild questions about my horses. I'd even begun to think that I should let my feelings get hurt by your seeming lack of interest. In answer to your question: I'm an entrepreneur. I do different things. I like management, and I'll take on any company so long as it's just getting underway, or better yet, needs to be picked up off the floor. And so long as the potential for profit is there," he added over the rim of his glass. Her expression had begun to grow very receptive as he talked, and he smiled again. "Business interests you, doesn't it?" he commented.

"Yes, a lot," Ashley said readily. She shifted against his leg, smiling. "When you go into a company, do you get involved financially or just go in and run it?" she asked.

"Both," he answered. "I never get involved where I don't put my money, and I never put my money where I don't have complete control, either as sole owner of the business or as full partner with absolute authority for decision-making."

"What are you doing now?" she went on interestedly.

He smiled. "At the moment, nothing. I don't stay with a venture any longer than I have to. Or I should say, any longer than I *want* to." At her curious look, he explained himself, relaxing more against the couch with one elbow crooked on the cushion behind him. "For me, Ashley, the challenge of being a businessman is in getting a concern going, or rejuvenating one, and taking it to the point where it's producing at its maximum potential. That's what I enjoy—the chase of success. And once I've gotten a company to hit its peak and hold, it's time for me to move on to something new, something that will offer me the renewed challenge."

Ashley said nothing immediately. The chase of success. Such an aspiration fit him, she thought as she considered everything she knew about him now, and she had no doubt that he attained that success every time he went after it; the evidence was all around him. Once again, thoughts of Grant Copeland and his vibrant personality supplanted everything else in her mind, and her eyes shone as she looked up at him. "And what companies have you brought from nothing to something?" she asked.

Grant saw that her reserve with him had slipped away completely, and he let his right hand drop down to rest against her neck; with the backs of his fingers then, he began to softly stroke her chin line. "So far, I've bought and sold two companies," he answered. "Steel in Pennsylvania and oil in Oklahoma. The steel took a little longer than I'd have liked, but we finally made it."

Ashley's pulse had accelerated with his light caress, and not really consciously, she tilted her head toward his hand. "You don't have anything in the offing right now?" she inquired.

"I didn't say that. I just meant that I wasn't involved at the moment," Grant answered. "It's been six months since I was. Frankly, I've enjoyed the time off. It's only when I'm not working that I can live here at Coconino full time, which is what I prefer."

Grant's eyes had been roaming her face throughout the exchange, as if his thoughts were elsewhere, and Ashley had noticed. "Are you baiting me?" she asked lightly.

One of his eyebrows twitched imperceptibly. "Now why would I do that?" The suggestion of a smile passed across his face as her expression went laughingly skeptical, and he lifted his glass then, taking a swallow of bourbon.

"Actually, I'm not dodging your question," he said. "I do have something in the offing, but I haven't even begun to take a really good look at it. And I make it a practice never to discuss the prospects I'm considering before I get into them. I also try to keep people from finding out about my involvement until I'm actually in charge—when I hit the streets, so to speak," he added with a grin.

"Why is that?" Ashley asked in surprise.

"Oh, it's just the way I like to operate," Grant answered lightly.

A smile of comprehension bloomed on Ashley's face then. "Oh, I see," she said. "Very much behind the scenes until you can just spring your formidable presence on everyone, is that it?''

Grant laughed. ''That's not quite how I'd put it. I just believe in buying myself a little temporary advantage, that's all. When you come in unannounced, the competition has to spend time checking you out, watching you to see what you're all about, while you can get on with the job because you've already done your homework.''

''And so, you've been sitting here closeted in your hide-away, getting ready to do your background work, while your poor competitors are somewhere going merrily on their way, unaware of what's about to hit them. Not bad, Grant. Not bad at all!'' she complimented laughingly.

He was smiling too. ''You make it sound as though I were a force to be reckoned with.''

''Are you?'' Ashley asked outright.

''I hope I know what I'm doing as a businessman,'' he said quietly. ''I like to think I do.''

''I'm very sure you know what you're doing,'' Ashley said softly.

Their eyes caught and held, and for the second time, Grant took her glass away from her, ridding himself of his own. And then he gently pulled her to him. ''You're sure of that, are you?'' he murmured.

Ashley could barely breathe as her arms went around him. There was a more urgent quality to their embrace this time, and she knew that if she let this go on, let him actually kiss her, there might be no turning back. ''Grant—'' she began, and tried to move back slightly.

''Ashley, has anyone ever told you that you talk too much sometimes?'' he said in a tender voice and very gently kissed her neck.

An involuntary smile touched her lips at the sensation of his mouth on her neck, and she closed her eyes as she felt the warmth of his lips travel up to her jaw; reflexively, she moved back against him and tightened her grasp around his neck. ''Oh no, do I really?'' she said with a soft laugh.

Grant raised his head to look into her face. ''Every now and then,'' he said with a slow smile.

She opened her eyes at that and let them roam his face lovingly. Reaching up, she gently touched the scar on his cheek. ''How did you get hurt?'' she asked quietly.

''Dakota gave that to me. He took a swipe at me when I

was breaking him,'' he said absently, and then, as he saw the caring for him in Ashley's eyes, he said intently, "Ashley, you're beautiful, do you know that?''

She dismissed the compliment with a smiling shake of her head, then looked at him quizzically for a moment. "Grant, why does Nick owe you ten dollars?'' she asked.

"I don't know what you mean,'' he said, coming out of his languor long enough to frown in puzzlement at her.

She toyed with the collar of his shirt, mildly self-conscious. "Yesterday, after I'd walked right into the path of your bale of hay, he came to the door of the stable while we were talking and said he owed you ten. It had something to do with me, didn't it?''

Comprehension had dawned on Grant's face, and he began to smile slowly. "Yes, it did.''

"He bet you that I'd have some other mishap before I got halfway down the stable corridor, didn't he?'' She laughed slightly and watched her fingertip tracing the edge of his collar.

Grant was nonplussed by her supposition, then abruptly threw his head back and laughed. When his amusement subsided, he shook his head disbelievingly. "Is that what you think the bet was about?''

"I can just hear the two of you making it,'' she answered ruefully.

"Well, you're wrong,'' he said with a complacent smile. "What I bet him, before you'd even gotten up probably, was that he'd think you had the most beautiful violet eyes he'd ever seen. Obviously, you know now what his opinion is. And what mine is.''

A breath caught in her throat, but she could only murmur, "Grant . . .''

"Ashley, I don't want to talk anymore. Not right now,'' Grant said, his eyes going darkly passionate, and he slowly put his mouth down on hers.

Every fiber of Ashley's being came to life as the warmth of his lips met hers, first gently, then with a more insistent demand as the kiss grew. She responded to every pressure of his lips, of his body against hers, and after a time, she trailed her fingers sensually along the back of his neck. It made him groan softly and shift his hand to her back, to bring her even more urgently against him. Then he lightly drew the backs of his fingers across her breast, stroking her with a softness that was like the brush of a dove's wings, and more powerfully exciting than any imperative touch could ever have been. Ashley couldn't repress her own soft murmur of desire as his hand lingered on her body, and at the sound of her moan, he pressed his hand over her breast, then raised his head abruptly.

"Ashley, I want to make love to you," he said, his eyes smoldering and heavy-lidded. "Come to bed with me."

Ashley clasped the wrist of his hand still so excitingly on her body, then abruptly sat up away from him, trying to regain her breath. Her pulse was racing, and after a moment, she felt him move behind her and get to his feet. Without looking at him, she too got up, then slowly turned around.

He was standing a short distance away, his broad shoulders tensed, his breathing shallow. He was looking at her through eyes narrowed with heavy desire, and when she said nothing, he slowly extended his hand. "Ashley, come to bed with me," he repeated in a low, ragged voice.

Don't, Ashley, don't. You'll only be compounding your troubles, and there'll simply be more guilt you'll have to add to all the rest in your life. The inner voice of restraint implored Ashley again to turn and walk away from him, but she no longer heard it as she gave in to her yearning for the heat of Grant's body once more against hers, saw Grant's eyes hold the promise of what was so right for both of them. And she reached out and took his hand.

Chapter 8

GRANT CAME LIGHTLY down the staircase from his loft bedroom the next morning at nine o'clock. The sun was shining through the unshaded windows, and the bright, clear day infused the big living room with airiness. As he swung off the last step to head at a brisk walk across the room, he caught sight of Michael in the dining room doorway.

"Mr. Copeland," the man said, "Marina's holding breakfast for you whenever you're ready."

"Shortly, Michael." Grant continued on, striding across the living room and down the far hallway, stopping finally in front of Ashley's bedroom door. He rapped once, listened, knocked again when there was no answer, then opened the door and walked in. She wasn't there, and the room was as neat as a pin, the bed crisply made—unslept in as he knew, of course, he'd find it. He checked the bathroom briefly for good measure, stopping when he'd come back out to stand indecisively for a moment in the threshold of the door.

He hadn't felt Ashley leave his bed earlier, whenever that had been—sometime between dawn, when he'd awakened to her breath on his neck and her hand sliding arousingly along his chest, and eight thirty when he'd finally awakened again after having made love to her one more time. The memory shot through him like an electrical impulse, and he unconsciously rested his weight up against the doorframe, losing himself briefly to the recollection of the night before.

His hand had closed over Ashley's when she'd put hers in it, and they'd walked together up the stairs to his paneled bedroom in the loft above the main room. He'd lit a fire in the small hearth across from his big, wood-frame bed, then by the light of it, kissed her lengthily again before slowly beginning to remove her clothes. She'd let him disrobe her without speaking a word or even once dropping her passion-filled eyes from his, and when he'd finished, she'd stood before him unselfconsciously. As they'd stood by the glowing firelight, his eyes had roamed her elegant, naked woman's body held regally and willingly motionless for his appraisal; and then, suddenly unable to resist any longer, he'd swept her up and carried her to the bed. He'd lain down beside her after placing her gently on the mattress. She'd seen to removing his own clothes then as slowly as he'd discarded hers, and when she was through, he'd leaned over her and pulled her into a hungry embrace, wanting her with an inferno of passion, needing her more than he'd ever needed any woman in his life.

He groaned softly in response to his memories, and as he remained resting up against the doorframe, the words, "I love you," echoed through his mind. How many times had he and Ashley shared those words throughout the long, slow, beautiful night? So very many—each time he'd made her completely his in the bed across from the flame-filled hearth, and, too, when they'd been simply lying quietly together, replete with satisfaction; once, they'd said the words right along with one another, their lips pressed lovingly together, except that Ashley had added, a small catch in her voice as she'd touched a gentle hand to his face, "Always remember that." A smile emanating from somewhere deep within him lifted one corner of his mouth; he would always remember that, for as long as he lived.

He roused himself from the languorous reverie and crossed to the window, pulling back the drapes to look out into the sunshine reflected glaringly off the snow-covered ground. The horse barn and long cement stable jutting off from one side of it caught his eye, and an unconscious smile once again passed across his face.

Ashley might've gone out there already, he thought, if she wasn't waiting for him over breakfast. She'd told him she wanted to take a last look at his horses before they left to drive into town for her car; she'd been lying against him when she'd said that, her head resting on his chest as they clasped their free hands together, their fingers entwined in a tight hold. The fire had turned to embers by then, casting only a dim light, and he'd decided not to mention at that moment that she'd be going into town only after they'd had a long talk and gotten a few things straight between them. For now he'd speak only of his love and his wanting for this woman who gave herself to him unreservedly, seeking his pleasure almost more than her own, her desire close to abandon in her open passion for him. He smiled consciously at that thought, then once and for all put aside the private memories for another time. What he needed to do now was find Ashley and sit her down someplace so he could go about separating the fact from the fiction of everything she'd told him about herself.

He turned away from the window and strode out of the room, crossing the length of the house to the dining room. Ashley wasn't there, either, but the Bonnards were, and at the sight of him, Nora perked up.

"Good morning, Grant. I hope we're not getting you up too early," she said, repeating her concern of the night before.

"No. I'm usually up before now as a matter of routine. Michael and Marina have seen to everything you wanted for breakfast, I hope?"

Dwight nodded. "It was fine." He pushed back his chair. "What time did you plan for us to get going? Of course, you'll want to eat first, and the drive into town is at your convenience. I just want to make sure we have everything ready."

"Well, actually, I was going to ask Nick Peters to take you in. There are several things I have to see to. I'll speak to him now, and if you've finished with your breakfast and gotten your things together, I'm sure you could be off in half an hour or so."

"Oh, that would be fine," Nora assured, looking somewhat crestfallen. "Someone should tell Ashley Welles, so she can be ready."

"Don't worry about that. She'll be going in sometime later. There was a problem with her car," he went on, improvising to forestall any curious questions from Nora. "Now, if you'll excuse me, I'll go talk to Nick."

The kitchen was empty, even of Marina for the moment, and he'd just turned to walk back through the house to exchange his leather shoes for his boots before going on out to the stable in search of Ashley when the back door opened.

Nick came in stamping the snow from his boots. "Jesus, the roads are bad!" he said when he saw Grant. Registering to the fact that Grant was in wool slacks and a turtleneck sweater, he lifted his eyebrows. "Why are you dressed like that?"

Grant smiled crookedly. "I have a date with a very beautiful lady."

"Oh yeah?" Nick eyed him uncertainly. "I thought you'd be out on the range by this time, at least halfway up the east fence.

"Not me. Not today. You can go out, if you want to. After you drive the Bonnards into town." He grinned. "I've volunteered for you. I have other things to do." He dropped the light manner then. "If you want to wait until tomorrow to check the fence, that's fine. I'll go with you then. Oh, and I'll be driving Ashley into town. Whenever," he added for his own benefit and turned again to leave the room.

"Grant." Nick was frowning in earnest now, and waited for his friend to turn back. "I've already taken Ashley into town," Nick said slowly then. "I'm just getting back from there."

Grant didn't move. "What are you talking about?"

They were staring at one another from across the room, and Nick was aware of the tension that had come into Grant's manner. "Look, Grant, I don't know what's going on—" he began carefully.

"Just tell me what you're talking about," Grant interrupted evenly, though a cold feeling had crept into the pit of his stomach.

"All right. I was out in the stable early, about seven thirty, I guess. Anyway, I was tacking up Cherokee to go on out on the property, like we agreed," he hastened to add, "and Ashley came in. She said the plans had been changed, that you said I should go on and take her into Flagstaff while *you* went ahead and started the inspection. I told her it was fine with me, whenever she was ready to go. She said she was ready right then . . ." He broke off because of Grant's expression, and shook his head in confusion.

Grant had begun to frown heavily, and a muscle was working tensely in his jaw. "Go on," he said in a flat voice.

Nick pushed his Stetson up from his forehead. "Well, I did wonder about things. She seemed very upset, in a hurry to leave. I asked her if she was all right, and she said she was, that she'd gotten a phone call—something urgent at home— that she had to leave immediately." Grant's silence had become stony, and Nick was certain then that Grant hadn't known Ashley was leaving. "She had her bag packed and ready at the front door when I brought the Bronco by," he finished quietly.

Grant was looking at Nick expressionlessly now. "Where did you take her? To Selby's?"

Nick nodded.

"When was that exactly?"

"We got there about eight-thirty, I guess. Grant . . ." Nick looked at his friend in concern. He'd been aware right from the start of Grant's attraction to Ashley Welles, and he didn't need to be told that his feelings had developed into a lot more than casual interest. However, he didn't understand exactly what was going on now, and he walked over to lay a hand on Grant's shoulder. "I'm sorry. I didn't know you weren't aware that she was leaving. Didn't she tell you about the call?"

"There was no call!" Grant said harshly, anger now displacing his initial shock at Ashley's having walked out on him. "Just like there was no change in plans. It was all a lie." The word reverberated in his car. She'd had to lie, one more time.

"Oh." Nick wasn't going to probe the depths of the situation right now. Grant would tell him in time, if he wanted to. "Well, look. You can find out what was wrong when you get in touch with her," he offered in consolation.

"Get in touch with her!" Grant nearly shouted, then dropped his voice immediately, conscious that the Bonnards were probably nearby. "I can't get in touch with her!" he said hotly under his breath.

"Why not?"

"Because I don't know who the hell she really is or where she even comes from, that's why!" Grant snapped. "She lied about all that, too."

Nick was nonplussed. When he realized the full import of what he'd done, unknowingly, he said again, "Grant, I'm sorry."

Grant massaged his forehead briefly, then looked at Nick with a resigned expression. "It's not your fault. You didn't know." His mind was already beginning to work deductively, figuring out what he was going to do, where he was going to look first in an attempt to find Ashley. He'd be damned if he would simply accept this disappearance from her, not after last night. "She'd have to drop the car off somewhere," he said, narrowing his eyes in thought. "I'm pretty sure it was a rental." He looked back at Nick. "Did you wait around Selby's or just leave?"

"I just left. And Grant, it wasn't a rental car. I asked her that. It belonged to her friend," Nick said, hating to have to reveal the dead end facing Grant.

Grant just looked at him, then headed for the door. He'd nearly reached it when Nick spoke up one last time, even more reluctantly.

"Grant, Ashley asked me to give you a message."

Grant stopped, then turned around slowly. "What?"

Nick hesitated. "She said to tell you that she meant everything she said. And for you to always remember that."

Grant stared at him, then turned on his heel and walked out of the room.

PART II

Alas, how love can trifle with itself!

William Shakespeare

Chapter 9

"NO, WALTER, I don't think just one or two successful sales are going to be enough to put DuBrand's back in the running as one of the top auction houses in the country. They'll be an enormous help, obviously, but it's going to take a lot more than that."

Grant Copeland was standing with his back to his uncle as he looked out through the big office window with its view of New York City's Central Park three stories below. It was April now, and the sounds of the noisy city filtered in through the plate glass as Grant watched the scene below. The park sidewalks were alive with people strolling along under the warm afternoon sun—couples with children by the hand, shoppers in smart outfits, a man with a Labrador retriever on the end of a leash and a newspaper under his arm. The trees had come into bud, and though Grant had had occasion over the past fifteen years of his professional life to view spring in New York City, it had never been from this particular window or in the capacity of sole executive officer of DuBrand & Company, Auctioneers of Fine Art and Antiques. The lavish office in which he was standing, with its decor of pastel blue carpeting, Jefferson swag draperies, and Federal period furnishings, had just that very day become his own, and after watching the leisurely scene below him for another few moments, he turned back to look at Walter DuBrand.

"You've let things slide for too long and DuBrand's has fallen too far behind in the industry to make rejuvenation of the business a simple matter of picking up one or two prominent collections to sell off," Grant went on without rancor. "You know all of that yourself. It's going to take work. Real work. And a lot of changes in the way things have been done up to this point."

Victor DuBrand stood up abruptly from his perch on the arm of a velvet wing chair. "You sound as if the shape of DuBrand's business right now was something Father and I saw to on purpose."

Grant eyed him. Victor was blond, slightly overweight, and though he was exactly Grant's age—thirty-nine—the residue of boyishness in his face and his customary air of uncertainty made him seem far younger.

"If I thought for one minute you'd seen to DuBrand's failings on purpose, I'd hardly have gotten involved with either of you as a business partner," Grant said mildly.

"It was Father's idea that you get involved in the first place, not mine!" Victor said, still in an attitude of belligerence. "I was never given the opportunity really to take things in hand. I resented his getting in touch with you three months ago and bringing you into the company. You might as well know that right now."

"Victor." Walter's expression was constrained as he spoke in a placating voice to his only son. He was a slender man of sixty-four, with thatches of gray edging the temples of his dark hair, and he walked over to the two men, laying a hand on Victor's shoulder. "This won't get us anywhere."

"I asked you to give me a chance!"

"Vic, please," Walter implored. "Grant has very kindly offered us his capital to get our company back on its feet, and if we're going to—"

"Very kindly offered his capital!" Victor exploded. "He's taken over the whole Goddamn thing!" He strode the length of the room, then turned back as he laid his hand on the doorknob. "You've been trying to brainwash me into thinking you've salvaged everything for me, but you didn't. You just gave away the whole damn company!" he said hotly and left the room, slamming the door behind him.

Walter pursed his lips, then turned apologetically to Grant. "I'm sorry . . ."

"Don't worry about it," Grant said easily, sitting in the leather swivel chair behind his desk. He smiled with a measure of sympathy. "It's tough for anyone to have to admit defeat, you know."

"Yes, how well I do know," Walter said with a sigh, then pulled a chair closer to the front of the desk and sat down. "I thought when Alex died three years ago that I could step into his shoes. I thought that Victor and I could maintain DuBrand's as Alex had made it—one of the top houses in the auction field. Seems, however, that neither I nor Vic have the same golden touch my older brother had. And I had no idea how easy it was to lose ground in this business. And by the way, how's Marion?" he asked abruptly.

Grant smiled. "Mother was fine, the last I heard. She's been in Europe for several months. Rome, I think. Frankly, I'm not certain. I don't see her all that much, you know."

"The merry widow," Walter remarked and shook his head ruefully. "When Harland died five years ago, I was really worried about my sister. Everyone in the family was. He'd always done everything for her, but she's taken herself in hand just beautifully." He shook his head again. "They're all going, one by one. First your father, then Alex. Makes a man feel old, you know, watching his contemporaries die off like that. Old and very, very mortal."

Grant sat forward, propping his elbows on the desk. "Walter, we've got a lot of things to talk about. And don't worry about Victor. He'll come around."

Walter studied his nephew. Grant seemed completely relaxed and at home in the seat of authority behind the big desk. Walter smiled. "You know, you're just like your father. All business. No wonder you've done so well for yourself, just as he did. You were both about the same age when you made your first million—his in tobacco, of course, yours in steel."

Grant was growing mildly impatient. "Thanks for the compliment. My father was a man anyone would want to emulate."

"Which you do. You made him very proud. Yes, very proud," he repeated in a murmur.

"Walter."

Walter looked up at Grant's pleasant but no-nonsense expression. "Oh, yes. Of course. What shall we talk about first?"

"All right." Grant eased back in his own chair, absently shifting papers around on the desk in front of him. "From what I've seen, the auctioneering of art and antiques can be a fabulous enterprise. There's tremendous potential for prestige and profit if it's done with finesse and forethought. But as I said, you've let things slide. Every auction house needs its steady supply of articles to sell and its steady supply of people to buy. There are plenty of both out there, but they're not coming here anymore. Yes, you've held onto a few of the important collectors who've always been loyal to DuBrand's, but you've lost some others. You've allowed DuBrand's to handle art and antiques of inferior quality, you've let some of the big estates with the important collections slip through your fingers. Your financial statements are lousy. You've got no cash flow, because you've let dealers and buyers who are well able to pay for what they purchase live on credit. That practice makes for pleasant business relations, certainly, but it doesn't pay the bills. I believe in giving a little bit of leeway for payment, but not to the extent you've carried it. All of this you've heard from me before, but I thought it bore repeating.''

"Yes," Walter said, studying his hands.

Grant was aware of his uncle's discomfiture and had no desire to perpetuate it purposely. "All right," he said again and sat forward, clasping his hands on the desk in front of him. "On to specifics. As a first priority, I intend to overhaul the staff here. It's time to get more specialists into our ranks, people who are indisputably knowledgeable about every area of collecting: the different furniture periods, silver, carpets, artists, porcelain, the works. We've got to be able to assess everything that's out there, determine its authenticity and value with crack precision. That's how we're going to be able to persuade sellers to bring their things here. If we can't do that, then we might as well quit right now.''

Grant stood, caught up in his thoughts, and went back to stand at the window, gazing down at the park.

"I want people on our staff who know the difference between what's simply the fashion of the moment in collecting and what's enduring in value and style," he went on. "People who have an eye for quality, and I might add here, people who know forgeries when they see them. You've had several bad experiences, which I don't intend to repeat," Grant said bluntly, turning to look at Walter.

"Yes, yes, I know," Walter, conceded, uncomfortably shifting in his chair. "We didn't realize. They were very well done . . .''

"Exactly. You didn't realize," Grant said. "Your people just didn't have the expertise they should've had. A lot of Alex's people went elsewhere, and you didn't replace them as well as you should have," he added, then held up a hand to stop what he suspected was going to be Walter's further attempt at justification. "I'm not interested in placing blame for those past mistakes. That's not a game I play. I simply plan to see that it doesn't happen again. It's bad publicity,'' he said dryly.

Walter got up from the chair. "And so, what you're telling

me is that you're going to fire an entire staff of employees, is that it?'' he inquired.

"I'm going to fire people, yes, but selectively."

"I don't know, Grant. That seems rather harsh to me."

Grant watched his uncle begin to pace the room. "It's not harsh, Walter," he said quietly. "It's simply good business practice to retain people who are of value to you and let go of the ones who aren't. Don't get me wrong," he went on, cocking his head. "I don't plan to go around with a hatchet in my hand and blindly ax anyone who happens to step in front of me, but I certainly do plan to get rid of those people who aren't pulling their weight. And I'm going to need your help. I think you know who those people are who aren't up to the jobs they've been given to do. You have insights, and I'd like to be given the advantage of them."

"I understand what you're saying, and I suppose it needs to be done. It's just that some people have been here a long time, and—"

"Walter do you want to have a good company or not?" Grant asked tersely then. When Walter looked back at him, apparently indecisive, Grant left the window and perched on the edge of the desk, facing his uncle. "If you want to see this company really running again, then you're going to have to make some tough decisions and stick with them.

"Oh, I know it's rough to be handed your walking papers," Grant went on before Walter could speak again. "I have sympathy for that. I'm not a hard-hearted man. However, I have to keep my mind strictly on what's good for my business, internally and externally. I do whatever needs to be done, conscientiously and within the boundaries of ethical conduct, to see that any company I'm associated with runs as well as possible. I'm not underhanded; I don't double-deal. I'd like you to know that here and now. But I do make the most careful decisions I can, and above just about every other consideration, I keep my personal feelings out of it. That's how I intend to operate here. If you're not going to be able to accept that, then we can dissolve the partnership right now."

Grant concluded his brief monologue and sat with one forearm resting on his thigh as he waited for Walter's response. It was a rather sheepish smile as the elder man returned from the far side of the room, where he'd gone to mix a cocktail at the well-stocked bar located behind a sliding mahogany panel in the wall. He motioned with his glass to Grant. "Can I get you something?"

"No, thank you."

"Grant, I'm sorry," Walter said then, sitting down again in the chair at the front of the desk. "You see now why DuBrand's has gotten in the position it's in. Perhaps I haven't been able to separate my own personal feelings from the things I do as a businessman."

"Perhaps."

At Grant's simple response, Walter squared his shoulders. "What else do you want to discuss?"

Grant slid off the edge of the desk, and resumed his seat behind it. "Actually, I think that's about all we need to go over right at the moment," he said. "Restaffing the company is the first thing I want to work on. But I should advise you that we're going to physically move the location of DuBrand's in the near future."

"Move?" Walter said in surprise.

"Absolutely," Grant said and leaned back, propping one foot on the corner of a low desk drawer standing slightly open. "This is a very glamorous business we're dealing with here," he went on. "Glamor feeds on glamor. People like to come into beautiful surroundings when they're going to buy beautiful things. It sets the proper mood, and besides, all jewels need a fancy setting. We could go ahead and refurbish the galleries and auction rooms here, but I feel that a brand-new location would be better."

"That's going to take a lot of capital, Grant," Walter cautioned.

"I've got it," Grant replied mildly. "And you don't make money without spending money. That's a cardinal precept in business, which I know for a fact you understand."

Walter laughed. "Yes, that much I do understand." He began to chuckle suddenly. "Ross Galbraith better look out. Alex was able in years past to give him a bit of competition on occasion, and it looks like he's in for it again. Finally," he added graciously.

Grant slid down more comfortably in his chair, clasping both hands behind his head in an attitude of easygoing self-assurance. "Yes, Ross Galbraith," he murmured.

Ross Galbraith owned and ran what was going to be Grant's

principal competition, Galbraith Galleries. Long the recognized forerunner in a field abounding with auction galleries large and small, Galbraith's was a refined, majestically dignified establishment with a posh Park Avenue address, and it had had as its only real rival over the years DuBrand's itself, in its more profitable days. Ross Galbraith was a man in his late fifties, as influential in this, his particular field, as Grant Copeland had made himself in others, and Galbraith Galleries had been in his family for generations. However, Grant had found very little in print about Ross Galbraith himself. And he had begun to suspect, from the few Ross Galbraith statements he had read, that Galbraith Galleries in recent years might have been maintaining its pre-eminent position more because of reputation than anything else. He'd never voiced that guess to Walter, however, because at this point it was only conjecture.

Grant came out of his momentary reverie and looked up from the desk on which lay two recent sales catalogues, one from DuBrand's and one from Galbraith's for comparison. "I'm looking forward to meeting Ross Galbraith," he said.

"I'm sure he'd be looking forward to meeting you, too, if only he knew he should be," Walter replied. "As you requested, nothing at all has been said yet about your association with DuBrand's, even within our organization here. Actually, you'll probably get the opportunity for an introduction to Ross at the dinner party tonight," Walter went on. "Philip Townsend, the executor of the Van Holt estate, will be there, and Ross wouldn't miss a chance to see him. That estate will be sold soon, and the auction house hasn't been chosen yet."

"I know, and I'll be pitching for DuBrand's," Grant said immediately. "I want the Van Holt collections. They're the most prestigious collections of paintings, furniture, and rare books on the horizon at the moment, and they'll bring in top dollar. Not to mention giving our reputation a real shot in the arm." He glanced at his watch abruptly and stood up. "But that's enough talk. . . ."

"Yes. Just one last thing, though," Walter said as he got up also. "Grant, it's black-tie tonight. I did tell you that, didn't I?" he asked somewhat worriedly.

Grant repressed a smile. He was accustomed to his family's unhappiness with his unconventional ways and was tempted to tell his uncle that he planned to show up in his Stetson. "Yes, Walter," he said, "you told me. I've pulled my tux out of mothballs. I'm fully aware that this business revolves around social functions and that they call for finery. I think my attire will be entirely appropriate for a stroll around a lavish Westchester estate. However, if you think the satin lapels on my jacket look a little frayed tonight, just tell me. I'll buy another one." He broke into a grin.

Walter smiled. "That's all then?"

"Yes, except that I'd like you to go down now and make the announcement about me to everyone," Grant said. "Let's do things right. I don't want our employees to read in tomorrow's paper that DuBrand's has a new chief executive. That makes for bad morale. And while you're doing that, I have a phone call to make. However, when I'm finished, I want to talk to whoever's responsible for this catalogue." Grant picked up the DuBrand sales catalogue lying on the desk.

Walter was frowning worriedly again. "That would be Karen Ryland. Grant, you don't intend to let her go, do you? She's very—"

"Good?" Grant finished for him with an easy smile. "Yes, you're right. She *is* very good, which is precisely why I want to talk to her. Catalogues are extremely important. They're our drawing cards for the sales, and I want to meet the individual who was responsible for this one. It's as good as, if not better than, Galbraith's."

Walter relaxed visibly. "Yes, I thought so, too. I'll speak to everyone, then send Karen up. You'll like her. She's very bright, conscientious, has an eye for cataloguing and exhibit setup. She's helped Victor and me quite often in setting up the presale displays down in the galleries."

"Good. I want to meet her." Grant resisted the urge to check his watch again as his concern about the telephone call he needed to make grew more pressing. "Now, if you'll see to everything . . ." He let the sentence trail off suggestively.

"Of course." Walter turned to leave, then abruptly came back, extending his hand across the desk. "Grant, thank you. For deciding to help us out, I mean. Your reputation for bringing a business back from the grave is well known, and I don't mean just in the family."

Grant returned the handshake firmly as he smiled at his uncle. "I'm not doing you any favors, Walter. I'm in this for myself, you know. The challenge of putting this company back on its feet looks like it's going to be an interesting one. However, I'm glad to be able to help you in the process.''

"Which you will," Walter said confidently, then left to share his news.

Chapter 10

GRANT LEANED BACK in his swivel chair as he listened intently to the voice on the other end of the telephone. He was scowling heavily, and finally, at a statement made by the other man, he abruptly tossed the pencil in his hand out onto the blotter.

"Damnit, don't tell me there's nothing you can do!" he said angrily into the phone. "There has to be! People don't just vanish off the face of the earth. She had to leave some kind of trail that you can pick up. You're just not looking in the right places." The man on the other end of the line said something else, and Grant sighed impatiently as he stood up and guided the telephone cord around the end of the desk. He walked with it to the window, where he stood looking out unseeingly, and after listening for a time, he forced himself to answer evenly.

"Yes, Joe, I understand you have almost no information, but you've had three months—you and your agency—to come up with something. No, her name isn't Welles. I'm willing to bet money on that. It might not even be Ashley, but I think it is. People don't respond immediately to a name that isn't theirs, and she did. And for Christ's sake, stop looking for her in the Midwest. She doesn't come from there. I've told you that over and over again!" Grant exploded again, his frustration getting the better of him once more.

The other man spoke again, and Grant lightly massaged his forehead. As the man repeated the sketchy information Grant had heard once a week, every week since Ashley had disappeared, he sighed again. "Yes, I know there are dozens of cabins in the mountains and that any one of them could belong to her friend. Yes, I understand that they're mostly vacant now. But check the real estate records at the court house! No, I know we don't know what name we're looking for. What about the information from the airlines? Have you been able to obtain passenger names yet?" He listened, then erupted again. "Goddamn it, she had to get to Flagstaff somehow! And get back out. Why don't you—ah, never mind! Yes, I know you're doing the best you can. All right. Keep me posted,'' he said and turned away from the window as the private detective hung up. He strode over to the desk to slam the phone back down in its cradle, then he stood by the desk, staring off across the room.

It had been three months now since that day when Nick Peters had told Grant Ashley was gone. Three months of searching for her through a detective agency and on his own as best he could, all of which had so far gotten him nowhere.

He'd driven into Flagstaff himself, immediately after Nick had explained what had happened, but there'd been no sign of Ashley, nothing to learn about where she'd gone. She'd left Selby's right after reclaiming the car that belonged to her friend. That was all he knew for a fact. He'd gone to the airport and found no silver Datsun in the parking lot, spoken to the ticket agents in the small airline facility without result; no one had seen a woman fitting her description, and they would've remembered. There wasn't that much activity there. He'd even inquired through his friends in the control tower about private planes, but none had landed there in the past week. After driving slowly through Flagstaff, keeping an eye out for her car—to no avail—he'd finally been forced to return to Coconino. He'd made the same trip several days later, thinking perhaps she'd gone up into the mountains to see her friend, then left, but there'd been the same upshot: nothing.

His thoughts of Ashley wouldn't leave him alone. He'd exhausted all his own methods before finally seeking professional assistance in his search for her. By now he had to admit he might never find Ashley again. He'd gone on with his life, as he'd had to, but with a certain emptiness, and the hurt of all those lingering unknowns. He felt alternately angry and disconsolate about Ashley, as he replayed through his mind their night together, then its aftermath; he'd been see-sawing between those two emotions throughout the last three months. And had remained completely and irrevocably in love with her.

He was still heavily preoccupied with his thoughts of Ashley when a knock came at his office door. Forcing his mind back to the business at hand, he called loudly, "Come in."

The paneled door opened to admit a pretty young woman with long dark hair. She looked to be about thirty, Grant thought as she closed the door behind her, and she was dressed in a plaid skirt and smart navy jacket. The door clicked softly as she shut it, and she walked directly over to him.

"You're Grant Copeland, the new boss. I'm glad to meet you," she said, extending her hand.

Grant appraised her as he accepted her firm handshake. Her eyes were brown, set wide apart, and she had a nice smile, though it was rather fixed at the moment. He smiled at her forthright approach. "Yes, I'm Grant Copeland. And you're Karen Ryland?"

"That's right. You wanted to see me?" She lifted her eyebrows slightly, almost defiantly, Grant thought.

"Yes, I did. About this." He leaned over and picked up the catalogue. "You do very nice work."

"Thank you." She stood stiffly before him, her hands clasped in front of her.

Grant eyed her thoughtfully, then moved around behind his desk, gesturing toward the chair Walter had occupied earlier. "Have a seat. I want to talk to you."

She eased herself down slowly, perching on the very edge of the cushions. "Yes."

Grant sat back, cocking his head. "Miss Ryland, you can relax, you know." He smiled pleasantly, but his words seemed to have an effect on her exactly opposite from the one he'd intended. Instead of easing the tension etched in her expression, he seemed to have increased it.

"Mr. Copeland," she said in a formal voice, "I like my job. I do it well, I think. I'm quite sure that you plan to clean house around here. Every new executive seems to feel the need to do that, whether it's necessary or not. I doubt seriously you'll be any different. I would like you to know that I'll of course respect your wishes if you want me to leave, but I won't like it. And I think you'd be making a big mistake if you let me go. I just wanted you to know right off how I feel."

Grant looked at her, then threw his head back and laughed. "Miss Ryland—Karen, if I may—I think we're going to get along very well. You speak your mind, which is the kind of thing I like to see. And if I do feel the need to clean house, as you put it, you can count on the fact that you won't be one of the people swept out the door."

She gave him a gauging look, then finally relaxed, easing back into the chair. "That's good," she breathed.

Grant was still smiling. "I meant what I said. You do very nice work. I intend to put DuBrand & Company back into the running as a major auction house, and I'm going to need your help. Catalogues are vitally important. You've done a beautiful job with what you've had to work with, but you're going to have more. I'm going to spend a lot of money on catalogues. I want more photographs, more color, more detailed descriptions of the articles for sale. And a larger subscriber list. The time for sitting around waiting for buyers to come to us is long past. I want to aggressively pursue attendance at our sales, and to do that, we've got to have effective publicity materials."

Karen's face had begun to light up, and she sat forward eagerly. "That's just what I think! I've been telling Walter and Victor for a long time that we have to take that kind of approach. Granted, it's my own bailiwick I was trying to promote, but you're right. That is what has to be done. That and a lot of other things. I have ideas—"

"Karen." Grant spoke pleasantly but with a firm edge to his voice. "I appreciate your outspokenness, just as I appreciate the fact that you have ideas, interest. However, at the moment, I'm doing the talking."

"Yes, of course," she said, settling back again in her chair, but she couldn't resist adding, "Catalogues *are* important, though. It's all part of the beauty and glamor. And I don't know if you're aware of this or not, but Galbraith's lost its best cataloguer three years ago. She was really super. I don't mind admitting that myself, as much as I don't mind admitting I'm glad she's gone," Karen added with a grin. "It's greatly eliminated the competition in catalogues, and maybe in other aspects, too. She could've really done things for Galbraith's if she'd had the opportunity to move into other areas. I feel very loyal to DuBrand's, and before she left, I was beginning to develop a healthy dislike for her, although I never met the woman."

Grant was leaning back in his chair, digesting her comments and responding in a very different way than Karen had intended. Perhaps the woman she'd talked about was still available, he thought, then narrowed his eyes slightly as he looked at Karen. If she was ever going to get anywhere, Karen would have to learn to deal with what was definitely a bent toward antagonistic competition, he thought. And she might have to start very soon if he did offer a job to the cataloguer who'd left Galbraith's. "And what happened to the woman?" he asked. "Where did she go?"

Karen gave him a wry smile. "She didn't go anywhere. She married the boss after his first wife died. Apparently she prefers a life of luxury to toiling in the fields, because she gave up her job when she became Mrs. Galbraith."

So much for that, Grant thought and straightened. "I see," he remarked absently. "Well, Karen, I merely wanted to meet you, to introduce myself, and to tell you that we've got a lot of hard work ahead of us. I see that I can count on your help."

"Absolutely," she said with a smile that was inspired now by more than simply the reassurance that her position at DuBrand's was secure. She studied Grant Copeland, sitting so easily behind the elaborate desk—his handsome face, the set of his broad shoulders in the jacket of his beautifully cut suit—and she unconsciously brushed her hair back from her face. "I think I'm really going to like working with you," she said sincerely and stood up. "This is an exciting business, especially when it's really going."

"I'm sure it is," Grant said, and he watched her with a thoughtful smile as she crossed the room and disappeared out the door.

Chapter 11

THE WESTCHESTER HOME of Gaylord and Priscilla Eldridge, patrons of the arts, was a breathtaking estate. Nestled within acres of rolling, residential land, the white-columned home sat on top of a knoll, and a long macadam drive wound up to it from the main, tree-lined road nearly a half-mile away. Grant, Walter, and Victor arrived that evening at eight o'clock, and they were stopped directly under the wide portico of the house by an attendant who took Walter's car keys and escorted the threesome toward the majestic sweep of steps leading up to the house. A host of elegantly gowned and tuxedoed guests was already thronging the large porch, wandering in and out of the double front doors thrown open to the warm evening, and there were groups of people standing out on the lawn sharing champagne and animated conversation. The lavish Eldridge buffet dinner party was a social affair, undeniably, yet more than a few business deals would be struck over a glass of sherry or champagne in the drawing rooms inside; Grant knew that, and he hoped that one of the contracts initiated during the evening would be his. He intended to at least make headway toward potential negotiations with Philip Townsend, the executor of John Van Holt's estate.

Inside, they were announced by a formal manservant at the portal of the expansive living room decorated in gilded Louis XV furnishings and hangings. The Eldridges greeted them warmly, and Grant's introduction into the society that had become, for a time, his professional affiliation, began. He was a stranger to most of the people in the room, for this was very much the art collecting crowd—mostly impresarios, theatergoers, dilettantes with whom he'd had little contact during his years in the steel and oil industries. But though the faces and occupations were different, the process was the same, and he handled it with the same finesse that had made him so successful in everything else he'd done. After nearly an hour of circulating through the guests with Walter and accepting congratulations for his entry into DuBrand's, the two men stepped out of the mainstream, near the open terrace doors, and accepted another glass of champagne from a passing servant.

"They have quite a crowd here," Grant remarked as he scanned the people milling around.

"The Eldridge parties are famous," Walter said. "Everyone who's anyone in this territory is invited—and makes an effort to attend, I might add. Which is why I was so eager for us to come. It's the very best opportunity for you to be introduced to the widest possible number of our potential clientele." Grant nodded absently as he continued to survey the room, and after a moment, Walter went on, uncomfortably.

"Grant, I'm sorry about Victor. In the car on the way over, I mean."

Grant gave his uncle his full attention then. "Walter, I told you this afternoon: He'll come around. And if not, well . . ." He hadn't made that inference earlier, that if Victor couldn't accept the inevitable, there was little to be done about it. Grant would make the effort to bridge the gap between them, but he would go only so far. Tonight Grant would've preferred to come alone, but he'd bowed to the need for an initial effort at togetherness and had left his gold Maserati in the garage below his newly acquired apartment on Central Park South. Victor had been openly short-tempered and abrasive on the drive out from town, and though Grant had ignored him, the trip had been decidedly uncomfortable.

"Don't worry about him," Grant said again. "Just give him time."

Walter dropped the subject and let his gaze follow Grant's out toward the roomful of people. "The Galbraiths aren't here yet, at least as far as I can see," he commented.

Grant, too, had been keeping an eye out for the man and thought he would've recognized him if he'd seen him. He'd come across a picture of Ross Galbraith in a business publication he'd been reading for information. Galbraith was an aristocratic-looking man, with sharply defined features and silver hair, a handsome man, in a mature, distinguished way.

"You know," he said, "I just realized, I've run across only one picture of Ross Galbraith in all the reading I've done on this business. That seems a little odd in a business where public relations is so crucial."

"It won't when you get to know him," Walter replied, smiling at an acquaintance who passed by in front of them.

"The man abhors personal publicity. It goes against his grain. The Galbraiths are blue bloods," he remarked. "Descended from the English nobility, so they say."

Grant raised an eyebrow at that. "Meaning?"

"Meaning nothing, really," Walter answered and motioned them out of the way of a servant laden with a tray of hors d'oeuvres. They stepped back, closer to the row of tall, French doors. "They take their lineage very seriously, and all of them have been extremely conscious of reputation, from Ross's grandfather right on down to Ross himself, who is, by the way, the last of the Galbraiths—he has no children. Of course, Ross knows the value of publicity as well as the next man, though even that's kept to a minimum, but whatever publicity he allows never includes anything personal," he explained. "Even strictly professional photographs of himself are permitted only now and then. I find this predilection for a low profile a bit obsessive myself, but it's the way the man handles himself," Walter said with a shrug, and added, "Galbraith Galleries is a very low-key organization."

"Yes, I got that impression from my reading. I also got the feeling that that quiet, unprepossessing attitude has pretty much been the style of all the auction houses."

"To a degree," Walter conceded.

Grant didn't tell him all that was about to change for DuBrand's; he merely sipped his champagne.

"Ross remarried about three years ago," Walter went on. "He married one of his employees. It was all done very quietly, without a word about it to the press. I can understand why, actually, knowing Ross's attitudes," he added, and flashed Grant a wry look. "The man's always mortified by insinuation, whether it's valid or not."

Grant was watching Walter in mild curiosity. "Yes, I was told he'd married the woman who did his cataloguing. What's so wrong with that?"

"He was afraid the press would have a field day with it, I suppose. You see, the woman is twenty-some years his junior, and he'd only been widowed a year when he married her. Now, if you were a newsman in search of a story, what would that sound like to you? A young woman after an old man's money? A lonely man bewitched by a predatory female?"

Grant laughed. "Maybe she *was* after his money," he said.

"Well, I don't know," Walter murmured. "She's a lovely woman, from what I know of her. No, I really don't know—"

he repeated, then abruptly ended the conversation when a couple approached. They were all soon engaged in conversation, and shortly, a second couple joined them.

It was sometime later, after Grant and Walter had left the foursome and continued to circulate through the room, that Walter nudged Grant. "There. Coming through the door," Walter said, motioning slightly. "Herbert Willingham."

Grant followed the line of Walter's gaze across the room and saw the stout, balding man entering alone. "Ah," he murmured, downing the last of his champagne and setting the glass on a nearby table. "Ollie, they call him, right?"

"Right," Walter said. "Ross Galbraith's right-hand man. He's a nice fellow, knowledgeable, too."

Grant continue to study the man. He was somewhere near Ross Galbraith's own age, Grant decided, pleasant-looking, with a shiny pate and a wide smile. He shook hands jovially with everyone within range as he stepped into the living room, and Grant had just looked away and accepted another glass of champagne from a waiter when the butler's voice announcing the newest arrivals drifted into his consciousness. The name Galbraith registered immediately, and Grant quickly thanked the waiter as he turned back toward the doorway. His expectant expression drained away instantly, however, as soon as his gaze found the portal of the living room. His breath lodged in his throat, and he could do nothing but stand stock-still, his champagne glass suspended in midair as he stared at the couple across the room.

Like every other man there that evening, Ross Galbraith was attired in a black tuxedo with snowy white shirt and satin cummerbund. He appeared to be a fit man for his age, trim, and his silver hair shone against his fair complexion in the bright light of the overhead chandeliers. He was of moderate stature, yet commanding in presence—because of his polished, charming manner, Grant thought as he watched Ross graciously take the hand of his hostess and smile warmly at the guests moving up immediately to greet him.

But though Ross Galbraith was an eye-catching figure, it wasn't because of him that Grant was unable to look away from the scene of cordial greeting going on in the doorway across the room. It was because of the woman on Ross's arm.

She was nearly as tall as Ross, and was wearing an exquisite, off-the-shoulder black gown that accentuated her statuesque height and slender figure. Her short black hair was swept back from her face in a style that was simple but flattering to her narrow face. At her throat was a sparkling choker of diamonds, around her wrist a matching bracelet, and to Grant, who watched her smilingly accept Gaylord Eldridge's handshake, she was the most beautiful vision of an elegant, sophisticated society woman he'd ever seen.

And she was the woman who'd told him her name was Ashley Welles.

Chapter 12

ASHLEY'S THROAT WAS SO dry she was certain she'd never be able to speak. Her breath was coming rapidly, the bodice of her elegant black gown rising and falling unnaturally fast, and as she, Ross, and Ollie stood in a small group of people halfway down the length of the grand Eldridge living room, she felt as if someone had suddenly tossed a blanket over her, suffocating her. There was nothing she could do at the moment, however, about getting away from the handsome man standing directly in front of her, and when it came her turn finally to respond to Priscilla Eldridge's introduction of Grant Copeland, she managed to extend her hand toward him.

Grant's own hand closed over hers without hesitation. It's familiar warmth was transmitted to her in an impulse that was almost painful, and she heard him say smoothly, "Mrs. Galbraith, it's a pleasure to meet you."

"It's a pleasure to meet you, also, Mr. Copeland," she said woodenly, immediately drawing her hand out of his. Grant was smiling at her with seeming ease, but she could see the shimmering intensity in his eyes as they remained on her. She dropped her own gaze, and when Ross spoke up on her other side, she again avoided eye contact with Grant and stared at her husband instead.

"What is your profession, Mr. Copeland?" Ross asked interestedly.

"I'm in the auction business," he replied, and took a sip of champagne. "I've just taken over DuBrand's. Today, as a matter of fact," he added with a smile as polished as Ross's.

Ashley's eyes shot to him then. Grant's gaze locked with hers for one brief minute before drifting languidly back to Ross.

"Oh, really?" Ross was saying. He was watching Grant with new curiosity. "I hadn't known DuBrand's was in the market for new management. There've been no rumors."

"No, I'm aware of that," Grant said.

"What business were you in before?" Ross now wore a

faintly quizzical look, and as Ashley watched him, she had a sudden mental image of her husband, busily thumbing through magazines, phoning around, trying to get a line on his new competitor. *No homework.* Ashley tore the vision out of her mind, making an involuntary, jerky motion of her head.

"Steel and oil," Grant replied.

"A little far afield," Ross said, relaxing visibly, and now there was a faintly superior edge to his smile. He accepted a glass of champagne from a servant without giving the uniformed man a look. "Art and antique auctioneering is rather a long leap away, I'd think."

"Perhaps," Grant said easily, "although it's always been my premise that every business is merely a matter of proper marketing. I consider certain techniques of running a company to be universal. So far they've worked beautifully."

Ross inclined his head noncommittally, and Grant smiled again. With exaggerated solicitude then, he turned his full attention to Ashley. "Mrs. Galbraith, are you feeling all right? You seem a little pale," he said.

He was wearing a suave smile, though his eyes were slightly narrowed, and Ashley wanted suddenly to reach out and slap him for what he was doing. Toying with her. Retaliating for what she'd done to him. Her momentary anger vanished in the face of that understanding, and she glanced nervously at Ross. He, too, was watching her now.

"Ross, I'm fine," she said with a reassuring touch on his arm. She turned back to Grant then. "Thank you for inquiring, Mr. Copeland, but I'm perfectly all right," she said lightly, then added quickly, "Now if you'll all excuse me, I have something to take care of." She smiled at Ross. "I want to find Elizabeth Maitland," she explained.

Ross raised his eyebrows at her abrupt departure, but Ashley turned quickly and was soon lost to view in the throng of guests. She'd known that if she didn't get away from Grant, from the shock of seeing him at all and then the further stunning news that he'd taken over DuBrand's, she might've collapsed right where she stood. A swooning woman; something you've never been in your life, Ashley. The inward attempt at humor was no help, and her need to reach the terraces leading out to the Eldridges' formal gardens only increased. She wanted fresh air and solitude—and time to think, to get a grip on the emotions that were pulling her in so many different directions all at once.

Her progress toward the bank of French doors on the far side of the room was slow; she was waylaid at every step by friends and acquaintances—among them Elizabeth Maitland, to whom Ashley had nothing of consequence to say. Yet she spoke breezily to the woman, as she did to them all, laughing lightly, all the while praying that she could control the tight spring of tension inside her. It took nearly half an hour to wend her way across the room, but she finally reached the open doors and stepped gratefully out onto the terrace.

It was a wide expanse of gray slate that stretched the entire length of the back of the house. A long, shallow flight of stone steps led down toward the gardens, and at the moment, the patio was free of guests in the immediate vicinity. There were several groups of people engaged in conversation toward her right, some distance down, and as a uniformed servant carrying a tray of champagne passed by on his way toward them, Ashley reached out abruptly and took a glass. The man stopped deferentially, and as he watched with pretended disinterest, Ashley downed the champagne in two swallows. She set the empty glass sharply back on the tray and promptly picked up another one. This time the waiter looked distinctly curious, and she tried to smile nonchalantly.

"That will be all, thank you," she said.

He nodded and continued on his way. Left alone again, Ashley moved forward slowly toward the flight of steps, raising the champagne glass to her mouth and taking another healthy swig. She was just about to down the rest of it when a voice spoke up casually behind her.

"I suspect Ross Galbraith would be horrified if he knew that his wife was out here on the terrace drinking like a sailor."

Ashley nearly spilled the champagne as she spun. Grant was standing in the threshold of one of the French doors, the light of the bright room behind him, silhouetting his powerful figure. "Grant, what are you doing here?" she whispered, biting her bottom lip as she quickly scanned the area for spectators to their encounter; there were none at the moment, thank God.

Grant smiled darkly. "I told you inside. I've taken over DuBrand's. I do that, you know. Run companies?"

Ashley felt simultaneously hot and cold, and not because of the jarring events of the evening. Her dismay was solely because of the way Grant was regarding her—with an unpleasant, sardonic expression. It looked unnatural on him and probably was unnatural to him, she thought with a stab of desolation, except right at the moment. Because of her. Because of what she'd done. "Grant, I—" she began softly.

"And tell me," he interrupted in the same nastily urbane tone, as he stepped out of the doorway and slowly approached her. "Is the eminent Mr. Galbraith aware that you can hold your own with a rifle? For some reason, I can't think he'd find that knowledge terribly pleasing."

Ashley opened her mouth to speak, then shut it abruptly, spinning away. She downed the rest of her champagne, set the glass on a nearby concrete bench, then rushed down the long flight of steps, holding up the hem of her gown as she headed into the garden. Tears were stinging the edges of her eyes as she ran from Grant and his ugly manner, and she followed the brick walkways through the maze of plantings to the deepest point of the elaborate garden. High hedges surrounded her on both sides, and at length, she disappeared around the edge of one.

She found herself in a small secluded alcove with a black wrought-iron bench nestled at the back. She went to it but didn't sit down. Instead, she merely stood there, taking deep breaths, then abruptly buried her face in both hands.

Moments later she heard the sound of footsteps coming along the walk, then halting at the opening of the alcove behind her. She knew it was Grant, and when he didn't speak, she raised her head finally and slowly turned to face him.

In the moonlight, she could see that there was nothing mocking about his expression any more; it was seething with explosive intensity.

"Grant, listen to me . . . ." she began again.

The sound of her voice seemed to compel him to move. He strode to her, taking her bare upper arm in a grip that was painful. "Why didn't you tell me you were married?" he demanded harshly.

Ashley could barely speak, barely move in the face of his palpable wrath. "Grant—"

"I *said*, why didn't you tell me?" he repeated angrily. "I don't tread on other men's property!" He grabbed her left hand, jerking it up roughly as he eyed the large cluster of diamonds in her wedding ring. "It's beautiful. Why weren't you wearing it?" he demanded and flung her hand away from him.

No, not like this; I never, ever wanted it to be this way.
Ashley closed her eyes in anguish at the point they'd arrived
at, then opened them and tried to speak as calmly as she
could. "I never wear my ring when I ski or do anything like
that," she explained. "It's a Galbraith family heirloom, and
Ross would be apoplectic if I lost it." Her expression grew
imploring. "Grant, I felt I couldn't tell you I was married
because—"

"Couldn't tell me!" he erupted, then dropped his voice; it
literally shook with fury as he went on. "You couldn't tell
me that little bit of information but you could certainly hop
into my bed without a second thought. Why didn't you just
say that all you wanted was a casual roll in the hay? If I'd
known, I might've handled myself differently!" He flung the
words at her, then abruptly let go of her arm, turning on his
heel to walk a few feet away from her. He stopped there with
his back to her, his hands balled into fists.

Ashley stared at his tense shoulders, every cell in her body
crying out for her to rush to him, to take him in her arms and
hold him tightly, so she could try to somehow comfort his
hurt. But she knew she couldn't do that; he was closed away
from her, bitterly furious, and she suddenly sank down on the
bench, dropping her face into her hands again. She'd hurt
them all by what she'd done: Ross, though he wasn't even
aware of it; herself, because she had to live with the knowledge of her infidelity, and Grant. Oh, she'd known so clearly
how hurt Grant would be if he found out the truth, she'd
known from the moment she'd gone into his arms! As they'd
made love that last night at Coconino, she'd nearly cried out
in remorse when Grant had said, "I love you," his heart in
his gaze all the while, but she'd let him say it, let him go on
with his avowals of love because she'd needed to hear them
and return them more than she'd ever needed anything in her
life. She looked up at his back again, her sorrow for the pain
she'd brought to him more unbearable than ever now that
she'd had to witness it vented in fiery anger, and finally her
tears overflowed.

She fumbled at the silver evening bag she'd brought along
that evening, getting the clasp open at last and pulling out a
tissue. She remained sitting on the bench, pressing the tissue
to the corners of her eyes, and she felt Grant's presence near
her again before she actually saw the trouser leg of his
tuxedo.

"Stop crying," he said coldly. "I don't feel like listening to it. And I want answers, Ashley. I want them now." He paused when she didn't respond, then, because he couldn't help it, he said, "Did you marry the man for his money, or are you honestly going to try to make me believe you're in love with him?"

Ashley's tearfulness evaporated instantly at his question, and she rose, her back rigid. "Don't you ever say that to me again," she said, her voice trembling suddenly with her own anger. "You can call me anything you like, but don't you ever insinuate that I married Ross Galbraith for his money!"

"For some reason, self-righteousness doesn't seem to fit you at the moment," Grant shot back, his anger rekindled.

"You don't know what fits me because you don't really know me!" she defended.

"Don't know you?" Grant's tone was incredulous. "Oh, Ashley, I know you. I know you very well. You gave yourself to me completely, as openly as if you'd been doing it all your life. Or is that how you act with any man who happens to come along?"

Ashley's hand flew out to slap the side of his face, but Grant caught her wrist in midair. They stood in violent confrontation then, seething, raging at one another with flashing eyes, until suddenly something shifted inside each of them. Their eyes still clashed but flickered. And then, abruptly, they both melted. Grant dropped Ashley's wrist and his arms slid around her back at the same time she reached out for him; she fell into his embrace as he pulled her to him roughly and held her there, possessively, as she held him around the neck. They couldn't even break apart to kiss, so strong was their need just to hold one another, and they clung together, Grant's face against Ashley's hair as he closed his eyes to the feel of her, Ashley's face buried in his neck.

"I slept with you and gave myself to you the way I did because I couldn't help it," Ashley said brokenly, pressing herself more closely against him. "I couldn't help it, don't you understand that? There aren't other men! I'm not like that!"

Regret for the vicious exchange that had occurred between them was already etched into Grant's face, but at her words, he raised his hand to the back of her head, holding it protectively to him. "Ashley," he groaned. "I'm sorry, Ashley. I didn't mean it."

She'd begun to cry in earnest now as she held onto him desperately. "I wasn't playing a game with you," she went on. "I wasn't. You can hate me for anything else, but don't hate me for that," she wept into his shoulder.

"I don't hate you," he whispered. "Oh my God, Ashley, I don't hate you." He drew a long breath, and after a moment, he lifted her face up to his. Her cheeks were wet and he felt only gentleness as he watched her struggling for control. He leaned down and kissed her then, softly, briefly. Raising his head finally, he gazed at her with quiet but still troubled eyes. "I don't hate you, Ashley. I love you. Didn't I say it enough times? But Jesus Christ, why didn't you tell me you were married before I went and fell in love with you?"

"Would it have made any difference?" she asked uncertainly.

He was silent for a long moment, then said, "No."

"Grant, I love you," Ashley whispered then and slid her arms back around his neck, closing her eyes as she felt him catch her back into a full embrace.

They remained that way for a very long time, holding each other, letting their emotions grow quiet. After a while, Grant brushed his lips across her hair and said, "Ashley, I want answers. I need them."

Ashley lingered in his arms a moment longer, then raised her head and stepped back from him. "Yes, you do need answers," she said tiredly and sat back down on the bench. She was exhausted by the extremes of emotion he'd inspired in her; he always would take her feelings to extremes, she realized. Never, ever had one individual been able to affect her so intensely, in every way. She dabbed at her face with the tissue, then looked up at him. "Do I look very bad?" she asked.

"It doesn't matter," he brushed aside, crouching down in front of her.

"Oh, Grant. It *matters*," she said, trying to dredge up a dry humor she didn't feel in the least. "It matters a lot, to Ross."

At that, Grant's jaw tightened. "Ashley, do you love him?"

"Grant," Ashley said, letting her hands lie quietly in her lap, "there are different kinds of love."

His expression darkened. "Don't hedge with me anymore, Ashley. I want the God's honest truth from you, from here on out. No more lies."

"No, Grant. No more lies," she said quietly.

"Do you love him?" he pressed.

"You mean the way I love you?" she asked with the whisper of a tender smile. "No Grant. I could never love any man the way I love you. But as for Ross—" her troubled gaze drifted over toward the wall of high hedges—"I have a fondness for him. I did when I married him, and I do now, though sometimes it's hard—" She broke off, shaking her head. "I can't explain it all to you now," she said, meeting his eyes again. "Not with Ross just inside."

She saw his expression of annoyance at being put off again, and her own temper aroused. "Grant, I'm well aware of my failings, but I want you to know one thing," she said, frowning unhappily. "I don't take the matter of infidelity lightly. Despite what you may think, I didn't hop into your bed without giving it a second thought—not even *your* bed. I fought with myself the whole damn time, and if you don't want to believe that, then you don't have to!"

"Ashley." Grant took her hand immediately as she turned her face away from him. "I'm sorry I said those things. I was angry. I was hurt. I apologize from the bottom of my heart." After a moment, he couldn't keep an involuntary smile from his face as he watched her tight expression. "And tell me, just how does the dignified Mr. Galbraith cope with your sharp tongue? Do you curse at him, too, or is that reserved solely for me?"

When she saw his grin, her defensiveness evaporated. "Well, Ross and I do have our moments," she remarked, her rueful smile faintly dimpling one cheek. "And though my cursing certainly isn't reserved for you, I doubt you'd have any compunction about handing it right back to me."

He laughed. "You're right."

Her smile lingered a moment longer, and then she sighed. "Grant, I want to explain everything to you," she said. "You can't imagine how agonizing the last three months have been, because of what I did to Ross, of course, but more, because of what I did to you."

"You think I can't imagine how painful they were? After you simply walked out on me the way you did?" he countered.

She reached out and rested both hands tenderly along the sides of his face. "Oh, Grant, I do love you so," she said softly. "And I'm so sorry for the way I've hurt you."

Grant's physical desire for her had been dangerously close to the surface. Now it got the better of him entirely, and he rose, pulling her up and against him. With one hand behind her head, the other low on her back, he kissed her deeply. Ashley understood the demand in the pressure of his mouth, in her own response to it and the way his hands moved across her back, and though it was the very last thing in the world she wanted, she broke away from him quickly. "Grant, I have to go back inside," she said. "I've been gone too long already. I can't take the time to explain everything to you now. It's very complicated, and I want to do it right. But I will explain," she promised.

Grant didn't want to relinquish her, but he knew he had to. "All right," he consented, letting her step back from him. "But it's going to be tomorrow."

"No, not tomorrow. Tomorrow is impossible." She just wouldn't be ready to face him that soon. She had so much thinking to do.

"The next day then."

Ashley nodded. "Yes, Friday."

"We'll go to my apartment," Grant said, brushing one finger lightly down her cheek.

"No." Ashley fleetingly touched his hand, then took another step back, and though she saw Grant's expression darken again, she was unyielding. "No, Grant. Not yet. There are a lot of things I have to think about, a lot of decisions I have to make, and . . . Grant, please," she said beseechingly, "don't put any more pressure on me than is already there. Just let me explain."

He had little choice but to accept her terms. "All right, Ashley. Where do you want to meet?"

"I don't know." Their rendezvous must be at some place innocuous, and where it was unlikely that either of them would be known. After a moment, an idea came to her. "At the zoo. I'll meet you at the Bronx Zoo," she said turning around to him.

Grant's annoyance surfaced completely. "For God's sake, Ashley! What the hell kind of place—"

"At the zoo, Grant," she repeated, coming back over to take his hand briefly and squeeze it. "Meet me in front of, let's see . . . the elephants. Every zoo has elephants. I'll meet you there at eleven o'clock."

"Ashley!" Grant made an effort at further protest, but it got him nowhere, for she had turned abruptly and disappeared around the hedge, and he could hear the fading sound of her brisk footsteps as she hurried back to the house.

Chapter 13

THE NEXT MORNING was sunny and bright, and Ashley sat alert in the English saddle, scanning the fences on the hilly, open hunt course of Shadow Knolls. She was wearing her formal black riding coat, rust-colored breeches, and boots, and finally sure of her route over the obstacles, she picked up Sharif's reins in her gloved hands and moved her big, black horse forward with her heels to his sides.

"You be careful now," Andrew Cantrell cautioned, slapping her leg as he moved back out of her way. Andrew was the owner of Shadow Knolls, the exclusive riding stable in Westchester where Ashley had boarded Sharif for the last three years; he was a tall, lanky, easygoing man in his early forties, and he and Ashley had been good friends from the start of her association with the club.

"Always," she said and tossed him a wink over her shoulder.

"Take it slow! This is only a practice run; there's no clock on you!" he called with his hands cupped to his mouth, but Ashley was already off and away. He shook his head in fond exasperation as he saw her push her horse into a fast canter downhill to line up for the first jump, and, going over to lean on the white-railed fence, he watched her.

She was soon over the stone wall at the bottom of the grade, pulling up on Sharif, then heading him at a sharp angle toward the wide water jump. "Jesus," Andrew murmured when he noted the horse picking up speed, his thundering hooves scattering clods of dirt out behind him as he approached the difficult fence. But Ashley had him over it with room to spare and sailed on to the triple bars, jumping a ditch in between, pushing the thoroughbred even faster to another wall, over a broad jump at the top of a sharp incline, and finally to a completely clean round with a handy negotiation of the high post and rail. Breathing hard, her cheeks flushed with high excitement, she brought Sharif down and was relaxedly swaying in the saddle, her reins dropped over the horse's withers, when the animal finally ambled back over to Andrew.

"You're going to break your fool neck one of these days," Andrew muttered, taking Ashley's hand as she dismounted lightly, then began walking beside him back toward the stable, Sharif behind her on the end of his reins.

"Oh, no I'm not," she countered good-naturedly, and she glanced back over her shoulder at the course. "Andrew, the bars are loose on the post and rail. We should have Randy fix them, or if he's busy, I'll try. *That's* all that's dangerous—unsecured equipment—not how the riders go over the field," she said facetiously, grinning back at him.

"Yeah, you think," he chided and frowned. "You ride that course too fast, Ashley. Slow it down. A little healthy fear would do you some good."

"I've got my share, thank you. I just don't show it off," Ashley remarked as she brushed back a lock of hair blowing in the light wind. She smiled warmly. "I'm okay. Don't worry so much, and anyway, you know that I'd have better sense than to ride like that on muddy ground. Today there was good footing." She grew thoughtful as they neared the barn, bustling with activity—riders leading mounts, stable hands with buckets, several curious spectators.

"The vet was coming to take a look at the leg on that new mare, wasn't he?" she said. "I think I'll find out if I can help. You busy?" she added, glancing at him.

"Yeah. I've got to tend the books," Andrew responded in a manner resembling a groan. "That is, unless you might want to take care of it," he added with a hopeful lift to one eyebrow.

Ashley laughed. "That's what I like about you, Andrew—you're so subtle. Yes, I'll switch chores with you," she said comfortably. "Give me the key to the office." Andrew handed it over with a complacent smile, and giving him a look of mock exasperation, Ashley veered off toward Sharif's stall while Andrew went in the other direction.

She stabled her horse and remained with him for a while after brushing him down, cleaning out his stall and refilling his water and hay. She hopped down finally from her perch on the feed bin, brushing off the back of her jodhpurs, and on her way to the office to attend to the matter of finances for the small operation, she stopped in at the tack room to have lunch with her friends, ensconcing herself comfortably on a dusty trunk, one booted foot propped on the lid while she talked horses with her cohorts and shared a good portion of her tuna fish sandwich with the stable dog, Fritz. By the time she'd gotten to the office and settled down to the paperwork, it was one o'clock, and she finished it at four-thirty. Noting the time, she quickly put away the heavy ledger books in the battered file cabinet in the corner of the office, retrieved her purse from the bottom drawer of Andrew's desk, and pulled out her car keys. Leaving the office key for Andrew under the outside mat, she headed toward the parking lot.

In the nearest pasture of the well-kept riding establishment, Ashley caught sight of Sharif grazing leisurely, and she altered her course and went to stand for a minute at the fence. He was a beautiful animal, Sharif—the finest of horseflesh and expertly schooled. More evidence of what Ross has done for me, of what I have because of Ross, she thought, and her eyes grew cloudy as she glanced toward the turf on the far side of the fence. She remembered the hour, however, and drew herself out of the pensiveness, walking briskly across the gravel walkways, past the row of tall shade trees lining the macadam parking lot, and to the car that Ross had given her to drive—a beige Mercedes sedan.

A half hour later, she reached the house and drove in through the heavy iron gates at the foot of the drive. The Galbraith home was an eighteen-room stone mansion located on fifteen acres of land, and the big, imposing house itself was hidden from view by a thick copse of trees encircling it. Ashley rounded the circular drive to the front door and pulled her automobile into the end space of the eight-car garage. Once there, she felt a tug of relief. Ross wasn't home yet.

Inside the house, she called a friendly ''Hi'' to Alicia, one of the six domestics in the household, and briskly crossed the ornate entry hall, trotting lightly on up the curving, white-banistered staircase. In the upper hall, she bypassed the door to the bedroom she shared with Ross, going down two more doors to her own sitting room. There she shrugged out of her dusty riding jacket, tossing it across the arm of the velvet-upholstered couch.

The small sitting room was strictly for Ashley's use, and she liked it particularly. She'd removed some of the marble and brass accoutrements that had been in the Galbraith family for generations, not because she had no appreciation for them but to make room for her own personal memorabilia. Above a carved shelf she'd hung her old riding ribbons from long-ago competitions, faded now and curled with age, and below, along the shelf itself, sat the newer engraved trophies she'd earned with her riding achievements over the past three years. Beside the silver show ring goblets and trays were two tall ski trophies she'd been awarded in her college days, and on the far wall, she'd traded several of Ross's Old Masters drawings for three watercolor landscapes she'd done one high school year as she'd recuperated from a broken ankle gotten while playing tennis. The back corner of the small desk near the window held her photographs of Georgia, Brett, and Grif, and she studied the pictures of her family as she sat down in the chair in front of the delicate writing table.

Grif, at sixteen years of age, was smiling as he sat perched on the upper rail of a pasture fence, and Georgia and Brett were standing side by side on the porch of their modest Pennsylvania farmhouse, Georgia smiling her quiet, matronly smile, Brett looking as gruff as ever. Ashley grinned involuntarily at her uncle's familiar dour expression—beneath which lay the most sentimental of hearts—and on a sudden impulse, she picked up the telephone. After three rings, she heard a click, then Georgia's soft voice.

"Hello," Ashley said, smiling as she unconsciously leaned back in her chair. "You sound rushed. Did I get you away from something?"

"No, dear," Georgia answered. "I was just at the door with the postman. The phone and the doorbell came at once."

"Always," Ashley laughed.

They talked for nearly thirty minutes, about friends, Georgia's needlework class, Ashley's most recent show with Sharif, an interesting dinner party she and Ross had held at the house the week before, and when Brett got on the line at the last, Ashley smiled at his predictable inquiry.

"You all right, girl?" he asked. "Ross treating you okay? You can always come on home if y'have to."

"Yes, I'm fine," Ashley said. She'd never fully confided her and Ross's problems to Brett and Georgia; it would only make them worry, and Ashley hated doing that. They'd been hit hard enough when Grif died.

"You eating enough?" Brett went on in his rumbling voice.

"Stop sounding like an old hen!" Ashley chided fondly. "Yes, I'm eating enough, and you'd better look out. Your

sensitivity is showing," she added. The teasing comment, as
always, brought a harrumph from her uncle, and after promising a visit in the near future, Ashley bade them a warm
good-bye and hung up, simply sitting for a minute at her
desk; it always gave her such a feeling of well-being, talking
with them. The hands on the small gold clock at one side of
the desk caught her attention, however, indicating that six
o'clock had come, and wanting to be sure she was out of her
riding clothes by the time Ross arrived home, she popped up
from the chair. Scooping up her jacket from the arm of the
couch, she left the study and headed back down the hall.

The master bedroom in the Galbraith home was a luxurious
suite of two rooms: an imposing bedchamber and an adjacent
study for Ross. It was decorated in gilt-and-painted heirloom
French furnishings, with a color scheme of lemon yellow; an
ornate cut-glass chandelier hung from the center of the ceiling. Brocade draperies hung at the deeply alcoved window
across from which were the twin beds, each covered by a
yellow satin quilt to match the tufted, satin headboards rising
halfway up the wall. The entire mansion that had been in the
Galbraith family for more than a hundred years was furnished
in the rich rococo style, and when Ashley entered the room,
her riding coat slung haphazardly over one shoulder, she
stopped abruptly just inside the door. "Oh!" she exclaimed
in surprise.

Ross stood in the door to the study, wearing a monogrammed, green silk dressing gown and holding several papers
in his hand. He took in her appearance for a moment, then
smiled in welcome as he removed his wire-rimmed reading
glasses. "Good evening, dear," he said in his cultured voice.

"Hi," she returned and moved at last. Crossing the Oriental carpet, she went directly to him and kissed him on the
cheek. Stepping back, she smiled through her discomfort at
being caught at this late hour in her riding attire. "I didn't
think you were home," she said. "Your car wasn't in the
garage." She gave him a fleeting look of puzzlement.

"Sanders has taken it down to the garage," Ross answered,
slipping his glasses into the pocket of his dressing gown. "It
was running poorly, and I left the office early to have it
repaired."

Ashley nodded, then turned to walk quickly into her dressing room. Once inside, she shucked her boots, breeches, and
white shirt covered with a thin film of dirt, slipping into a

satin mocha-colored negligee; as always, they would be dressing formally for dinner. Ashley returned to the bedroom, sat
down at her skirted dressing table, and began to brush her
hair vigorously.

Ross came to stand behind her and put his hands on her
shoulders. "You look lovely in that dressing gown," he said
fondly to her reflection in the lighted mirror above the dressing table. "I've always thought so."

"Thank you," she said, smiling as she continued to brush
her hair.

"The Bennets will be in town next week," he told her.
"We got a card from them. I left it downstairs in the drawing
room for you to read." He watched her as she laid down the
brush. "In his note, Earl mentioned our bridge game the last
time they were here. He was quite taken with you as a
partner," he went on and smiled reflectively. "I don't blame
him. The two of you beat Carol and me quite soundly. The
next time, I think I'll keep you for myself."

Ashley smiled again and studied Ross in the mirror. At
fifty-seven, he was still an attractive man, and to look at him,
Ashley thought, one would never suspect that he was a man
suffering from a serious heart condition; his complexion was
clear, and his gait was still youthfully brisk. She herself
hadn't known about his weak heart until she'd married him,
when she also learned that the problem had grown more
serious in the last few years, the angina attacks more frequent
and unnerving. He'd finally been forced to give up playing
tennis altogether, an activity he loved and the one that had
kept him fit throughout his life; Ashley was reminded of that
fact, regretting it for him, every time she looked out on the
empty tennis courts behind the turreted mansion.

Ross's eyes had strayed thoughtfully toward an Oriental
silk hanging on the wall beside the dressing table mirror.
"Last night's dinner party was particularly nice, don't you
think?" he asked. "Priscilla's parties always run so smoothly." He was caught up for a moment in silent admiration of
what he considered to be Priscilla Eldridge's superlative social
graces, then Ashley saw the shadow of a frown pass abruptly
across his mirrored brow. "I was really quite surprised at the
news about DuBrand's," he said. "Quite surprised."

Ashley picked up her brush again and lifted it to her hair;
she'd been pushing away thoughts of Grant all day, keeping
constantly busy so that she'd have no time to think and could

let her system adjust to the shock it had received the night before. It was inevitable that he'd finally come to the very forefront of her mind, however; that was where he'd been, without relief, every waking moment for the last three months.

She'd left Coconino in a distraught rush that morning after the long, glorious night in Grant's arms, running away in that stark manner because she'd felt that she had to. Though the ultimate intimacy with Grant had given her a sense of total serenity, as if all the pieces of herself had finally fallen into their proper place, there'd been so many other emotions working on her, too, and painfully, she'd felt she had to leave before Grant wakened. She'd slipped quietly from his bed, just as dawn was breaking, and after getting dressed, she'd come back to stand beside him for a moment, tears streaming down her face as she'd lovingly studied his sleeping figure sprawled out under the sheets. At length, she'd reached down with trembling fingers to tenderly caress his forehead, softly brushing back a lock of his tousled hair; it had been her silent, anguished good-bye to him. She'd torn herself away then, faltering only once in her resolve to leave, and after looking back at him one last time, from the doorway, she'd finally hurried from the room, returning home to the life with Ross that had only been made that much more complex by the new guilt she'd added to it with her infidelity. Grant had become simply a heart-rending memory—of the man she would forever love and who had given her the same inner fulfillment she knew she'd given him. And then, last night, he'd walked back into her life, and in one single evening, her life had acquired complications she'd never even dreamed of.

"Odd," Ross murmured.

Ashley was pulled from her reverie by the sound of Ross's puzzled voice, and she looked back up to his reflection. He was frowning, his manicured hands still resting absently on her shoulders.

"Odd," he repeated, his perplexed frown deepening. "I wonder why the man didn't announce his association with DuBrand's before now?"

Because that's the way he does things! Ashley wanted to exclaim but didn't, of course, not only because of the significance the response would have had but because she knew that Ross hadn't really asked the question of her. He wouldn't consciously discuss such a matter with her; he had simply been talking aloud to himself. Yet, she did respond, in a careful way. "Ross, Galbraith's is in good shape," she said, the flicker of a concerned frown on her brow. "You don't need to worry about anything."

"Of course not," he murmured abstractedly and patted her shoulder.

"Although I . . . you should probably keep a close eye on what's happening over at DuBrand's," she added quickly.

She knew better than to say more, had spoken at all only because she was feeling a sudden, real alarm about the future of Galbraith Galleries. This was Grant Copeland who had come to run the rival company, not just any man. She couldn't be sure, of course, that he constituted a serious professional threat, but she sensed that he did; she believed in him, instinctively. How ironic their conversation of three months ago now seemed. She'd been genuinely impressed by his habit of slick entrances, and she closed her eyes briefly in pained chagrin.

"Now, Ashley, you mustn't concern yourself with my business," Ross chided and reached forward, resting his hand against her cheek.

"Ross, I only meant—"

"Ashley, *don't* go on about it!" Ross's voice lashed out like a bullwhip. "You know I can't abide my wife involving herself in my business affairs. It isn't your place to do so." His hazel eyes snapped as they bore into her reflection in the mirror, and then, abruptly, he was once more wearing a smile that held all the debonair charm in the world. "What you need to be concerning yourself with are the social obligations of Mrs. Ross Galbraith," he went on fluidly. "Such as this afternoon. You were out when Greta Jorghenssen called for a visit. Fortunately, I came home early and was here to receive her." The rebuke this time was far more subtle, but there all the same. "And Madeleine Carruthers spoke to me last night at the party," he continued. "She said they missed you at the last meeting of the Garden Club. I had thought you'd gone," he added with a quizzical frown.

Ashley was staring at him in the mirror, her eyes flickering. The chameleon—Ross Galbraith. So charming, so magnanimously gracious on the surface; below, a man rigid as steel, and capable of the most stinging severity. She'd been stunned the first time she'd seen it, in that same lightning-fast transformation. In all the years she'd worked for him, she'd never suspected what austerity lay beneath his exterior of *savoir-faire;* no one would, until they knew him well. She continued to look at her enigmatic husband, a man who could sometimes be so sincerely generous, then rose from the chair, easing her shoulders out from under his hands as she moved away. Her long negligee flowed around her slender figure as she walked to a spot beneath the crystal chandelier, and she turned back to face him, her arms at her sides. "Well, Ross, I . . . just didn't go," she said levelly.

Ross regarded her steadily. "Why not?" he inquired.

"Ross, I dislike those meetings," Ashley said in the same even tone, already knowing the script of what was to follow; the sequences were so predictable, repetitive. She might've laughed at the knowledge that she could recite the impending exchange almost verbatim if it hadn't been so depressing that she could, so *sad.* "You know how I feel. It's difficult for me to sit for hours just chatting idly. I don't have a lot in common with the woman there."

He thrust his hands in the pockets of his dressing gown as he gazed down at the toes of his leather slippers. "Yes, I know you've told me that, and it's nonsense that you have nothing in common with them. You are all women of position," he responded, looking back up. "And I know as well that I've told you how important it is to me that the Galbraiths be represented civically."

"Ross, please—"

"Ashley, I'm not asking you to devote all your time to these activities," he interrupted in a matter-of-fact tone. "I don't want that at all. But I do expect you to make the proper appearances around town in your capacity as an influential member of this community. And I don't understand your attitude toward these volunteer associations. There's nothing wrong with them."

"I know that, but they're just not the kind of thing I, as a person, enjoy."

Ross cocked a disapproving eyebrow. "Ashley, we all have to do things we don't like to do sometimes," he said. "I do it all the time. I would like to see you learn how to put your personal feelings aside and meet a few of your obligations."

There it was—the patronizing tone she liked least of all. "Please don't talk down to me like that, Ross," she said in a tightly controlled voice, her back suddenly stiff. "No one deserves condescension, and I won't accept it." Her chin lifted. "I do meet the obligations I feel are important and many that I don't. It would be nice if I could sometimes pursue my own interests without always being taken to task for them," she said, frowning now.

Ross turned away, speaking over his shoulder as he went to the small bar near the dressing rooms. "Ashley, we're quarreling again, and I don't like that," he said. "You do nothing but put us both on edge when you argue this way. Besides, it sets the servants talking." He slid back a panel in the wall and revealed a collection of shimmering crystal glasses and cut-glass decanters. He poured himself a small glass of port, and turned back to look at her; her lithe figure was tense under the beautiful fabric of the brown negligee. "However, since we have gotten onto the subject of your own interests, we'll discuss it. Obviously, you spent the entire day at Shadow Knolls."

"Yes, I did spend the day there," she admitted, purposely going over to the night table and picking up a copy of *Art Review*.

"Ashley, you know how I feel about your activities at Andrew's," he said.

She began to flip through the pages of the magazine, keeping her eyes trained on them.

"I don't mind that you ride. It's a perfectly suitable pastime for a woman of breeding, which is why I purchased Sharif for you. You look well on him, and I'm quite proud of your achievements with him in the show ring. But you *must* stop hanging about the place like a common stable hand," he went on. "It isn't an image that I care for in my wife. I know you muck stalls and fork hay over there. I've had reports of it."

"I don't fork hay, I *pitch* it, Ross," Ashley retorted and slapped the magazine back down on the stand, really angry now. "And I wouldn't have to spend so much time at Andrew's in an effort to save my sanity with some semblance of work if you'd just let me go back to my job at Galbraith's," she added.

"Ashley, you have got to stop bringing that issue up! That matter is closed," Ross said sternly and set his glass down sharply on a nearby table. "Ross Galbraith's wife doesn't work. You know that, and I won't pursue any discussion of the subject with you. And I don't care what you call working with hay—forking, pitching—the point is, you do it, and I don't like it." Abruptly, his expression became stony.

"Ashley, you may not be aware of this, but people are beginning to talk about you and Andrew because of the amount of time you spend over there. I know, of course, that your relationship with the man is above reproach, but others aren't so certain of that fact. It doesn't look good, and I won't endure insinuations of any kind, nor a situation which invites them. I was subjected to scandalous rumor once, and I don't ever intend it to happen again!" He stalked over to the study door, tightening the knot of his dressing gown sash with a jerk as he turned around to face her. "Ashley, I would think that you'd have a little more regard for my feelings in these matters, after all I've done for you!" he said angrily.

As she stood looking at him across the span of the beds, it seemed to her that this was all they ever did anymore: argue. And always about her, about what she did, what she said, who she wanted to be. She knew he was at fault, too, with his inflexible insistence upon propriety and his refusal to see another point of view, but the fact that she was always the central issue of every dispute that arose between them some-how seemed to tip the scales of blame for their arguments to her side. And yes, it was true he had done a great deal for her. If she now found the mold he kept trying to force her into confining, well, she'd stepped into it of her own free will. Her shoulders dropped, and skirting the end of the bed, she went to him quietly.

"Ross, I didn't mean to anger you. I'm sorry. Of course I have regard for your feelings," she said, a troubled look in her eyes as she did her best to smile at him. "And you know there isn't anything but friendship between Andrew and me." She hesitated briefly, then added, "I won't do anything but ride at Shadow Knolls from now on. I promise."

Ross relaxed, his smile reappeared, and he reached out and took her hands in his. "That's much better, my dear. I knew you would never intentionally embarrass me by behaving like a field hand." He kissed her on the cheek, then drew back, a light suddenly coming into his eyes. "And now, I have something for you. I was going to wait until later to give it to you, but I've changed my mind." He let go of her hands, then turned and disappeared into the study.

Ashley, you're one hell of a woman . . . She was barely aware that Ross had returned as the echo of Grant's rugged, masculine voice rang through her mind, but she managed to smile on cue as Ross laid a blue velvet jeweler's box in her hand.

"Open it," he instructed expectantly.

She did and drew out an elegant diamond-and-emerald bracelet. Ross's eyes were sparkling as he took it from her, then fastened it around her wrist, and he cocked his head as he waited for her reaction.

"Ross, it's beautiful," she said, forcing herself to give him the enthusiastic smile she knew he wanted to see; she herself didn't covet the elaborate jewelry he often gave her, but she conscientiously wore it to please him. "It's lovely," she repeated, smiling again as she brushed her fingertips along the glittering surface.

"As you are, wearing it," he replied gallantly. His eyes took on another kind of light as he abruptly put his arms around her. "Dinner isn't for another hour," he said. "There is the time, I think, for us to properly make up for these minor disagreements we've had."

Ashley felt an immediate stab of anxiety at the suggestive remark. Ross's sexual advances weren't all that frequent, and though she'd once been able to respond to them without real difficulty, it was all she could do now to keep from flinching at his intimate touch. At the time she'd married him, this aspect of their relationship had been unimportant; she'd been at her lowest emotional ebb, with little sexual desire of her own, so that Ross's now-and-then interest had been all right. But she'd recovered both her emotional stamina and her youthful woman's needs. Because of that and the fact of now having been with Grant—a man so attuned to her own natural sensuality—Ross had no physical appeal to her at all. There was a world of difference between Grant's virile, impassioned lovemaking and Ross's disciplined approach. To Ross, sex was something to be accomplished quickly, and his caresses, when there at all, were more token than anything else, not a source of excitement, like Grant's. In the Galbraith bedchamber, there were no such things as long, provocative nights and rumpled bedsheets, and as Ashley had a sudden, all-too-familiar vision of Ross lying beside her in the narrow twin bed, holding her as he remained almost fully clothed, she knew she was going to refuse him.

"Ross . . . I . . . it's been a long day, and I'm tired," she said in a low voice.

Some of the warmth once again drained from his face.

"Ashley, this is the second time now that you've denied me," he said, dropping his hands. "I will understand—again—since you say you're tired, but I expect your cooperation. Soon."

Cooperation, Ashley thought as she turned away and walked slowly toward the bathroom. That's just exactly what their lovemaking amounted to. She quelled her paradoxical feelings of guilt for being unable to respond physically to her husband and anger at being expected to give her body to him, or to anyone, upon instruction. She was just about to close the bathroom door when she turned to him suddenly. "Ross, did you remember to take your heart pills?" It was strange how even an unpleasant scene like the one they'd just experienced did not alter her constant concern for his health.

"Don't be concerned about it, dear." He didn't look up from the pad on which he was making notes to himself.

"Ross, I do worry." Too much, she added silently. It was probably a legacy of what had happened to Grif, this near-phobic anxiety she had about someone close to her being ill.

"Yes, I've taken my pills," he said impatiently. "Now, go on and draw your bath." He smiled perfunctorily, then quickly became absorbed again in his notations.

For a moment longer Ashley watched her husband, now completely caught up in matters of business, and as she closed the bathroom door behind her, she sighed.

Chapter 14

THOUGH THERE WAS a nip in the morning air, Ashley wasn't cold as she stood waiting for Grant in front of the elephant cage at the Bronx Zoo. She'd dressed with particular care that morning, finally choosing from her extensive wardrobe a smart wool suit of deep turquoise; the jacket was draped casually over her shoulders, and the gauzy blue scarf she'd added around her neck fluttered in the wind against one shoulder of her white silk blouse.

She was feeling oddly unsettled about the rendezvous with Grant now that it was all but upon her—nervous about some of the things she had to explain to him, yet thrilled at the prospect of being alone with him once again. Schoolgirl, she chided herself silently as her pulse raced, and she checked her watch another time. It was ten forty-five. Fifteen minutes to wait. She leaned across the black iron railing, tossing a handful of peanuts into the enclosure in front of her.

She was stifling her impulse to look at her watch again when she felt a whisper of warm breath against the back of her neck. "You look gorgeous," Grant said in her ear.

Ashley caught her breath, and she turned. Grant was directly behind her, wearing a dark pinstripe suit and silk tie, and there was a wide smile on his face as he stepped back and gave her an undisguised once-over. "I was wrong," he said. "You don't look gorgeous. You look stunning. And sexy," he added with a slow smile.

She felt a warmth rising in her cheeks as she smiled. "Thank you. You're early," she added, needing something inconsequential to say.

"So are you."

She flushed again and turned back around to look at the elephants. "Yes, well, I guess I am." He came to stand beside her, and she laughed slightly as she looked at him. "The fact is, I've been here all morning."

He raised an eyebrow. "Oh, zoos hold such fascination for you?" he inquired.

"No," she said, laughing again. "I had to tell Ross something, so I told him I was spending the whole day with a good friend of mine. That obliged me to leave early." And more important, I needed to be here in this place where I'd be seeing you, she added silently, strangely reluctant to admit the real reason she was so early.

"You weren't lying to Ross," Grant answered mildly. "You are spending the whole day with a good friend."

He took her by the arm and began to walk them in the direction of the gate. When his brisk pace didn't let up, Ashley glanced up at him with a perplexed look.

"Grant, where are we going? I thought we could just sit down over there—" She motioned toward a tree-shaded wooden bench that they were already passing.

"No," he said. "We're going someplace where we can really talk."

Ashley stopped in her tracks, drawing her arm away from his. "Grant, I meant what I said the other night about wanting to be careful."

"Yes, you told me that the other night," he said. "But I have no intention of talking to you in this place, while you stand slinging peanuts to a pair of pachyderms. I had no choice before but to cater to your paranoia, or whatever it is, but today is a different story. Now, if you want to stand here and argue about it, fine, but I think you'll be defeating your purpose if you do. I won't give in, and what you'll get is simply an enormous scene that will make us as conspicuous as hell."

Ashley looked at his implacable expression and couldn't help the tiny smile that crept into her face. Shaking her head then in exasperation, she took his arm again and they headed toward the gate.

They left Ashley's Mercedes in the parking lot and went on in Grant's car to the first restaurant they saw. It was a small luncheon establishment, with a quiet atmosphere and low lighting, and Grant saw to it that they were seated at a corner table, a circular booth, at the back of the room. They ordered drinks, and once they'd been served, he slid his arm along the back of the seat just above Ashley's shoulders. "I want to apologize again for the things I said to you the other night," he told her quietly.

"It's all right, Grant. I . . . it was a difficult moment,"

she answered and studied him thoughtfully with her head to one side. "You know, I almost don't know you without your Stetson."

He kept a hold on his smile. "You thought it was pretty funny once."

She dropped her eyes. "No, I didn't. Not really. I was just terribly aggravated at the moment I made that remark to you," she murmured and picked up her drink, taking a healthy swallow of it. At the sound of Grant's chuckle, she looked at him.

"You know, I'm beginning to learn about you," he remarked. "Whenever I want to know if you're agitated about something, all I have to do is watch you with your liquor."

She flushed, setting down her glass. Smiling sheepishly then, she said, "Well, I really *was* in a bad mood that night you picked me up."

"I know. I remember," he said softly. "Ashley, shall we get down to the serious talking?" he said.

"Yes, serious talking," Ashley echoed. "But where do I start so that I can make you understand everything?"

"Why don't you try at the beginning—with why you married Ross Galbraith in the first place," he prompted, reaching for his bourbon.

"It starts before that, Grant," she answered. "It really starts with Grif."

"Grif?"

"Griffith. He was my brother," she said softly, and her gaze drifted away to the dimly lit room scattered with empty tables set for luncheon diners. Grant could feel the sudden melancholy that had dropped down over her, and he laid his hand on the back of her neck.

"Ashley," he said quietly. "Tell me. All of it."

She couldn't allow herself to relive all that pain. She had to get on with her story. "Yes, I will," she said and tried to gather her thoughts.

"It begins even before Grif, actually. My parents died when I was very young, Grant. I was thirteen, Grif was seven. There we were, two orphans, and my aunt and uncle took us in. We were raised by them, on their farm in Pennsylvania." She smiled. "It was a nice life. Georgia and Brett are good people. But the loss of my parents was still very traumatic for me, and it was even worse for Grif. He was an extremely sensitive young boy. After Mom and Dad died, he developed problems—feelings of insecurity, things like that.

"I always felt very responsible for him, Grant, even when we were children. Though Georgia was always there, and very kind, I guess I felt almost like Grif's mother myself." She paused for a minute, in her mind's eye seeing that young boy again: thin, leggy, with his engaging smile and startling red hair. "I looked after him," she went on at last. "I worried about him a lot. I vowed to myself I'd do everything I could to see that he got what he wanted out of life, as a way of making up to him for what he'd lost, I suppose. I even played basketball with him every afternoon when school let out, though that might've been as much for my own benefit as for his."

She laughed when she saw Grant's amusement. "You might as well know now," she said, a rueful smile dancing on her lips, "I was quite a tomboy when I was growing up. That's when I learned to ride, shoot, do all those other unlady-like things. I did manage to grow up into a real female, but I think Georgia had her doubts for a while."

"She needn't have," he commented, and Ashley blushed as his appreciative gaze dropped down to the sleek bodice of her blouse before moving back up to her face.

"Well, anyway," she said evenly, "the point is that Grif and I were unusually close right from the beginning. I went off to college finally—I put myself through school because Georgia and Brett couldn't afford to send me themselves. I studied art history, got a bachelor's degree, and a master's, and then I went to work for Galbraith's. In the meantime, Grif had decided he wanted to be an architect. I had never known him to want anything so badly. I had every intention of putting him through school, too. Well, actually, I did for one year, and he'd gotten a partial scholarship too. Uh, he was there . . . he finished that first year at school, before . . ." She broke off, trying to find the easiest words to say what had to be said. "He had cancer, Grant. Bone cancer," she said in a monotone, as she fingered the spoon at her place setting. "We found out about it that summer after his first year at school."

Grant had been aware all along that Ashley was speaking of her brother in the past tense, and he'd been expecting a disclosure along the lines of the one she'd just made. Yet, it still rattled him; the death of one so young was always shocking. "I see," he said softly.

As she sat staring at the spoon under her hand, Ashley had a picture in her mind, the one she hated and would carry forever: of the once broad-shouldered Griffith Welles, eaten away by disease, his life reduced to nothing but pain as he lived out his last moments in a hospital bed. "I won't go into the gruesome details," she went on in the same carefully controlled voice. "It's not necessary, and frankly, I can't. The disease ran its course fairly rapidly, though not quickly enough, as you come to understand once you've watched someone disintegrate before your very eyes. I'd been at Galbraith's several years by the time Grif had to go into the hospital. He lingered on there for months, living on machines and enormous doses of pain-killers. Ross enters the picture at about this point. I mean, as an important entity in my life," she clarified with a brief look upward at him. "Of course, I'd known him professionally for several years by then. I was working rather closely with him by the time Grif became really ill. I was in charge of the cataloguing, and I'd gotten into other things, too—exhibition management, some of the advertising."

Impatient with herself for the unnecessary digression, she waved it away and turned her face up to Grant, the low light of the pewter carriage lamp above them bathing her complexion in an amber glow. "A number of months after Ross's first wife died of a heart attack—Kathryn was her name—he began taking me to dinner. At first, it was only when we'd been working late together at the office, but then his invitations became purely social. I went with him because I found Ross to be a charming man, and also, it was easy—platonic," she explained. "Up to that point, when I started seeing Ross privately, I'd kept Grif's problem to myself. But I began to confide in Ross because, well, it got so that I had to talk to someone."

Grant took her hand, and she looked down at it; he was running his thumb across her long, graceful fingers, caressing them sympathetically, and when her eyes traveled back up to his face finally, they held his in a long moment of silent communication. She extracted her hand quietly then, so she could go on in a clear way with the narrative.

"Grant," she said, "I've always been a strong person emotionally, able to cope, to handle what came my way, but when I found out that Grif was terminally ill, I really stumbled. And then when he finally died, I fell apart completely. It was a horrible time in my life, frightening to me really," she said in an undertone, her eyes trained on her hands in her lap. "I wasn't even getting through the days. I didn't go to work for a week after the funeral. I couldn't." An almost imperceptible shudder ran through her as she recalled the debilitating sense of despair she'd felt. Finally, she raised her head again. "Not only had I lost the brother I cared for so deeply, but my entire immediate family was gone at that point." Grant was watching her with pain in his eyes, and she smiled, as if to tell him it was all right now. "I only add that so you can fully understand why I went on to do what I did," she said.

"At any rate, Ross was there the whole time as a shoulder to lean on when Grif died. He'd just been through illness and death himself and could empathize. Oh, I was offering him something, too," she added, and looked up as the waiter brought the fresh drinks Grant had ordered with a motion of his hand. "I fully understood that," she went on when the man had left again. "He was lonely with Kathryn having been gone not even a year, and my companionship and problems gave him something else to think about. He came to Grif's funeral, too. It was very simple. Just my aunt and uncle and me. The jolting 'morning after' happened the next week," she said with a humorless smile. "I got the bills then for the balance of Grif's hospital care—the doctors, equipment, all of it. By that time, my insurance coverage had run out, and I was left with slightly over ten thousand dollars to come up with. That might not sound like much to you, but to me, Grant, it might as well have been a million dollars," she said, looking at him with shadows in her eyes. "I had no idea how I'd ever pay what was due. I had no savings left, and Georgia and Brett couldn't help out."

"But Ross Galbraith does have money, and he paid the bills for you," Grant interjected and sat back against the seat cushion, studying her anew as he considered the information that had just abruptly put so much into perspective for him.

"Well, it wasn't exactly that cut-and-dried, but you're on the right track," she said and turned to face him squarely again. "Grant, I would never have asked Ross—or anyone else—to pay those bills for me. But I did tell him about them when he took me to dinner several nights after I'd received them. I needed advice. At that point, I'd been able to pull myself together enough to make inquiries at several banks about a loan. I didn't have the resources to qualify on my own, and every place I went, I was advised that they would extend the loan only if I had a cosigner. I told Ross that, too, and he said—right out of the blue—that he'd do that for me. He would cosign the loan.'' Her expression as she looked at Grant held a faint trace of the bemused wonderment she'd felt at the time. "I was stunned, but I had nowhere else to turn. After thinking about it all through dinner I told him I'd accept his offer, but it was to be a formal agreement. I wanted papers drawn up to state that this was simply a financial arrangement between the two of us. He went along with that.

"I went into work finally the next day, for the first time since Grif had died," she went on, studying her highball glass on the table and absently tracing the rim with one fingertip. "I'd been in my office barely ten minutes when Charlie Halperin appeared—he's Galbraith's treasurer. He handed me a check, written on the Galbraith company account and signed by Ross. It was for the exact amount I owed the hospital," she said, giving Grant that same look of amazement. "I had no idea what was going on, and I went directly to Ross's office to talk to him. He said he—Galbraith's, really—was making the loan to me, and it was to be at a rate substantially lower than the one the banks would have charged. He said he'd known it would put a strain on my finances to make the monthly payment. Again, I was stunned, I didn't know what to say or what to do.''

"So you married him when he asked you to," Grant finished for her.

"Yes," she said quietly and picked up her drink. "Grant, we were filling a need for one another in so many ways. Ross is the kind of man who can't be unmarried. For him, a wife is part of a proper life-style, although he did care for me. I know he did and still does. As for me," she said, almost wearily, "I was emotionally incapable of going on alone at the time, and yes—before you have to say it—I was grateful for what he'd done for me financially. How could I not be?" she implored, then sighed again before filling in the rest of the details quickly. "Ross asked me to marry him several weeks after Grif's funeral, and I accepted. There was no fanfare about it. We just went down to the courthouse and got married. I was in the process of having legal papers drawn up for the loan between us, but, of course, at that point, it didn't matter anymore. The money ceased to be a loan. It was more—what?—an outright gift, from husband to wife.''

Grant was watching her steadily. ''And so, that was three years ago,'' he said.

Ashley glanced at him in surprise. ''How did you know that?''

''Oh, I've got my sources, although I didn't realize until I saw you standing in the doorway of the Eldridges' living room the other night that I should've been listening to them with a bit more interest than I did,'' he remarked dryly.

''Yes, that was three years ago,'' she answered matter-of-factly. ''I had a fondness for Ross when we got married. I told you that the other night. I know it sounds as if my motivation for marrying him was strictly because of what he'd done for me, and, yes, that was a very large part of it. Had I been more emotionally stable, maybe I could have withstood the pressure of my gratitude, maybe not. I don't know. But I wasn't totally mercenary about the whole thing,'' she said intently. ''I *did* have some warm feelings for Ross, platonic though they might've been. And my marrying him had positively nothing to do with any further financial benefit I'd have!'' she stressed, her eyes suddenly beseeching. ''Please don't think that, Grant.''

Grant took her hand, holding it tightly. ''Ashley, I don't think you married Ross for money. I said what I did the other night out of anger. And frankly, I don't give a damn why you married the man, so long as it wasn't because you had a flaming passion for him.''

Ashley was watching him with a soft smile and said quietly, ''No, Grant, I had no passionate love for Ross. Nor do I now.''

''All right. And so, what about now, three years later? You said the other night that you still have some fondness for him, but you weren't entirely convincing. What kind of life have you had with Ross? I can't help but feel, knowing what I do of you and the little I've gathered about Ross, that it's your marriage to him that's responsible for your being unhappy.''

She looked at him curiously. ''I suppose unhappiness can't really be hidden, but I didn't realize that mine was so obvious. Is it?''

''To me,'' he said, his expression softening. ''There was

something bothering you terribly that last night at Coconino. It was very evident at one point.''

She tilted her head, as if to study him. "Are you always so observant about people?''

"Yes. But I'm particularly observant when someone interests me, as you did from the very first.''

"Why did you find me so interesting?'' she asked with a trace of unaccustomed shyness.

His eyes flickered. "Ashley, you're a very beautiful woman. Certainly that was one reason. But even more than that, anyone who's more annoyed than afraid at being stranded alone on a highway in a driving snowstorm has got to be someone very special,'' he said with a slow smile. "Someone I definitely need to know.''

Ashley laughed lightly. "Well, I have to admit I did have a twinge or two of anxiety,'' she said, "but yes, I *was* annoyed at getting stuck.''

"As long as we're on the subject of the night you arrived at Coconino, there are a few things I'd like to know,'' he said then. "Why couldn't you tell me right away who you were? Why did you have to lie about it? Sure, the Galbraith name would have meant something to me, but you couldn't have known that. And what would it have mattered anyway?''

"It was a problem in my own mind, Grant,'' she said quietly. "Ross is obsessively concerned about the Galbraith reputation.''

"Yes, so I've heard,'' Grant remarked and picked up his glass to down a healthy portion of the bourbon.

"Well, then maybe you can understand.'' She went on to explain about the misadventure on the Penrys' yacht. "Ross said to me afterwards that I should've considered all the possible situations that could develop before I accepted the Penrys' invitation to go out with them and Blair. 'Be *aware*,' '' she quoted. At Grant's still-skeptical look, she looked at him pleadingly. "Grant, you have to understand how it is with Ross and me. We argue so frequently—almost always because of me—that I just . . . try to keep the sources of discord to a minimum to spare both of us the ordeal of his distress,'' she said unhappily.

"Why is Ross so concerned about the Galbraith name?'' Grant asked. "It seems to me that there has to be something more behind his obsession about his reputation than simple family pride,'' he observed.

"Grant, don't kid yourself. In Ross's mind, pride and honor are synonymous with the name Galbraith. But yes, you're right. There is more to it."

She went on to tell him a story related to her by Ollie Willingham. As a much younger man, married to Kathryn only a few years, Ross had become the subject of rumors in Westchester linking him with an attractive young widow. The two had been working together on a civic function and spending what seemed to some people an inordinate amount of time with each other. The upshot had been that the gossip got back to Ross's father, who told Ross he had disappointed him deeply and disgraced the family name.

"Ross sets very high standards for himself, and I think he never got over it," Ashley concluded. "He's still trying to regain his father's approval, I suspect, even though the man has been dead for a long time. Ross was his only son and he adored his father."

"All right," Grant said. "I accept your explanation for lying to me initially, but I still need to know why you couldn't tell me who you were and that you were married once things between us got so serious. Ashley, you told me you loved me. Don't you think you owed me some honesty at that point? I do."

"Yes, I did, but I . . . I felt I couldn't give it to you," she said in a voice that was all but lost to the clatter of silverware on dishes and the chatter of lunchtime diners now filling up the tables.

"You couldn't tell me because of your worry that I might know Ross or someone who knew him?" Grant sounded angrily incredulous. "Do you imagine I go around boasting about my conquests, which, by the way, isn't a category you happen to fall into?"

"No, of course not!" Ashley protested. "Grant, I couldn't tell you because I couldn't face your hurt."

"Oh, for God's sake!"

"No, hear me out, Grant," Ashley pleaded, clasping her fingers tightly around his arm. "Don't you understand? There was no way for me to alter my circumstances. I had to leave you and go back to Ross no matter what you and I felt for each other." She wasn't making herself clear, she saw, and went on urgently. "Grant, I would've told you I was married if there'd been some way for me to ease your hurt about it, if I could've said, 'But even though I'm married, that's okay. I can easily end that and give myself to you, the way we both want.' But I *couldn't* tell you that because it isn't possible for me to do it.'' Her shoulders dropped. ''And so, because there was nothing for me to do but leave you anyway, I . . . just didn't have the courage to tell you the truth, to have to see you hurt and for me to be the object of what I knew would be your anger. I'm not proud of what I felt, but there it is. And I left before you woke up because I knew you'd press me for details about myself and try to make plans for us to be together again.''

Grant's annoyed expression hadn't altered, and suddenly Ashley felt hopeless about trying to reason with him. ''Look Grant,'' she said, ''no one could claim I've handled myself well in any aspect of this situation. I certainly wouldn't. Actually, if I'd handled myself *well*, I'd have stayed away from your completely that last night at Coconino. I had no business going out with you at all that day, after I'd acknowledged to myself that I was so attracted to you. I have no business being in love with you at all!'' She scooped up her jacket and slid away from him to the edge of the cushion. ''Grant, I think it's time to go,'' she said in a quivering voice.

Grant reached for her quickly and caught her just before she stood up. ''Come back here. I didn't mean to—''

''It's easy for you to be so judgmental!'' she exclaimed suddenly as she looked at him with widening eyes; she could feel the emotional upheaval welling up inside her, but there was nothing she could do to stop it. ''You're not in the same position I'm in! It's easy for you to say what was right and wrong to do. You haven't got a wife to whom you've been unfaithful. Do you realize how much I've hurt everyone? Do you know just exactly how much more difficult my life has become? Do you understand—'' She choked on a sudden gulp of air and then, to her horror, burst into tears.

Grant glanced around quickly as he pulled her back to his side. Several heads turned in their direction at the sound of Ashley's distress, but only briefly, and Grant put his arm around her, holding her close.

''Ashley, calm down. Honey, it's all right,'' he soothed, reaching into his pocket for a handkerchief. She had hidden her face in her hands, and he put the linen cloth to her fingers, watching her take it and press it against her eyes. She was sobbing quietly, and he continued to hold her, speaking softly into her hair, brushing his lips against it. When she'd finally calmed down, she wiped her eyes and kept them downcast.

"I don't know what I see in you anyway. All you ever do is make me cry," she muttered. "Oh, God, what a mess I've made of everything!"

"I hope the reason I make you cry is because I affect you deeply," Grant responded with a smile, then kissed her on the top of her head. "Ashley, it's not a matter of whether you have a right to love me or I have a right to love you. These things aren't prescribed, you know." He was doing his best to calm her and to express what he himself felt. "I know it's easier for me to say what should've been done, tell you that you shouldn't have walked away. But you have to remember that it was the last thing I expected you to do. The last thing I wanted you to do was leave me, just as I don't want you to leave me now."

Finally she looked up at him. "Can we go someplace else?" she asked abruptly. "Please, Grant?" She pleaded with her eyes, miserably self-conscious about the scene she'd made.

"All right. We'll take a drive," he said.

"Make sure it's somewhere out of the way," she cautioned, then bit her lip in chagrin.

He laughed humorlessly. "Of course."

Chapter 15

THE NEW YORK City skyline shimmered in the bright sunlight across the Hudson River as they drove along the Palisades Parkway. The trees on the banks of the palisades were coming into full leaf, and the view through them was beautiful: skyscrapers cutting jaggedly into the blue horizon, the George Washington Bridge in the distance behind them, small boats drifting lazily along the river. Grant was a fast driver, with a fast car, and as they sped along the beautifully landscaped two-lane road, Ashley watched the scenery flash by.

Grant glanced across at her, sitting quietly in the passenger seat. "There's something I've been meaning to ask you," he said. "Just how did you get in and out of Flagstaff so that a whole agency full of detectives couldn't get a line on you?"

"Detectives?" she repeated incredulously. "You've had detectives looking for me?"

Grant smiled. "You didn't really think I'd just sit back and let you disappear from my life, did you?"

Ashley felt a rush of inner joy at discovering that Grant had had such an urgent need to find her, yet she was grateful too that she'd been unaware of the investigators before; she'd have been panicked. "Well, Grant," she finally answered, "I didn't come in and out of Flagstaff."

"What did you do then?" he asked, and thought of all the dead ends he and Joe Farnum had run into. No wonder.

She told him then—about having done a favor for Margaret by flying into Phoenix instead of Flagstaff so she could pick up her friend's car, which had been left at the airport there a week before when Margaret flew from Phoenix to visit her family. Ashley hadn't minded; Margaret had done her many favors, and besides, it had eliminated the need to contend with a rental car.

"I see," Grant said when she'd finished the explanation. "And going out again?"

"I drove on to Margaret's because I wanted her to know I was all right," she replied. "She was really worried about me at that point, though she'd realized I had to have stopped somewhere because of the storm. I reached her just before she'd have gone into Flagstaff to get in touch with Ross,'' she said with a meaningful look at Grant, then added, ''I stayed with her overnight.''

''Does she live up there year 'round?'' Grant asked curiously.

''No, it's just a vacation cabin for her,'' Ashley explained with a brief smile. ''She goes up there often, but she actually lives in California.''

''I see,'' Grant said again and changed lanes to pass a car slowing down for the upcoming exit. ''And so, what airport did you fly out of?''

''Las Vegas.'' She didn't have to add that she'd put all that distance between Flagstaff and her point of departure in order to make herself harder to trace; the inference was perfectly clear.

Grant merely nodded, and some distance down the parkway, he pulled off onto a gravel lookout point. He cut the engine of the Maserati, then relaxed back in the driver's seat, positioning himself against the door. ''It's time we talk about where you stand with Ross, don't you think?'' he said.

''Grant, I'm not sure I know the answer to that,'' she said. Sighing moodily, she let her gaze stray to the windshield.

''You're not happy,'' he observed.

''No.''

''Then leave him.''

When she looked back at him, she found he was watching her steadily, and she gave him a troubled frown. ''That's easier said than done, Grant. Leaving just like that, I mean.''

No, Grant admitted to himself, nothing was ever quite that simple. He shouldn't have spoken so bluntly. ''Ashley, tell me why you're unhappy with Ross,'' he said. ''I'd like to know.''

She tucked one leg up under her. ''Grant, there are so many reasons,'' she said with a cloudy expression, ''from the simple and obvious one like the fact that he's so much older than I am, to others that are more complex. Our attitudes toward life are entirely different. I like to be—well, you know how I am,'' she said with a small laugh. ''I speak my mind, I like a very informal outdoorsy life-style, for the most part anyway. Ross likes ritual, elegance, reserve. Oh, I know that being completely opposite in nature isn't always such a terrible strike against a relationship, but it can only work when there is tolerance by each person for the other's point of view. And that's one of the problems with Ross and me. He has no tolerance for who I am and what I may want as an individual. Maybe I don't have as much tolerance for him as I should,'' she allowed, "but if that's true, it's because I've given up. In the past, I have tried. Really I have, Grant,'' she said earnestly. "Ross never did, though, and I don't think I'm being unfairly critical in saying that. Right from the start he had his own idea of what I—what any wife of his—ought to be, and I suspect no one could ever change it.''

"And what *is* his idea of what you ought to be?'' Grant asked.

"A stay-at-home wife,'' Ashley answered without hesitation. "An appendage to him. His wife is a woman who oversees the servants and the household, who makes all the correct appearances at the clubs and committees in town, who doesn't dare meddle even conversationally in his business life—under pain of his biting reproach if she's so foolish as to try—and who, above all else, doesn't veer one iota from his perception of what constitutes femininity. Which, by the way, doesn't include about three quarters of the things I like to do,'' she added humorlessly.

"And you mean to tell me you weren't aware of all this when you married him?''

"I wasn't thinking so clearly as I might've been at another time in my life,'' Ashley reminded him quietly. "But even if I had been, it wouldn't have changed the fact that—no, I wasn't aware of Ross's attitude about a wife when I married him. I wasn't aware of a great many things about Ross then.''

At Grant's curious look, she went on. "Grant, Ross Galbraith is an enigma. Beneath that charming veneer of his is a totally inflexible person. And he can lash out at you with a swiftness and contempt that are, well, if not exactly frightening, at least stunning. I'd never seen that facet of him in the years I worked for him. We'd actually been quite companionable when we were working together. It was a total shock to learn how cold he can be. He doesn't let anyone get really close to him, not me and not even Ollie, who's been his staunch friend for years. And yet, on the other hand, he can often be extremely generous, sincerely so.'' Her expressive face held a look of bemusement as she tried to explain her husband.

"The worst thing of all is that he won't let me work,''

Ashley continued. "Won't hear of it, won't talk about it—it's a closed subject. This issue came up about a year after we were married. Up until then, I honestly hadn't cared about doing anything. I was emotionally drained after what happened with Grif, and during that first year, before I got back on my feet, things weren't bad between us," she said with a faint wistfulness. "But I did recover, and I brought up the subject of returning to my position at Galbraith's. Little did I know what Ross's reaction would be! He—well, to put it in a nutshell, he had a fit.

"Grant, having a professional life is very important to me. I have a lot of goals in life for myself, but that's one of the major ones. I worked very hard to get where I was at Galbraith's, and to be deprived of the chance to do something I'm good at sets up a tension in me that I can hardly stand sometimes." She stared at her hands, which had tensed into fists, then looked back abruptly. "Ross is fully aware of how strongly I feel," she said. "He's capable of understanding my interest in the business world—he *knows* how good I was!—and yet that cuts no ice with him. Ross Galbraith's wife doesn't work, period. My only salvation for the past year and a half or so has been helping a friend of mine run his riding stable. Shadow Knolls, it's called. That's where I board Sharif. It's not what I really want to be doing, but it's been a way of putting my brain to use, at least in some manner."

"Ross Galbraith is missing a good bet," Grant said then. "It's too bad his company has to be the victim of his narrow views."

"What do you mean?" Ashley asked uncertainly.

"I think you'd make someone a hell of a business partner."

Ashley's color heightened noticeably, but she didn't look away from him. "I sincerely appreciate the compliment, but you can't know that about me," she demurred.

"Yes, I can. I make it a practice to study people, as you know, and I've studied you a great deal. And worked with you once. You know all about cooperation. You can take pressure. You're intelligent, interested, and you've got a hell of a lot of courage. Those are the qualities you need. You can take them and put them into any kind of business and be successful, with a little homework on the technical end of things."

"Grant, I . . .'' Ashley murmured, flustered that praise like that was coming from him.

Grant smiled. "That wasn't idle flattery, Ashley," he said. "I don't go in for that sort of thing, not even with you." He reached for her hand and took it firmly in his own. "All right," he said. "You've told me why you're unhappy with Ross. Now, what are you going to do about it?"

They were back to that question again, Ashley thought, and, somber once more, she looked out to the distant New York skyline. She'd asked herself that same thing time and time again, for nearly two years now, and still she had no definite answer. "I don't know, Grant," she said slowly. "It isn't easy for me to just walk away from Ross. It isn't ever easy, but with us, there are so many things involved, so much . . .''

"Guilt?" Grant supplied.

Ashley looked over at him. "Yes," she answered quietly. "I have a lot of guilt about Ross—guilt that I don't really love the man I married, guilt that I can't honor my commitment to cherish him as I vowed. That's a terrible thing, Grant, to feel no passionate emotion for the man you've taken as your husband," she said in a strained voice as she dropped her eyes again to her hands. "I'm one of those people who believes in marriage. I suppose I feel that there ought to be *some way* for me to make it work, simply because I got myself into it." She looked back up to him. "Yet, I'm the one who's the cause of all the dissension," she said. "I'm always the issue of the arguments, and I . . . I always seem to be letting him down. No matter who's in the wrong, I hate upsetting him so much."

"Ashley, marriage is a two-way street," Grant said. "It's never one person who causes all the conflicts. You can't honestly believe that."

"No, I know," she conceded, feeling confusion envelop her as it always did when she tried to come to terms with her feelings toward Ross. "So much of the problem is Ross's absolute refusal to see any but his own viewpoint. And yet, he *has* been very good to me in so many ways. He was there to help me out when I desperately needed someone, and he's given me a very comfortable life, free of worry of any sort—well, financial worry anyway." She expelled an unhappy breath. "How can I turn my back on him after all he's done for me?" she asked. "What an ingrate I'd seem— no, I'd *be*, wouldn't I?—throwing his generosity back in his face like that.

"And there's another thing, Grant. Most people aren't aware of this, but Ross has serious heart trouble. How can I walk out on a man who's ill? Who'd be all alone? Grant, he has no children," she said, the pain of empathy now in her eyes. "His marriage to Kathryn was barren, and his two sisters are dead now. No one knows better than I what it feels like to be alone on this earth, with no one else, and how could I do that to him?" She turned to stare unseeingly out across the water beyond the tree-studded cliffs.

"Ashley, I want to tell you something," Grant said seriously. "If you keep feeding all your guilts, they'll devour you. You can't allow them to rule your life, and they will if you let them. Guilt is a very powerful emotion, and it can make even the strongest, sanest person react peculiarly. Be careful of it, Ashley. Don't let it distort your thinking."

Ashley turned on him in displaced anger for her own inability to resolve her feelings. "Don't preach to me about things you haven't experienced, Grant. You can't understand how difficult it is to walk out of a marriage, even a bad one."

"Can't I?"

Ashley stared at him. "You were married once?" she breathed.

"Yes."

"I—I'm sorry." In that moment she felt a stab of jealousy for that other, unknown woman pierce her entire body, and she was able to comprehend firsthand Grant's volcanic reaction several nights before, when he'd learned she belonged to another man. "When?" she asked, completely off-balance.

"A long time ago," Grant said. "When I was in my early twenties. It lasted about two years. We were as incompatible as you and Ross." A brief smile passed across his face. "Actually, Ross would've liked Mara. The only thing she ever wanted was to live a life of extravagant ease as someone's pampered *hausfrau.*"

"Grant, I'm sorry for what I said," Ashley reached over to lay her hand on his, and he took hold of it. "I had no idea."

"I know you didn't," Grant answered. "I don't talk about it because there's no need to. It's water long under the bridge. But, Ashley, I do know the guilt associated with getting out of even a lousy marriage, and I know that at some point you've got to make a decision to let go of that guilt. Or keep the guilt and let go of yourself. You can't have both.''

No, you can't have both; she knew that. She so often felt that somewhere along the line she'd lost the woman she used to know well when she looked in the mirror, relinquished her to her feelings of confusion about Ross. She sighed and said, ''Grant, let's not discuss this anymore, all right? Not now.''

He eased his hand from hers and reached out to rest it against the side of her throat. ''When am I going to see you again?'' he asked softly.

Reflexively, she pressed her hand to his. ''Oh, you'll see me,'' she said, trying for a little humor. ''Our lives have become rather intricately entwined all of a sudden. But, Grant—'' She took his hand and held it with both of hers in her lap, as another thought struck her. ''I don't think you realize that Ross's business means everything to him,'' she said worriedly.

''Hmm,'' he murmured. He was studying her hair, remembering so well how it waved at the temples, how the highlights shone blue black in the light.

''Grant, you aren't listening to me,'' she said more intently. ''Galbraith's is Ross's whole life. It's been the family business for generations, and to him, it's the most important thing in the world.''

Grant said nothing and simply watched her doubtfully.

She knew she was talking around what she really wanted to say, and finally came out with it directly. ''What I'm trying to say, Grant, is . . . don't take it away from him.''

''Ashley!'' Startled, he laughed. ''I don't want Ross's company. I've got a company of my own to run. That's all I intend to do.''

''Yes, and put it at the top of the auction field,'' she said immediately.

''If that's in the cards.''

''There's not room for both of you.''

''I'm not so sure about that,'' he said when he saw that she was truly disturbed. ''But if I do get DuBrand's back into a position where it's vying credibly for what's out there in the auction business, and if that results in Galbraith's losing some sales—which, if I read you correctly, is what's worrying you—it will have come about simply because I've done what was in the best interests of my own organization. That's all I ever do." He smiled then. "You seem to have an awful lot of faith in my professional abilities. "I'm flattered," he added.

Ashley didn't return his smile. "Grant, I suspect you can accomplish just about anything you want to, but it must not include hurting Ross's business. Grant, listen to me," she went on earnestly, clasping his hand very tightly. "Ross isn't like you. For you, the auction business is only a passing interest. You don't have the same emotional tie to DuBrand's that Ross has to Galbraith's. And you're a younger, stronger man than Ross," she said. "It's not fair for you to take him on."

"What is this, Ashley? More guilt?" Grant said, one eyebrow slightly cocked. "That it's the competition you've fallen in love with, and that if I'm effective to the detriment of the husband you can't love, you'd have a hard time living with that?" Ashley drew back immediately, and Grant grabbed her hands as she pulled them away.

"Honey, don't take offense," he said mildly. "What I said seems fairly obvious to me." He looked at her affectionately. "Ashley, you can't predict what may or may not happen because of Ross's heart condition. It's beyond anyone's control, except possibly his own. I realize it's natural for you to be sensitive to illness, after what happened with Grif, but don't let that dictate to you, huh?" He concluded with a light touch to her face.

"Please, Grant, don't lecture me," she objected. "I admit that Grif's illness still influences me, but I can't help that. It left such a deep scar in me. Maybe I never will get over it, I don't know. And yes, it bothers me that it had to be you of all people who has taken over DuBrand's. But Grant, those things are beside the point. The real issue is that you have to take into consideration what consequences your professional actions may bring to another man. And in the case of Ross, I just want you to keep in mind how he feels about Galbraith's, what it might do to him if he were to see his company failing." She hesitated, then looked at him earnestly. "In other words, Grant: back off. Please. It's important."

Just what we needed, Grant cursed silently, another obstacle in this murky situation. Apparently this was a matter Ashley couldn't be objective about, and he didn't intend to pursue it now. "Honey, don't worry about it," he said finally and repeated, "When am I going to see you again? And I don't mean just 'around.' "

At that Ashley looked down to his strong hand clasping one of hers. She felt the heat of it, and the sensation sent an ache of longing through her body. "I don't know, Grant," she said in a low voice. He raised her face with a hand under her chin, and as his eyes searched it, her own filled with deep unhappiness. "I can't meet you alone anymore, not while I'm still living with Ross," she said. "I can't be unfaithful to him again. I won't be. But more than that, Grant, I have to make my decision alone—whether to stay with my husband. I can't be as impartial as I'd like to try to be if I'm with you in the meantime."

"That's a very admirable attitude, Ashley, but it doesn't do a whole hell of a lot for me," Grant said, unable to repress his frustration.

"No. Nor for me," she admitted. "But it's the way I feel." She studied his moody expression and smiled gently. "Grant, I don't want to hurt you. It's just that I need this for myself. I'd like to be able to behave with some amount of integrity in all of this, toward both you and Ross. I haven't done terribly well up to now. And I can't meet you on the sly, Grant. I don't want that kind of relationship with you. Please understand."

"I'd forgotten how difficult it is to move you off dead center when you make up your mind about something," he remarked, pressing her hands before letting them drop.

Ashley's eyes were flickering. "Grant, I asked you the other night not to put any more pressure on me than is already there. Can't you respect that?"

Grant looked at her, then expelled a long breath. "I'm sorry. I'm being foolish." He reached out again and laid his palm against her cheek. "Yes, I can respect that, and I will."

Her smile of gratitude was subdued, and she checked her watch. It read three o'clock, and she was startled at how quickly the hours had gone by. It would take them some time to drive back to the zoo, and she still had to go from there on home. "Grant, we'd better go," she said. "It's getting late."

"Yes, we will," he said, "but I want to say good-bye here, where there's at least some privacy. Today is going to have to last me for awhile, it looks like." He opened his door and got out of the car, coming around to open her side and hold his hand down to her. "Come on. Let's take a walk."

Ashley stepped out with him, and Grant led her by the hand down the wooded path in the small copse at the edge of the palisades. Just before the embankment where the mossy earth disappeared in a sheer drop to the Hudson River below, he turned and pulled her to him, sliding his arms around her back; she immediately slipped her arms around his neck.

"Someone will see us," she murmured as she laid her head in the cleft of his neck and shoulder, thrilling at the scent of him, the feel of his strong arms holding her tightly.

"No, they won't," he said. "The path bends around. Ashley—"

"The last time, I was the one who kept talking too much," she interrupted. She smiled as she raised her head from his shoulder, and before he could say another word, she put her mouth to his. He crushed her to him, feeling the heat of his passion for her envelop him completely as he dropped his hands down her back and pressed her lips to his.

"Remember?" he whispered with his lips still warm on hers, and his eyes were heavy-lidded as he broke their kiss. He moved her backwards then, two paces, up against a tree, pinning her there with his body.

"Grant," she said and caught a breath as she arched her neck back to his kiss on the side of her throat. "Don't, please. I'm not made of stone," she said with difficulty, and she brought her hand up to his neck, unable to keep from rubbing it softly.

"I know that," he said and smiled slowly as he continued to run his lips along the soft skin of her neck. "Oh, how well I know." He moved back just slightly as he raised his head again, and putting both hands at the sides of her waist then, he ran them slowly up her torso, sending a shudder of desire through her whole body as they skimmed her breasts lightly before going all the way up to capture her face. "Ashley, I love you," he breathed as he held her face with both hands. "I've never loved anyone the way I love you."

"I love you, too," she whispered, straining against him as she tightened her arms around his neck. "Grant, hold me," she implored.

He took her in his arms again, possessively. At length, their lips found one another's again, and they kissed deeply, communicating in a very private way, saying to each other what words would never have adequately expressed. Finally, Grant broke them apart again and stepped back from her, letting his hands slide reluctantly all the way down her arms, then completely away. "One more minute and the limitations you've imposed on us will be nothing more than words. I'm not made of stone, either," he said, his voice constrained.

Ashley felt dazed, and empty when bereft of his arms. She wanted to throw her own restrictions to the wind, and as she stood looking at Grant's tense figure, she almost did. Yet, she had made a resolution and forced herself to remember it. She stepped back onto the path. "I know," she said unsteadily. "We'd better go." She ached as she thought of the separation looming ahead of them, and reached out her hand to him. He took it, and they walked silently back to the car.

When he had the engine of the sports car running, he looked across at her. "Ashley, I want to tell you something right now," he said. "Some day you're going to marry me. I don't know when it will be, but you can count on it. I'm a patient man, and I'll wait as long as I have to for you to leave Ross and come to me. What exists between us will endure forever, no matter what happens."

"Like Coconino sandstone?" she said softly, her smile quiet in her eyes.

"Like Coconino sandstone," he echoed and threw the car into gear.

Chapter 16

GALBRAITH GALLERIES WAS crowded. It was the first Friday in October, overcast and chilly in the city, and the heavy bronze revolving door on the Park Avenue side of the building rotated steadily as patrons, spectators, and sightseers came and went from the elegant auction establishment. In the marbled reception area just inside the door, several newcomers unfamiliar with the premises were seeking information from a uniformed male clerk, and above—up the imposing serpentine staircase, behind which hung two massive Renaissance paintings—people milled around the main floor, catalogues in hand, some waiting for the morning's auction of leaded crystal and china to begin, others there simply to look and stroll around the presale displays. Galbraith's interior was richly ornate, with high-ceilinged rooms, thick crimson carpeting, and brass railings throughout, and the main floor display room, situated on the near side of the large velvet-draped sale arena, was studded with tall glass cases inside which sat dozens of objects on felt-covered shelves—silver, gold, porcelain, crystal, all expensive, many priceless.

On the third floor was located the large, open gallery room where the furniture and paintings to be sold were displayed. On that day, some twenty people were slowly moving through the area to the muted strains of Chopin coming from ceiling speakers. The viewers talked in an undertone as they carefully examined the heirloom artwork hanging about the walls, each picture tagged in the bottom right-hand corner with the artist's name, a lot number, and the estimated sale value. On the far side of the last fabric-covered display partition was a heavy black door. The sounds of a company at work could just barely be heard filtering out from it, and on beyond that door, past the noisy clerical desks and slamming file cabinets, was Ross Galbraith's imposing office. He sat behind his Louis XV desk, telephone receiver to his ear, and jotted down notes on a pad of embossed paper. Herbert Willingham stood by one corner of the ornate French writing table and watched his employer intently. Ross had begun to frown, and after listening another brief minute, he finally said a curt "Thank you," then "Good-bye," and very gently replaced the receiver into its cradle.

"It's happened again," Ross said softly, but the shimmer in his hazel eyes as he looked up at his associate belied the calm tone.

"Which one is it now?" Ollie inquired in a controlled voice.

Ross pushed back his winged desk chair. "The Jordan collection of rare books," he answered, "which includes the last known copy of the Gutenberg Bible. That was Lucien Daley, the executor of the Jordan estate. He apologized very graciously," Ross said bitingly, "but he's giving everything to DuBrand's. Their book auctions have been doing extremely well lately. It's the auctioneer—so *Lucien* says. He feels that the man knows how to run up the bidding."

Ollid said nothing as Ross got abruptly to his feet and moved around the desk. It had been six months now since Grant Copeland had arrived in New York to take over the running of DuBrand & Company, and the effects of that occurrence were beginning to be felt at Galbraith's. Ollie watched his friend and employer of three decades begin slowly to pace the opulent office, and as he stood by the corner of the desk, he let his thoughts travel briefly back over the past half year.

There had been important changes in DuBrand's with the coming of Grant's fresh, dynamic leadership: new staff, new location, a flurry of publicity. All that had been accomplished during the first several months of Grant Copeland's new management, but though Grant had quickly managed to achieve for DuBrand's a renewed visibility and a more polished image within the newsy world of art and antique collecting, the summer months had seen only a moderate increase in the company's actual business. Galbraith's had continued to be the center of the most important auction activity, until two weeks ago. And then the results of all Grant Copeland's behind-the-scenes work had begun to come to light.

Without a doubt, Grant was a sharp negotiator, and the Galbraith executives had become painfully aware of that fact when, one by one, phone calls had begun coming in to Ross. They'd been calls of regret, every one of them, from people Ross had known and dealt with professionally for years. The

gist of the messages had been the same each time: that
Galbraith's abilities were appreciated but better terms and
potential for profits were being offered by DuBrand's. The
loss of the Jordan collection created a total of four highly
prestigious sales that would be taking place at DuBrand's
sometime in the very near future, each one newsworthy, each
one containing *objets d' art,* books, paintings, and furnishings
that would be coveted by the most discriminating collectors in
the country. Each one was of a caliber that would attract
similar business to DuBrand's, especially if the sales brought
high prices and good crowds. In just six months, Grant
Copeland had effectively produced the momentum needed to
break Galbraith's near monopoly on the auction field, and if
things continued this way for very long, there was no doubt in
Ollie's mind that there could be rough times ahead for Galbraith Galleries.

"Well, Ross," Ollie responded finally, "if Grant Copeland
was able to convince Lucien that his book auctioneer is so
good, maybe we ought to give some thought to bringing in
more auctioneers, too. Grant Copeland's premise that a sedate
auctioneer in a flamboyant crowd doesn't inspire as much
bidding activity as a more outgoing personality—and vice
versa—has some merit to it," he went on.

Ross stopped his pacing directly in front of the fireplace on
the wall opposite his desk. On the carved mantle sat a large
porcelain vase that had once belonged to Ņapoleon, and Ross
fingered it absently as he spoke. "We don't need more than
one auctioneer," he said, a slight edge to his voice. "Harold
Brighton is just fine. He's been with Galbraith's for decades
and knows his business—in all areas." He turned to give
Ollie a direct look, one silver eyebrow slightly arched. "I
don't intend to bring a loud-mouthed, showy auctioneer onto
Galbraith's premises. Not only would a man like that offend
me, but he'd offend Harold," he said shortly. "And anyway," he went on with a dismissive frown, "book collectors
are a quiet crowd. That's Harold's style, and he can handle
them as well as Copeland's man. Grant Copeland just did
some fast talking, that's all," he added and went back to his
unconscious admiration of the vase.

"Well, yes," Ollie said, walking slowly across the room
toward Ross. It was decorated in the same opulent French
rococo style as the Galbraith mansion itself, with gilded,
satin-upholstered chairs, a long velvet divan, and marble-top

coffee table. "I do agree about Harold in that regard," Ollie conceded and stopped several feet from his employer. "But you know, Ross," he went on carefully, "I've been wondering if maybe we shouldn't proceed a little more aggressively now, as Grant Copeland has been doing. He's—"

"Aggressively!" Ross spun around as he snapped out the word, then abruptly looked over at the door. It was opening slowly, and in a moment, the blond head of a young woman tentatively appeared. "Come in, Elizabeth," Ross said in a mellow tone. "Ah, yes. The letters. Thank you, dear," he said and accepted the letterhead sheets she held out to him. He read them over carefully, and smiled at his secretary. "Perfect, as always," he complimented and walked briskly to his desk to sign the letters with a silver fountain pen. "These can be mailed now, Elizabeth. Oh, and pull the door closed when you go, please," he added with another smile as she took the letters and left. When the door clicked shut, he faced Ollie again, and his expression had lost all its congeniality.

"Herbert," he said sternly, using Ollie's given name, as he did only when angered, "aggressive isn't a word associated with Galbraith's. We are not—*I* am not—aggressive. I'm not going to handle myself or my business in the manner of a cold-call salesman. I never have before, and I don't plan to start now. Galbraith's reputation will continue to be one of decorum and refined behavior in all respects."

"Yes, of course," Ollie responded in a clear voice and braced himself to go on. It wasn't easy for him to appear to question Ross's absolute authority at Galbraith's nor to speak out against the methods of the man who'd employed him for so long.

"But Ross, the conservative approach we've always taken in our business dealings may no longer be what's called for. There's no getting around the fact that Grant has beat us to the punch. I strongly suspect that while you and I were quietly nudging our old business associates to come to some kind of decision about how and when these collections would be sold, refraining from talking to them except at what seemed like suitable intervals, our friend Mr. Copeland was making repeated contact with them, not only over champagne and hors d'oeuvres but with frequent visits to their offices. Whatever it was, he's done something right," he added feelingly.

Ross's eyes narrowed slightly. "Herbert, are you suggesting that we are at fault?'' he asked slowly. ''That I am at fault for these estates having gone to DuBrand's?''

Ollie drew a deep breath. ''Yes,'' he said quietly.

Ross turned away from him, and Ollie thrust his hands into the trouser pockets of his suit and resolutely went on. ''Ross,'' he said, ''times have changed. It used to be that the whole mood of this business was one of soft-sell. Everybody dealt that way. There was only a small group of affluent, important buyers and sellers who made up our clientele, and they responded to an air of refinement when it came to the handling of their most precious possessions. In that kind of climate, Galbraith's way of operating was particularly effective.''

He paused for a moment, thinking of what he might've added: that Ross had been particularly effective when an aura of aristocratic elitism had characterized the business of auctioning fine art. He'd fit perfectly into such an environment, known how to deal in it, lead it—*epitomize* it. Ollie didn't vocalize those thoughts, however; saying such things would have constituted out-and-out disloyalty to Ross, and he would never have gone that far, even for the sake of making a point. Besides, he liked Ross Galbraith and had no desire to insult him.

''But Ross, things aren't like that anymore,'' he went on, although Ross hadn't once looked at him; instead, he stood silently gazing up at the portrait of his father, a man as distinguished in looks as Ross was, with intelligent eyes looking steadily forward. ''We haven't noticed the change up until now,'' Ollie continued, ''probably because we didn't really have to notice. Galbraith's has been established for a very long time, and it's been years since we've had any serious competition. Oh, Alex DuBrand gave us a run for our money every now and then,'' he allowed with a wave of one hand, ''but not like this. Not in so short a time and with such impact all at once. Four sales, Ross!'' Ollie's consternation surfaced completely. ''Four really important ones, with art and antiques of the highest quality.

''We have to face the fact that collecting no longer belongs only to the select. It's big business now and involves a wide range of people. A new breed of people.'' Still he talked to Ross's back. ''And Grant Copeland belongs to that new breed, as much as he belongs to the ideologies of big business. He's employing the techniques that have worked for him before. That's what people respond to now. It doesn't put them off, Ross, it makes them sit up and listen.''

At last Ross turned to him. "I am a Galbraith," he said, his head held high. "There has always been a code of conduct in our family, in our personal lives as well as in our business. Am I to destroy all that Galbraith's has stood for over the decades because of the flashy tactics of a man with nowhere near the breeding I have?" he asked, his eyes trained on his associate. "A man who couldn't learn in a lifetime what I know about this business from having been raised with it and having dealt in it for over thirty years? From having made it what it is! Yes, Ollie, that's right. I and my forefathers have made the business of auctioneering what it is.''

"Grant Copeland hasn't been flashy," Ollie protested. "Assertive, yes, but hardly flashy. Ross, you've observed the man," he went on in a cajoling tone. "He's got as much *savoir-faire* as anyone. And for a man who'll never understand anything about this business, he's doing all right for himself. He knows *something*, and I'd say it's how to market what he's got, if you ask me.''

"I didn't ask you!" Ross snapped. "And don't continue to talk to me as if I'm not aware that DuBrand's has become a problem for Galbraith's. I am.''

"Then hear me, Ross!" Ollie exclaimed, trailing his employer as he walked angrily back to his desk. "We've got to make moves to counter these recent gains of DuBrand's, and make them quickly. We must change our style to fit the new ways of thinking. Do you imagine for a moment that others of Grant Copeland's kind can be far behind him?" he demanded.

Ross turned to face Ollie, and now he was smiling indulgently. "Ollie, I've been more than able to handle my business in the past," he said fluidly. "I will be able to handle it now. In my own way—the Galbraith way.''

Ollie couldn't let it go so easily. "This isn't the past, Ross," he countered levelly and wondered briefly if Ross was getting tired, if his age and years at work, as much as his self-image, were clouding his professional vision. "We can learn something from Grant Copeland's methods.''

Ross's eyes widened momentarily, and he turned on his heel. "I do not need to watch a younger man to understand how to run my business!"

His anger had the upper hand again, and he abruptly sat

down behind his desk and immediately picked up his silver pen and a note pad. Scowling down at the paper before him, he felt a sharp tightness in his chest.

That constricting pain across his breastbone had been insistent now for weeks, since that first unbelievable phone call about the important sale lost to DuBrand's; Ross had no intention of telling Ollie about his discomfort, however. Or anyone else. It wasn't their business. Besides, it would be as good as an open admission that DuBrand's sudden emergence as a strong competitor had him really worried—afraid—when he considered what it might be like to lose his position as master of the pinnacle of power in the auction world.

"Ollie," Ross began when he'd regained his composure, "I don't deny the man has been effectual," he allowed, dropping the pen on the desk. "Unfortunately, I can't deny it. The proof is upon us. Frankly, I hadn't thought he'd be able to adapt his skills to our business as well as he apparently has," he added thoughtfully. "After all, there's a vast difference between dealing in the rough-and-tumble businesses of oil and steel and knowing how to operate in the world of art and antiques." The disdain had crept back into his voice. "But I see that the man does have versatility."

He got up again to stand at the window and absently fingered the edge of the rich satin draperies. It was true that he viewed Grant Copeland with a good deal of professional distaste, but what was most disturbing to him was the fact that old friends and associates had fled Galbraith's, had, in essence, turned their backs on him and his company. *Faithless.* The word stuck in Ross's mind, and he said over his shoulder, "You know, Ollie, I would've hoped that our old friends might have had a little more regard for our past relationships than they have demonstrated with their defection to DuBrand's."

"It isn't a matter of regard for relationships. It's a matter of dollars and cents, as always," Ollie responded bluntly.

"Yes," Ross murmured and continued to stroke the curtains. "Yes, dollars and cents suddenly mean more than remembering old loyalties, giving due to past favors. I've done a lot for these men, Ollie!" Ross looked around sharply. "They owe me loyalty for my help over the years."

"Ross!" Ollie was incredulous. "They owe loyalty to their own interests, as anyone does. You know that."

"And I am the one who has seen to it that their interests

were handsomely taken care of,'' Ross responded. "Yet, they have seen fit to turn their backs on me and my company. Well, let them,'' he added shortly. "We don't need them. There are many others who will not have such short memories or such low regard for the name of Galbraith.''

Ollie extended a hand in frustrated supplication. "Ross—''

"Ollie, this discussion is over for the moment,'' Ross said abruptly and returned to his chair to sit down again. As he'd stood at the stately window, he'd felt his pulse begin to accelerate, the pain in his chest radiate over to his left arm. He had to compose himself. "You needn't worry that Ross Galbraith can't protect his own business,'' he said. "And don't forget the Van Holt collections. Once we have those on our auction block, everything will be back in perspective. It's taken a long time to negotiate for that estate, longer than I'd anticipated,'' he added with a brief frown. "But I hope Phil Townsend is going to decide soon as to when he wants the sale to take place. Frankly, I'm tired of his dragging his heels.''

"I'm sure Grant Copeland has been working right along on that one, too,'' Ollie warned.

"He won't get it,'' Ross said flatly. "I can count on Phil as an executor with good sense, and as a man who respects old friends,'' he added.

Ollie made no response to that, but instead looked at Ross closely. The man's usually clear complexion looked somewhat mottled to him, and his breathing seemed more rapid that normal. "Ross, are you feeling all right?'' he asked in concern.

"Of course,'' Ross said, looking up. "Why?''

"Your color, that's all,'' Ollie hesitated, knowing how touchy Ross was about inquiries into his health. "Have you seen your doctor lately?'' he asked.

"Yes, and there's nothing to worry about,'' Ross said firmly.

Ollie wasn't totally convinced. "Maybe you ought to take the afternoon off—''

"Ollie, I'm fine,'' Ross insisted, the flicker of a warning light in his eyes. "Ashley is meeting me for lunch today, so I couldn't leave anyway. It's just as well; I have something to discuss with her,'' he added, as if to himself really. "And please remember that I don't want her to know about these matters with DuBrand's,'' he went on, giving Ollie a keen look. "These things don't concern her. Nor do I want any of your false worries about my health brought up. Understand?"

"Yes, Ross. Of course," Ollie answered, then couldn't help but add, "but don't you think Ashley might like to know what's happening here?"

"My business isn't her concern," Ross repeated strictly. "Kathryn always understood that."

At the mention of his first wife's name, Ross thought briefly of her. They'd been married for thirty years and had had a good life together, despite the disappointment of never having children. They'd shared the kind of existence Ross liked, one of serene companionship, an understanding of their proper roles in life, and he'd envisioned that same kind of life with Ashley. Well, it hadn't quite worked out that way. She was a lovely woman, and he was very fond of her, but he sometimes wondered if he'd made a mistake in marrying her; he'd thought at the time of their wedding that she'd fit into his life, that she'd want to. Well, she would fit in, he thought as he pulled over a stack of papers with deliberation. He wanted her to, because he cared for her—and because there were no other options. They were wed now, and he would never divorce her; no Galbraith had ever left his wife.

"But Ashley isn't Kathryn," he said, coming out of his reverie. "She's a delightful young woman, and I care very much for her, but she sometimes forgets who she is now."

Ollie didn't agree with Ross's refusal to let Ashley return to her position at Galbraith's. His and Ashley's was a warm relationship, dating back to the time when she'd been simply Ashley Welles: bright, energetic, and unusually gifted. His personal opinion was that she could be as good for Galbraith's as she once had been, if only Ross would give her the opportunity. But he knew better than to comment.

"No, Ross, I won't say anything to Ashley," he responded finally. "By the way, why don't we go on downstairs and take a look at the exhibition of tomorrow's sale?"

"A good idea," Ross agreed. He laid a companionable hand on Ollie's shoulder as the two of them began heading for the door, but though the pain in his chest continued to nag him, still Ross said nothing as he walked with his old friend out of the room.

Chapter 17

ASHLEY STOOD OUT on the wide lawn of the Galbraith estate, the wind of the cold October day wrapping her raincoat around her pant legs. Dark clouds hovered threateningly in the cinder gray sky above, and as the sleek, gray dog ran back up to her, tail wagging, she leaned down and worked the stick from his mouth. By her side was eight-year-old Diana Bullard, Alicia's shy daughter, and when Ashley had the stick free from the dog's teeth, she straightened and hurled it as far as she could out across the long stretch of grass in front of her.

"Fetch it, Gus!" she called.

The dog wheeled and bounded after the stick. He was a Saluki, a handsome dog resembling a greyhound, but long-haired. He was Ross's pet, a graceful animal worthy of residing in the Galbraith household and just as deserving of the name Ross had given him: Caesar Augustus. Ashley watched the beautiful sight hound retrieve the stick, then smiled down at the girl beside her. "Okay, Diana. Your turn next," she said. At the young girl's pleased yet hesitant expression, Ashley added the encouragement she knew the child needed. "He's nowhere near ready to quit, and my arm's a lot older than yours. It's getting tired. Now go on," she said, giving the girl's shoulder a gentle push.

"Thank you, Mrs. Galbraith." Diana smiled happily and ran to meet the dog halfway on his return trip, her dark hair bobbing as she tossed the stick again, then skipped after the dog when he ran for it. Ashley watched the tableau, a quiet smile on her face.

"Mrs. Galbraith!"

Ashley turned to see Alicia coming toward her from the house at a hurried walk. Smiling, the woman held a hand to her neatly arranged hair, trying to protect it from the wind. "I called from the house but couldn't get your attention," she said, then frowned worriedly. "I hope Diana's not giving you any trouble."

"Of course not," Ashley dismissed warmly, her gaze going

back to the child and dog; they were wrestling with the stick. "She's a darling girl."

"I appreciate your letting me bring her along today," Alicia went on. "It's hard to get a sitter on short notice, and I'd completely forgotten that school was out for the day." She smiled toward her daughter, then glanced back at Ashley, her expression going uncertain again. "Mr. Galbraith won't be angry, will he?"

"No," Ashley said, placing a reassuring hand on the woman's arm. There was a certain friendship between them, and as often as Ashley went out of her way to be helpful to Alicia Bullard, the divorced woman reciprocated whenever she could. "It's no problem, really," Ashley repeated. "Did you need me for anything in particular?"

Alicia looked at her somewhat quizzically. "You told me to tell you when it was eleven, so you wouldn't be late for your luncheon in town with Mr. Galbraith," she prompted.

Ashley put a hand to her forehead, smiling sheepishly. "I'm sorry! It went right out of my mind. I'd gotten so caught up with walking Gus out in the fields, then playing with . . ." Her explanation trailed off as she shook her head at herself. "Thank you."

Alicia nodded and turned, starting back toward the house. Ashley watched her go, and when she glanced around for one last look at Diana and the dog still playing happily on the slope of the lawn, her eyes had grown somberly shadowed.

These moments of carefree fun had become so rare in her life that when they came to her, she got lost in them, Ashley thought as she thrust her hands deeply into her coat pockets and began to walk slowly in the direction of the house. In the past six months her relationship with Ross hadn't changed at all—it was no better, no worse—and though she was doing her best to be as fair toward her husband as possible, to give the marriage a full chance without being prejudiced by her love for Grant and her need to be with him, that hadn't been such an easy thing to accomplish. She saw Grant all the time at social functions in New York that she attended with Ross, and her feelings for him were constantly being fueled. Their encounters were perhaps the hardest part of it all, these public moments of cordial formality and exquisitely painful pretense. They both wanted nothing more than to fall into one another's arms, but instead they spoke briefly and impersonally before going their separate ways, and Ross had never suspected that

they might be anything more to each other than casual acquaintances. We both ought to be nominated for Academy Awards,
Ashley thought as she crossed the drive toward the front
steps, but her attempt at humor sank like a stone thrown into
a river. It was getting harder with each passing day to keep up
the charade with Grant, and though she hadn't resolved her
feelings about Ross, she knew the time was approaching
when she was going to have to make a decision; tension was
building in her to a critical point—the tension of needing to
move in *some* direction. There was nothing more debilitating
than indecisiveness, and she'd been living in that state of
limbo for months now.

She sighed as she mounted the front steps and went into the
house, giving a friendly nod to the young, uniformed maid
dusting the large marble table in the hall by the drawing room
doorway. She headed directly for the central staircase, resolutely putting away her heavy-heartedness, and when she
reached the steps, she picked up her pace, hurrying so she
wouldn't be late for her lunch with Ross; it had been her own
idea, the luncheon date before she went shopping, and as she
trotted lightly up the last flight of steps to her room, a bleak
smile touched her lips.

She was trying.

An hour and a half later, Ashley walked in through the front
door of Galbraith's and stopped just inside the revolving door
to shake her dripping umbrella. Drizzle had increased to
serious rain right after she'd left Westchester, and the drive
through the congested New York City streets had taken longer
than she'd anticipated; the traffic had slowed to a honking
crawl just past Fifty-first Street, and when she'd finally reached
the underground parking lot around the corner from the gallery, she'd been exhausted and on edge.

Her tension left her completely, however, as she stood in
the elegant reception lobby of Galbraith's. She was always
overtaken by a sense of excitement when she stepped into the
auction house, and waving to the man behind the circular
entry desk, she headed up the winding staircase at a light trot,
receiving a surprised and warm welcome from several old
cohorts on her way up. She made her way on through the
crowded main floor waiting room, but didn't go directly up
the second flight of stairs to Ross's office; instead, she con-

tinued down the long hallway to the sale room, stopping in the doorway to watch the auction in progress.

There was only light attendance at the daily sale, though an air of hushed expectancy prevailed in the large room. Rows of comfortable metal chairs fanned back from the carved auctioneer's podium up front, several feet from which was the skirted display table for small objects; a stage for larger items was directly behind that, and royal purple velvet draperies sheathed all four walls. Ashley leaned against the doorframe, an unconscious smile on her face as she watched Harold Brighton calling for bids on a pair of ivory elephants from China. He was a slim man, dressed in a tuxedo, and his style was businesslike but graceful as he repeated the starting price of $2000, then looked around the room for bids. Three at $500 increments were quickly received, and after watching the items knocked down for a final price of $4000, Ashley pushed herself from the doorway and headed for Ross's office.

When she entered, after a courteous knock, she found Ollie sitting on the velvet couch beneath the portrait of William Galbraith, papers strewn across the marble coffee table in front of him. Ross was behind his desk, on the far side of the room, and at the sight of her, both men stood.

"Ashley, how nice to see you," Ollie said as he skirted the coffee table and walked to her. He caught her hands and kissed her warmly on the cheek. "You look a little damp," he observed as he stepped back, then glanced to the window. "It's really begun to rain, has it? I hadn't noticed. We've been busy."

"Yes, I'm a little wet," Ashley said in understatement; in fact, the hem of her chartreuse shirtwaist under her raincoat was soaked. "It's pouring. And of course, I had to pick a rainy Friday to come shopping," she added with a small resigned smile.

"My dear, I was getting worried about you," Ross said as he came up, and he, too, gave her a kiss on her cheek. "I expected you an hour ago."

"I'm sorry, Ross. The traffic was terrible," she explained, shrugging out of her coat and hooking it over one peg of a brass coat stand by the door.

"Well, I think I'll grab something to eat now, too," Ollie said. "It's later than I thought. Will you be returning after lunch or going on home with Ashley?" Ollie knew better, of course, but he wished Ross would take off early today.

Ross smiled pleasantly, though his eyes were steady on his associate. "I will be returning to the office, late perhaps, but I will be back. We have a staff meeting at four o'clock."

Ollie nodded, said good-bye to Ashley, and left. Ross turned once he was gone and strode back over to his desk, picking up the memorandum lying on top of several papers. "I'll only be a minute, dear," he said across his shoulder. "I just want to get this read. Oh, and I thought I'd take you over to the Plaza for lunch."

"That'll be nice, Ross," she said, and when he again busied himself with his work, Ashley walked over to the desk to stand beside him. On the corner of the writing table was a catalogue, and she picked it up when she saw the DuBrand emblem on the corner.

The thin brochure was a work of art itself, with excellent photographs and concise descriptions of a porcelain collection. She thought of Grant and her initial concern that Galbraith's—Ross—would suffer at his hands; that worry had long since been allayed when months had passed and nothing had changed for Galbraith's. Well, that wasn't really surprising. Grant Copeland was the most sensitive man she'd ever known. She closed the catalogue and stood perfectly still as she stared down at its glossy cover, one finger unconsciously caressing the shiny surface. He *was* the most sensitive man she'd ever known, and the most exciting, and . . .

"Ashley?" Ross said quizzically.

She dropped the catalogue onto the desk like a hot iron, color flooding her face; she felt as if she'd just been caught with Grant himself, in his embrace. "I—I'm sorry, Ross," she said. "I didn't hear you. I was just looking at that DuBrand catalogue. It's very well done."

He smiled, at the same time taking the catalogue and tossing it to the far side of his desk. "I said, you look wonderful in that dress," he repeated. Its classic lines fit her slender figure perfectly, a narrow belt called attention to her waist, and she'd turned the collar up in the back so that it lay just against the edge of her short dark hair. "It will be my pleasure to have you on my arm at the restaurant."

"Thank you," she said. "Ready to go?"

"In a moment," he demurred. "There's something I want to talk to you about first."

Ashley clasped her hands in front of her, smiling. "What?"

Ross moved away then, his manner deliberate, and went

over to stand near the fireplace. "Madeleine Carruthers called me this morning," he said, "about the Town Development Committee in Westchester."

Ashley tilted her head inquiringly.

"She's stepping down as chairwoman," he advised.

"Oh." Ashley continued to watch him, and he moved over to a drop-leaf table where he became heavily preoccupied with the study of a Steuben ashtray on its surface. "They need a replacement," he went on.

"That's nice." When Ross didn't look up but continued to give his full concentration to the heavy crystal object in his hands, Ashley began to get a cold feeling in the pit of her stomach. "Ross, I hope you're not thinking what I'm afraid you are," she said carefully.

At that, Ross set down the crystal object and looked over at her with an inquiring smile. "Which is?"

"That you feel I should take over the job."

"That's precisely what I think."

Ashley's shoulders tensed involuntarily. "Ross, I can't do that," she objected. "It's a full-time volunteer position—"

Ross interrupted her with an abrupt movement forward. "Ashley, you've been agitating for two years to work," he said and spread his hands. "This is the perfect opportunity for you to do what you keep saying is so important to you."

"Ross, that's not what I meant, and you know it." Ashley had begun to breathe more rapidly; she couldn't believe that they were about to go through this again. "You know what I mean by working," she said as evenly as she could. "I want to work here, at Galbraith's. Or, if that can't be, then somewhere else, in something I can make a career of."

"Ashley, dear," Ross returned indulgently, "you can have a lovely career in—"

"Stop it!" The exclamation escaped from her as her frustration mounted. "You act as if we don't even speak the same language. Ross, we've talked about this so many times. I've told you how I feel about those committees, but you won't hear me!"

"No, you won't hear me!" Ross dropped his mild manner abruptly. "Ashley, it's time we got a few things settled once and for all. I want you to participate in the social and civic functions of our community. It is part of the life that is now yours." His hazel eyes had grown stern, and he frowned heavily. "Ashley, I am making a concession here. Keep that in mind. You know how I feel about your working at something full time, but I'm willing to compromise. I expect your cooperation in return," he stated.

"Making a concession! Your concession is to allow me to do something I have absolutely no interest in doing! Ross, how can you even make that statement?" she demanded, pressing a hand to her brow as she watched him with troubled, angry eyes.

"Your interest will grow as you get involved," he said, his voice unflustered again. He passed by her as he walked over to the desk and pulled out a telephone book. "Let me make a reservation at the restaurant before we go, so we aren't kept waiting." He smiled. "I know you want to get on with your shopping."

Ashley felt like a coiled spring with no room to expand. Was he simply going to drop the subject, just like that? She shook her head in confusion. "Ross, I don't want to take over that job. I won't do it," she said.

He was still leafing through the Manhattan phone book, then running his finger down a column of names and numbers. "I have already told Madeleine that you will," he said matter-of-factly.

Ashley stared at him. "What did you say?"

"You heard me, dear," he murmured without looking up and jotted down the phone number.

Ashley continued to stare at him, then all of a sudden felt her anger explode inside her as Ross continued to ignore her. Her voice shook with a deep, inner rage when she was finally able to speak again. "How could you do that?"

Ross finally looked up, seemingly startled when he saw her rigid stance. "Now Ashley—" he began.

"How could you do that?" she repeated angrily and unconsciously walked toward him several paces. "How could you tell someone—anyone!—what I will do, and then simply advise me of it afterward as if it weren't my life you were arranging?" she demanded.

Ross began to frown again. "Ashley, you're overreacting. You simply must learn to keep your emotions in hand."

"You can't run my life like this, Ross," Ashley said, and she trembled with the intensity of her outrage. "You cannot make me into what you want me to be without asking me how I feel. I'm not a possession!"

"You are my wife," Ross said, regarding her steadily.

"Is that the same thing?" Ashley countered with raised chin.

"Ashley, I haven't got time to go through this argument again today." He was frowning heavily as he walked over to her and stood directly in front of her, taller than she was by an inch or two.

"You don't have time?" Ashley's hand had crept to her throat, and she shook her head as she stared at his implacable expression. "There isn't time for any discussion of how I might feel about things?" Ashley felt suddenly as if she might cry, out of hurt, out of frustration, because there was no other way to vent the total disbelief she felt at his attitude. "Ross, I won't do this!" she objected.

"Ashley, I have given you everything you could possibly want," Ross said then, looking at her with eyes slightly narrowed. "You have a more luxurious life than most people could dream of. Is it so much for me to expect that some of what I've given you be returned with respect for my wishes?"

"What do you want?" Ashley whispered. "Repayment with my soul?"

"Ashley, stop it!" Ross said with an angry motion of his head. "This has gone far enough—"

"Yes!" The answer rushed from her as she stood staring at him. She backed away from him, her eyes flashing. "Yes, this *has* gone far enough," she echoed. "I just don't care anymore, Ross. About any of it!"

"Well, I do," he said, misunderstanding her meaning completely. "I won't have you continuing to carry on this way. You are my wife," he repeated.

"Not for very much longer!" Ashley exclaimed, then turned on her heel, walking briskly over to the coat rack to rip her raincoat from the brass prong. She pulled open the door, giving Ross one last furious look over her shoulder, and stalked out.

Chapter 18

GRANT WAS STANDING with Karen in front of his desk, sorting through a handful of photographs. They were shots of Ming vases, T'ang dynasty porcelain, and examples of other Oriental artwork, and after studying each photograph, he passed it to Karen. When he'd finally come to the last one, he nodded with a smile of satisfaction.

"Beautiful photos," he said. "Tell Jim he can have a raise."

Karen's look followed his progress back behind his desk. "Oh, God, Grant. If I tell him that, he'll think you really mean it!" she laughed.

"I do," Grant answered. "He's a superior photographer. Between the two of you, the catalogues around here have become collector's items in their own right. Maybe you need a raise, too." He grinned as he sat down comfortably in his swivel chair and leaned back. He'd removed his suit jacket and rolled back the cuffs of his white shirt, baring his muscular forearms, still tanned from his trips back and forth to Coconino throughout the summer.

Karen was watching him eagerly. "Thanks. I'll take one."

"You got it." He kept his expression bland. "How about five a week?"

Karen flipped her long hair back behind her shoulder. "Thanks but no thanks. I thought you meant a raise, not an insult."

He laughed. "Actually, I am serious, and I'm talking about real money. I don't know what I'd do around here without you."

Karen smiled prettily, as she always did for Grant Copeland. Their relationship didn't extend beyond business, but she'd welcome something more with him if it was ever offered. There were men in her life, but beside Grant, they'd come to seem so insubstantial.

"Well, if I wasn't here, you'd still have Victor."

Grant rolled his eyes. "Yes, I would have Victor, wouldn't
I?" he said.

The rift between them had never been repaired; Victor had
been unwilling to give an inch in his attitude toward Grant
and spent his time now moodily going about the duties that
had been given him. As Grant's full partner, along with
Walter, he should have been his closest confident, but he
wasn't. Grant had no faith in the man's intuitions, and though
Walter was more astute, he was seldom around anymore to be
included in discussions. Walter had never really wanted to
run the business, Grant had decided, and had only stepped
into Alex's shoes because of his sense of duty. Grant didn't
mind his uncle's withdrawal, and over the months, Karen had
become his sounding board. Victor had been relegated to a
slot of merely overseeing the everyday minutiae of running
the organization. He didn't like it, but Grant had had no other
choice; he hadn't wanted to dissociate the man altogether, but
neither had he been able, in good conscience, to give him full
say over anything more important. There would come a time,
Grant knew, when he would probably buy them both out, but
that point was down the road yet. Six months to a year, he
thought, then came out of his preoccupation as Karen walked
around the desk and perched on the edge.

"Grant, what's happening with the Van Holt estate?" She
smoothed the fabric of her soft wool skirt down over one
knee. "Have you heard anything more?"

"No. Nothing. Philip Townsend and his lawyers are still
trying to make up their minds."

Karen smiled complacently. "I can't wait to hear the screams
from Galbraith's when we get it," she said. "Believe me,
they're going to yell. And I'll love every minute of it!"

Grant eyed her. "Keep your mind on what's good for
DuBrand's, not what's bad for Galbraith's," he warned.
"And don't be so sure we're going to get it in the first
place."

"Oh, come on, Grant. Of course we'll get it. Look at what
we've landed already—what *you've* landed. And Philip
Townsend has been carrying on talks with you for months.
He wouldn't do that if he wasn't seriously leaning in our
direction."

"True," Grant allowed, "and actually, I do anticipate that
he'll bring the collections to DuBrand's. But let's just wait
and see what happens before we start counting on anything."

She shrugged. "Okay. But Ross Galbraith is absolutely going to flip when he loses this one," she added, seeming to need to get in the last word.

Grant sat back, thinking of Ross, wondering at the man's attitude. He'd suspected from the outset that Galbraith's had been riding on its reputation for a long time; nonetheless, he'd fully anticipated that Ross would react to any significant challenge from a rival firm. The signals that Grant was serious about reestablishing DuBrand's had been there right from the start; as a businessman, Ross had to understand them. Yet in all the negotiations that Grant had concluded successfully, he'd been one step ahead of Ross. He really didn't understand where the man's mind was, unless Ross honestly believed that his business was impregnable. And if he did think that, then Grant was disappointed in him; no business was impervious to effective competition, no matter who was in charge.

Karen slid off the edge of the desk. "Well," she said with a sigh, "I've got to get back to work. I'm going to run these pictures down to production. When do you want this catalogue done?"

"It ought to go out by the middle of next month."

"Okay. And remember," she added with a good-natured arch of her eyebrow. "I'm going to hold you to that promise of a raise."

Grant smiled. "I'll remember. As it happens, I'm a man of my word."

He watched her leave, and when he was finally alone, he leaned back in his chair again, clasping his hands behind his head as he looked toward the window and the overcast sky beyond. It was raining hard now, and as he sat there staring at the patter against the plate-glass window, he thought of Ashley.

I'm a patient man, he'd told her six months ago; it had been true, and since he fully understood her situation, he'd been able to maintain a genuine attitude of forebearance about not seeing her except when he encountered her by accident. His patience had lasted through the spring and summer months, through all those difficult moments of being with her and feigning indifference; it had even lasted through those unfulfilling hours spent in the company of the other women he'd casually dated at intervals over the past half year. He'd never taken any of them home to Coconino with him, though;

in his mind—and heart—there was only one woman with whom he would ever again want to share his private retreat. But though his patience had been sincere, it had begun to wear thin as time passed and still Ashley hadn't made a decision. His own needs and wants had begun to assert themselves over his more intellectual understanding, and it was becoming harder and harder to maintain that careful distance, to control the impulse simply to claim her. He shook his head ruefully. As if Ashley would let him get away with anything so high-handed. . . .

He expelled a long breath and with effort put her out of his mind. In front of him on the oak desk was a long piece of ledger paper, and he sat forward again, turning his attention to the numbers. DuBrand's newest financial figures looked promising, he decided after briefly scanning the far right column. He'd just taken up a pencil to get busy on a more in-depth study of his company's financial position when the buzzer on his phone sounded. Absently, he reached over and pressed the intercom button. "What is it, Denise?" he asked.

His young secretary's voice sounded hollow over the speaker. "You have a visitor, Mr. Copeland," she announced.

Grant frowned and cast a glance at the appointment book open near his elbow; the afternoon portion of that day was blank. "I wasn't expecting anyone."

"No, I know, Mr. Copeland. She told me she hadn't called ahead."

Grant was mildly annoyed for the intrusion but resolutely accepted it. "All right. Who is it?" he inquired.

There was a pause on the other end of the line, and then Denise's voice finally filtered through again, this time in faint awe. "Mrs. Ross Galbraith."

Ashley stood on the opposite side of the office door, her lips pressed tensely together, her violet eyes full of fire. Her anger at Ross was still raging inside her, having found no release in the ten-minute drive from Galbraith's to here, where she'd come straight from walking out on Ross, and she'd just reached for the brass knob on the paneled door when it was yanked open in front of her. Grant stood before her then, in shirt-sleeves, his tie hanging loose around his neck, and his expression as he regarded her was a mixture of surprise and pleased welcome. She summoned the restraint to speak evenly.

"May I talk to you for a moment, Gra—Mr. Copeland?" she asked, forcing a smile.

"Of course." He moved back and waved her in immediately, tersely instructing Denise to hold his calls, before closing the door.

Ashley went directly across Grant's modern office to the wide plate-glass window, and when she heard the door click shut, she turned around.

"How would you like to buy me a drink?" she asked shortly.

"I'd love to," Grant returned as he crossed the room to her, studying her alertly. Everything about her was tense—her shoulders, the set of her mouth—and her eyes were glittering. He frowned in concern when he reached her, putting both hands on her arms. "Ashley, what's the matter?"

"Nothing! Nothing's the matter!" she said in a clipped tone and broke his light hold, walking around him to pace back across the carpeted floor. "There's nothing wrong except that Ross Galbraith has just blueprinted my whole life for the next several years!" Her anger was fanned back into high flame, and she whirled when she reached the far wall, throwing her chin up as she put both hands on her hips over her rain-soaked coat. "Ross has decided what I'll do with my time," she went on, "made all the arrangements with everyone involved, then let *me* know about it, like an afterthought!"

"Ashley, take it easy," Grant soothed, slipping a hand in his trouser pocket. "What does he want you to do?"

"That's not the point!" Ashley began pacing, and her voice was still sharp with anger. "It's not so much what he wants me to do—although I'd hate it—so much as the fact that he simply went ahead and set it all up without even asking me about it. He thinks I'll simply accept it because he says I have to. You can't do that to people!" She flung out her hand, her expression angrily entreating. "You can't make life decisions for other people—husband, wife, sister, brother, anyone! And I'm not a piece of property! I—!" She broke off, then let out a breath of unhappy frustration, and turned abruptly to face the wall. She closed her eyes tightly as she wrapped her arms across her body and gripped the sleeves of her coat. "I can't take it anymore," she said, her voice suddenly much lower, and trembling.

Grant was across the room at once and turned her around by the shoulders. Her face was no longer tense or filled with

anger, but etched with weary strain. Grant's eyes searched
her, and then he made the easiest decision he'd ever made in
his life. "Ashley, I'd love to buy you a drink," he repeated,
"just so long as we go somewhere out of the way."

She looked away from him tiredly, her hands at her sides.
"Grant, it doesn't matter if it's out of the way or not. It
doesn't matter to me anymore."

He cocked an eyebrow. "It doesn't, huh?"

"No."

"Good. I just have one phone call to make and then we can
leave."

Ashley watched him cross back over to his desk and pick
up the telephone. "Who are you calling?" she asked with a
quizzical frown.

"The flight tower." When he'd dialed the number, he
shifted the receiver to his ear as he stood watching her from
across the room, a quiet smile on his face.

"Why?" She was beginning to come out of the fog of her
emotions and looked at him more alertly.

"Because I'm going to take you for a ride in a plane."

Ashley suddenly understood what he was planning to do
and said nothing for a long moment. Finally, she made a
decision of her own, and a smile she couldn't help came to
her lips. "In a silver phoenix, maybe?" she inquired lightly.

Grant was still waiting for someone to answer on the other
end, and he raised his eyebrows at her. "Who told you that?
Oh, never mind. I know. It was Hank, wasn't it?"

Her smile widened as his did, and she walked over to him,
sliding her arm around his back as his went around her
shoulders. "Of course Hank told me," she said, looking up
into his face. "We're going to Coconino, aren't we?"

He kissed her on the lips. "You're very perceptive."

She smiled again, though a trace of worry crossed her eyes.
"Grant, I'll have to call, too—home. I can't leave town
without letting Ross know, no matter how angry I am. I'll
have to give him some reason why I won't be home." She bit
her lip with a thoughtful frown. "I'll leave a message with
Alicia."

"Tell her you're spending some time with a good friend,"
Grant suggested.

Ashley glanced up, then laughed softly. "Yes, I can tell
her that, can't I?" Grant was smiling down into her eyes, and
she tilted her head against his arm. "I do want to see Coconino

in the fall,'' she said, ''but really, Grant, don't you think Arizona is a little far to go just for a drink?''

''Yes, but it's a hell of a distance out of the way,'' he said, and grinned before responding to the voice that had just spoken up in his ear.

Chapter 19

SILVER PHOENIX TOUCHED down on Coconino property at four o'clock. They'd gained three hours in the trip across country, and the late afternoon sun shone red across the Arizona range and mesas off in the distance from the airstrip. Grant had called ahead, and Nick was waiting with the Bronco jeep at the hangar when the jet taxied up. With his Western boots and his blond hair whipped by the open range wind, he seemed a reassuringly familiar sight to Ashley as she stepped from the cockpit with Grant, and after warm greetings, they got on their way in the jeep. It took another fifteen minutes to cross the steppe plains that were blooming with October flowers, and Nick dropped them off in front of the house. Ashley felt a surge of emotion at the sight of the long, buff-colored sandstone structure; it looked so different in the fall setting, with the surrounding green grass no longer snow-covered, the tall pine shading nearly the entire wing off to the right. She let Grant guide her across the low wooden porch, and when they entered, she stopped just inside the front door.

Everything in the big, comfortable living room was just as she'd remembered it so many times over the long months—the stone fireplace they'd sat before on her last night, the colorful Indian rugs scattered about—and she stood silently looking around, a lump in her throat for the feeling of belonging that washed over her. She turned abruptly to Grant and found him watching her. He still had on his dark brown leather flight jacket, and Ashley put her hand on his arm, feeling the smooth texture of the well-worn cowhide under her palm. "I feel as if I've just come home," she said with a catch in her voice.

"You have," Grant said simply. He smiled and reached out to run his hand into her hair at the nape of her neck. "This is as much your home as mine, Ashley." He'd just leaned down to kiss her when Michael appeared, and the caress that Grant had meant to express his deepest emotions turned out to be merely a brief brush of his lips to hers.

"Mr. Copeland," Michael said in a smiling greeting, "we were expecting you a little later."

Grant dropped his hand from Ashley's neck, and returned his smile. "It was an easy flight. And we got a runway earlier than I'd anticipated," he said.

"Will you be staying for the weekend? Marina wasn't certain when she got the message."

"Yes." At Ashley's quick, startled glance up to him, Grant gave her a level look, then began drawing her raincoat from her shoulders. "Would you tell Marina to make dinner fairly early, Michael?"

"Of course." Michael passed on through the living room, and when he was gone, Ashley turned to Grant; he'd draped her coat over the back of the fan-back chair near the door and was shrugging out of his jacket.

"Grant, I didn't realize you were planning to stay the weekend," she said uncertainly. It was one thing to walk out on Ross and disappear for the night, but for an entire weekend?

Grant walked to her and raised her chin. "You don't want to stay?"

"That has nothing to do with it," she answered, her troubled eyes on his face.

"Then what does have to do with it?" Grant asked. "You told me earlier that you can't take it anymore with Ross. And if you're going to tell me that the problem is you're having a sudden guilt attack about walking away from him, I might understand, but I won't accept it as an excuse. I can't, Ashley. Not anymore. And if that is the case, then I'm afraid you should've thought about that before you came through my office door." His expression grew intent. "Did you think for a minute I wouldn't take you away with me somewhere?"

In the face of Grant's obliquely expressed desire and the fact that she could no longer deny herself the time with him she needed so badly, her hesitancy fell away. She slipped her arms around his neck, and he immediately pulled her against him. "Well, my message to Alicia was pretty vague," she capitulated. "Just that I was going to be with a friend and wouldn't be home tonight. It should cover the weekend." She studied him a minute, then inquired sweetly, "I'm a prisoner here, then, until Sunday?"

His momentary tension slipped away. "That's right," he answered, tightening his embrace. "Unless you plan to walk all the way back across country. Your pilot is on R and R for two days.''

"And tell me, just what do you intend for your prisoner to wear for the next two days, since you saw fit to whisk her away with nothing more than the clothes on her back?" She knew she was flirting with him and loved every minute of it.

"Clothes, my love, aren't something you're going to have to worry too much about."

"Oh, really?" She held his look, and they were both aware of the instant, moments later, when their provocative playfulness slipped to more earnest sexuality. Grant brought his hands up to run them slowly through her hair, and as Ashley closed her eyes to the feel of his exciting touch, she managed to speak reasonably. "Really, Grant," she said. "I've got to go buy some clothes or something."

"I'll take you into town in the morning," he murmured as he put his lips to her face, kissing her cheek softly, then moving to her mouth. He pressed his own to hers and was well on his way to being lost entirely to his pent-up desire for her when Ashley broke them apart abruptly.

She stepped back, feeling a passion for him that needed release as much as his did. Yet along with it came a sudden buoyancy—an absolute exultation at being with him, and especially at being with him in this place she loved as much as he did. She caught his hands, holding them tightly as she threw her head back to laugh.

"Come back here," he said, pulling her over by the hands.

She kissed him quickly on the chin, then stepped away. "There's time for that later," she said softly, then smiled. "I vote we go into town right now, so that there are no chores for tomorrow. Of any kind."

"I didn't realize there'd been a ballot taken," Grant said dryly.

"You weren't paying attention, that's all." When he didn't respond completely to her capricious attitude but continued to regard her with smoldering eyes, she smiled quietly. "Grant, I want to get all of the necessities over with. First. So that there is nothing else to think about except us. And anyway," she went on, the light coming back to dance in her eyes, "I have a mind to ask you to tell Michael and Marina to find something to occupy them for the weekend. Away from here. I'll do all the cooking, which would mean a trip to the grocery store. There was a time, you know, when I did that kind of thing without the aid of footmen and ladies-in-waiting, and actually, I'm rather a good cook.'' She saw him begin to grin finally and bit her lip. ''What do you think?'' she asked with a hopeful smile.

''That you're crazy,'' he said immediately. ''And marvelous. And that it's an excellent idea to give the Redchiefs some time off, especially when I need very much to be alone with you.'' He eyed her for a moment. ''And you're not the only one, you know, who's able to handle a frying pan. I've served my time over a hot stove.''

She laughed. ''Your talents are never-ending, aren't they?''

''Of course.'' He chucked her lightly under the chin, resigned to her determined plans and not entirely immune to her infectious enthusiasm. ''Put your coat back on while I go find Michael, and let's get this over with.'' He began to walk away, then abruptly came back to her, his expression momentarily cloudy. Lifting her left hand, he drew the diamond-studded wedding band from her finger and laid it in her palm. ''Put this away. It doesn't belong there.'' He refrained from adding, ''It never really did.''

Flagstaff was lit up for Friday night when they arrived downtown forty-five minutes later. They'd driven into the city in Grant's black Jaguar. It was the automobile of Ashley's dreams, she told him, not adding that Ross had never allowed her to have one because he considered it too flashy. When they stepped out into the parking lot, he caught her attention over the top of the sleek automobile. ''For the drive home,'' he said, and to her delight, tossed the keys to her.

They joined the steam of evening shoppers crowding the Main Street sidewalks, and their first stop was a saddlery shop where Ashley purchased boots, jeans, and several fitted Western shirts while Grant idled the time in conversation with the proprietors, whom he knew well; at her lighthearted direction, they went next to a cosmetic boutique, then a lingerie shop, but it was Grant who engineered the final stop before the grocery store. Just on the near side of the brightly lit supermarket, he detoured them into an exclusive evening wear establishment, one with fashionable dresses in the window and plush carpeting on the floor.

''Buy the most elegant dress in here. And make it low-cut,'' he told Ashley softly. ''I'm paying.''

Ashley couldn't fathom his intent but was titillated at his

specific instruction. "Grant, I hardly think designer clothes are necessary for a quiet evening in front of the fireplace," she said with a small laugh, then added firmly, "and you're most certainly not paying for anything."

"No, designer clothes aren't necessary for an evening at home," Grant concurred, "but they are for nightclubs in Las Vegas, which is where I'm taking you tomorrow night. It's time you started living it up. And since this is a dress that's to be suited to an evening with me, I'm buying it. Now go on, find something remarkable."

Ashley needed no more persuasion; she was exhilarated by the thought of spending a real night out on the town with Grant. And with the prospect of dressing up for him—to his taste. With dancing eyes, she handed him the bags in her arms. "You're on," she said merrily, and while he settled himself in a comfortable armchair to wait, Ashley and the saleswoman began to search for a dress.

What she finally came up with a half hour later brought Grant to his feet; appearing from behind the dressing room curtain with a flourish, her elation barely in check, she stood before him for inspection in a brilliant crimson velvet gown that tightly hugged the contours of her supple body from the shoulders to the hips; below, it spread out in a full, flowing skirt to the floor. The long sleeves were like gloves on her slender arms, set just at the point of her shoulders, and the only detailing on the entire gown was the scalloped edges of the bodice; they lay softly against her skin in a vee that was cut wide and very low, baring the full rise of her breasts. On her shapely figure and next to her dark coloring, the blood-red gown was breathtaking. Grant was speechless. And bought the dress at once. Next she bought evening shoes, and selected a shawl Grant insisted she would need, and they concluded their shopping excursion with a fast trip through the grocery aisles. In high spirits, they returned to Coconino, Ashley at the wheel of Grant's onyx Jaguar, her window down and the October breeze in her hair.

Later they ate by candlelight, completely alone in the house, and the soft flickering points of light at each end of the long oak table in the rustic dining room cast haloes around their faces as they sat over the steaks they'd prepared together. When they were finished, they left the dishes to be done later, and in a mood quieted by the intimate dining, settled down on the couch in the living room to share a brandy. And to talk seriously.

"Ashley, tell me exactly what the argument with Ross this afternoon was all about," Grant said, stretching his legs out on the coffee table in front of him.

She kicked off her shoes, propping her legs next to Grant's as she shifted more comfortably in the crook of his arm, then recounted the exchange in full for the first time. When she'd finished, he said, "Ashley, how much more evidence do you need that it can't ever work between you and Ross? That you can't ever be happy?"

"No more, I guess," she said with a heavy sigh and looked down at her hands.

"You don't sound convinced." Grant frowned at her sudden somberness.

She glanced up quickly. "It's not that, Grant," she said, and raised her hand to touch his face, wanting to remove his moody look. "I am convinced," she assured. "It's just that it's not any easier now to do the actual leaving than it wouldn've been six months ago. I'd hoped that with time I could come to terms with my feelings, but I haven't." She rested her head against his shoulder, and watched the fire burning low in the hearth. "The guilt about divorcing Ross after all he's done for me just lingers on and on," she said. "And Grant, despite it all, despite all the things Ross does that infuriate me sometimes, I don't want him to be hurt. And he will be, when I go."

"You're a soft touch beneath all your spit and fire, you know that, Ashley Welles?" He called her by her maiden name because that's who she would always be to him, and though his words held a touch of reproof, they were said lovingly.

"Yes, I guess I am sometimes," she conceded with a faint smile. "It's time to leave, though. Far past time, really."

That was what Grant wanted to hear, flatly, without coaching on his part. He kissed her hair as he tightened his arm around her shoulder. "I want you to marry me, Ashley," he said.

She laughed slightly. "Well, I will, but I have to get unmarried first."

"Live with me until you do."

She lifted her head from his shoulder and looked at him. His expression was serious, and she sat all the way up then, setting her brandy snifter on the coffee table. Perching on the edge of the couch, she turned toward him and took his hands in both of hers. "I can't do that, Grant," she said quietly.

He frowned. "Honey, these aren't Victorian times."

"No, I know that, and I'm not terribly Victorian in most of my attitudes," she said with a trace of a smile. "But Grant, you aren't taking everything into consideration. I am Ross's wife. You are Ross's competitor. If my moving in with you wouldn't be a newsworthy event, then I don't know what would be. And the fact that we were living together would get around. It would have to. I wouldn't like that kind of publicity myself, nor can I think that you would either, personally or professionally. And I simply would never be so insensitive to Ross," she added. "The gossip we'd cause would destroy him."

Grant reached over and caressed her face. "You're right, of course," he said. "I'm just tired of waiting, that's all."

"The waiting's over, Grant," she said softly. "For the most part. We'll see each other, though I guess a certain amount of discretion—to use that overworked word of Ross's —will be necessary. But we will be together."

Grant set his own glass on the table, then reached for her and guided her into his arms so that she lay facing him in his lap; he'd held her that way once before, and smiled at the memory. It was one that had been with him for a long time. "Say that again," he said. "It's music to my ears."

Ashley smiled as she settled her cheek against Grant's shoulder and encircled his neck with her arms; she had her own memories of their night together so long ago, and they were vivid as she again felt the heat of his body against hers.

"How about if I sent it to you in a singing telegram?" she teased. At his low chuckle, she smiled again and lightly began to trace the hollow of his throat exposed by his open-necked shirt.

"Grant, I'm going to tell Ross I'm leaving when I get home Sunday night," she said.

He was beginning to feel the effects of her feather-light touch on his skin; whether or not she really meant to arouse him, she was doing just that. Simply to be with her was arousing. "Then what will you do?" he asked.

"Get an apartment in the city, I suppose."

"Until you move in with me," he murmured. He began to

finger the edges of the lapels of her dress, then slipped his hand beneath the fabric.

Her skin was tingling under his touch that moved erotically along her chest, skirting tantalizingly close to her breasts before traveling away again, up one side of her lapel to her neck, back down the other side. She could not continue talking, and after a moment, she closed her eyes to the sensations of his caress; she felt him ease her down all the way, so that she lay across his lap, her head falling back languidly to the couch.

Grant watched her, letting his gaze roam the length of her from the slender column of her neck arched backwards, down to her shapely legs, one stretched out along the couch, the other crooked at the knee, making the skirt of her green dress slip back toward her thigh. She was elegantly supine below him, graceful, sensuous, and he abruptly ended his light fondling and unbuttoned her dress down to the waist, unhooking the delicate clasp of her lace bra and separating her clothing away from her body, freeing her breasts. He didn't touch her then but merely continued to look at her, openly, hungrily. "You're beautiful, Ashley. I'd forgotten just how beautiful," he said in a husky voice.

She opened her eyes to see that his had darkened and his breathing had gone shallow; his slow, ardent appraisal thrilled her, sensitized every nerve ending in the part of her body that was bared to him. Waiting for his touch became exquisitely painful when moments passed and still he didn't put his hands on her, and she was compelled finally to sit up abruptly and press herself against his chest. "Grant, take me to bed," she whispered.

"Later." He took her head in both hands, entwining his fingers in her hair, then kissed her passionately, parting her lips with his tongue; after a time, he brought his hands down and pulled her back into an embrace, leaning over her as his lips traveled from hers, down to her throat, across the point of one shoulder, then back to her neck; he lingered there, his breath warm against her skin, and then he moved on downward, his hand coming up to cup her full breast at the same time his mouth finally reached it.

Ashley involuntarily cried his name at the caress; her body had yearned for him for so long, and she hugged his head to her, burying her face in his hair as he continued to kiss her breast. She let out a soft moan of protest when some minutes later he finally raised his head, and he ran his hand through her hair again, gripping it.

"Ashley, you drive me crazy," he said raggedly, and he crushed her mouth under his again.

"Grant, take me to bed," she begged when the pressure of his mouth eased slightly.

He eased her away and got to his feet, but instead of pulling her up beside him, he pushed her gently back down on the wide cushions and stretched out beside her; she was pinned between him and the back of the couch then, and as he began unbuttoning his shirt, he caressed her with his eyes. "I will take you to bed. Later. But right now, I'm going to make love to you here."

Ashley's eyes were half-closed in desire, and she watched him strip the shirt from his shoulders. His broad chest and upper arms were muscular from years of physical activity, and she ran her hands over them, remembering the sight and feel of him as he flung the white shirt to the floor. "You're a handsome man, Grant Copeland," she breathed as he moved back to her and slid one arm under her back. "And I didn't mean to be so literal about the bed."

"Then say what you mean," he answered.

"What I mean is just—*take* me."

She strained against him intimately, pulling him closer to her with her hands low on his back, and the only response he was able to give was a groan as he shifted her forward and abruptly rolled over on top of her.

Chapter 20

ASHLEY AND GRANT rose at ten the next morning. The day was fresh and balmy for October in the high country of Arizona, and after their leisurely breakfast, they wandered hand in hand around the ranch house grounds, both dressed in jeans and checked shirts. The pine trees were rustling along the lane leading out to the main road a half mile away, and as they walked along it, Ashley stooped every now and then to pick up a rock and toss it off into the trees.

"Are you going to let me work for you after we're married?" They were some distance down the gravel drive, and Ashley looked up at Grant in smiling inquiry.

"No," he returned mildly.

"Grant!" she exclaimed with a laugh and stopped. His placid expression didn't change as they stood in a circle of shade by the side of the road. "You'll never work for me," he clarified. "You'll work with me. And it's not a matter of letting you but asking if you want to. I'd like for you to, but that's a decision you'll have to make on your own."

"It's been made already. I want to," she answered smilingly.

"Good," he said comfortably. "And why do you have to wait until after we're married?" He caught her arms and whirled her around, then pulled her against him, sliding his arms around her waist. "It so happens I have an opening right now for a woman who's exceptionally beautiful, more sensual than anyone I've ever known, and brighter by far than most people."

She held onto his forearms, resting her head back against his shoulder. "What do you want me to do, mop your floors?" she inquired playfully.

"Hardly," he returned. "I don't waste good talent. I want you to run DuBrand's with me."

At that, Ashley eased out of his embrace and reached for his hand, starting them walking again as she looked pensively toward the ground. "I don't know about that, Grant," she said quietly. "Because of Ross."

This was an issue she hadn't thought of before, and undoubtedly there would be many other unanticipated problems connected with leaving Ross. She had never been unduly afraid of the unknown, yet there was in all people, she knew, a certain hesitancy about breaking with things that were familiar. She was gripped briefly by that feeling, then abruptly raised her chin against it; she'd made her decision and would stick with it. After all, it was the one she really wanted.

She was quiet a moment longer, then ventured, "Grant, would you consider getting out of DuBrand's?"

He was sorry this subject had been broached; this was their time together, a new beginning for them as a couple, and he had wanted it to be as uncluttered by outside issues as possible. He couldn't, however, ignore her straightforward question.

"I could pull out, Ashley," he answered candidly, "but I don't want to. For one thing, I'm very sincere when I say I want you to be my partner in everything, and this enterprise is one you have experience with and find enjoyable. But for another, I've sunk a lot of money into DuBrand's, and to walk away from it at this point would be absurd. I haven't gotten where I am now by compromising my investments."

"I know," Ashley said immediately, grimacing at her own shortsightedness. "That was a self-serving thing to say, because your leaving DuBrand's would make things easier for me." She smiled apologetically. "I'm sorry."

"Don't be," he said and slipped his arm around her shoulder, hugging her. "What do you say we save this discussion for another time, huh?" He'd had a taste of how strongly she felt about DuBrand's not giving Ross real competition, and it was too volatile an issue to be explored in their newly found mood of contentment.

She nodded and studied his tanned face, the one that was to become so familiar in her life; it was still hard to believe. "What time are we leaving tonight?" she asked.

"About six, I thought. It's a short run to Vegas."

She raised her eyebrows. "Not by car, it isn't."

"No, but by plane it is," he said. "We're taking the twin-engine."

She looked at him, then gave him her most charming smile. "I thought my pilot was off duty," she remarked.

"Depends on what you ask him to do," Grant returned smoothly and, turning them around, began strolling her back toward the house.

*   *   *

Their night in Las Vegas was one to remember. They flew in after dark, and as a couple made heads turn everywhere they went—the tall handsome man in his black evening clothes and his statuesque lady in crimson. They dined to a floor show at the Stardust, then tossed dice and played roulette at the crowded casinos; they drove along the flashing neon strip of Las Vegas Boulevard, from nightclub to nightclub, the top down on their rented Porsche, the wind blowing in their hair and both of them exhilarated and laughing in the chilly night air. They danced and sang to jazz bands and country music pianists, toasting the evening with champagne all night long, and when at last they returned to Coconino, dawn was breaking. Tipsy and laughing still in exhausted gaiety, Ashley climbed the loft stairs behind Grant, clinging to his hand all the way to the top. Once upstairs, she followed him directly to the bed, and they collapsed together on it, fully clothed, both of them falling immediately into a deep and satisfied sleep.

When Ashley finally awakened, the Sunday sun was high in the sky. Grant was gone, and she'd just sat up and begun to swing her legs over the side of the bed when the door opened.

Grant came in carrying a tray with a coffee pot and two cups. He was barefoot, and the tail of his dress shirt hung out of his trousers, unbuttoned and looking much the worse for wear. At the sight of Ashley sitting foggily on the edge of the bed, her hair in disarray, her exquisite gown wrinkled and off one shoulder entirely, he grinned. "Good afternoon," he said.

She watched him come over and helped him set the tray on the pine night table. Peering at him then with one eye closed to the bright shaft of sunlight streaming through the unshaded window, she put a hand to her head. "Do I look as bad as you do?" she asked with a small laugh.

"No." He sat down on the bed beside her and handed her a cup of steaming coffee. "Worse, I think."

"Oh, what a blow!" Reaching around behind her, she propped the pillows against the headboard and eased herself back down onto them. "God, it's going to take me a whole day to pull myself together. But it was a marvelous evening, wasn't it?" She gave him a look of total serenity. "Let's do it again."

"Absolutely. Next weekend," he said. He motioned for her to move over, then stretched out on his back beside her. "And you've got exactly one half hour to recuperate," he added. "We have to leave within the hour, so don't get too comfortable." He smiled at her, turning his head against the pillows.

At the mention of returning to New York and the reminder of what lay ahead of her that evening, Ashley felt a tightness come into her back; all the problems of her life—especially the difficulty of confronting Ross with her plans of divorce—had seemed so far away in the last two days, and as she imagined the impending scene with Ross, his hurt, his sharp, stinging anger, she had a fervent wish that it was yesterday instead of today. She rested the cup back on her chest and laid her head back against the pillow, tightly closing her eyes. After a moment, she felt the warmth of Grant's breath on her cheek and opened her eyes to see him leaning up on one elbow beside her. She smiled wanly at his concerned frown. "Reality comes crashing back down on me," she explained with a shaky laugh.

"Are you going to be all right?" he asked in a low voice.

"Of course," she said with more assurance than she felt. "Once I get it over with. The anticipation is always the worst part of anything. I hope," she added under her breath.

"I'll drive you straight to the house from the airport," he said. "We'll worry about your car in the city another time."

"Yes, I can deal with the Mercedes tomorrow, or whenever. But, Grant, I don't want you to drive me home." Her eyes were serious as she lay beside him. "I'll take a cab from the airfield. Honestly. I have to face this alone."

Grant looked at her for a moment, then acquiesced reluctantly. "All right. But I want you to call me in the morning, first thing," he instructed as he gently brushed the hair away from her forehead, his eyes still worried as he watched her. "And if you need me to come and get you, I will."

Her dread of the encounter with Ross receded a bit under Grant's protective attitude; she reached up and lovingly put her hand around the back of his neck. "I'll be fine, Grant. Don't worry," she said. "I'll call you, but you won't have to come. It'll be okay," she said softly.

"All right." He checked the clock behind him. "Finish your coffee. I'm going to shower and shave." He fingered the scalloped edges of the bodice of her gown for a moment.

"You're a gorgeous creature in this dress," he said. "Marina will press it, and it'll be hanging in my closet next weekend. For you to wear for me again."

Ashley flushed in pleasure at his open admiration, as she had the night before every time she'd found his eyes drinking in the sight of her. They shared an intimate smile, and as Grant made a movement to swing himself upright, she caught his arm. "This might be a little premature, but I want to tell you something." She hesitated, then said with an uncertain smile, "Grant, don't buy me any flashy diamond wedding rings, all right? I don't really like them. I'd rather we just keep it simple."

He eased back down beside her. "What would you like, a gold band?" he asked.

"No. That has no real meaning—to us, I mean." She thought for a moment, her eyes on his face the whole time. She smiled finally. "What about something Indian?" she said. "Indian silver, maybe?"

"Turquoise," he returned immediately. "I'll have them made for us at the Navajo reservation. Matching turquoise bands." His eyes were warm. "How do you like that idea?"

"I love it. Like I love you," she said and met his kiss, her hand again around the back of his neck. The caress made her tingle everywhere and threatened to spill her coffee on both of them, and finally, she reluctantly pulled her lips away. "Grant, we won't leave any time soon at this rate," she warned.

"No, you're right." He rolled off the bed and stood up before his resistance gave way completely. "My showing you again how much I love you will just have to stay on hold for awhile."

They arrived at the New York airport at eight o'clock; it was dark and raining—had it never let up for three days? Ashley wondered—and she pulled her raincoat closely around her as she sprinted with Grant from the *Phoenix* to the small terminal. Grant called the taxi for her, seeing her into it when it drove up sometime later, and as the Checker cab pulled away, Ashley rubbed a spot in the fogged-up window for one last look at him standing under the building's awning, his worried eyes watching her departure, before settling in for the nervous drive home.

The gates at the foot of the Galbraith driveway were open when they arrived there a half hour later, and the taxi driver took her directly up to the house. It was darkened, with only a light visible through the mullioned window of the large drawing room downstairs and one shining out of an upper bedroom window. Ashley paid the man when she got out, then stood in the middle of the circle after he'd gone—a lone figure staring at the stately stone edifice, the drizzle matting her hair, tension like bony fingers once again closing around her chest.

It had been one thing to maintain her resolve about telling Ross good-bye back in the warm comfort of Coconino—where her mind seemed so clear and her desires so certain—but was quite another as she stood now before the house that, for better or worse, had sheltered her for three years. Her legs didn't seem to want to move and there was a feeling welling up inside her that at any minute she would spin and bolt in the opposite direction, fleeing from the ordeal that awaited her.

A rivulet of rain water began to trickle down her forehead, and Ashley became conscious then of the fact that she was getting soaked. She made herself move forward and walked up the long flight of steps to the front door, stopping there for a moment to compose herself. She suddenly caught the faint aroma of Grant's after shave on the collar of her dress, left there when he'd hugged her one last time before helping her into the cab, and she felt an involuntary stab of dismay. She brushed it away immediately, however; there was no longer any need for her to feel guilty about being with Grant. She was starting her new life tonight, of which he was the principal part. She hadn't yet decided just exactly what she'd tell Ross when he asked her where she'd been, or whether she should mention Grant at all. *See how it goes,* a voice in her mind instructed, and she tried to smile at it. Yes, she would see how it went; that was the only thing she could do.

She fitted her key into the lock and opened the door finally, stepping inside. The cavernous center hall was shadowed. There was an eerie silence to the house, Ashley thought as she stood uncertainly in the big entryway, and she glanced finally to the curving staircase. She was all set to cross to it and go in search of Ross upstairs when she heard a footfall on the slate floor to her left.

"Oh, Mrs. Galbraith! Thank God!" Alicia came rushing toward her from the drawing room, one hand outstretched. She was in street clothes, not the starched black uniform Ross preferred her to wear, and her expression was a mixture of relief and consternation.

"Alicia. You're here late," Ashley commented, smiling as best she could past her nervousness.

"I stayed late," the woman explained. "I was hoping you might've returned."

Ashley put a reassuring hand on her arm. "Alicia, I'm all right," she said. "I . . . know I didn't call again, but I . . . well, I decided to stay a little longer with my friend than I'd anticipated, and—"

"No, it's not that," Alicia interrupted, her distressed frown deepening. "No one knew where to reach you. No one could get in touch with you to tell you. You never told me where you'd be exactly." Ashley's expression had begun to grow perplexed, and Alicia realized she was making no sense. She took a deep breath. "It's Mr. Galbraith," she advised in a quieter tone. "He's in Westchester Memorial hospital, in intensive care. He's had a heart attack."

Chapter 21

ASHLEY'S ENTIRE BODY was ice cold as she stood staring at Alicia in shock. She could say nothing at all for a time, then finally asked in a strained voice, "When did it happen?"

"Friday afternoon," Alicia answered. "He was on his way home from the city. He had the attack in the limousine, and Charles drove him straight to the hospital. Then I called Mr. Willingham, and he came right out to be with Mr. Galbraith." Her expression held compassion now for Ashley's acute distress. "Mrs. Galbraith . . ." she began consolingly.

Ashley didn't hear any more as she spun, stricken. She rushed to the narrow, gold-leafed table by the door, and jerking open the middle drawer that held the spare keys to Ross's automobiles, she frantically searched for the one to his black Mercedes. She didn't even want to wait to summon the chauffeur. She found the keys finally and bolted out of the house, running across the driveway to the garage. Throwing up the farthest door on the right, she jumped into the dark coupe and in minutes had it heading down the winding drive to the road.

It took fifteen minutes to reach the hospital through the traffic on the suburban roads. She raced into the building after parking the car in the rainswept lot, stopped long enough at the information desk to find out where intensive care was located, then hurried through the halls bustling with uniformed nurses, attendants, and visitors. She came to a stop finally when she'd reached the nurses' station on the third floor. Her heart was pounding wildly in her breast by then, and her stockings and the hem of her coat were splattered with mud. There was no one at the desk when she arrived, but in moments, a white uniformed nurse appeared around the corner.

"I'm Mrs. Galbraith," Ashley said breathlessly. "I want to see my husband. This is intensive care, isn't it?"

"Oh, Mrs. Galbraith," the gray-haired woman said calmly. "Dr. Spaulding is in with your husband at the moment. If you'd like to wait . . ." She trailed off as she glanced down the hall and saw the tall, white-coated doctor just stepping out of Ross Galbraith's room. "Oh, there he is. Doctor—"

She broke off again as Ashley pushed herself away from the desk with both hands and rushed off in the direction of Ben Spaulding. A gaunt man with thinning black hair, he'd been Ross's private physician for years. At the sight of her coming toward him, her heels clicking sharply along the tile floor, he smiled.

"Ashley," he said warmly as she approached.

She walked right up to him and gripped both of his arms. "How is he, Ben?" she begged.

His smile faded at her distraught expression, and he took her arm. "There's a lounge down the hall. We can talk there." He guided her by the elbow to a small room at the far side of the nurses' station and ushered her inside. It was a sparsely decorated waiting room, which at the moment was empty of other visitors. He motioned Ashley to a chair and watched her perch on the very edge of it. "I've been very anxious to get in touch with you," he said as he sat down. "Where have you been?"

Nowhere, except with another man, dancing and drinking and carousing the nights away while my husband lay all alone in a hospital bed, close to death. A small cry escaped her, and she pressed her lips together hard. "I—I went away for the weekend," she said, then leaned forward, grabbing hold of the ends of the chair arms. "Ben, *please!* Is Ross going to be all right?"

Ben peered at her closely through his tortoiseshell glasses. He'd come to know her fairly well over the past three years, and he'd never seen her look so pale. Or disheveled. "Ashley, calm down," he said soothingly. "I'm going to move him out of intensive care in the morning. He's had a serious attack, but he'll recover."

Ashley looked at him a moment longer, then fell back in the chair, closing her eyes. She swallowed hard several times, trying to relax, but too many things were spinning around in her mind. After a moment, she opened her eyes. "How long before he can come home?" she asked.

"It's too early to say, but if all goes well, as I expect it to, he should be able to return home in several weeks." He smiled encouragingly, then began to frown lightly when Ashley didn't react as he'd expected she would. There'd been no audible sigh of relief from her, no weak smile. She sat staring at her hands as they automatically rolled and unrolled the belt of her raincoat. "Ashley," he said, "are you all right?"

She looked up. "Ben, what caused it?" she asked in a constrained voice.

"Well, that's hard to say," he answered slowly. "It could be many things."

"Did he say anything about what . . . did he think . . . ?" Fear was in her eyes as she spoke haltingly.

"He hasn't been conscious, Ashley." When she dropped her head into her hands at that, Ben Spaulding leaned forward. "He is now. He is now, Ashley," he reassured quickly, "though when I left him he was sleeping. He's going to be all right," he reiterated as he saw Ashley press her lips together until they were white.

"We had an argument," she said in a voice barely above a whisper, raising her head.

"Yes, I know. Mr. Willingham mentioned something about that. Apparently, the secretary outside Ross's office was aware that the two of you had had words."

"I . . . I was very angry," Ashley went on. "I said things—do you think something like that could have?—" Her eyes widened as she was unable to go on for a moment, then suddenly she blurted out, "Was it my fault?"

"That's hard to say," he repeated.

Now that she'd said it openly, Ashley sat forward, watching the man intently. "Ben, if something had upset him very much, would it have caused this heart attack?" she asked clearly.

"It could have. But Ashley, you must remember that Ross has had a heart condition for some time now. There are many factors that go into these things. His checkups have been good, but one can never really know. Obviously, stress is something he must be careful to avoid as much as he can."

"But getting upset over an argument could have been a catalyst?" she pressed, her eyes trained on the doctor.

"As I said, it could have," Ben answered carefully. "But there might have been other things on his mind also." He smiled slightly. "You know Ross. He's a great one for keeping things to himself. And—"

"Ben, I have to know!" Ashley cried, her distress bringing her right up out of the chair. She'd begun to tremble, and Ben stood at once and placed a hand on her shoulder.

"Ashley," he said, "I cannot absolve you of what is

obviously your guilt about this. I wish I could for your sake, but I can't. I cannot tell you that one particular thing did or did not cause Ross's attack. These things simply aren't so cut-and-dried. And it won't do you any good to dwell on it.''

Ashley tried to smile then, taking several deep breaths to get herself under control. "I'm sorry," she said. "I—may I see him?''

"For a few moments," Ben agreed. "He's sleeping now, and I want him to rest. But yes, you can go in for a few minutes. He's in an oxygen tent now, but that will be gone tomorrow.''

Ashley nodded. Ben escorted her out of the lounge and down the hall, and at Ross's door, he patted her shoulder. "He's going to be all right," he said again, then left her as a nurse hailed him from down the hall.

When the doctor had gone, Ashley pushed open the door and slowly went into the hospital room.

Déjà vu hit Ashley like a fist in the stomach as she looked at the still figure lying under the white sheets, his head and shoulders obscured by the transparent oxygen tent over them. An IV bottle hung from a pole beside him, its rubber tubing draping down and attached to his right arm, and for a brief moment, Ashley was transported back to another hospital room where another motionless figure had lain attached to support systems, a shell of a human being, dying. She pressed her fingertips to her mouth hard, fighting back tears, and silently crossed the room.

She could see Ross's face more clearly when she stepped closer. There was no color in his complexion, and his features seemed sunken, ghostly. His eyes were closed, and after a moment, Ashley took his hand lying limply on top of the bed sheets; it felt cold to her, and abruptly she sank down to her knees next to the bed.

"I'm so sorry, Ross," she whispered, her eyes agonized as she brought his hand to her cheek, and they searched his face through the oxygen tent as if waiting for an answer. She knew one couldn't come, not then—maybe never—and suddenly she laid her forehead against his hand. "I'm so very sorry," she repeated in a strangled voice and then very quietly began to cry.

Ashley sat on the edge of her linen-sheeted bed the next morning at nine-thirty. The covers were askew, and she was still in her peach-colored nightgown, having gotten up only ten minutes before. The receiver of the ornate French telephone on the night table between the two beds was pressed to her ear, and she listened to Grant's terse question on the other end of the line.

"It happened on the way home in the car. He'd left the office early—and I know he hadn't planned to before. There was a four o'clock meeting he wanted to attend. Oh, Grant, it's all my fault," she went on, closing her eyes tightly. "If I'd just been able to hold my tongue for once, if I hadn't spoken so sharply and just walked out like that, none of this would have happened!" she cried.

On the other end of the connection, Grant was listening to her with a heavy frown, gazing unseeingly at the papers littering the top of his office desk. At Ashley's sudden self-recriminations, his scowl grew deeper. "Ashley, honey, stop it. It wasn't your fault. You can't know what caused Ross's attack."

"Yes, I can!" she objected. "It was me. It *had* to be!"

Grant massaged his forehead. "Honey, stop it," he repeated very calmly at the sound of her uncharacteristically tremulous voice. "You can't take the blame. You can't be guilty about this." Hearing himself, he abruptly made a decision. "Ashley, I want to see you. Now. This morning," he said. "We've got to talk about this face to face."

"I can't meet you, Grant. Not this morning. I need to get over to the hospital because they're moving Ross from intensive care. He's conscious now, and I have to be there. I want him to know I'm back. And that I'm sorry."

The door to Grant's office opened just at that moment, and Karen stuck her head inside. When Grant caught sight of her questioning look, he frowned at her immediately, shaking his head sharply. She backed out, looking somewhat miffed at his terse dismissal, and when the door had closed again, Grant thrust one hand into the pocket of his suit jacket. "Ashley, I have to talk to you as soon as possible," he said. "I'm worried about you. You've got all kinds of emotions working in you, and you've got to sort them out."

"I can't see you, Grant," Ashley repeated blankly. "Not today. Not for awhile. I can't leave Ross right now. I just can't. I have to stay with him."

Grant felt as if a stone mantle had just been dropped around his shoulders. *I can't leave Ross right now.* He tried to push the echo of Ashley's statement out of his mind; she was speaking in the heat of high emotional upset, and anyway, now was no time to dwell on the long-term ramifications of what had happened. One thing at a time. He thought vaguely that if he'd had any idea what this morning's conversation— which he'd been restlessly anticipating for hours—would consist of, he wouldn't have gotten out of bed whistling, as he had. "Honey, I want to talk to you," he said again. "We'll get through this together."

At his loving statement, Ashley felt some of the tightness within her loosen. The mental images of Ross switched to visions of Grant's face, and she smiled as she pressed the receiver of the phone more closely to her ear. "Grant, I have to go now," she said softly, "but I'll call you as soon as I can. I don't know when that will be exactly, but . . . just as soon as I can," she repeated. She glanced out the leaded panes of the window, saw the sun trying to push through the dark clouds, and like a mirage, a picture of Coconino drifted across her sight. "Grant, I love you," she said abruptly.

"I love you, too," he said, his eyes shadowed. After they'd exchanged good-byes, he hung up. He sat perfectly still for a time in the chair behind his desk, his thoughts in a turmoil for all the complications that had suddenly come back into his and Ashley's relationship, then abruptly picked up a pencil and snapped it in two.

When Ashley arrived at the hospital at ten-fifteen, she checked at the front desk for Ross's new room assignment, then went immediately to the second floor where he'd been transferred. She was wearing a gray wool suit she knew Ross particularly liked, with a high-necked white blouse that had delicate lace edging the collar; at her throat she'd pinned the emerald brooch Ross had given her for her last birthday, and she knew she looked very feminine and sophisticated, just as he liked her to. As she stepped out of the elevator on the second floor, she smiled abstractedly at two people entering the lift, then caught sight of Ben Spaulding down the hall.

"Dr. Spaulding!"

He looked up and waved to her, and when Ashley reached him, he smiled. "You look a hundred percent better this morning," he said approvingly. "I was a little worried about you last night."

"I'm fine." Her brief smile was quickly replaced by a worried look, and she asked, "How's Ross?"

"Weak. Tired. But he looks better, too." Ben smiled. "He's awake. I just came out of his room."

"Did you tell him I was here last night?" Ashley said anxiously.

"Yes. And he's aware that you were due here this morning. Now, why don't you go in and see him? He's in 213."

Ashley nodded, then hurried on down the hall, stopping in front of Ross's door for a moment before she opened it. She felt nervous, uncertain of what to do or say, but finally she pushed open the door.

Ross's new room, located in the private wing of the large hospital, was handsomely furnished. Her brief glance took in comfortable armchairs, a writing desk, and a lighted dressing area next to the bathroom. There were several paintings on the walls, and along the ledge under the window were colorful arrangements of flowers sent by well-wishers. But it was on the man in the bed that her gaze rested. Ross lay still in the white-sheeted hospital bed, but he was awake. And watching her.

"Ross," she said softly and went over to his bedside. "How do you feel?"

He was wearing a gold dressing gown that someone—Ollie, it must've been—had brought to him, and it was incongruous with his plain hospital gown. His hands were crossed over his chest on top of the sheets. At her question, his impassive expression didn't change. "I'm tired, Ashley," he said. "Very tired."

She pulled over the only straight chair in the room then and set it next to the bed. She sat down quietly, clasping her hands in her lap. "You look better than you did last night," she told him with a tentative smile. "You're not so pale."

Ross was watching her steadily. "Ben told me this morning that you didn't arrive until last night. Did you just get home then?"

Ashley felt the tension in her chest tighten. "Yes," she said in a low voice.

"Where were you all weekend?"

She swallowed. "I—I needed to get away, to . . . think, Ross. I—I" Oh God, did she have to go through this? Yes. "I flew out to see Margaret," she said, hardly able to hear her own words. "I was upset, Ross. I—" She broke off, abruptly taking both his hands in hers as her eyes clouded over in pain. "Oh, Ross, I'm so sorry that I argued with you."

"What did you mean when you left, Ashley?"

His tone was so very cold, and she could see by the veil over his expression that he was completely closed away within himself. "Ross, I——"

"What did you mean when you said you wouldn't be my wife much longer?"

He was watching her narrowly as he waited for her answer. He had only one thought on his mind anymore: All around him people were turning their backs on Ross Galbraith, including his wife. He'd become completely fixated with that concept when he'd received another intolerable phone call about an hour after Ashley had left; he'd been rooted to his desk after he'd hung up, feeling cast aside by yet one more of his colleagues, and it had been only a short time later that the pains in his chest had intensified to a degree that forced him to try to get home. His old friend's polite words of rejection came vividly back to him now as he continued to regard Ashley steadily, making him cough in sudden distress.

Ashley leaned forward, holding his hands more tightly. "Ross, please don't get upset!" she said fearfully. "It's all right. I didn't mean anything by what I said. I was only speaking in anger. I'm so sorry!"

She was suddenly very near tears again, and though she was certain she knew in her heart what the answer was, she wanted to cry out, "Did I cause this to happen to you?" Yet, she couldn't bring herself to search for vindication from him, not now when he lay weak and ill before her.

"Ross, I was speaking in anger," she said, making her voice calm, reassuring. "I didn't mean anything by it. I'm here, and I will be here—every day while you're in the hospital, then when you come home." His expression relaxed even more, and she committed herself clearly. "I won't leave you, Ross."

He closed his eyes then, turned his head on the pillow, and the strain left his face. After a time, Ashley carefully laid his hands back down on the soft wool blanket, then sat back in her chair, watching him quietly.

What she had told him was true: She couldn't go, not now and, she realized, probably not for a very long time. And with that knowledge came another feeling—a deep sense of inner desolation. The time for her and Grant hadn't come yet after all, and when it would finally come, she had no way of knowing; the decision had been taken out of her hands. A tight constriction filled her chest, and tears she couldn't contain pooled in her eyes, then dropped down onto her cheek. She thought of the past weekend at Coconino where she and Grant had talked, made plans, made love. She saw an image of Grant's face once more, of the expression in his eyes when he looked at her, and the echo of his quiet words that morning came back into her mind. *We'll get through this together*.

"We still don't have any 'together,' " she whispered to him in a voice that broke with despairing emotion, and sobbing once silently, she rested her head in her hand.

Chapter 22

ASHLEY REMAINED WITH ROSS all day, leaving only for a short time to have lunch at home, where she made a few phone calls—to Ollie, to Georgia and Brett, and to a road service to arrange to have her car brought back from the city to Westchester. When she returned to Ross's room she saw that another bouquet of flowers had arrived, and she took the large, beautiful arrangement of irises from the nurse, pulling out the card. Ross was awake and smiled with brief interest. "Who are they from?" he inquired.

Ashley was staring at the card. It was printed with the words, "Sympathy from," and below, in casual script was a handwritten signature: *Grant Copeland*. "They're from Mr. Copeland," she said in an even voice and set the vase on the sill beside the many other bouquets from friends and business associates, letting her fingers linger for a moment on the petals of the lovely flowers. She glanced at Ross then, for he'd turned to look at the opposite wall, and without another word, she went over and sat down again in the chair near the bed.

It was nearly seven o'clock when Ollie arrived. Ross had just dropped off to sleep once more after only picking at his dinner, and at the sight of a familiar face in the door, Ashley rose.

"Ollie." She extended both hands, and he took them firmly as he came over to the bed.

"How is he?" he whispered.

"Better." She looked at Ross with clouded eyes, then back to him. "Ollie, would you have dinner with me tonight? At the house? We didn't really get a chance to talk this morning, and there are some things I need to discuss with you."

"Of course," Ollie said warmly. He had no intention of delving into her whereabouts for the weekend, which must be what was bothering her. "Perhaps we ought to wait here a bit longer, though, in case Ross wakes up?" he ventured. "I'd like him to know I came."

"Well . . ." She glanced at Ross uncertainly, then smiled

back at Ollie. "He seems to sleep for quite a long time when he goes off, and I'll tell him you were here."

"All right. Shall we go then?"

She nodded, and after leaving word with the nurses as to where she'd be, they left.

Once at the Galbraith home, Ashley saw to instructions for dinner, then joined Ollie in the main drawing room downstairs. He looked up from the bar set out on a wheeled butler's cart as she entered, and extended a glass of sherry toward her. "I took the liberty of pouring this for you," he said. "I thought you might need it." He gave her a fondly admonishing look as she approached. "I suspect you've been at Ross's bedside without letup. You mustn't do that, Ashley. You have to get some rest yourself."

She brushed aside his concern with a brief smile and accepted the crystal sherry glass. Motioning him toward one of several silk-upholstered couches in the formal room, she sat down and watched him with a tense expression as he followed suit beside her, his own glass in hand. "Ollie, I want to talk about Ross," she said.

"Yes."

"I—Ollie, we had a fight on Friday. I know you know that," she began.

"Yes," he repeated.

"Ollie, I was very angry at . . . certain things Ross had said to me. It doesn't matter now what they were, but the point is, I—I lashed out at Ross and then just walked out. I left town immediately to see . . . a friend. I had to get away. I—Ollie, did Ross say anything to you? About me, I mean? After I left?" Her eyes were anxious. "Was he dreadfully upset?"

"Ashley, you mustn't blame yourself," he said.

At that, her shoulders slumped and she gave him an agonized look. "Oh, Ollie! How can I not blame myself?"

"Ashley, I think the attack had been coming on all morning. Ross didn't look well at all. His color was bad. . . ." he said, and lapsed into uncomfortable recollection. "I should have tried harder to persuade him to leave."

Ashley felt as if a hand had grabbed at her throat; why hadn't *she* noticed his color? "Oh, God. If I'd only paid attention to him!" she exclaimed.

"Ashley, you couldn't have known," he said.

"If you could be aware that he didn't look good, why

couldn't I?'' she demanded. "I was fully aware of his heart condition. I live with him. I know him well enough to know when things aren't right with him. Ben Spaulding was unwilling to commit himself as to what could've caused the heart attack, but I'm not. It had to be me," she said bleakly.

"Ashley, I don't know what Ross felt about the argument," he said truthfully. "He said nothing to me about it. I can't say that it didn't have an affect, but I can tell you for a fact that it wasn't the sole cause. Galbraith's has lately been having some problems, and if one needs to point a finger in any direction in search of some reason for Ross's heart attack, it would have to be at DuBrand's.''

"At . . . DuBrand's? What do you mean?"

"I mean that DuBrand's—Grant Copeland—is giving Galbraith's serious competition," he answered. "So serious that Galbraith's will have real problems if we don't do something soon." Ross wouldn't like for him to be telling her this, but Ollie felt she had to understand the pressures her husband was under.

Ashley was shaking her head slowly. "But that can't be, Ollie. Tell me exactly what you mean," she said carefully.

He did then, relating in full the events of recent weeks. Ashley sat perfectly still as she listened, and by the time Ollie reached an explanation of the phone call that had come just after she'd left, her emotions were in a turmoil. She got up abruptly and began to pace the room.

". . . and I was with him when he got the fifth call about losing a significant estate,'' Ollie was saying. "It was from Earl Parks, and he said he was giving over the Jensen estate to DuBrand's. It's not the biggest estate around, but there are some fine things in it, especially the Georgian silver. Well, you remember. I knew, of course, that Ross was upset when he hung up the phone. He told me what Earl had said, then, well . . . he asked me to leave." Dismissed me, Ollie thought with a touch of rancor, but laid it aside; that had always been Ross's way, to be alone when he was disturbed. "So you see, Ashley," he said in conclusion, looking over to where she now stood tensely near the fireplace, "if there was really anything that afternoon that set Ross off, it was the phone call. Coming right on the heels of so many others.''

"Just what is Grant doing, Ollie?" she asked intently. "All these people you mention have been dealing with Galbraith's for years. There hasn't been any great surge of business over the months at DuBrand's, not that I could see anyway, so they couldn't be influenced by that. Just what is it that Grant Copeland is doing to make them go over to the other side?'' she repeated.

Ollie sat back with a sigh. ''Well, he's been out there aggressively pursuing business, Ashley,'' he said. ''I don't know exactly what he's offering as terms, but they must be very attractive. He's stepped up publicity enormously, of course, and he's got himself a very impressive staff at this point. You know how important that is in this business,'' he added with a meaningful look at her. ''Sellers like to think that the auction house they choose has people who know exactly what they're talking about when it comes to what their merchandise is worth.'' He smiled humorlessly. ''He's even got Frank Wilson now.''

Ashley looked at him in total silence for a moment. ''But Frank is Galbraith's head of period furniture,'' she finally said slowly. ''He always has been. And he's the best there is.''

''That he is.'' Ollie's agreement was heartfelt. ''And we feel the loss. He went over to DuBrand's about a month and a half ago,'' he explained.

Ashley felt her breathing quicken, and she kept her voice level as she asked, ''Did Grant offer him the job or did Frank go on his own?''

''I don't know, Ashley. Frank didn't say. But he did divulge the salary he's getting over there. It's substantially more than we were paying him.''

Ashley stared at Ollie a moment longer, then abruptly looked down at the beautiful heirloom rug underfoot. She couldn't believe it. Grant had taken to heart none of the things she'd said to him six months ago. She was stunned that the man she loved could so thoroughly disregard Ross's welfare. When she finally looked back up, her eyes were shimmering with troubled anger. ''I can't believe this,'' she said.

''Yes, I know,'' Ollie agreed, reading her expression as understandable concern for Ross. ''It was a blow to lose Frank, but more to lose these sales that DuBrand's has gotten.'' He sighed as he stood up then. ''I'm the first one to admit that the turn things have taken is worrisome, and though Grant Copeland is directly responsible for it, one can't condemn his methods. To be perfectly frank with you, I had a talk with Ross Friday morning about our own tactics. I told him that perhaps we've let these things happen too easily.

Ross hasn't been as aggressive as perhaps he should've been. As Grant Copeland has been.''

"Yes, Grant's apparently been that all right,'' Ashley murmured.

"Well, there's no use looking back,'' Ollie said then as he set down his half-finished sherry on a nearby table. "We can only be concerned with what to do now. It was going to be difficult enough to put a halt to DuBrand's gains on us before, but what with Ross being ill now''—he shook his head—"I'm afraid Grant Copeland is going to be given even more lead time. Ross, as you know, has never given much authority to anyone else, including me. And there's the Van Holt estate to consider.''

"John Van Holt's estate?'' she asked alertly.

"Yes. You probably know it's been in negotiation for months now.''

"Through the grapevine,'' she answered. "How important is it?''

"Very important. Certain sales make a season, as you well know, and the ones from this estate definitely fall into that category. John Van Holt had an incredible collection of Old Masters paintings—a Rembrandt, a Botticelli—and his library has some very rare books in it. Many of the furnishings in the Newport, Rhode Island, house are one of a kind, from all over the world. The profits from handling this estate will be substantial, but even more important, the prestige of being the auction house to disperse it is incalculable. Like Ross, I can't help but feel fairly confident that Galbraith's will get the estate, yet it's insanity to think that Grant Copeland hasn't been doing his best to capture it for DuBrand's.'' He turned abruptly as one of the Galbraith servants called from the doorway.

"Mrs. Galbraith, dinner is served, if you are ready,'' the young woman announced.

Ollie looked at Ashley. "Shall we go in?'' he said.

"What? Oh! Yes, of course,'' Ashley smiled mechanically and took the arm Ollie offered. She hadn't even seen or heard Jeanette in the doorway, she'd been so deeply lost in thought, and her mind was focused on one thing alone: that it was definitely time to see Grant. Face to face.

Chapter 23

AT TEN O'CLOCK the next morning, Grant was standing with Karen and Victor at the very back of the largest auction room on DuBrand's second floor. The big open area had an ultra-modern feel to it, with a black marble floor, light silk-covered walls, and rows of gleaming chrome chairs stretching the length of it. At the front, to the right of the long teak auctioneer's podium, stood an enormous revolving display stage, which turned slowly as the auction moved from item to item. A sale was in progress, and the young, blond auctioneer in a fashionable suit had just begun calling enthusiastically for bids on an Oriental tapestry hung lengthwise in one lighted partition of the display stage. The response from the audience was immediately brisk, and when the $10,000 mark had been reached after only three bids, Karen leaned toward Grant.

"It's a good crowd today," she said in a stage whisper barely audible above the rising volume of the noise in the room. "Especially for a daily sale. And they look like good bidders, too," she added with a smile.

Grant nodded as he continued to let his gaze travel the room, noting with pleasure that all but the last two rows of chairs were occupied. Men and women of all ages and in all manner of dress were represented in the audience, and after watching the discreet signaling of a stocky, bearded man in the third row back, Grant nudged Karen.

"Watch the guy in the blue suit, the one with the cigar," he instructed. "He'll take most of the lot. The quiet ones usually do."

Victor frowned down at the file folder in his hand, and when finally Karen moved away slightly, he tapped Grant's shoulder. "These are the inventories. You said you wanted to see them," he said when Grant had given him his attention. "The only things not on here are the Tiffany lamps that came in yesterday. You've got them up in your office."

Grant didn't respond to Victor's reproving tone; he knew Victor meant to imply that he was impeding Victor's work by

198

keeping the new articles out of the mainstream even for a day. Grant didn't dignify the petulant attitude with a direct comment but did open the folder immediately to scan the contents of the typed sheets. He nodded approvingly as he flipped the pages and was unconscious of the fact that his secretary, Denise, had slipped in through the back double doors and come to stand beside him until she spoke.

"Mr. Copeland," she said, "you have a phone call. I was paging you, but I didn't realize you'd planned to look in on the sale."

Grant smiled absently as he listened to her with one ear and continued to study the inventory sheets. "I should've told you. Sorry," he said. "Who's on the phone?"

"She said it was your cousin," Denise answered, "from Welles, Pennsylvania."

"I don't—" His head snapped up as comprehension struck. He clapped the folder shut and handed it back to Victor. "Thank you, Denise."

"I switched it over to a line that could be taken down here—"

"No, I'll take it in my office," Grant called over his shoulder. He was already on his way toward the door, oblivious to Karen and Victor's surprise at his abrupt departure, and he strode out of the room. He went down the main hall, passing by the elevator and going to the stairs, which he took two at a time. When he'd finally reached his office, he closed the door behind him, went immediately to his desk, and pushed down the button that was blinking. "Ashley?" he asked anxiously when he had the receiver to his ear.

"Yes, Grant. I'd like to see you."

At that statement, Grant relaxed for the first time in twenty-four hours. "That's very, very nice to hear," he answered, slipping a hand into his trouser pocket. "Are you okay?"

On the other end of the line, in her study at home, Ashley was standing by her desk. Her expression was set as she looked unseeingly out toward the manicured lawn two stories below. "I'm fine, Grant," she said.

"How's Ross?"

"Improving. Grant, please. I want to see you. Today. And not at your office."

Grant smiled as he sat down on the edge of his desk and absently jingled the change in his pocket. "I wasn't about to invite you here," he responded. "I haven't spent every waking moment trying to take my mind off you and keep it on business just to have an office visit with you when I finally got the chance." He waited for her laughter, and when it didn't come, the shadow of a frown passed across his face. "That was supposed to be a joke," he remarked.

Ashley was still standing motionlessly by her desk, her tall figure very straight. "Can you meet me at a restaurant somewhere?" she asked.

Grant let pass the fact that she'd ignored his mild attempt at intimacy. "No. I'll meet you at my apartment. Where are you now, in Westchester?" At her affirmative response, he checked his watch. "All right. It's just past ten now. It'll take you an hour to drive in. I'll be waiting for you at my apartment soon after eleven."

It was a moment before Ashley answered, but she did finally. "All right. I'll come to your apartment."

At her hesitation, Grant frowned again. "Honey, are you sure you're all right?"

"I'm fine," she repeated and hung up the phone.

Grant was pacing the carpeted living room of his apartment when the buzzer on the door finally sounded at eleven ten. He answered it immediately, pulling open the door to find Ashley standing out in the skylit hall. She was wearing a dark leather coat, epauletted and belted at the waist, and at the sight of her, he broke into a wide grin.

"I forgive you for practically hanging up the phone on me," he said as he reached for her hand. "I don't do that for just anyone, you know."

"I didn't mean to be so short," she murmured, taking his hand. She went into the living room and stopped to look around.

It wasn't what she'd expected. Unlike Coconino, where the ambiance was one of comfortable, private living, this apartment was furnished for elaborate entertaining. Its mood was formal, and most of the furnishings were English antiques, all polished to a high sheen. The dining room opened off to the left, and she glanced at the table where six place settings were laid out. Apparently there was to be a dinner party later. Ashley took in everything, then turned to look back at Grant standing by the closed door, his hand on the knob.

"Your apartment is beautiful," she said with a tight smile. "Obviously you do a lot of work at home."

Grant was aware of some undercurrent to her compliment and made no direct comment. His easy expression had already disappeared when she hadn't met him with a hug, and he walked over to her. "Take off your coat," he urged, and draped it over a chair. He came back to her then. "Come on. Let's sit down," he said, taking her elbow.

She didn't go along with him but faced him instead. And confronted him then without a lead-in. "Grant, I thought you were going to leave Ross's business alone," she said. "I thought you were going to hold back on your competition with him."

So that was it; she'd evidently just learned about his new clients. Grant was relieved that there was at least an explanation for the strain in her manner, though he cursed himself now for not having taken up the subject when they were at Coconino, before her understanding of his position could be complicated by Ross's illness.

"Honey, sit down, and we'll talk about it," he said.

"Yes, we will talk about it," she agreed but instead of going to the couch he'd motioned her toward, she walked to the wide, draw-draped window that overlooked Central Park, standing there for a minute looking down toward the trees painted with the reds and golds of autumn. Finally, she turned around, and her expression now was etched openly with her troubled anger.

"Grant, we talked six months ago about Ross and Galbraith's," she said. "I asked you then not to hurt him. I told you at that time about his heart condition."

Grant realized that she wasn't going to relax and went over to perch on the arm of a wing chair near where she stood. "That's right. You did," he said mildly.

His answer seemed unfeeling to Ashley, and her frown deepened. "Is that all you can say, Grant?" she asked. " 'That's right'?"

"Ashley—" he began.

"Grant, I explained to you about Ross for a reason!" she went on. "I was very much afraid of what might happen to him if Galbraith's were to get into trouble. Ollie told me last night about the sales going over to you, sales that will have a real effect on Galbraith's. Ross has been getting phone calls for the last two weeks, informing him little by little of what he's losing to you, and he got another one right after I left on Friday. That was what set off his heart attack!" she said and shook her head, her unhappy eyes searching him. "Grant, how could you have done this to him after what you knew!"

Grant was taken aback by her distressed tirade and crossed his arms when she finished. "Well, well," he said. "So now I'm the one directly responsible for Ross's heart attack. That certainly gets you off the hook with yourself, doesn't it? Yesterday, you were the one to blame, by your reckoning, but I see you've found an out for this newest guilt."

Ashley stared at him for a moment, then turned away sharply, wrapping her arms across her chest. Grant was on his feet immediately and went to her. "I'm sorry for that, Ashley, but you asked for it. Now come on," he said, his voice softening as he put both hands on the backs of her shoulders. "Let's sit down together so we can talk intelligently about this and about where you and I are going from here."

She turned back around, her expression less fierce but not relenting. "That's what you think I'm trying to do, shift the blame away from myself?" she asked.

"I think that's pretty obvious," he said, dropping his hands from her. "I've never heard you so upset as you were yesterday. Your conscience was killing you."

"Well, you're wrong," she said in a low voice and walked around him. "I haven't exonerated myself for my argument with Ross. I'll never really be able to, because I'm sure I helped his collapse along."

"Then that makes it all the worse, doesn't it? Your self-reproach still has you in its grip, so that it can continue to muddle your viewpoint about what's going on."

"Grant, we are both to blame for Ross's heart attack, but you the more so. Oh, I'm not so foolish that I'd expected you to do nothing for DuBrand's," she continued with a brief wave of her hand, "but I had thought that you had some sensitivity, that you'd back off, not only because of our relationship but because you'd been made aware of Ross's health. Yet none of that seems to have mattered to you after all. You've gone right ahead and done everything in your power to get just about all the important collections around—with more to come? Like Van Holt? I fully understand that DuBrand's can't survive without a few of the prestige sales, but damnit, Grant!" she exclaimed, her eyes unhappily entreating. "Do you have to have all of them?"

Grant messaged his forehead; he didn't quite know where to start in trying to discuss this with her. He knew that her emotions were dictating to that strong mind of hers, making her look at things in a way he felt certain she wouldn't at a less complicated time in her life. Old hurts and so much guilt; they all had her in their grip.

"Please sit down, Ashley, will you?" He held her gaze, and when at length she obeyed, he relaxed slightly. He took the big wing chair opposite her. "Ashley, listen to me for a minute," he said quietly. "First of all, I am a sensitive man, which I think you really know in your heart. I feel very bad about Ross's heart attack, as I would about anyone's illness. I can't be as quick as you are to make a judgment as to what caused it, but if it was connected to the competition between Galbraith's and DuBrand's, then I'm sorry. I'm sorry Ross has let it get to him this way."

She looked as though she was about to speak, and Grant raised a hand to stop her. "Hear me out," he went on levelly. "Yes, I have done my best to get as much business for DuBrand's as I can, but I'm not going to be put in the wrong for doing that. I understand what's making you look at the situation that way. We've talked at length about your feelings toward Ross—your guilt—and I know that what happened with Grif still hangs over you, but you can't let your feelings get into this. You've got to stop putting a personal emphasis on my professional relationship with the man. What I have done over the months with DuBrand's, I have done because I am a businessman with a company to run. I never planned to do any more or less than that. Yes, I heard what you said to me six months ago, and I wish like hell I'd talked this out with you then, when you first brought the subject up," he said feelingly. "But I didn't, because I had other things on my mind. Like you," he said and smiled.

A mental vision of Ross's still figure confined to a hospital bed intruded into Ashley's mind, and a renewed coldness swept over her. "Then if you heard what I said, why couldn't you have heeded it? You should have, Grant."

"Because none of it had any bearing on what I did or didn't do with DuBrand's," he repeated. "Business is business, period. And as a point of information here, Ashley, Ross might not have lost a couple of those consignments if he'd been a little more on the ball. I don't know what his thinking has been over the months, but he certainly hasn't made as much effort as he could have to get hold of those collections himself."

"Well, how could he?" Ashley asked queruously at that. "He doesn't stand a chance against you, not if you're really working!"

"Oh, come on, Ashley. I'm flattered, but——"

"Grant, this isn't a light matter. Feel flattered if you like, but what you've done is wrong!" Grant was watching her steadily, his head resting against the wing of the chair, but he said nothing, and she went on. "Grant, why did you have to lure Frank Wilson away?" she asked suddenly. "He was one of Ross's most valuable employees. Is that consideration for Ross? Knocking a hole in his company like that?"

"Honey, the man came to me. I didn't approach him first."

She was taken aback, but countered immediately. "Well, you offered him a salary he couldn't turn down. It amounts to the same thing."

Despite his love for Ashley, Grant was beginning to feel slightly impatient with her. "Ashley, I pay people what I think they're worth. One should do that, you know, as a matter of good business practice."

"Don't be condescending, Grant," she said, her voice very low and trembling slightly, and she got up and walked to the window.

Grant saw that he'd hit a deep chord of anger in her and realized in the same instant that he didn't blame her for it. His answer had been couched unpleasantly, in direct response to her displeasure with him. "I'm sorry, Ashley," he said. "That was poorly put. The point is, I didn't lure Frank away. He came to me, wanting to work for my company, and if I felt he was worth more money than Ross did, well, that's not my problem. Or my fault."

Ashley sat down again, but farther away from him. "Grant, can we talk just plain business for a moment?" she said quietly. "Leaving out all of this about the relationships between you, me, and Ross?"

"Yes, we were going to get around to doing that at some point, weren't we?" he remarked with a brief smile.

She regarded him soberly. "Grant, to my mind, there's a simple concept you've disregarded with Ross."

"And that is?"

"The fact that business competition ought to have a little of the human element to it, no matter who's involved. You've got to give some thought to how what you do is going to affect your competitors, especially when it might go so far as to affect another man's health.''

Grant was watching her steadily. "You really believe that, without qualifications of any kind?"

"I do," she answered simply and clasped her hands in front of her.

"Well, you're wrong," he said, and pushed himself out of the chair.

"No, I'm not," she defended, her eyes on him as he went to a bar arranged on one half of the paneled bookcases next to the fireplace. "There's no reason why businessmen, or women, can't incorporate awareness of others into their decisions," she said.

"There's a very good reason, Ashley," Grant answered over his shoulder as he reached for two glasses. "It doesn't work. It's a nice theory and one that most of us would like to apply, but, unfortunately, sentimentality is destructive to business reason." He mixed Scotch and water for Ashley, poured a bourbon for himself, then crossed the room to hand her a glass.

She accepted it, looking up to him. "I don't buy that," she said.

Grant sat down across from her once more. "You don't buy that because, for one thing, your compassionate heart is getting in the way, but for another, and more importantly, you've never been there," he said, propping one leg on the other. "You haven't had to cope with running a company, so there are things you haven't experienced."

Ashley gave him a skeptical look over the rim of her glass. "I don't have to have 'been there' to know what I believe, what I feel," she said. "Grant, people get hurt all the time with your kind of thinking," she went on. "And I don't see that it has to be that way. There is such a thing as latitude. And compromise." She smiled despite her troubled look. "If both those things are put into practice, then everyone can have something," she reasoned.

How confident she is, Grant thought. Confident, clear-eyed, and filled with conviction. He realized that one of her strong opinions was coming into play here—something he hadn't understood six months ago—and found that knowledge extremely disturbing. He let out a slow breath and finally responded.

"Ashley, I want to tell you a few things," he said, resting

his glass on his thigh. "Personal feelings of any kind don't belong in business. I know you have the capacity to understand that and to accept it because you demonstrated that once. You knew full well why I had to unemotionally accept the death of one of my brood mares. I'd be out of business by now as a breeder if I let my sensitivity influence the things I do. You understood that, Ashley, and you know why?" he asked, cocking his head. "Because you've been dealing in that kind of thing for years. You've seen it, and you've experienced it."

Ashley frowned. "Grant, please don't tell me what I know or don't know—"

"Just listen to me," he answered, holding up a hand.

"—and we're talking about people now, not animals!" she continued earnestly.

"I said *listen* to me!" Grant's expression was suddenly stern. "The same thinking applies everywhere, Ashley, in every business. If you let personal feelings become part of the decision-making process, they'll only make you do stupid, sometimes disastrous things. Latitude and compromise? They're necessary and even called for in some cases, but when you start running a company on the concepts of compromise and consideration alone, you're as good as dead. Or worse, second-rate."

"Would that kill you, Grant? To be second-rate?" she said, piqued at his continued lecturing.

He heard the disapproval in her tone. "Yes. Like it would kill you, Ashley, or anyone else who seriously likes to achieve. Just as you're afraid it might kill Ross Galbraith to find himself second-rate. Which maybe he is when put to the real test."

Ashley's eyes widened. "You really hold a grudge against him, don't you?" she asked slowly.

"Oh, for Christ's sake, Ashley!" Grant was totally exasperated at her for having inspired him to make the pompous comment, then for misreading it.

Ashley's eyes were searching him uncertainly. "Is all of what you've done to Ross more a matter of getting back at him than a simple disregard for him as an individual? Grant, have you been jealous of him all this time?"

He set his drink down sharply onto the table beside his chair and stood up. "You know, you can be, without a doubt, the most aggravating, infuriating woman I know sometimes!"

he exploded. "Stubborn, dictatorial, opinionated. And conceited, on top of everything else? Maybe half *your* trouble in all of this is simply that I haven't done as you *told* me to do six months ago. Maybe you just don't like being disobeyed."

"That was totally unnecessary!" Ashley objected, hurt in her eyes as she too rose from her chair.

"What's the matter? Don't you like being insulted?" he demanded. "Well, neither do I, but as far as I'm concerned, that's all you've been doing to me ever since you got here. Now once and for all, you're going to hear what I'm saying—"

"Will you please stop lecturing me!"

"Damnit, you need to be lectured! You need to have someone knock some sense into you! I have *not* been jealous of Ross, I'm sorry to inform your ego. There wasn't any reason for me to be."

"Don't worry about my ego, Grant," she said, her eyes snapping now too. "It—"

"Shut up and listen to me!" Grant was furious and reached out abruptly, grabbing her arm and pulling her over roughly so that she stood directly in front of him. "Maybe Ross puts up with this kind of scene from you, but I won't!" he snapped. "You walked through that door determined to fight, and if that's what you want, then you got it! I've had about all I can take of trying to justify myself to your tangled perceptions and opinions. I've had enough of being put in the position where I have to explain myself at all, to you or anyone else," he railed on. "And I'm tired of your trying to pass off onto me your own damn guilt, which, as far as I'm concerned, is exactly what you're doing. I had thought you were a strong enough woman to handle your feelings, intelligent enough to be able to put them into their proper perspective, but it looks like I've been wrong all along about just how smart you really are!"

Ashley caught her breath sharply. She stared at him blindly for a moment, then turned, walked over to grab her coat and purse, and headed for the door. Grant reached it first, throwing his hand out against it.

"Oh no. You're not leaving!" he said furiously. "You can walk out on Ross in a temper, but not on me!"

"Yes, I am leaving, Grant. Right now," Ashley said tightly and clutched her coat against her. "I'm going over to the hospital to see Ross."

He looked at her a moment, his anger still burning hotly

inside him, then abruptly dropped his hand from the door, jerking it open; he waved her out. "All right, go on. Go on over to Ross. You belong there anyway, with a man who isn't going to expect you to shape up and start using your brain. Living with me might have been a little taxing for you after all."

Ashley's hand was at her throat as she stood out in the hall, staring at him. She opened her mouth to speak but then turned instead to rush away, at the very same moment that Grant let go of the door and kicked it shut in her face.

Chapter 24

"THE SALES WERE an unqualified success, all of them. The last one was over today, and though the complete figures haven't been published, they'll be impressive, without question. The final prices on most of the items were unusually high. I sent a couple of our people over to sit in on most of the sessions, and they came away—well—stunned at some of the bids the auctioneer was able to draw out. The Georgian silver and Impressionist paintings went particularly high."

Ollie Willingham was filling Ross in tersely on the business news. It was a Saturday in late November, and the two of them, plus Ashley, were sitting in Ollie's darkly paneled office on the third floor of Galbraith Galleries.

"Grant Copeland has done well for himself with these sales, there's no doubt about that. But that's all right. We can put it behind us," he said with brisk optimism. "Now, there are several things I wanted to take up with you while you're here, things I think we ought to consider getting into the works—"

Ross stood up, interrupting Ollie with the abrupt action. He was wearing a handsomely tailored navy blue suit, and he was looking much improved—the color in his face good, most of the weight he'd lost regained. His carriage was straight as he stood by Ashley's chair and said, "I'm going down to look over the galleries."

Ashley rose immediately and put her hand on his arm. "Ross, I don't think you should push yourself too hard," she objected. "It's your first day in the city. The galleries are fine. You can look at them—"

"Dear, I'm not an invalid," he said, stepping away. "And I want to see my galleries." He turned without a further word and walked from the room.

Ollie's bald head shone in the light of the window behind him as he sat at his desk staring toward the empty doorway through which Ross had disappeared. After a minute, he abruptly got up from the high-backed chair. "He wants to look at the galleries!'' he said, throwing up his hands as he paced over to an antique armoire near the bookcases.

Ashley sat back down slowly. Nervously, she kept smoothing the fabric of her coral wool skirt over one knee. ''Just give him time,'' she said quietly.

''Time? We don't have time!'' Ollie exclaimed, expelling a breath of frustration. ''I've been going out to the house regularly ever since Ross got home from the hospital, trying to get some answers from him as to how he wants to proceed, but I get only a deaf ear. I thought that his coming into the office meant he was finally ready to get on with a serious discussion of business, but all he wants to do is look at his galleries!''

Ashley's smile was both sympathetic and troubled. ''He's been closed away from everyone, Ollie. You know that.''

''Well, that's fine,'' Ollie nearly snapped. ''And in the meantime, everything at Galbraith's has come nearly to a grinding halt because Ross is unreachable. And won't turn over the responsibility for matters of importance to me.'' He ran a hand over his smooth pate. ''But I don't mean to take all this out on you, Ashley,'' he apologized wearily.

She gave him a tired smile. ''It's all right. This is a difficult time all around.''

She knew better than anybody. In the past month, she'd done everything she could for Ross: keeping him as comfortable as possible when he'd been bedridden, reading to him when he'd asked her to, and then once he'd been allowed to get up, she'd walked with him for short periods around the frost-covered grounds of the private estate, with Gus the handsome Saluki at their heels—all the while trying to draw him out of that introspective world he'd been locked up in, but to no avail. Ollie had come out three times a week, in combined personal and professional concern, but it had been with Ashley that he'd discussed matters of business in depth, for Ross's behavior on the occasion of his visits had always followed the same pattern; he'd greeted his associate, then immediately ask the single question: ''Has Phil Townsend called yet about the Van Holt estate?'' At Ollie's always negative response, the veil would settle back over Ross's eyes, and in the middle of whatever matter Ollie tried to discuss next, Ross would, as often as not, rise without a word and leave the room. As he'd just done.

''Damnit, Ollie, I wish Philip Townsend would hurry up

and come to a decision about the Van Holt business," she said. "I just feel that once that's behind him, Ross will be all right." She tilted her head hopefully. "Couldn't you call him?"

"Actually, I have," Ollie admitted. "His decision will be made 'soon,' he tells me. And, of course, Ross would feel much easier if that were resolved, but there are other things that need his attention too!" He sat down on the edge of his desk, exasperation written all over his face. "Because I was unable to get Ross to discuss bringing our commission rate down to the figure Grant Copeland has been using lately, we've lost another estate to him. I found out about it this morning."

At the mention of Grant's name, Ashley got up and restlessly walked over to the mahogany bookshelves, where she stopped to finger the rows of leather-bound volumes neatly aligned within. The last time she'd seen Grant had been that day, more than a month ago, in his apartment, for she and Ross hadn't been out and around since then. The memory of Grant's raw anger on that day, the echoes of the derogatory statements he'd hurled at her, made her fingertips tremble on the binding of the book she touched.

She had to admit it was true that she had entered Grant's apartment that day in an argumentative manner; she'd known that even as she'd run away from the place on the heels of the horrible exchange. But still, that didn't excuse what Grant had been doing to Ross—was *still* doing—didn't mitigate the things he'd said to her, how he'd . . . The image of the door slammed in her face was so sharp it might've been happening again right at that moment, and she turned away from it bodily, pressing her lips together so tightly they whitened as she raised her chin.

No, Grant couldn't be excused from his actions toward Ross, nor did she want to see or hear from him at all. She'd refused the two calls he'd made to the house—taken by Alicia, luckily—in the several days following their altercation and had returned his letter that had arrived a week after that. It had been hand-delivered, a small buff-colored envelope addressed, "A. Welles," and she'd taken it up to her sitting room, where she'd addressed a plain white envelope of her own. It had read, "Grant Copeland, Coconino Ranch, Flagstaff, Arizona," and after inserting Grant's unopened letter into it, she'd gone immediately to mail it, standing motionlessly in front of the mailbox for only a moment before she'd firmly impelled the letter into the chute. She'd hurried away from the big blue postal bin then, running by the time she'd reached her car; she'd been anxious to get home, that was all. She'd had so very many important things to get on with.

Ashley crossed her hands over her body, trying to alleviate the sudden chill that had come to her. "Ollie, Ross has to fight back!" she said.

"You're so right," he agreed, and looked up from the papers he was straightening on his desk. "And I'm going down to find him right now," he added, heading for the door. "In the first place, he ought not to be putting a strain on himself with too much wandering around, but in the second, I'm going to make him listen to me about a few things." He held the folders out meaningfully.

"I'm coming with you," Ashley said immediately.

He tucked the folders beneath one arm and headed with her toward the door. "Don't worry, Ashley," he reassured when they reached it, sounding more calm than he himself felt. "We'll get through this. And so will Ross. Between the two of us, we'll see to that."

"Congratulations again, Grant," Walter was saying nine days later as he, Grant, and Victor came out of the oak-paneled conference room at DuBrand's. He was smiling broadly at his nephew and clapped a hand on Grant's shoulder. "This is a real coup. Everyone had assumed that John Van Holt's estate was a shoo-in for Galbraith's. I guess Philip Townsend was impressed by the recent sales, huh?"

"So he said." Grant's return smile wasn't as easy as it might have been, and he looked from one to the other of his business partners as they stopped out in the hall. "Now, if the two of you will excuse me, I've got to get busy right away on the arrangements for all of this. I just wanted to let you know the news." He gave Victor his full attention. "You and I will be sitting down together soon, to go over everything."

Victor nodded, pleased at the inclusion, minimal though he suspected it would be. "There are a couple of reports we could go over now, if you have time . . ."

"Later." Grant smiled politely, but firmly. "I'll be tied up for awhile."

He left them then before anything more could be said and rode the elevator from the second floor up to the third. The doors slid open, and when he stepped out, he nearly ran into Karen as she came hurrying around the corner.

"Oh!" She broke into an immediate smile. "I was just on my way down to hover outside the conference room door. Well, how did they react to the news about Van Holt?" she asked eagerly, keeping pace with Grant when he began walking down the carpeted hall toward his office.

"They were pleased," he answered with a brief smile.

"Pleased?" Karen's excited voice rose another octave. "I imagine that's a masterpiece of understatement."

Grant said nothing as he pushed open the door to his secretary's office and strode on through to his own. He entered and Karen followed, watching him in growing bemusement.

"Why are you so subdued?" she asked, frowning. "For God's sake, Grant, this will be the biggest sale of the year. And you got it!"

"Hmmm." Grant was already behind his desk, shrugging out of the jacket of his gray wool suit. He unbuttoned his vest, loosened his tie, and unbuttoned the collar of his shirt before sitting down to get immediately involved in the stack of mail on the blotter.

Karen came and perched down on the arm of a chair in front of the desk. Her brown eyes were suddenly luminous in far-off speculation. "Man, what a flap there's going to be over at Galbraith's when they find out! Don't you just wish you could be there? I'll bet—"

"Karen, knock it off!"

Startled by Grant's sharp command and dark look, she got up from the chair and stood by it, her expression wary. "Grant, I was only—"

"Never mind," he said, annoyed with himself for being so short. And with her for being so vindictive. "But stop worrying about Galbraith's, will you? Worry about us. We're going to have a hell of a time coordinating all this." He forced a smile then. "Now, if you don't mind, I have a few things to get done, but I do want to talk to you later," he added.

She accepted his dismissal and oblique apology. "No problem. I have plenty to keep me busy." She left immediately, and when the door had closed behind her, Grant gave up the pretense of concentrating on work and stared moodily toward the blustery day beyond the window.

He wished he could be as unreservedly complacent as

everyone else about DuBrand's impressive step forward, but he couldn't. He was pleased, yes; he couldn't help but be and had felt a real surge of satisfaction when Philip had called first thing that morning and given the Van Holt collections to him. Yet, it had taken only a moment for all the other dimensions of the victory to permeate his pleasure, and as his mind focused entirely on them now, he stood up abruptly.

"Damnit, Ashley!"

He cursed her aloud, for so many things, and strode across the room to the bar, where he mixed a drink. When he had it in hand, he looked at the bourbon in the glass, glanced at the mantel clock sitting on one level of the expansive bookcases lining the wall, then dumped the alcohol into the sink. Ashley Welles could make him do a lot of unnatural things—and had—but he'd be damned if he was going to start drinking over her. Not first thing in the morning, at any rate.

He went back to his swivel chair and sat down, his thoughts hounded, as they always were, by the remembrance of his fight with her weeks before. He'd done everything he considered reasonable and acceptable to try and reach her. He *had* to see her again, so he could shake her for so stubbornly misunderstanding herself and all that was happening, and so he could, more than anything else, take her tightly into his arms and apologize for the awful things he'd said—things he'd never meant—and for slamming the door in her face.

"Christ," he groaned, leaning forward to put his head in his hands as he vividly saw his furious behavior all over again. He despised the fact that Ashley could provoke him to such anger, though he knew, too, the reason for it: He loved her with a passion approaching ferocity.

"That's a nice way to excuse yourself for behaving like a bastard," he said aloud, scowling at his desk. Actually, Ashley had pretty much the same problem with him, he felt. No, he knew. They were so alike in so many ways; her love for him was as strong as his for her. *Meant for each other.* The cliché passed through his mind, making him smile, but his momentary pleasure was dissipated immediately by the heaviness of his thoughts.

He couldn't condone his excesses of behavior, no matter what the reason for them, and he intended that there would be no more episodes of it. And he intended for Ashley to know that, just as soon as he could find some way to be with her again. He could've walked right up to her front door and demanded to see her, of course, but doing that would've been acting as unconscionably as he already had. So, he'd done the next best thing with his calls and his letter. For the hundredth time, he wondered if she'd read it.

He'd begun the letter of apology to her four times, tearing up each one immediately after it had been penned because they'd all sounded insincere, ineffective. He'd gotten up from his desk finally and paced around his apartment, the verbal slaps he'd given her reverberating in his head. At length, he'd decided to tell her *not* what he didn't feel about her, but what he did. He'd returned to his desk then and simply spoken from his heart on paper; it had taken only a half hour to cover three pages with words more lyrical than he'd ever known were in him to say, and finally satisfied, he'd slipped the written testament of his feelings for Ashley into the envelope, addressed it, and had it delivered by messenger the next day.

The buzzer on his phone rang sharply, startling him from his deep reverie. "What, Denise?"

"There's a call for you."

Impatient with the bother, he frowned. "Do me a favor, Denise? Switch it over to Karen. We were expecting a call from the printer. Let her take it."

Denise assented, and when he was alone again with his thoughts, Grant eased his head back against his chair.

It was more important now than ever for Ashley to understand his feelings for her, because he knew she would be outraged by the news about his having landed the Van Holt collections. In deference to her feelings, he was going to bow for the first time in his professional life to the personal side of an issue. He was going to wait for several weeks before making a public announcement of the stunning news about the Van Holt estate; he'd told Walter and Victor to keep it to themselves until he said otherwise, and he planned to inform the few others who knew to do the same. Holding up on the publicity for so long a time wasn't usual, for the advance notice that Philip Townsend had so much faith in DuBrand's would be a phenomenal drawing card of immediate benefit to the company. But he was doing what Ashley wanted: He was letting consideration for Ross's weakened health take precedence over his strict attention to what was best for DuBrand's.

The news was unquestionably going to come as a blow to Ross, even when delivered gently by phone call, which Philip Townsend intended to do after tomorrow; it couldn't be done

before then because Philip had had to leave town immediately
after his call to Grant that morning and wasn't going to return
until the following evening. The bank executive had expressly
told Grant he'd be unreachable while he was away and had
asked Grant to keep the news quiet until he could speak
personally with Ross. And that was the way Grant wanted it,
too; he never would have subjected Ross to the shock and
humiliation of learning of the event through the cold, hard
voice of newsprint. Grant felt sure the matter was being
handled as tactfully as possible: to allow Ross to hear the
news from Philip himself, then to give him several weeks in
which to absorb the shock, before the public announcement
was made.

Ashley, you ought to be proud of yourself, he thought.
You've got me crossing over the lines. *This time*, he added.

He had pulled from the pile of mail on his desk a manila
envelope sent by Nick from Coconino, and was just dumping
out its contents when his phone rang again. He reached for it
while he quickly read over Nick's brief note.

Grant—
*Meant to get these letters and things to you before now,
but I could never seem to get around to it. The snow's on
the ground already. Dakota kicked down his door again.
We've got two colts and a filly. How's your lady?*
                                                            Nick

My lady's hurt, Grant answered silently as he slowly lifted
the phone from the console, and when he finally got it to his
ear, he said, "Hello."

"My God, it took you long enough to say something once
you picked up," Karen chided lightly. "What are you doing?"

"Just having a conversation with myself," he remarked.
He picked up a plain white envelope from among Nick's
forwarded letters and began working open the back flap as he
gave Karen his complete concentration. "What's up?" he
inquired. "Did you talk to our laggardly printer? I hope he's
got some good reason for being so late on those proofs."

"Yes, as a matter of fact, I did talk to him," Karen
answered. "I'll tell you about it in a minute. But first, I
thought I'd make your day for you." She paused for effect,
then said with a lilt, "You know that call you switched to
me? Well, it was none other than a columnist from the *Times*

art section. Somewhere he'd gotten wind of the fact that Phil Townsend had finally turned over the Van Holt estate to us. Probably someone in Phil's office leaked it. Of course, I was happy to clarify the information for him. He's going to run the news in tomorrow morning's paper, with headlines. Headlines, Grant! Can you believe it? God, I'm so excited I can hardly stand it! I—Grant, are you there?'' she asked abruptly when her news was met only with dead silence.

In his office, Grant was sitting like a statue as he replaced the receiver. He was too stunned to speak, and after a minute, the envelope he was holding slipped from his hand. It landed on his blotter, drawing his eyes downward.

"Damnit to hell," he whispered when his cold mortification over what Karen and some unknown newsman had just inadvertently arranged for Ross Galbraith was compounded with the sight of the envelope's contents.

It was a letter to Ashley, unopened.

Unread.

Chapter 25

ROSS PICKED UP the early edition of the *Times* at nine thirty-two on the first Tuesday morning in December; Ashley would always remember that. They were sitting together in the sunny alcove of their opulent yellow bedroom, having breakfast at a small, linen-draped table set up in front of the bay window, and Ashley had glanced purposely at her watch when Ross picked up the paper and folded it out flat.

"Ross, we'd better hurry a little, don't you think?" she said, giving him an encouraging look across the table. "Ollie said the meeting this morning was going to begin promptly at eleven."

"Ashley, there's plenty of time," Ross murmured as he scanned the international headlines on the front page. He was wearing the trousers to his dark gray pinstriped suit, a crisp white shirt, and silk tie, and he looked up then with a trace of a smile in his eyes. "Gavin Caine has never been on time for an appointment in his life. I've told him that any number of times, but it doesn't seem to help."

Ashley was dressed for the trip into New York City in a tailored burgundy suit with belted jacket and black turtleneck sweater. Over the past week, she'd driven Ross into his office every day for a stay of several hours each time, and she and Ollie both were beginning to see signs of the old Ross. She'd decided that his burgeoning improvement in attitude was due to his finally getting back where he belonged: behind the handsome desk that had been his for a professional lifetime. He hadn't actually done that much while he'd been at the office, and he'd often slipped into a heavy silence as he'd strolled around the richly appointed room, fingering his possessions, touching the leather bindings of his books, or just standing beneath the portrait of his father, staring up at it. Yet, he'd instructed Ollie to set up today's meeting with the executor of an important estate that would be going to auction, and he'd agreed to attend himself. One step at a time, Ashley thought, and reached for the silver coffee pot.

She poured her husband another half-cup of coffee, glancing across the table set with crystal and fine English china; two covered silver serving dishes sat on either side of a fresh arrangement of carnations as a centerpiece. "Ross, while you're in the office today, why don't you call Philip?" she suggested with a light smile.

Ross didn't look up from the paper and continued slowly to turn the long pages, the light from the window streaking his silver hair with diamondlike highlights. "Phil will call me when he's ready," he responded. "He knows where I am. Ashley, dear, you're spilling coffee on the tablecloth." He dabbed with his napkin at the tiny brown stain on the embroidered cloth and flashed her a smile touched with remonstrance.

"It can be washed," Ashley dismissed, then pressed her train of thought. "I realize Philip knows where you are, but it couldn't hurt to prod him a little."

"Ashley, I don't intend to nag at my friend. And please remember my feelings about your involvement in my business affairs."

The old Ross. Ashley's gaze lowered to the table briefly, but when she looked up, she was smiling, if a little consciously. "We'd really better be getting on our way soon," she said. "The traffic might be a problem."

He nodded, then glanced up again, this time removing his reading glasses. "By the way, what was that all about earlier, with Alicia?" he asked with interest.

Ashley immediately busied herself with her napkin, folding and tucking it under the edge of her plate. Ross was referring to Alicia's appearance at their bedroom door not a half hour before with the information that Ashley was wanted downstairs; she had gone down to the front door where Alicia directed her and found there a uniformed messenger with a letter for her. Another one from Grant. She'd accepted it, but rather than taking it inside, she'd borrowed the messenger's pen, crossed out her name and written Grant's, instructing the man to return the letter to the sender. She'd come directly back upstairs then to her breakfast with Ross.

"It wasn't anything important. Just a slight problem with the postman." She pushed back her chair, saying quickly, "I'm going to put on some lipstick, and then I'll be ready. Shall I get your suit jacket out of the closet?" she asked, tilting her head inquiringly.

"Please," he returned with a smile for her solicitude. He

watched her rise, then replaced his glasses and went back to reading the paper.

As Ashley left the table her thoughts returned to Grant. The letter that morning hadn't been the only communication she'd received from him in the past two days. He'd called her also, late yesterday afternoon. He'd given the butler who'd answered the call a fictitious name, thereby luring her unsuspectingly to the telephone, and when he'd spoken her name, adding, "I've *got* to talk to you," that so familiar, deeply masculine voice had pierced all the way through her; it was the first time she'd heard it since the day of the argument. For a moment, she'd been unable to speak at all, had simply closed her eyes and given herself up to the pleasure of hearing him, but then everything else had come rushing back to her: the fact that he still hadn't let up on Ross, the remembrance of his cutting remarks that had hurt her so deeply. She'd drawn herself up and said, "We have nothing to talk about." She'd hung up right away then and turned immediately from the phone, going into the drawing room where she'd involved herself in chores, briskly, competently. A whirlwind of activity.

She reached the closet, drew out Ross's suit jacket, and after glancing over it to make sure it was as perfectly pressed as Ross insisted it be, laid the jacket carefully across his bed.

She sat down then at her dressing table, wondering, in spite of herself, why Grant had chosen this particular time to try to contact her again, and had just gotten her lipstick in hand and leaned forward toward the lighted mirror to put the soft wine color to her lips when she heard the tinkle of glassware coming from the other side of the alcove wall. She couldn't see Ross, and with her hand suspended in midair, she called out to him.

"Ross? What did you do, knock over a glass?"

She waited, but there was no answer. He hadn't heard her, she thought, and turned back to quickly finish what she was doing before going to investigate further. And it was then that she heard the heavy crash, the clattering of china plates as they fell, the sound of silverware being swept off a table.

Ashley dropped the lipstick and was up in an instant, racing into the alcove. "Ross!" She screamed his name when she saw him crumpled by the table, his chair lying on its side behind him, one of his hands still gripping the tablecloth, which he'd pulled nearly all the way off the table as he went down. Plates and glasses were strewn on the floor around him, and he was gasping for breath, his other hand encircling his throat, his face contorted in pain.

Ashley knew he was having another heart attack and dove for him, panicked, screaming unconsciously for Alicia. She fell to her knees beside him, fumbling at his tie, getting it undone and off finally, opening his collar buttons with hands that trembled almost uncontrollably. His complexion had gone beet red, and Ashley began to cry then, out of fear, watching her husband writhe in distress as she grabbed his shoulders.

"Ross! Ross! Alicia! Somebody, help me! Oh, my *God!*"

Minutes went by but no one answered her screams, and powerless to stop what was happening, Ashley finally put her arms around Ross and pulled him to her, crying helplessly as she cradled him close to futilely try to comfort his suffering. He continued to fight for air, clutching once at the bodice of her black sweater, struggling for several more moments, and then suddenly it was all over. There was a final shuddering of his entire body before it went limp in Ashley's arms, his head rolling against her breast, one hand dropping to the floor, and Ashley just sat for a moment, shocked.

"Ross?" She whispered his name this time, disbelieving that he was now so still. So slowly that it was like a lifetime to her, she loosened her embrace enough so that she could look down at him. His face was in repose now, his eyes open but unseeing, and the hand that had clutched his throat had slipped down to lay motionless on his chest, against the fine fabric of his shirt.

Ashley knew that he was dead, and with a moan that rose from the very depths of her, she pulled him back up against her, holding him tightly, her mind torn between her refusal to believe and her understanding of the truth. Alone, she sat with him in her arms in the desolate quiet of the sun-dappled room, completely dry of tears suddenly, as if they'd been ripped out of her with the passing of Ross's spirit. She wanted to cry, to scream again, but she could do nothing except hold him, and she rocked back and forth as the innate despair for a life gone left her hollow inside, anguished.

Nearly five minutes passed before Ashley finally relinquished him, and it was when she lowered him gently back to the floor, arranging his arms beside him, that she at last became aware of the newspaper. It was lying open by the leg of the table, on top of the wrinkled tablecloth, next to Ross's reading glasses, and all across the top of the first page of the art section was splashed the bold, black headline that Ashley knew as soon as she saw it had killed her husband. It read:

DuBrand's to Represent Van Holt Estate on the Block—
Copeland Pleased to Accept Townsend's New Allegiance.

Ross's funeral was on Friday. Ashley saw to all the arrangements herself, going through the motions of phone calls, meetings, and the topsy-turvy minutiae of everyday living like an automaton. Ollie was there the whole time, from the moment he'd received her agonized phone call on Tuesday morning and sped in cold shock to the Galbraith home. Georgia and Brett had arrived Thursday evening. Reporters swarmed the grounds of the estate like locusts crawling in the grass, and finally, in desperation, Ashley called in security guards to patrol the gates.

Over a hundred mourners came to the spired chapel that Friday morning to pay their last respects to Ross. It was a cold, windy, gray day, and Ashley in her black dress and belted black wool coat sat between Georgia and Brett in the first pew at the front of the church, Ollie to the far side of her uncle. Flowers overflowed the altar—in vases, on stands— and across the bronze casket itself lay Ashley's own tribute to Ross: a blanket of brilliant red roses, the shade that had always been his favorite.

The service at the huge, vaulted cathedral was lengthy, and when it was at last concluded, Ashley walked on Brett's arm, with Ollie and Georgia following, to the chauffeured black limousine parked at the end of the walkway; in it, they drove behind the hearse to the cemetery. No other mourners came to the short graveside ceremony; Ashley hadn't wanted a crowd there. The several dozen closest friends and business associates of Ross, including Philip Townsend, had been instructed to go on to the Galbraith home and wait there for what was to Ashley the barbaric custom of an after-funeral reception. She hadn't wanted that, either, but she'd known it would be expected and so had made those arrangements, too.

Finally, the brief ceremony on the immaculate grounds of the tree-studded cemetery was over. Ashley thanked the minister and pallbearers, and as she turned to leave, Brett once more took her arm.

His rough, leathery face was worried as he patted his

niece's hand. "Come on home with us, Ashley," he instructed. "We'll drive down tonight."

"Yes, please dear," Georgia's soft voice chimed in. Her concerned eyes searched her niece. "You need the rest," she encouraged.

Ashley's smile was grim. "I'm fine," she answered, putting her hand to her forehead to shield it from the cold, blowing wind. "And I couldn't leave, not right now. There are things I have to see to."

Ollie, too, was watching her anxiously. She'd been rigidly collected throughout the ordeal, yet he knew she hadn't been sleeping. She'd told him that, and he could see the shadows of exhaustion on her face. "Ashley, they're right," he interjected. "A few days away won't hurt. They'll do you good. And though there are people waiting back at the house, I know everyone will understand if you leave soon."

Ashley summoned up the strength then to give all of them her most reassuring smile. "I really will be all right," she said, reaching up to put her hand on Brett's shoulder; anyone who didn't know him would think his scowl meant he was angry. It was the kindest of expressions, really, the frown of a very heartfelt concern. "Brett, stop worrying so much, please?" She turned to Georgia then, taking her aunt's hands in hers; Georgia was smiling at her sadly, and Ashley tilted her head. "I love you all for being so concerned about my welfare, but I really do have to stay. There are so many legal details to see to. Ross's estate is very large, and—"

She broke off. And it belongs to me now, she added silently. Ross's will hadn't been officially read yet, but the only unknowns in it were the technicalities, and the miscellaneous bequests he might've left to servants, friends, and the few distant relatives he had. Everything else went to Ashley, as Ross had once advised her: the house and grounds, the staggering investment income. And Galbraith Galleries. She'd never thought that Ross's estate would matter to her; she'd never coveted his wealth or possessions. But as she stood there just in front of his gravesite, she knew that it did matter to her now, for one single, very deeply felt reason; it had begun to matter the moment she'd seen that newspaper headline.

She looked back at her aunt and squeezed her hands. "You and Brett must feel free to go on home without me tonight," she said. "I'm going to be okay."

She smiled once more and glanced over at Brett and Ollie,

but her gaze was halted by something she glimpsed past Brett's shoulder, off in the distance. Her smile faded away, and she stood perfectly still, not speaking, simply staring.

The black limousine was still parked under the leafless maple trees lining the macadam drive leading into the cemetery, but in front of it now was a gold sports car. A man was standing by the driver's side, his head bare, his topcoat open and flapping in the wind, and he was looking fixedly across the cemetery lawn toward the small group of people clustered at the gravesite.

It was Grant, and he remained stationary for a moment longer, then slowly began to walk toward them. Nothing in the last four days—not any event nor any person—had been able to touch Ashley's emotions, which in that moment when Ross had expelled his dying breath in her arms had become hellishly imprisoned inside her. But at the sight of Grant they began to stir, like the warning rumble of the ground before an earthquake. She watched him coming closer and closer, only barely aware that the three people around her had also turned to watch him approach, and at last Grant reached them.

"Ollie," he said in constrained greeting and extended his hand. The two men shook hands briefly, and because Ashley was standing like a statue, Ollie made polite introductions; he felt a coldness toward Grant now, but it wasn't enmity.

"Georgia and Brett Welles, Grant Copeland," he said. "Mr. and Mrs. Welles are Ashley's aunt and uncle."

Grant nearly said "I know," but caught himself in time. "It's a pleasure to meet both of you," he said, and after warmly taking Georgia's hand, then sharing a firm handshake with Brett, he looked at Ashley, his dark eyes intense. "Ashley, I'm so very, very sorry," he said. "I'd like to talk to you for a moment, if I may."

Ollie was the one who reached out and put a fatherly hand on Ashley's shoulder. "Mr. Copeland, this was a private service," he objected.

"No, Ollie." Ashley's voice had come to her at last, and she raised a slender hand to the older man without taking her eyes from Grant. "I'll speak to Mr. Copeland," she said slowly. She looked then to her companions. "Would you mind leaving us for a minute?" she asked, forcing a smile. "I'll meet you back at the car."

After a momentary hesitation, the trio acquiesced. Ashley watched them until they were all the way to the limousine, then finally looked again at Grant. "Why are you here?" she asked in a voice that suddenly trembled.

Grant's expression held open pain now as he looked at Ashley's complexion, so pale against her short, raven hair and black coat. "My God, Ashley," he breathed. "Did you think I wouldn't come?"

One by one, Ashley's emotions were coming unchained. "No, I wouldn't have imagined that you'd come," she answered, her strained voice quivering even more as she raised her chin. "I wouldn't have thought that you'd want to pay your last respects to a man you had no feeling for or that you'd feel any need to comfort his wife, a woman so far beneath your intellectual level."

"Ashley . . ." Grant spoke her name as a moan and took hold of her arm.

"Don't!" She pulled away, the dam inside her on the verge of bursting completely. "There is nothing you can do. He's dead now. He's—" A yellow room, a sun-streaked floor strewn with sparkling shards of broken glass and shattered china flashed before her eyes, and the horror of Ross having died in her arms swelled over her entirely. A trembling cry escaped from her and then, at long last, she burst into the wrenching sobs that had been bottled up inside her.

Grant hurt for her so much he couldn't even speak. He knew what she'd gone through in that big house up on the hill; the newspapers had been avid in their reporting of the details of Ross Galbraith's death—the widow alone with him, frantic, helpless. He reached out to take her protectively into his arms—spectators be damned!—but she pushed him away so roughly that it sent him off balance. She turned her back on him then as she put her face into her hands, her weeping emanating from the very core of her, so that it shook her whole body, choked her.

Grant was forced simply to watch the agonized release of her emotions, and her torment possessed him as if it were his own; it *was* his own. When at length her sobs died away and she was simply standing with her back to him, he pulled out his handkerchief and walked up beside her, extending the linen cloth.

She looked over at it, then turned away again. "I hate you for witnessing that," she said in a low voice. With the pent-up aftermath of death finally eased, she now felt only her profound outrage with Grant, which had settled deep within her when she'd read the headline in the paper, and caring nothing for her tear-streaked appearance, she turned to face him.

"Ross died reading the newspaper, did you know that?" she asked, and her voice was tremulous again but this time in suppressed anger.

A pained frown came to Grant's face. "I could figure it out. Ashley—" he went on intently.

"Do you know *what* he was reading?" she interrupted.

"Ashley—"

Her anger surged into her eyes. "He was reading about the Van Holt estate having gone to you. Reading it, Grant! In the paper!" Her shock at the cruelty of the incident overcame her entirely for a moment, and she looked at the ground. At length, she raised her eyes again to Grant, and they were filled with condemnation. "You couldn't have waited until he'd been told personally before putting the news out, could you?" she said. "You were so self-satisfied at having gotten those collections that you simply had to grandstand your success, didn't you? Well, I hope you can live with yourself and the effect it had."

Grant took her accusations without flinching; he'd expected all of them. "Ashley, I didn't put the news about Van Holt in the paper," he said quietly.

"I don't believe you," she answered. " 'Copeland pleased to accept Townsend's new allegiance,' " she quoted in that low voice trembling with bitter emotion. "Oh, Grant! Couldn't you have saved the gloating commentary?"

Grant put both hands on her shoulders then, holding her eyes intently with his own. "Ashley, I didn't say that. I never even spoke to the press. It was a mistake, all of it, done by someone else in my office. I knew that Phil hadn't talked to Ross," he explained, "and I would never have done this kind of thing. Ashley, I did everything in my power to stop the news from getting to Ross like that," he went on, looking around at her face when she turned it away from him again. "Phil was unreachable, but I tried anyway. I called the paper, but they were determined to print. I called *you* then, to tell you not to let Ross have the paper, to keep him away from any news at all until Philip could get back, but you wouldn't talk to me. I even, as a last resort, tried to send you a hand-delivered note to the same effect, even though I knew after your refusal to speak to me on the phone that you probably wouldn't read it, but I had to try anyway! That got nowhere either.'' He watched her in despair—how could he find the words to reach her? "Ashley, I had every intention of holding off on publicity about this for weeks. Weeks, honey,'' he stressed. "Just so Ross could be let down easy.''

"I don't believe you,'' she repeated and stepped back, forcing Grant to drop his arms from her shoulders. "Everything you've done to Ross has been totally unfeeling, but this last is . . . I—'' She shook her head as she looked away, at a loss. "Well, it defies description,'' she said finally.

Grant could see that there was no use talking to her now, she was too upset. Yet he had so many things he wanted to say to her. "Ashley, you're wrong about me, about everything. So very wrong.''

"Am I?'' she challenged, her hands pressing the collar of her coat tightly against the long column of her neck.

"Yes.''

"I don't think so.''

"Ashley, I didn't mean to hurt you, all those weeks ago at my apartment,'' he said then. "I know that memory isn't helping what you think of me at the moment.''

"What happened there that day doesn't matter,'' she answered tonelessly.

"I don't believe that; I can see your hurt in your eyes, and you've already flung one of my insults back in my face. Honey, I didn't mean a word of those insults I threw at you that day. I was hurt, in the way only you can hurt me. I couldn't take your disapproval of me, and I lost my temper.'' He smiled but there was no humor in it. "Only you can make me do that so easily, too.'' He studied her face, saw no sign of relenting.

"Ashley, I wish you'd read my letter, the one I sent you after our argument. I tried to explain everything about that day to you. No, not explain, I tried to tell you what I really feel about you, what I'll always feel,'' he amended, and a soft smile briefly curved his mouth. "It was a love letter, Ashley, and if ever you've wanted to know how much a man can love a woman, then you'd have known if you'd read that letter.''

The apology, eloquent though it was, couldn't penetrate Ashley's indignation, her conviction that he had done a terrible thing. She scarcely heard what he was saying, so caught up was she in her own rage.

"It doesn't matter to me what you said or did that day," she repeated. "And I have nothing more to say to you, except for one thing." She paused, her eyes steady on him. "As far as I'm concerned, Grant, you are responsible for Ross's death. I didn't love him, but I had compassion for him. He was a human being, and he didn't deserve to have done to him what you did with your ambition and your callousness. You can't be allowed to get off scot-free for that, Grant, and I'm going to see that you don't."

Grant started to speak, then changed his mind; there was no use now.

"Galbraith Galleries belongs to me now," she went on. "I'm not an aging man, Grant, who is ill and no match for you, but a young, strong woman. I'm going to take Galbraith Galleries, and I'm going to run it myself," she said, her eyes locking with his. "And Grant Copeland, I'm going to ruin your business just like you ruined Ross Galbraith's. Payment in kind. That's what you deserve."

She stood looking into his stunned face a moment longer, then turned and, without a backward glance, walked away.

PART III

Journeys end in lovers meeting,
Every wise man's son doth know.

William Shakespeare

Chapter 26

"TAYLOR, I THINK you're going to be very pleased with the results of this sale," Ashley said. "Mrs. Berenson's estate has some very good late-eighteenth-century cabinet pieces in it, and they'll appeal to collectors. We've noticed quite an interest lately in furniture of the Federal period, and I don't think it's just a brief trend."

Ashley sat in the lower Manhattan office of Taylor Kirby, the trust officer of Chase Manhattan Bank handling the administration of the late Edna Berenson's estate. For the meeting she had worn a vivid citron-colored suit and ivory blouse tied in an ascot at her throat, and she knew she looked every inch the self-assured professional woman. She was sitting relaxedly in the armchair in front of Taylor's leather-inlaid desk, and when he raised his eyebrows approvingly at her remarks, she went on.

"Galbraith's sold a Hepplewhite sideboard several weeks ago for thirty thousand dollars," she said. "You might've read about it in the paper."

The dark-haired, urbane-looking man nodded. "Yes, I did, which is heartening," he answered. "As a matter of fact, I find Galbraith's estimated values for everything in the Berenson estate extremely encouraging."

"And they're quite accurate, I think," Ashley replied promptly. She sat forward in her chair. "Drew Langley, who is handling our appraisals for period furniture now, has an excellent eye for values. If his estimates are off at all, they might err a little on the conservative side." She smiled as she took up the contract that had just been executed by the bank and Galbraith's. "I'd like to get this sale on our calendar for next month," she said then as she inserted the agreement into the black leather case at her feet. "I'll check the schedule when I get back to the office and give you a call with a definite date."

"Fine." Taylor was watching her as she snapped the locks on her attaché case. He knew Ashley Galbraith rather well,

from his years of socializing with her as Ross's wife, and he
lounged back in his desk chair, giving her an approving
smile. "You know, Ashley, you're quite an impressive
woman," he said. "In six months' time, you've taken hold of
Galbraith's with amazing adeptness. In fact, to be frank, the
whole art world is astonished at the changes you're making at
the gallery. I find your competence at handling the firm in so
brief a space of time rather remarkable, considering the fact
that you were relatively inexperienced in management when
you stepped into Ross's shoes last December."

Ashley relaxed back in her chair. "Thank you," she said
warmly. "I've worked hard at it," she added with a light
laugh and thought to herself that just how hard she'd worked,
Taylor could never know: long nights spent under the brass
reading lamp at her bedroom desk while she'd poured over
textbooks of all kinds, business publications and professional
manuals on everything from marketing to taxation; learning
sessions with Galbraith's accountants; skipped lunches, hours
at the library, breakfasts inhaled over a financial newspaper
every morning. They'd all been part of her effort to supplement
her good working knowledge of the field with all those other
things she'd needed to know: issues of top level management
that she'd only been superficially exposed to before taking
over Ross's place at the company. It had been a trying six
months, without a doubt—she'd had no life at all except for
Galbraith's—but the strain of carrying out the grueling regi-
men of self-education at the same time as she'd seen to
business as usual at the auction house had been worth it; she
had a real grasp now of what to do with Galbraith's—how to
promote it, how to competently oversee its many operations,
how to negotiate in its best interests. *With a little study up on
the technical side.* Ashley frowned as the phrase echoed in
her mind and focused back on Taylor.

"I've really worked hard at it," she repeated. "There's
a debt I have to pay."

Taylor lifted his eyebrows curiously. "Oh?"

She hadn't meant to say that; it wasn't a subject she ever
discussed with anyone, not even Ollie—the motivation behind
her determination to become the sharpest businesswoman she
possibly could. "I just want to see Ross's company continue,
that's all," she said.

"Well, he'd be very proud of you if he could see you
now," Taylor complimented. He returned Ashley's gracious

smile, and when she got to her feet, he rose also. "Is there anything more we have to discuss about the Berenson estate right now?" he asked.

"No, not at the moment." She picked up her attaché case, settled her purse over her shoulder, then began walking with the bank officer toward the door of the oak-paneled office. "Once we have the sale date, it's simply a matter of putting everything together. I'll let you know when the truck is going out to Long Island to bring the contents of the house to the gallery. Probably in a week or so," she advised.

Taylor nodded, and after bidding him a friendly good-bye, Ashley went quickly out of the building. Her next appointment on that sunny, late spring morning was with Peter St. John, the youngest partner of the Manhattan law firm of Caton Walsh & St. John, which had always handled the Galbraith's legal affairs; Peter had been charged with the intricate matter of administrating Ross's estate, and as Ashley stood out on the busy street corner in front of the towering bank building, her dark hair tousled by the wind, her arm raised to hail a cab, she abruptly realized that she'd neglected to bring from home the legal documents she was supposed to be returning to Peter.

"Damn," she muttered crossly, and when a cab finally responded to her signal and pulled over to the curb, she gave the driver not Peter's address but her own, on Fifty-third Street. It took slightly over half an hour to make the drive uptown through the snarled, stop-and-go traffic, and she felt harried by the time the taxi finally pulled up in front of her narrow row house, just behind the sleek, silver Jaguar she'd purchased with elation several months before. She quickly got out of the cab, asking the driver to wait, and she dashed through the filigreed gate of the wrought-iron fence surrounding her small courtyard, up the three steps of the concrete stoop, in her haste dropping her keys before finally getting the door unlatched.

She stopped for a minute just inside the house, her edginess momentarily dissipating as she felt a sense of simple pleasure at being home; she loved the renovated brownstone she'd bought in late January. She'd moved out of the Galbraith mansion a week after Ross's funeral, to get away from the stark memories associated with it and the ringing hollowness the immense house had taken on without Ross's presence. She would have left it quickly even without sad associations; the imposing residence simply wasn't to her taste, nor did she have any patience for the daily commuting of an hour each way. While temporarily lodged at the Plaza Hotel, she'd managed to work house-hunting into all her other activities, and had found the quaint townhouse on the quiet, residential street, falling for it immediately when she'd wandered with the realtor through the miniature, high-ceilinged rooms and stood musing over the decorative possibilities of the narrow stairs winding up the three stories. She stood just at the foot of that steep staircase now, and shaking herself free from her brief room-gazing, she hurried on up to her third-story bedroom.

It was a warm room, outfitted with a four-poster bed, a colorful but faded Turkish carpet, and white frilled curtains at the windows; there was a reading chair and floor lamp next to her bureau. Beside the closet door, Sharif's saddle rested on its cantle, his bridle draped haphazardly over it, and she smiled briefly as she passed it, thinking of Andrew's generous caretaking of her horse still boarded at Shadow Knolls. She crossed the room immediately to her desk in the far corner and grabbed up the blue-backed legal papers sitting squarely in the center of the blotter—where she'd so carefully placed them the night before so she couldn't possibly forget them—then turned hastily to go back downstairs. She'd just reached the doorway when a scratching at the window caught her attention and she glanced over to it; she smiled at the sight greeting her there.

"Oh, all right, Baker. Come on in," she said resignedly to the big yellow cat standing on the outer sill; he seemed only to be mouthing his meows until she raised the window. "Why can't you use the front door like everyone else instead of the fire escape all the time?" she groused good-naturedly as she stroked his head, then gently shooed him off the windowsill so she could reclose the sash. "Too much of a street man still, huh? You like the back alleys and rooftops, I guess." She smiled down at the stray cat she'd adopted not long after she'd moved in, and crouched for a moment to stroke him, then straightened again as she realized she was dawdling once more.

"Sorry, Baker, but I've got to go," she told him. "I'm not supposed to be here in the first place." She lightly hurried down the stairs and back out to the cab.

In another fifteen minutes, Ashley arrived at the modern office building on Madison Avenue, and after paying her cab fare, went through the double glass doors, directly to the banks of elevators in the center of the public hall. Peter's office was on the ninth floor, and after pressing the button, she stepped back to wait impatiently for one of the five elevators to descend. She was oblivious to the businessmen and women who passed her by as she checked her watch for the third time and someone addressed her from behind her shoulder.

"Ashley?"

At the sound of the deep, masculine voice she recognized instantly, the legal papers she'd never put into her attaché case fell from her hand. Grant reached down just as she did to retrieve them for her, got them in hand first, and smiled down into her eyes as they straightened together; he handed back the documents. "You look a little rushed," he observed.

Ashley glanced at him only briefly as she accepted the papers with a formal nod of thanks. "I am," she replied.

Only civilly; that was how she spoke to him now. Grant contained his sigh and went on with resolute friendliness. "Nice day for appointments out of the office, isn't it?"

Ashley didn't respond this time and, with her back very straight, stepped immediately into the elevator that opened up in front of her, intending to end the accidental encounter as quickly as possible. She hit the button for the ninth floor, then turned to find Grant right behind her. He selected twelve, then took a position by the wall, leaning up against it. Though the elevator remained open a few more seconds, no one else entered, and finally the doors closed, sealing them alone together.

There was a palpable silence as the lift began its sluggish ascent, and Grant finally spoke into it. "I talked to Taylor Kirby yesterday," he said. Ashley was standing in the farthest corner from him, her attaché case in one hand by her side, the papers clutched to her chest with the other, and she kept her eyes trained on the row of numbers above the doors slowly lighting up as the elevator moved from floor to floor. "I understand that Galbraith's is getting the Berenson estate," he continued. "Congratulations."

Ashley said nothing for a minute, then finally gave him her attention. She looked over, her expression perfectly calm but her eyes alive with the glittering anger that they held for Grant since the day of Ross's death. "Thank you, but it isn't nearly large enough," she told him, her chin raised. "It's nice, and it'll turn a profit for Galbraith's, but it's not nearly the caliber of sale I want—one that you're really going to feel when you lose it, that's going to set your company back painfully. I'm waiting for that one, Grant. Impatiently!'' She regarded him with steely challenge for a moment longer, then went back to her uncommunicative study of the numbered board overhead.

Grant's eyes stayed on her another instant, then dropped to the elevator floor. God, in all his life he would never have dreamed that he and Ashley could come to a point like this—Ashley no longer his lover but his antagonist! It was no easy thing for him to accept her angry coldness toward him when he sometimes literally ached for her passionate tenderness, but he did accept it. Or rather, he bore it, without remark, because he'd made up his mind that he would. His love for her was too strong for him to just let go, even now, and he simply couldn't believe, after all that had been between them, that she wouldn't finally come around, see all that had happened with Ross in its true light—somehow, sometime. And, he hoped, before she made good on her vow to ruin his company. The ghost of a smile flickered across his face at the rueful thought, but disappeared almost immediately. He didn't relish the prospect of having his business cut into, nor did he dismiss as impossible the chance that Ashley might be able to do just that; she'd picked up the reins of Galbraith's with an initial proficiency that astounded even him, someone who'd always believed she had it in her to be a top-notch professional. *She's a natural,* he thought with approval.

"That was a good-looking ad you put in *Antiques Marketplace,*" he said, determined not to accept the silence she tried to impose between them. "Nice color." He paused briefly, then added, "You're doing a terrific job with Galbraith's all around, Ashley, better than a lot of people might who've been at this game a lot longer than you have. I like to see you achieve this way."

At that moment, the elevator came to a gentle, whirring stop at the ninth floor. The doors slid open soundlessly, and without a word or look in response to Grant, Ashley smiled briefly at the two businessmen entering the car, then walked out.

Chapter 27

"YOU KNOW, ASHLEY, you look great in yellow."

Peter St. John smiled appreciatevely as he contemplated Ashley's lithe figure; she stood across the room from him near an inset of overstuffed bookshelves. Peter was an attractive, well-dressed bachelor of thirty-seven, an Ivy League man with sun-bleached blond hair and thoughtful blue eyes. Ashley wasn't listening to him, however, but was pensively studying the wheat-colored carpeting, her arms crossed as one hand unconsciously smoothed the fabric of her jacket sleeve, and Peter continued, trying his best to capture her attention. "It's your dark coloring, I think. That makes the yellow so striking on you, I mean."

"Hmmm? Oh." Ashley looked up, flushing under the compliment as it finally sank in, and though she smiled, there was still an edge of abstraction to her expression. "Thank you." She inclined her head immediately toward the legal papers she'd brought with her, which were now lying on Peter's desk. "I signed everything you gave me. What else do we have to do today?" she inquired.

Peter straightened away from the desk where he'd been perched, and went around to the chair behind it, reluctantly abandoning his attempt at creating a more personal mood. He tried to inject personal comments into their conversations whenever he could; for a long time he'd wanted his and Ashley's relationship to move on to something more than just a friendly acquaintance between attorney and client, and though that state of affairs hadn't developed yet, he was working on it. He was a confirmed New Yorker who loved the city's vital cultural life and had several women to share it with, but it was Ashley Galbraith, above all others, with whom he'd like to spend his private time. He liked professional women who took themselves seriously, and he'd never, ever seen anyone pursue a goal as hard as Ashley had in the last six months.

"Well, actually, there's not much else," he answered. "Let's see—" He began to sift through the voluminous files on Ross Galbraith's estate. "Eventually, we'll have to get to the tax returns, and of course, the accounting will have to be done." He flipped several more pages, his brow knit. "There are a few bills to pay that came in the oth—Ashley, is something bothering you?" he asked abruptly, as he glanced up and discovered Ashley staring fixedly ahead of her, at nothing in particular.

You're doing a terrific job . . . better than a lot of people might who've been at this game a lot longer than you have. . . . The professional praise coming from Grant Copeland sang one more time through Ashley's mind, then finally faded away completely, and she at last made herself concentrate fully on her attorney. Her encounters with Grant always left her this way: feeling unsettled inside, unable to focus on anything around her for a time. "No, of course not," she answered, smiling apologetically. "I'm sorry, Peter. I don't seem to be able to keep my mind from wandering today. What were you saying?" she asked.

"Oh, nothing really." He pushed the Galbraith file aside and rested his forearms on the desk. "I was simply mentioning a few things we still have to do. Future items." He motioned toward the chair at the side of his desk. "Sit down. There is one thing of immediacy I want to talk to you about."

Anxious to make amends for her impolite distraction, Ashley came immediately to the armchair and sat down, crossing her legs as she offered Peter her most receptive smile. "What?"

"The house." Peter lounged back in his swivel chair, locking his hands behind his head. "I spoke to the mayor, and the township has granted the variance for turning the Galbraith property into a museum. He called me the other day, but I wanted to wait until I saw you in person before I gave you the news."

Ashley's expression was blank for a moment, as if she couldn't quite believe what she'd heard, then all of a sudden lit up with a deeply relieved smile. She hadn't known what to do about Ross's home, and for months had simply let it sit, in the hands of caretakers, while she'd deliberated uncertainly over the matter. Something had prevented her from simply selling the estate that had been in Ross's family for so many generations and dispersing the possessions that had meant so much to him, and the idea of turning the house and grounds into a public museum had struck her one night as she'd lain in bed, pondering the subject for the hundredth time. It had jelled instantly. Unquestionably, the heirlooms in the elegant home were worthy of such reverential treatment, but more compelling to her was the thought that this was a plan that would've pleased Ross so much if he could have known about it: being memorialized, and in a manner so closely related to his family's lifelong enterprise. Feeling a restless need to have the commemoration to Ross put into the works as soon as possible, she'd called Peter first thing the next morning, seeking his help; he'd seen to all the preliminaries, giving her periodic updates as the weeks passed.

"That's wonderful," she breathed, her eyes shining. "So now it's only a matter of setting up an organization to maintain the premises?"

Peter nodded. "And if you'd like, I'll take care of seeing to that, too." he offered.

She smiled gratefully. "I'd love you forever if you did! I just can't see how I'd have time."

"No, I'm sure you wouldn't, not with the pace you keep up," he observed dryly. "How did it go with the Berenson deal this morning?"

"Fine." The whisper of a frown flitted across her brow as her encounter with Grant came back to her. She'd sincerely meant her challenge to him; she was impatient to find the means really to begin meting out justice to him and was growing more so all the time. Six months had passed and she had yet to make even a small dent in his business; in fact, DuBrand's was more successful than ever, pulling top billing in the industry. She bit her lip as she gazed moodily toward the floor. "I just wish it was bigger," she murmured.

Peter shook his head in bemusement. "I thought you told me it would be a nice one to get," he noted.

Annoyed with herself for speaking so precipitously again, she tried to explain away the inadvertent comment. "Oh, it is. It's just that we auction people are always after the sales that make a really big splash, that's all," she said, not untruthfully. "You know, along the lines of DuBrand's Van Holt auctions this spring."

Peter unclasped his hands behind his head abruptly and quickly reached for a textbook slipping off a precarious stack of others on the edge of his desk; he set it back in place, relaxing again. "Well, there's the Maynard estate you and Ollie have been talking about so enthusiastically," he offered.

"That's certainly a major estate. And you'll get it," he added with a wink. "I have no doubt about that."

Ashley smiled to his expression of confidence. "Yes, it's major all right, but our getting it is merely avid speculation at this stage." As she sat toying with a ballpoint pen lying near the corner of the desk, she thought briefly of the estate left by Henry Maynard, pre-eminent author, playwright, and patron of the arts who'd died unexpectedly several months before at the age of fifty-two; it included not only his magnificent residence in Tarrytown, New York, filled with all manner of valuable possessions, but a highly important collection of rare Old Masters.

"It's not even at the negotiation stage yet," Ashley added wistfully, "although I have made a phone call to Leland Bartholomew, the executor." She smiled wryly. "I understand that Cathleen Maynard, Henry's widow, is a bit on the eccentric side, and I get the feeling that Mr. Bartholomew is a character in his own right. I don't think I've ever talked to anyone who comes across as quite so precise and . . ." She searched for a descriptive word. "Decisive!" she said finally. " 'Yes, Mrs. Galbraith. No, Mrs. Galbraith. We'll undoubtedly talk when and if the time is right.' And then he hung up," she said.

Peter laughed. "Well, you're on the ball anyway," he remarked and, as the moment seemed propitious, he went on hopefully. "I'd say your successful acquisition of the Berenson estate calls for a celebration. How about dinner tonight?"

Ashley's light smile dimmed, and she shifted in the armchair. "Oh. Well . . ."

"Ashley, please don't tell me you've got work to do," Peter admonished affably.

Tensely, she rose and moved across the room to stand before a tall plant placed decoratively before the plate glass window; she fingered the spreading leaves. "Well, actually, there are a couple of things I was planning to do tonight," she answered. There really were: ad changes she wanted to go over, schedule adjustments, things she knew she wouldn't be able to get to during the workday. Yet, she understood also that there was more to her hesitation than simply prior commitment. She was reluctant to get involved personally with Peter, or any other man for that matter. It was just . . . too soon.

Peter sensed that she wanted him to drop the subject, but

he couldn't. "Ashley, you've got to stop being so single-minded about Galbraith's," he chided as he sat forward toward his desk and rested his forearms on it again. "I'm sure whatever there is to do over there could wait until tomorrow. You know, the place would still be standing the next morning if you were ever to leave at a decent hour," he added lightly.

She looked over at him with a laugh. "Yes, I imagine that's true," she allowed.

"Then we have a date?"

"I . . . may I have a raincheck, Peter?"

He forced himself to smile nonchalantly. "Of course. Though you can plan on my issuing it in the very near future." He searched for a topic to alleviate the awkwardness between them. "Have you read the *Times* yet this morning?" he asked.

Ashley's tension left her, and she sat down again in the leather armchair. "No, I haven't," she said. "Why?"

Peter had begun to scout around under the assortment of documents and books scattered over his desk and finally located the newspaper under them. "I think it must be some kind of commentary on my growing interest in your business that I've taken to reading the art section before the stock listings," he said with a grin. He found the article that had caught his attention and extended the paper to Ashley. "I thought you'd be interested in this. Nothing like trying to insure that your merchandise gets accepted by the auction house of your choice with a little blatant prepublicity, huh?" he added with a chuckle.

Smiling at him curiously, Ashley accepted the newspaper. Quickly she read the short article in the lower righthand corner of the page.

London, England—Sir Isaac Baylor, executor of the estate of Dame Meriweather Chilton, the Englishwoman who gained a scandalous reputation as the mistress of some of the most famous men in England, including a prime minister and a bestselling novelist, has announced his intention to sell at auction the full contents of Chilton Castle on the Dover Cliffs of Kent, England. Arrangements have been made with the prestigious London auction firm of Appleby's for dispersal of the bulk of the household goods, but Sir Isaac has expressed his hope that Dame Meriweather's vast collection of bronze statu-

*ettes can be handled in the United States by the estab-
lishment of DuBrand & Company. This well-known assemblage of unusual pieces has toured Europe under the
auspices of the London Museum of Decorative Arts, and
final dissolution of the collection is being offered to the
citizens of the United States, where most of the statuettes
were crafted. According to Sir Isaac, negotiations are in
progress with Grant Copeland of DuBrand's.*

Peter was watching Ashley as she read, and when she
finally let the paper fall to her lap and turned a pensive gaze
toward the window, he felt a sudden stab of dismay and
leaned forward toward her. "Ashley, I hope you don't think I
was rubbing anything in, about DuBrand's being preferred
over Galbraith's in this case. I wasn't," he said, frowning in
worry. "I just thought it was amusing, that old Sir Isaac
Baylor, whoever the hell he is, felt he had to use tactics like
this to promote himself. I simply thought you'd be interested,
that's all."

*Vast collection . . . well-known assemblage of unusual
pieces . . . negotiations are in progress with Grant Copeland
of DuBrand's. . . .* With difficulty, Ashley roused herself
from her speculations and answered Peter. "No, I didn't
think you were," she said with an absent smile and stood up
quickly. She picked up her attaché case. "Peter, I have to get
going. I have an eleven o'clock appointment, and if I catch a
cab right away, I just might make it. We are through here,
aren't we?" she added hastily.

"Yes." Peter had risen also and came around the desk to
stand beside her. He wasn't altogether convinced he hadn't
made a gaffe in pointing out the article, and after walking her
to the door, he stopped her progress with a hand on her arm.
"Ashley, I really didn't mean anything by pointing out that
article," he repeated earnestly. "I just thought you'd be
interested in it for humor's sake."

"Stop worrying about it," she reassured with a laugh.
"I'm not that thin-skinned. But you're right, I am interested.
And not just for humor's sake," she added as the speculative
look came back into her eyes, and with a smile that was
abstracted again, she left him then.

Chapter 28

GRANT WAS RUNNING late. He'd worked longer than he'd meant to with Lloyd Patterson, the firm's accountant, going over the figures for the six-month period just ended; they were impressive with the Van Holt sales figured in, and Grant wanted them to be published as quickly as possible. He'd intended to be finished with Lloyd an hour ago, so he could get on his way for the business trip that would keep him out of the office for a little over a week, and as he stood by the desk in his office, rapidly tossing papers into his open attaché case, Denise came in briskly.

"Here you go, Mr. Copeland," she said. "The two proposals you're taking with you, the letter to Delabeaux that you wanted to sign before you left and the file on the Chilton estate."

Grant gave her a quick smile. "Thanks," he said as he took the letter, signed it, then handed it back. "Oh, and do me a favor," he added as Denise started to move away. "Give Karen a buzz and tell her I'd like to see her."

"I'm here." Karen stood in the doorway. She was looking unusually elegant in a simple black dress with a white scarf tied around her neck and secured to the collar by a gold pin, and she came right in, giving Denise a friendly smile as the two women passed each other. She went to Grant's side, watching as he continued inserting materials into the leather attaché case. "I didn't think you were leaving this early," she commented with a glance at her watch; it was two o'clock.

"As soon as I can," Grant replied brusquely.

Karen moved away and went over to sit down on the leather couch opposite his desk. Settling herself with legs crossed, she smiled up at him inquiringly. "What did you want to see me about?"

Grant frowned thoughtfully as he scanned the contents of the attaché case, ran his eyes over the desktop one more time, then, satisfied he'd gotten everything, sat down behind his desk. "Just a few last-minute things. First of all, you are going to be at the opening of the new wing of the museum on Thursday, right?''

She nodded. ''Of course. I even bought a new dress for the occasion,'' she confided with a teasing smile. ''To make sure DuBrand's representative makes a good appearance.''

''You will,'' he said without hesitation. ''And also, see if you can get in touch with our import broker and find out what's happening with that shipment of mirrors from Italy,'' he went on with a brief frown. ''It should've gone through customs by now. I can't imagine what's holding it up.''

''I called once already, early this morning, but I'll push them again tomorrow,'' she answered.

Grant nodded, looking to the scrap of paper on the blotter where he'd scribbled several notes. He mentally checked off the things he'd already taken up with her, reading the final item. ''One last thing. Check up on the catalogues for the Wilson-Bremerton sale. I'm not sure I trust the printer on this. They've already gotten the coloring on the cover wrong once.''

''I've already made a note on my calendar for Wednesday.'' She tisked good-naturedly. ''You can stop worrying about all these last-minute details now,'' she told him. ''I'll take care of everything. Have no fear.''

He glanced up, then broke into a grin. ''Sorry. I know I'm leaving things in good hands,'' he added mildly.

He was sincere with the expression of confidence. He had no qualms about leaving DuBrand's under her direction while he was gone; she'd always been competent and had grown even more so as time had passed and she'd absorbed the additional responsibilities he'd turned over to her. He was the sole owner of DuBrand's now; he'd bought out Walter and Victor two months before—for a fair and handsome sum—and Karen was his top assistant, and a good friend. He looked at her thoughtfully a moment longer, then shot a look at his desk clock.

''Time to get moving,'' he murmured and stood up. ''You've got my agenda so you can reach me if you have to?'' he asked.

Karen shifted to the edge of the couch and nodded. California for one day, Coconino for two, then back here on Thursday to Kennedy Airport for the flight to London; Karen mentally rattled off his itinerary, then tilted her head. ''You'll be staying at the Connaught in London, right?'' she inquired.

"Right." Grant crossed the spacious room and picked up his canvas suitcase. He deposited it near the door, then reached for his flight jacket, hanging in a small closet just inside the door. As he shrugged into the jacket, he said, "I'll be at the St. Francis in San Francisco tonight."

"Okay." Karen rose, strolling over to his desk. "You said there were some things you had to take care of at the ranch. I hope nothing's wrong," she said, turning around to look at him with a tentative smile.

"No, not really," he answered. "Nick just wants to go over a couple of matters with me. He probably could've told me about everything over the phone, but the fact is, I need to get home for a few days. It's been a long time since I was there. Longer than I like."

Karen dropped her eyes and traced the smooth edge of the desk with one fingertip. She was always bothered by talk of Coconino, for the very simple reason that it meant so much to Grant yet was a part of him she knew nothing about. The ranch—what it looked like, what he did there, and his friend Nick—were completely beyond the scope of her knowledge of him, and she could barely tolerate that fact, because if there was anything she wanted above all else in the world it was to know and share everything with Grant—his work, his thoughts. His life.

She sighed inaudibly. She was in love with him now, completely, and her greatest longing was for him to feel the same way about her. She knew he liked her; there was often masculine appreciation in his eyes when he looked at her, and they bantered freely over lunches, late hours at the office, and once even an impromptu dinner after a particularly long day. But she wanted a relationship with him that went far beyond that. She'd never be the one to make the first advance; something in Grant—his decisive, self-contained manner— wouldn't allow her to do that, but she'd certainly accept any advance he made toward her. And would go on and on accepting them for the rest of her life.

She was uncharacteristically silent, and Grant finally glanced over at her as he picked up his case from the desk. "Karen, is anything wrong?" he asked in concern.

She came to immediately, giving him a quick smile. "No, no. I was just thinking about . . . about your trip!" She felt very self-conscious, as if her thoughts had been visible to him. Disconcerted, she spied the itinerary lying on his desk and reached over to pick it up. "I was thinking about London," she elaborated and, remembering the article she'd read, she smiled skeptically. "Which reminds me: Did you see this piece in the paper about our friend, Sir Isaac Baylor, and what he had to say about the Chilton bronzes?"

Grant expelled his "yes" with a short laugh.

Karen's equanimity returned; there was a certain kind of intimacy in their business exchanges. "Do you suppose he thinks we really might handle those things just because he's spread the word that he wants us to?" she asked wonderingly.

"I think that's his angle," Grant replied. He perched down on the edge of the desk briefly, resting his attaché case beside him.

"You're not planning to see him while you're in England, are you?" Karen asked then.

"Yes, I thought I would. I'd at least like to look at the things, as long as I'm going to be over there anyway."

She shrugged as if to say, "Why bother?" and when he made a movement to get up again, she quickly picked up one of Galbraith's catalogues lying on a stack of papers; it was a means of delaying, if only a bit longer, his departure for this trip that would keep him away from her so long. She inclined her head as she gave the Galbraith's booklet a fast once-over. "You know, the colors used on this cover for Galbraith's carpet sale last month are almost exactly the same as those we selected for the Wilson-Bremerton sale," she observed. "It's a striking combination, pale pink and gray. And you can really see the hand of Ashley Galbraith in this. I've got to admit it's an eye-catching catalogue."

At the mention of Ashley's name, Grant eased back down on the desk. Scarcely realizing what he was doing, he took the catalogue from Karen and sat gazing at it somberly, his thoughts on his brush with Ashley that morning.

". . . surprised she's gotten into so many things at Galbraith's right off the bat."

Grant started slightly and laid the catalogue back down on the desk. "Who, Ashley?" he asked.

Karen nodded. "I thought she'd go a little slower."

He got to his feet, resolutely this time, and strode back over to the door. "Well, the changes are called for," he said over his shoulder. "Galbraith's needed the more progressive image she's giving it. I'm glad to see she recognized that."

Karen walked toward him, frowning sharply. "Glad to see

it?'' she complained. "Don't forget who you're talking about. The competition.''

"I don't forget that. Ever," Grant said under his breath, and the sudden pain reflected in his eyes was hidden by the dark glasses he put on. He gave Karen a smile as she stopped beside him. "I've got to get moving."

"I know, but there's one more thing you should hear about before you go," she said, very seriously.

Grant picked up his suitcase. "What's that?"

"It's about Ben Geary."

Karen had just gotten Grant's full, undivided attention, and he frowned. Benjamin C. Geary was a magic name at DuBrand & Company. Reputed to be one of the three wealthiest men in the country, he was a steel magnate, a man wielding enormous influence throughout the world's business and financial community. His hobby was collecting—anything, everything, from hundred-dollar watches to million-dollar paintings—and he patronized DuBrand's exclusively. He was often found among the notables who joined the other auctiongoers and the sightseers filling the gallery on sales days, and he often attended the auctions in person, with his dog-eared scratch pad covered with lot numbers in every category. But despite his casual manner, he was a financial mainstay for the auction house. He represented hundreds of thousands of dollars in buyer's income and more in seller's assets, and though Grant had nurtured for his company a healthy clientele of moneyed regulars, Ben Geary was undeniably a pivotal contributor to steady profits; Grant didn't like even to contemplate what Ben's leaving DuBrand's would do to his company's financial position. He'd just seen Ben the week before, unexpectedly wandering through the jewelry exhibition downstairs in the first-floor gallery room, and he watched Karen now intently.

"What about him?" he asked.

Karen sighed. "Well, he called up this morning and spoke to someone in accounting," she said. "He was complaining about his bill. He said it was inaccurate."

Grant frowned again, this time in mild annoyance with the unpredictable billionaire who spent part of his time in New York and the rest at his palatial home in Grosse Pointe, Michigan. "Why the hell didn't he call me directly if he had a problem?" he murmured, then focused on Karen again. "So, what happened?"

"Nothing really," she said. "Ralph Baines, who talked to

him, didn't quite know what to do. That's why he came to me. You were out at the time,'' she hastened to add before Grant could ask in some irritation why he hadn't been advised immediately of the situation. "I haven't had a chance to go over his account,'' she went on. "I know he owes us a lot.''

"Well, get on it,'' Grant said tersely as he checked his watch again. "Whatever you do, just keep the man happy. If his outstanding tab is really incorrect, then fix it. And,'' he added with a pointed look, "if his unpaid bill is over five hundred thousand dollars, get in touch with me. I'll call him myself about getting some of it taken care of.''

Karen nodded, then smiled quietly. "I hope you have good flying weather,'' she said, flipping her hair back behind her shoulder. "The last time you went west, you said it was really stormy. Please be careful.''

Grant pulled open the door, allowing the sounds of the busy outer office to intrude. "The weather report was clear all the way. Thanks for the concern, though.'' He smiled briefly. "I'll give you a call tomorrow, late afternoon probably,'' he added as he went out.

Karen stood at the edge of the door, watching as Grant stopped briefly at Denise's desk to bid his secretary farewell, then headed for the main door. "Do that,'' she said softly and didn't move until Grant was completely out of sight.

Chapter 29

ON THURSDAY, ASHLEY didn't get into Galbraith's until eleven o'clock from an early morning appointment that had run long. She checked in on the day's sale, watching with a smile as her newly hired auctioneer, Francis Barclay, called for bids on two Chinese ivory pieces displayed at the front of the crowded room on a table near the podium. Francis was a young man, in his thirties, with curly brown hair and an engaging, outgoing personality, and Galbraith's auctions were far less reserved under his direction as he joked intermittently with his audience and spiced his descriptive orations with anecdotes. Ashley had been enormously relieved when, shortly after Ross's death, Harold Brighton had said he wanted to retire, because she knew he would have been hurt by her bringing in a much younger man; yet it was a move she could not have avoided. She relished watching Francis work and remained long enough to see the items get struck down for just slightly over the estimated value of nine thousand dollars before finally going up to her office.

The rich decor of the room was just as Ross had left it. The gold satin draperies remained at the windows flanking the ornate desk, the same plush blue carpeting was there, and the elegant accoutrements were in the exact spots in the table-tops and along the fireplace mantel where Ross had once so meticulously placed them. Though she was systematically making changes at Galbraith's, in this office she had an odd reluctance to alter anything at all. Or not so odd, she thought as she set her attaché case down next to the desk; she didn't feel as if this was her office really, but Ross's still. She wasn't replacing him, simply carrying on for him until justice could be served, and she considered for a moment that she'd felt more like Ross's wife in the last six months than she ever had when he'd been alive.

She stopped unconsciously turning her diamond-studded wedding band, which she still wore, and got down to business. She was absorbed in a memorandum sent to her from

Galbraith's Tiffany specialist when, sometime later, a knock
came at the door. She called, "Come in," without looking
up, and quickly finished the brief memo about an increase in
forgeries of genuine Tiffany articles before glancing up to see
who had entered. It was Ollie, dressed as usual in a dark suit
and starched white shirt, and he was smiling as he came over
to the desk.

"Good morning, or afternoon almost, I guess," he said.
He was carrying a large manila envelope under his arm and
sat down in the chair in front of her desk.

"Good morning. Sorry I'm so late. I hadn't expected to be
that long going over the new publicity campaign with Norm.
He wanted to run through it all in detail." She shrugged in
weary resignation.

"No matter," Ollie said. "There've been no great emer-
gencies."

Ashley laughed. "That's a pleasant piece of news!"

Ollie smiled as he studied her briefly, sitting behind Ross's
desk; she looked lovely, he thought, in her tailored blue silk
shirtwaist dress, and quite at home in the seat of authority.
He'd felt no resentment toward her when she'd come in to
take over the firm, although some had; she'd had a few
battles in the beginning, challenges to her position from
several people unwilling to accept an old cohort as a superior,
but she'd handled the problems with firmness and finesse. As
the months had passed, his respect for her had only increased,
and in many ways, working with her was far easier than it
had sometimes been with Ross. Not that he didn't miss Ross;
after nearly thirty years as friends and colleagues, it was
impossible not to miss him.

"You're awfully quiet," Ashley observed. "Something on
your mind?"

Ollie leaned forward and tossed the manila envelope onto
her desk. "The material you requested from Isaac Baylor,"
he said. "It came in this morning."

"Have you looked everything over?" she inquired quickly.
"Oh yes."

Ashley gave him a keen look at his dry tone, then eagerly
opened the envelope and drew out the contents. There was a
stack of eight-by-ten color photographs with a handwritten
letter on top, and with her lips pressed together in high
anticipation, she picked up the first photograph. She scanned
it, then took up the next picture, then the next and the next.

There were fifteen photographs in all, of bronze statuettes about twelve inches high mounted on oversized wooden bases—among them a rearing horse, a ballet dancer, and an old bearded man with a pipe sitting on a tree stump—and by the time Ashley had finished giving each of them a cursory inspection, her enthusiastic expression had faded considerably. She put down the group of pictures, looking back across the desk at Ollie with a deeply quizzical frown. "What *are* they, anyway?" she asked.

Ollie was sitting with his hands locked around his knee. "Newel post ornaments," he advised, one eyebrow slightly cocked. "That's what the wooden bases are, the top of the post. It's a Victorian form of decoration."

Ashley mouthed the words, *newel post ornaments,* as she glanced uncertainly at the photos again. "Well," was all she could say after a moment, and blinked twice.

"Yes, *well,*" Ollie echoed and grimaced. "Monumentally unattractive, aren't they?"

Ashley had begun to frown and didn't answer directly but instead picked up the letter from Sir Isaac Baylor. "Did you read this?" she asked without looking up.

"Yes."

Again, Ashley said nothing and simply read the communication from the Englishman. It was written in a flourishing hand and went on at length, in a chatty style, about the forty-three statuettes that comprised the mint condition collection, about their having toured the Continent, and about Dame Meriweather herself, a woman, he advised, who'd had the same affinity for husbands she'd had for antiques; there had been four in all. He related details of the intrigue in Dame Meriweather's life, numerous love affairs, including one involving a highly placed member of the nobility that had caused a sensation when made public. Concluding the letter was Baylor's comment that although he was in contact with Grant Copeland about the auctioning of the articles, he would be more than happy to pursue a discussion with her. Ashley finally finished reading and slowly put the five pages of heavy bond paper back down on her desk.

"Well," she said again, glancing up at Ollie with a somewhat bemused look, "it certainly sounds like Miss Meriweather went about life with zest."

"Apparently," Ollie answered and shifted in his chair. "I

can't say, however, that I care much for her tastes in collecting,'' he added, nodding toward the pictures.

At that, Ashley's expression grew pensive and she got up, walking around the desk. ''We have only the pictures to go by, of course, but these statuettes don't appear to be very good quality, do they?'' she said reluctantly.

Ollie reached across the desk and picked up several of the photographs again. ''No. Certainly not the quality that Galbraith's runs through its auction rooms.''

''Hmmm.'' Ashley's moody frown deepened as she got up and came over to stand looking over Ollie's shoulder at the glossy photos in his hand; he was studying an image of a pirouetting ballet dancer. ''The detailing doesn't seem very distinct, on this one anyway,'' she said. ''The others seem to have the same problem,'' she added, going to the desk to pick up the rest of the photos again. She went through them a second time, very slowly, letting out an audible sigh when she finished. ''No, none of them is really well executed. There's a certain charm to that little girl with the lamb, except that it's out of proportion. The lamb is the size of a pony.''

Ollie put down the pictures in his hand and stood up. He shook his head in mild disgust. ''I can't conceive of coming down the stairs first thing in the morning to be greeted at the bottom with one of these things staring me in the face,'' he grumbled. ''But then, there's no accounting for Victorian tastes, is there?''

Ashley laughed. ''You know something, Ollie? You're a snob. There's quite a market for Victoriana, no matter what opinion you might have of it,'' she chided.

''Indeed. Good Victoriana.'' He eyed the photographs, then gestured dismissively with his hand. ''Toss this stuff in a file somewhere and close the drawer,'' he pronounced. ''We both—''

''Yet, they *are* just pictures.''

Ollie's eyes returned to her in surprise. She'd gone back to a heavily thoughtful study of the pictures, and he propped a hand on his hip. ''You sound as if you're working up to an argument in their favor.'' When Ashley didn't respond, he frowned. ''Ashley, I find no reason to continue giving this matter any thought at all. I agree, because of the intriguing write-up they were given, that it was worth our time to inquire, but''—he shook his head once more—''I don't think these are anything we want to take on, nor, frankly, can I think that Grant Copeland would either.''

Ashley suspected he was right. Despite its uniqueness, the collection was disappointingly mediocre, nowhere near the caliber of heirlooms that Galbraith's dealt in. Nevertheless, the fact that DuBrand's had been publicly chosen to handle them rankled. She arched an eyebrow, then resolutely turned, walked back around the desk, and sat down.

"Ollie, I'm going over to England to look at the statuettes in person," she said.

He stared for a moment, watching her pick up the telephone. "To what purpose?" he asked finally.

Ashley had buzzed Christine, her secretary, and as she waited for the young woman to answer, she regarded Ollie. "To see—Chris?" Her eyes fell to the manila envelope as she spoke. "I'd like you to make plane reservations for me. To London. I'll go tomorrow night, on the evening flight. That will get me in on Saturday, in time to see Isaac Baylor," she added, looking again at Ollie. "Oh, and also make hotel reservations for me at . . . oh, the Connaught, I guess. For Saturday night. I'll take it from there if I have to stay any longer." She listened for a moment, then smiled. "Fine. Get back to me."

She hung up, immediately raising an imperative hand to Ollie. "Don't look so disapproving," she objected. "I'm just going to take a look at the things," she explained honestly. "I simply don't want to dismiss this matter quite so summarily."

"Why?" he asked with a quizzical frown.

Ashley busied herself with the rearrangement of her calendar and paperweight. "I just don't, that's all," she murmured.

Ollie had known her too long not to recognize the expression on her face; her mind had been made up. "All right," he relented with a sigh. "Want me to come along?"

"No. I can handle it." She smiled up at him then. "It's probably not going to be much more than an inspection anyway." Ollie nodded, and after he'd left, Ashley buzzed Chris again and set her on the task of getting through to Isaac Baylor in London.

Ashley arrived at Heathrow Airport late Saturday morning. It was a drizzly, cold day, and she flipped up the collar of her dark leather raincoat as she hurried out of the airline terminal to a taxi. This wasn't her first trip to London; she'd accompanied Ross several years before on a business trip that had taken them to Appleby's and Worth's, the two largest auction firms in England, and they'd done a round of London's exclusive antique dealers, then gone out into the picture-postcard countryside for sightseeing. They'd stayed at the Connaught then also; Ross had preferred its quiet English elegance to the atmosphere in some of the more glamorous hotels.

At the entrance to the hotel she was assisted from the taxi by a tall, uniformed attendant, and her suitcase was carried in for her. Inside the lobby she went directly to the desk to check in. As she waited for the desk clerk to process her reservation, she thought longingly of a bath and a long nap.

"Mrs. Galbraith, if you would just sign here, please," the man said in his pleasant accent.

She turned immediately and smiled. "Of course." She quickly signed the registration card, then laid down the pen. "I have an appointment in Kent this afternoon. I'd like to have a driver to take me out there, if you could arrange it for me," she said.

"Ah, the second in two days," he remarked conversationally. At Ashley's curious look, he smiled. "We had another guest make the trip to Kent yesterday," he explained. "What time did you want to leave?"

Ashley glanced at her watch. "Well, I have to be there at two o'clock. How soon should I leave to get there by then?" she asked uncertainly.

"Within the next half hour, I should think," he advised. "I'll arrange for a car to be here in a quarter of an hour." He smiled again as she nodded her thanks, handing her a room key. "You're in 103. I'll have your bag taken up."

Ashley followed the porter up the curving staircase and down the hall. Inside the door, she tipped the man, and when he'd left, she looked around tiredly at the charming room with its heavy, dark old furniture. Quickly she unpacked the few clothes she'd brought, then sat down for a moment to catch her breath.

It had been an all-night flight from New York to London, and she felt fatigue gnawing at her as she rested her head briefly in her hand. She liked to travel now and then, though not on so rush-rush a basis, and she'd just involuntarily let her eyes drift closed, settling more comfortably against the wide wing of the chair, when the jangle of the telephone made her sit bolt upright again; she answered it. Her car was ready whenever she was, the man at the front desk advised over the line, and feeling anticipation once more come over her, she swiftly changed into fresh clothes, attended to her hair and a touch-up of her makeup, then left the room and headed downstairs to the car.

Chapter 30

BY EIGHT O'CLOCK that evening, Ashley was back at the hotel and dressed for dinner in a black, street-length cocktail dress; it was elegant in its simplicity, fastening in a halter effect around her neck to leave her shoulders bare, and she'd added as a last touch a choker of pearls around her throat.

She'd arrived back from Kent an hour before, tired and damp from the steady light rain that had followed her all the way out into the countryside and back again, and though she'd wanted nothing more than to stretch out on the feather bed and go to sleep, hunger had insisted that she defer the longed-for rest for awhile longer. It was just as well, she thought as she stood in front of the mahogany dressing table, brushing her hair. This would give her the opportunity to have at least one meal in the Connaught's famous restaurant; if she didn't take it now, she wasn't going to get the chance at all, because she would be leaving London in the morning. There was no point in staying longer.

She cast a glance at her appearance in the oval mirror above the dresser, then laid down her brush and went over to the desk to pick up her small evening purse. She left a lamp burning but flipped off the light beside the inviting bed, then left the room, her thoughts heavily preoccupied with the afternoon's business.

It had been a very disappointing trip out to Kent; the scenery had been beautiful, Meriweather Chilton's turreted castle sitting just on the edge of the White Cliffs of Dover was quite breathtaking, even set against an overcast sky; as a sightseeing tour, the afternoon had been enjoyable. But from a business standpoint, it had been anything but satisfying. Sir Isaac Baylor—who had turned out to be a thin, humorous old gentleman with white hair, long by American standards, and well-worn tweeds—had given her a brief, chatty walk-through of the drafty castle, elaborating further on the amazing and titillating escapades of Dame Meriweather, then had escorted her to the gallery wing where the newel post bronzes were displayed in a long glass case set in the center of the room. Ashley had studied them carefully, and when she'd finished, she'd realized that the pictures she'd been sent had done the objects justice after all; their workmanship was no more impressive in actuality than the two-dimensional images had suggested.

Ashley sighed audibly as she passed down the long hotel corridor. She'd been noncommittal to Isaac Baylor's direct inquiry as to whether or not she was interested in having Galbraith's handle the heirlooms, telling him that she would have to give the matter some further consideration. And she had thought about it continuously from the moment she'd gotten back into the chauffeured car that had returned her to London.

There *were* positive aspects to the bronzes, suggesting that a sale of them could be an above-average event. The ornaments were unquestionably rare, even unique; it was an unusually large collection and carried the prestige of having been on exhibition. And then there was the matter of Meriweather's reputation; Ashley knew full well that the fame, or better yet infamy, of an owner lent an attractiveness to her possessions that might not otherwise be there, and in fact, as far as she was concerned, that point of interest was the collection's greatest asset. Yet, there was just no getting around the fact that the statuettes were not of the quality that a fine arts auction house readily took on.

She frowned as she reached the head of the stairs, feeling a certain aggravation with herself for having made such a long, exhausting trip for nothing, but she resolutely put aside her annoyance, determined that she was going to enjoy her dinner. She began her descent, moving to the banister to avoid a couple dressed in evening clothes ascending past her, and she was nearly halfway down the staircase when she abruptly stopped, so suddenly that the man behind her bumped into her. She exchanged embarrassed apologies with him, then turned her incredulous gaze back to the man coming up the stairs directly below her.

It was Grant. He was dressed in a white turtleneck pullover, navy blue blazer, and gray slacks, and he looked absolutely dashing. He'd seen her at the same moment her eyes had fallen on him, had slowed his pace immediately, and he continued to mount the steps until he stood directly in front of her.

"Well, hello." His deep voice held pure pleasure at the surprise of encountering her here, and his eyes slowly took in the dress she was wearing—the low vee of the bodice, the way the soft fabric hugged her waist then flared to a full skirt—and when his gaze went back to her face, he smiled. "You're just about the last person I expected to run into on these stairs," he said.

Shock was holding Ashley completely mute as she stood looking into his dark eyes, one hand gripping the polished banister. It released her finally, and she gave him a cool smile in return. "Yes, I guess I could say the same thing," she answered.

Grant continued to look at her steadily. "Here on business, or is this strictly a pleasure trip?" he inquired.

"I had a few things to do, yes." Ashley's tone gave away nothing, and after waiting for a threesome to pass, she made a move to step around him and continue on her way.

He caught her arm; an intensity had come into his eyes, and he held her gaze as he smiled again. "Ashley, we're both a long way from home. Let me buy you a drink," he offered. "There's an excellent bar."

"No." Frowning, she drew her arm out of his hold. "I'll buy my own, thank you."

"Ashley—"

"No thank you, Grant." She gave him a sharp look, and without another word, she left him then, walking around him and going on down the stairs to the lobby. It was crowded, and she made her way through the chatting guests to the doorway of the restaurant, stopping to stand with the cluster of people waiting for admittance. She was still frowning from her encounter with Grant, and though it was pleasantly warm in the hotel lobby, she felt chilled. She stood with her arms wrapped around her body, and after a moment, her eyes were drawn to the spot on the staircase where the two of them had been standing; Grant was gone. An unwelcome awareness came to her then, of the waste of a Saturday evening in one of the world's most fabulous cities. Once she and Grant would have shared its excitement, but now they went their separate ways, like strangers. The subtle sense of loss persisted until all of a sudden a delayed reaction hit her: *What was Grant doing in London?*

The Chilton collection. That had to be it. What had the desk clerk said to her when she'd arrived earlier in the day?

"We had another guest make the trip out to Kent yesterday." That remembrance triggered another one, of something Sir Isaac Baylor had said that afternoon that hadn't penetrated until just now. "I don't usually leave the case unlocked," the Englishman had commented when he opened the glass case for her inspection of the bronzes, "but I was showing them yesterday." To whom? Ashley wondered, but she knew even as the question passed through her mind what the answer was. It had been to Grant. She heard the echo of a third voice, Ollie's this time, as he'd said, ". . . nor can I think that Grant Copeland would be interested in these bronzes either." Can't you, Ollie? she asked him silently. Well, you were wrong. He's interested in them all right. He wants them. *He wants them!*

Ashley was suddenly galvanized. She spun around, smiling apologetically at the people she brushed past in her anxious rush back toward the staircase, and reaching it, she ascended hurriedly, picking up her pace even more when she got to the upper hallway. She walked briskly to her room, giving the door a brusque push closed once she was inside, and thumbed rapidly through her appointment book until she found Sir Isaac's number. Waiting impatiently for the call to go through, she felt a rising tension at the thought that maybe he wasn't home, that no one would answer, until finally the ringing stopped and Sir Isaac's voice said, "Hello" on the other end of the line.

"Sir Isaac?" Ashley sank down into a chair in relief, winding the telephone cord around her finger. "This is Ashley Galbraith. I'm sorry for the late call, but I wanted to reach you tonight." Smiling, she listened to his polite dismissal of her apology. "Well, I know I seemed a little uncertain about the bronzes this afternoon, but I've been doing a lot of thinking, and I've come to a decision. I'd like very much to meet with you tomorrow, if you're amenable. I think we can do business, Sir Isaac, and I'd like to talk to you about making arrangements for Galbraith's to handle the statuettes at auction.

"Ollie, it will be *fine!*"

On Tuesday morning Ashley sat with Peter and Ollie at the long oak conference table in Galbraith's paneled board room, a shaft of sunlight streaming through the window, catching her shoulder as she sat at the head of the table. "You've got to take all the merits of the collection into consideration,'' she went on with an earnest smile. ''You can't just dwell on a single aspect and dismiss everything else.''

Ollie sat back heavily in his chair, hiking down the vest of his pinstriped suit. He'd been vaguely disquieted earlier when Ashley had popped into his office, her spirits positively buoyant, her only response to his inquiry about the Chilton collection a bright, ''Later,'' and now that he'd plainly heard her say she'd made a deal to have Galbraith's sell the bronzes, his disquiet had blossomed. Into full-fledged distress.

''Ashley, as far as I'm concerned, there aren't any merits to the collection. You've admitted that you weren't any more impressed by the quality of the statuettes when you saw them.''

''What I said,'' Ashley countered smoothly, ''was that the photographs were a fair representation of them.'' She sat forward eagerly. ''And if you'll just please listen to me for a moment, I know you'll agree that I was right to go ahead and secure this sale for Galbraith's,'' she pressed.

''Ollie, we might as well hear her out about the matter,'' Peter interjected. ''It's a *fait accompli* at this point,'' he added dryly.

''Thank you,'' Ashley said with a nod and turned her full attention back to Ollie. She felt compelled to bring him around to her side; just exactly why she didn't know. ''Ollie, the more I think about this, the more certain I become that this is a sale that's not only going to do well but that will really make headlines for us.'' She launched then into a recitation of all the rationalizations she'd been drumming into her own mind since Saturday night.

''And then, of course, there's the point of Meriweather Chilton's reputation,'' she said finally ''That's what will play the biggest role in making the sale go over. You know how people love a good scandal and how quick they are to snatch up something that once belonged to someone who caused a sensation,'' she said cajolingly and gave him an encouraging smile. ''Gossip, Ollie. The human creature loves it, in any form.''

Ollie was watching her stolidly. ''I think you're giving far more weight to that concept than it deserves,'' he said. ''But even if you aren't, you seem to be forgetting that Dame Meriweather's reputation doesn't stretch across the Atlantic. I daresay few people have ever heard of her. I certainly never had until now," he muttered.

"We'll make it stretch," Ashley answered blithely, leaning back in her chair. "We'll publicize her escapades to the hilt, and we can do a complete background on her in the catalogue. You know, a précis on her life on the inside front cover." She took a sip of the coffee Christine had brought them, then gave Ollie another bright smile over the rim of her cup.

"Ashley, I don't know," Ollie said heavily. "You seem to have convinced yourself, for whatever reason, that all these peripheral considerations are able to override the fact that what we're dealing with here are inferior antiques."

Ashley could field this objection; she'd practiced innumerable times on her own inner voice of reservation. "What I'm convinced about, Ollie, is that we have a good sale in hand, and if done properly, it will be what we've needed for a long time—a news event," she said optimistically. "And I know for a fact that Grant Copeland considered it worthwhile," she added before she could get it back.

"Oh? How?" Ollie inquired immediately, looking at her keenly.

"I just know, that's all." She could see that Ollie was going to press the matter, so went on to elaborate. "He'd been out to see the collection," she told him, her eyes on her fingertip as it made invisible circles on the table. "And Ollie," she said with a sudden glance upwards, "Grant's got good instincts for what makes a successful sale."

Ollie arched an eyebrow. "You say that as if it's another selling point for the collection," he commented.

"Well, no one can deny he's got good intuition," she murmured, then looked back up with a very firm smile. "Ollie, it's going to be fine," she reiterated.

Ollie studied her, finally accepting the inevitable with a long sigh. "Well, maybe it won't be so painful if we mix the things in with other pieces," he said. "We have some Art Deco miscellanea scheduled for—"

"No, Ollie. I'm not going to do that," Ashley broke in decisively. "I've already been jotting down ideas. This is going to be a sale on its own, with its own day, its own ad campaign. This is an important sale, Ollie. I'm going to treat it as one. I've already decided to schedule it for the end of next month, July thirty-first. I'll get the publicity going immediately, and I'm going to see Janet about the catalogues just as soon as we break here.''

Peter had remained silent while they discussed the quality of the collection, a subject he didn't feel qualified to talk about. But now he asked, ''What about the contract, Ashley? Any special provisions?''

She kept her eyes on the pad. ''It's already done,''she answered. ''Sir Isaac has an office in London. I wrote up the terms and his secretary typed out the contract. He was given standard terms with . . . just—'' She paused for a fleeting moment, then chastised herself for the hesitation; he was going to have to know at some point anyway. ''With just a moderate cut in the commission rate,'' she finished.

Ollie's eyes snapped back to her. ''You cut the commission?'' he breathed.

''Yes.'' She felt decidedly uncomfortable under his sharp look of disapproval.

''Why?''

''It was necessary.''

''Why?'' he pressed.

Because Grant was there, and if I hadn't come in under what he usually charges for commissions, I wouldn't have been able to get this sale from him. Ashley nearly said it, but caught herself in time. ''Because it was the way I worked out the deal, that's why. Now,'' she said in a tone meant to end the discussion once and for all, and folded her hands on the edge of the table in front of her, ''there's only one other thing I wanted to tell you about, not on this subject at all.''

She settled back relaxedly in the armed chair at the head of the long table. ''I stopped by Appleby's on Monday, and I spent several hours with Wilfred Dalton.'' She smiled. ''He's a fascinating man, and I think knows the auction business very well. He sent you his regards, by the way,'' she added, tilting her head.

Ollie smiled. ''Yes, he's a very knowledgeable man,'' he concurred.

''He took me to lunch,'' she continued, ''and told me something that I found extremely interesting. He's thinking of instituting buyer's premiums at his firm. Were you aware of that?'' she inquired intently.

Ollie's gaze had sharpened. ''No, I wasn't,'' he admitted slowly.

Peter frowned, sitting forward toward the table. "Stop a minute," he interjected. "What are buyer's premiums?"

Ashley rapidly explained the concept whereby the buyer of an article sold to him at auction would be required to pay a fixed percentage of the final sales price to the auction house. It was an innovative departure from the existing method, which was for the seller of an auctioned item to be solely responsible for the commission due the auction establishment—a hefty figure. Under a system of buyer's premiums, the rate charged a seller could be substantially lowered, for the buyer would now be sharing the burden of commission payments; it would benefit the sellers by reducing their financial outlay, and would benefit the auction house in two ways. Not only could such a practice readily attract more sellers and their merchandise to whatever company offered the cheaper service but the auction house could collect a higher total commission.

"Sounds reasonable," Peter remarked when she'd finished.

"And difficult to get across to the buying public, which has never had to *pay* to be able to purchase at auction," Ollie rejoined immediately, frowning as he shook his head. "You'd have to educate them to the notion of paying money on top of the sales price, and I'm not sure they'd go for it, either in England or here. The system as it is now has stood for a long time. Forever, in fact."

"Well, I think it's a very intriguing idea," Ashley commented, then glanced at her watch. "Gentlemen, we've all got work to do." She smiled at them both as she stood up, and when Ollie rose beside her, she laid a hand on his arm, giving him a searching look. "I hope you won't be depressed about the Chilton sale for the whole next month until it's over. I don't like to see you with a long face."

"Have you ever known me to be like that?" he countered, managing a slight smile.

Ashley eyed him, then grinned. "Yes."

Ollie laughed at that but sobered quickly. "I'll back you up on this, Ashley. You know that. But I feel this wasn't a wise thing to do. You'll simply have to prove me wrong."

"Which I will," she said confidently and watched him as he smiled thinly then headed for the door.

When he was gone, Ashley turned to Peter. His presence at the short conference had been accidental; he'd dropped by just as Ashley and Ollie had been entering the board room, and she'd invited him to join them. Now, however, she was feeling a twinge of guilt for having subjected him to what had been, at moments, a somewhat uncomfortable meeting.

"Peter, I didn't mean to put you in the middle of Ollie's and my disagreement," she said, smiling apologetically as she started around the table.

He ushered her past him with a hand at her back, walking with her toward the door. "There's nothing to be sorry for," he responded. "The most interesting part of any business is always the back-room discussion. And don't let Ollie's pessimism get to you," he added. "As long as you follow your instincts, you'll do fine."

Doubt fluttered in Ashley for the briefest moment, then died away. She gave him a brilliant smile, turning to him when they reached the door. "This sale is going to work, Peter. I want it to, and I'm going to make it," she declared.

He nodded, then said abruptly, "We have a raincheck for dinner, you know."

Ashley shifted uncomfortably and dropped her eyes to the floor. "Yes, I know. Peter, I . . ."

"Ashley." He put his hand on her shoulder, frowning slightly. "Why are you so reluctant to go out with me?"

Ashley looked back up at him and, disconcertingly, an image flashed across her eyes: that of a broad-shouldered, handsome man standing on a staircase directly in front of her, his tanned face lit by an easy smile. She shook her head, dissolving the vision, and once again saw Peter clearly, his own attractive features, blond hair, blue eyes. Troubled blue eyes. "Peter, I'm not reluctant," she said slowly.

He studied her, then let his hand fall from her shoulder. "I could say, 'Oh, okay. I was mistaken,' to that, but I can't react that casually with you any longer," he answered. "You are hesitant, and I'd like to know why. I think it must be obvious to you by now that I find you extremely attractive and that I'd like very much to get to know you on a more personal basis. I don't always approach these things so directly," he added moodily, "but you leave me no other choice."

Ashley determined that she would try to answer him as honestly as she could. "Peter, it isn't that I don't like your company," she said and smiled gently. "I do. It's just that, right now, Galbraith's is the most important thing in my life. There's so much I want to do with it, and that takes time."

He frowned. "Ashley, you can't go on living the kind of life you have been up to now, doing nothing but working.

You're handling Galbraith's beautifully now. Don't you think it's about time you started having some kind of real life again?''

"Peter." Ashley still spoke quietly, but an intensity had come into her expression. "Everyone has priorities in their lives. Those priorities change as circumstances in your life change, and right now, Galbraith's is my first. It simply . . . is. Please accept that. And I'll be busier now than ever, getting this Chilton sale put together. It's going to occupy all my time and energy. I *want* it to, so I can be certain it's done right," she finished, her eyes imploring him to understand.

He laughed ruefully. "Well, I have to say that's the most polite put-off I've ever gotten," he commented. Ashley looked away from him, and he backed off. "All right, Ashley. I'll accept it. And I admire your energy." She smiled faintly, and he raised his eyebrows curiously. "By the way, you never did say how much you cut the commission on this Chilton sale."

Ashley was grateful that he'd changed the subject but wished he'd chosen some other topic. "By a third," she admitted.

Peter didn't respond immediately, and Ashley quickly added, "Yes, I know that's a rather substantial cut, but it was necessary. And we'll make it up in the profits."

Peter opened the door, smiling automatically at several Galbraith employees passing by in the hall. "They'd better be pretty hefty profits, Ashley, since you're planning to put so much publicity into this one," he observed.

"They will be," she answered without hesitation, and she'd just made a movement to step through the door when Peter caught her arm.

"I'm going to drop this subject, Ashley," he said when she'd turned back to him. "But I only want to say one last thing. When you're ready to come out of this narrow existence you're leading, you let me know. I'll be waiting."

She smiled. "I'll let you know," she replied, then walked with him from the room.

Chapter 31

CHILTON BRONZES FAIL TO SELL
By Mark Rooney

Galbraith Galleries' sale of bronze newel post statuettes belonging to the late Dame Meriweather Chilton was held on July thirty-first in the large auction hall of Galbraith's gracious Park Avenue building. Heralded by a massive advertising campaign that centered primarily around the scandalous life of the Englishwoman, the sale of forty-three bronze staircase ornaments began at ten a.m. and was, by any standards, an enormous failure.

Presale viewing had been encouraging, and though attendance at the auction itself was respectable, the audience was made up more of curiosity seekers than actual buyers. Only twelve of the statuettes sold at all, the bronze of a young girl with her lamb bringing the highest price of $4400, while the lowest price gotten was $1200 for the statuette of a rearing horse. The bronzes had been estimated, over-optimistically, at $10–15,000 apiece. The session lasted for two hours, and though each bronze was duly presented to the audience for sale, all but the twelve that were eventually purchased had to be bid back in by Herbert Willingham, on behalf of Galbraith's and the Chilton estate.

It seems obvious that Ashley Galbraith believed the focus on Dame Meriweather's disreputable past would shift attention away from the fact that the articles were of poor quality, but it was a grave miscalculation. Final figures for the sale have not been published yet and may not be at all. On the face of things, however, it would seem that enormous losses were sustained by Galbraith's in this sale, considering the scope of the advertising surrounding it, the cost of the catalogue, and the fact that Galbraith's usual commission rate was reduced, as has been discovered. Mrs. Galbraith has been unavailable for comment.

Grant Copeland of DuBrand & Company has also declined to comment about the Chilton auction, but it has been learned that he refused to handle the collection for DuBrand's. Mrs. Galbraith should have had the same foresight and will have, we trust, in future sales.

"Well, that has to be the most embarrassing article I've ever read!" Karen breathed as she let the latest issue of *Antiques World* drop to her lap. It was August fifth, and she and Grant were sitting together in the back seat of a taxicab as it headed up Madison Avenue. They were returning to the office from a long morning meeting with DuBrand's import brokers, and she'd pulled out the paper she'd had in her briefcase to pass the time on the long uptown ride.

"I'd just die if something like that was ever written about me!" she went on feelingly and glanced over at Grant. "Do you want me to read it out loud to you?"

He was sitting with his shoulder up against the car door, swaying with the motion of the cab jolting along the potholed city street, and his pensive gaze was turned out the window toward the passing storefronts and office buildings. "I've already seen it," he murmured.

Karen's eyes left him and went back to the paper as she slowly shook her head. "The press is really crucifying her, though I think this write-up is worse than any of the others." She tisked as she brushed her long hair back behind her shoulder. "I suppose I ought to feel sorry that Ashley is being raked over the coals the way she is, but after all, it is her own fault!"

"Karen, leave her alone," Grant said, still frowning out the window.

She was too absorbed in Ashley's misfortune to hear him and grimaced wonderingly. "What do you suppose possessed Ashley to get involved with those awful things in the first place?" she mused.

Grant's eyes flickered, but he didn't answer the question. Instead, he asked, "Did you get the estimates on those Impressionists?"

Karen's bemused expression had drifted into a smile of satisfaction. "Well, anyway, this ought to set Galbraith's back a bit, to say the least," she commented.

"Karen, pay attention to me," Grant said shortly and

scowled as he looked away from the window and directly at her.

Her startled eyes came up from the paper. "What?"

"I asked if you'd received the estimates on the Monets and Renoirs we're selling the first of next month."

The cab swerved out around another car at that moment, throwing her against him, and with a hand against his shoulder, she righted herself. "Yes. And why are you in such a bad mood?" she asked with a quizzical frown.

Grant didn't answer that either, and as he caught sight of Sixty-fifth Street coming up at the next light, he leaned forward and spoke to the cab driver through the opening in the plexiglass shield. "Drop me off at the next corner, please." He reached for his wallet as he settled back, glancing over at Karen, who was watching him in complete perplexity. "It's past noon," he said in answer to her expression. "I'm going to grab some lunch. I'll meet you back at the office. If Leland Bartholomew should happen to call while I'm out, tell him I'll be back in about an hour."

She was acutely disappointed that she wasn't being asked to go with him, but in light of his darkly pensive mood, she didn't invite herself along. "Okay. And is Bartholomew talking seriously about putting the Maynard estate out to auction now?" she asked as the taxi pulled over to the curb and came to a standstill.

"I don't know. I can't get the man to really discuss anything with me. I just keep trying," Grant answered absently as he stepped out of the cab. He reclosed the door and leaned down to speak to her through the window. "I'll see you later."

"I meant to tell you," she said quickly, catching his wrist around the cuff of his jacket. "I heard some speculation the other day that if the contents of the Tarrytown house are sold off, they might just sell the property along with it. That could be a real point in our favor since you've gotten into the auctioning of real estate, huh?"

Grant nodded vaguely and straightened. Karen watched him step up onto the curb, then walk away without saying anything further, and expelling a small sigh, she settled back against the seat and instructed the cabbie to drive on.

Grant strode along the sidewalk with his eyes to the ground. His destination was Templeton's, a popular restaurant on East Seventy-first Street, five blocks from his office and several over from where he'd gotten out of the cab, and although the day was dreary and overcast, threatening to rain any minute, he'd gotten out of the cab as abruptly as he had because he'd been in the mood for a walk. And wanted to be alone.

He was disturbed about Ashley and her Chilton sale—bothered because everyone was slamming her so hard, and even more because she'd taken on the things in the first place. Disturbed most of all because he knew exactly why she'd gotten herself into this. So damn needlessly, he thought, and his frown tightened. His heavy preoccupation enveloped him, and he came to from it only once, at the jarring blare of a car horn; startled, he looked up to see that he'd walked directly in front of an oncoming car as he was crossing Sixty-ninth Street, and ignoring the driver's angry oath, he stepped back to let the automobile pass, then kept on going.

When he reached the restaurant finally, he consciously roused himself from his moody reflection, and pushed through the glass doors monogrammed with a gold *T*, standing for a moment just inside to let his eyes adjust to the dim lighting. Templeton's wasn't a fancy restaurant, but it had excellent food, a pleasant airy atmosphere with its long wall of windows overlooking Seventy-first Street, and it was crowded even at twelve-fifteen. He passed through the narrow entrance lobby and went to stand directly in the portal of the big dining room, waiting for the hostess to return after seating a party of two.

Almost all the tables scattered across the carpeted floor were taken, and Grant's gaze passed abstractedly over them, coming finally to a small, round table for two, directly by the windows in the far corner; it locked there, and he stood silently watching the lone woman occupying the table, her somber gaze turned toward the window.

It was Ashley. She was dressed in a sleeveless white summer dress, her ebony hair clipped back from one temple with a thin, gold barrette, and one arm was resting listlessly on the table in front of her. She looked so vulnerable to Grant, sitting there with dejection written all over her.

"One?" the hostess inquired pleasantly, a menu in the crook of her arm as she stood smiling at him.

"Yes," he answered, startled at being addressed, and his eyes strayed back to Ashley in the far corner.

"I have a table over here, sir." The woman gestured straight ahead.

Grant glanced at Ashley once more, then smiled back at the hostess. "No, as a matter of fact, I see someone I know. If you don't mind, I think I'll join her," he said and, after a courteous nod, began making his way across the room toward Ashley's table.

Chapter 32

ASHLEY HAD BEEN at Templeton's for half an hour now, forcing herself to eat the better part of the shrimp salad she'd ordered only because she'd felt she ought to, not because she was hungry. She might never be hungry again, she thought unhappily as she watched two shoppers strolling down the sidewalk beyond the window. Not, at least, until she'd thought of a way to live down the fiasco that the Chilton sale had turned into.

She closed her eyes tightly as recollection of the painful auction stabbed her again. It had been a worse day than she could have dreamed possible, that bright sunny July day a week ago, when she'd stood at the back of the velvet-draped sale room at Galbraith's, watching with a needlelike pain all across the back of her shoulders as statuette after statuette had been brought to the display table at the front of the room only to *sit* there, with no bids being offered, the room all but silent except for the rustle of people shifting uncomfortably in their seats and the voice of the auctioneer. Francis Barclay had handled the debacle as well as could be expected; he'd somehow managed to keep his composure, even through Ollie's calls to bid back in for Galbraith's all but twelve of the bronzes—sweet, generous Ollie who'd never once said, "I told you so." Ashley had wanted to leave time and time again during that eternity-long, two-hour period, but she'd resolutely stayed and watched.

She picked up her glass of chablis and dispiritedly sipped at it as she tried to blank out of her mind the images of that horrible day. She wished she hadn't read the article in *Antiques World* that morning; the acerbic comments of the columnist, repeating everything she already knew, had been demoralizing enough, but then to be stunned by the disclosure that Grant had never wanted the bronzes after all. . . . She downed almost three quarters of her wine in one gulp and set the glass on the table. Salt to the wound—and deserved, she thought miserably; if she just hadn't *assumed* Grant had been in

271

London negotiating for the bronzes, if she'd just listened to
her own instincts instead of . . .

"Hi."

Oh God, no, not him; it was effort enough just to show her
face in public. Ashley flushed crimson as she watched Grant
pull out the straight-backed chair on the opposite side of the
table and sit down. He looked relaxed and self-assured—the
consummate executive—and the only thought on her mind
when he smiled at her was that she had to get away from him
or die of embarrassment. "I . . . was just leaving," she said,
keeping her eyes averted, and she pushed back her chair;
Grant reached across the table and clamped a hand on her
wrist.

"No, you weren't."

"Grant . . ."

"Sit still, Ashley. I'm tired of your instant exits." The
smile had gone out of his eyes, and they locked with hers.
Something in his manner finally compelled Ashley to capitulate,
and as she settled back tensely in her chair, he let go of her
arm, smiling up at the waitress who'd just appeared. "Bourbon
and water," he told her. "And another glass of wine for the
lady, please." The woman nodded and left, and Grant turned
his attention back to Ashley. "I want to talk to you. About a
couple of things," he said.

Ashley was staring fixedly at her hands folding and refold-
ing the linen napkin by her plate. "We have nothing to talk
about," she answered in a constrained voice.

Grant eased back, resting one arm on the back of his chair.
"That was quite a disaster you staged at Galbraith's last
week," he said matter-of-factly. "Ashley, you've got better
sense than to get involved with something like those Chilton
statuettes," he added with a disapproving frown.

Ashley's eyes widened as she looked up at him. It was hard
for her to take a statement like that from anyone, but coming
from him— *To look the professional fool in front of Grant
Copeland* . . . The thought stung fiercely, and she looked
back down at the table, swallowing.

Grant's eyes softened as he watched her suffering under his
biting comment. "You asked for that, Ashley," he said. "I
came over here wanting just to have a quiet talk with you, but
unhappy though you are, you could do nothing but hand me
the same old line." He broke off briefly as the waitress
returned to serve their drinks, then picked up again when she

was gone. "So now that we've gotten the harsh commentaries out of the way, let's talk. I'm sure in your present frame of mind you'll find this hard to believe, but I'm probably just as upset about this Chilton affair as you are. I could never want to see you go through what you've suffered over this. And I know why you got into that sale. Others may not know, but I do."

Ashley silently searched for something—anything—to say in her defense. "Grant, I—"

"You were trying to deal some swift blow to me. I know," he finished quietly. "Baylor had spread the word that he was hoping to give the collection to DuBrand's, and you thought I wanted it. You saw me in London and figured I was there to strike a deal with Baylor. So you went after him, cutting your commission to make sure you got the bronzes from me." Ashley frowned tightly, and Grant grimaced across the table in fond admonishment. "Don't look at me like that," he said. "You can keep up whatever pretenses you want with everyone else, but there's no need to do it here. This is just the two of us, and we both know what happened."

Ashley had no response to that because, yes, they both did know what happened. Grant knew *exactly*. With that understanding, her humiliation was complete, and she propped her elbow on the table, putting her forehead in her hand as she looked bleakly at her wineglass. "Grant, what do you want?" she asked in a voice that was hardly above a whisper.

He sat forward, his expression serious. "I told you. I want to talk to you. I tried once before to impress upon you that personal feelings don't belong in professional judgments, that mixing the two only leads to trouble, and that's exactly what you did here. You were so stuck on the idea of hurting me and my company that you didn't listen to your good business sense. And I can't believe that in your heart you didn't know those statuettes were almost unsalable; you've got too much training in this field, plus too much savvy. I knew it, which is why, after I'd seen the things in person, I turned my back on them." Ashley finally looked at him then, and he smiled. "Take some advice, Ashley, meant only in the friendliest way. In the future, just stick to worrying about your own business, and if you're going to make errors in judgment, let them be errors honestly made."

So she had been right about one thing: he had looked at the bronzes in Kent; the small vindication was of no consolation whatsoever to Ashley, and she sighed heavily. "Grant, I'm not up to one of your lectures today," she said despondently. "And thank you for rubbing it in—that your judgment was so much better than mine."

He frowned. "I'm not doing either. I'm simply trying to help you learn a lesson."

"Well, I don't want your help," she said down to the table.

He sat back again in his chair, studying her. The white dress she was wearing with its small patch of colorful appliqué just beneath the collar was very flattering to her figure and her coloring, and after a moment, he picked up his drink, downing a good portion of it before he set the glass back on the table. "Ashley, the other thing I want to talk to you about is us."

Ashley's need to get out of Grant Copeland's discomfiting presence was growing so urgent it compelled her to make another attempt to leave. "There is no 'us,' " she answered, pushing back her chair.

Once again, he quickly reached across the table and took her wrist in a tight grasp, preventing her from getting up. "Oh, yes there is. You know, there aren't many women in this world for whom I'd wear my heart on my sleeve," he told her as he let his fingers slide down from her wrist to her hand, which he covered warmly with his own. "You happen to be the only one." His expression suddenly grew intent. "Ashley, I love you," he said. "That still stands despite all that's gone on, despite how you feel about me. How you say you feel," he amended.

"Grant, please let me go," Ashley pleaded in some desperation, trying to extricate her hand from his hold; his grip merely tightened.

"No," he answered. "I'm not going to let you go. It's time to talk about this openly. I've kept my distance for six months now, living with your attitude because I've been trying to give you time to get far enough away from all that happened with Ross so you could have a chance to see things with a clearer perspective. But my patience is wearing thin. Ashley, this has got to stop, this business of your behaving like an angry opponent. It's all wrong."

"Grant, please let me leave!"

"Honey." Grant's eyes grew gentle at her distraught expression, and he cocked his head. "Relax. It's only me. And this has got to be talked about." He paused, and when he finally went on, there was a certain quiet inner confidence in his eyes. "Things aren't over between us, Ashley. You can't convince me of that. And though I meant it when I said my patience in waiting for you to come around again is getting a little ragged around the edges, I'll keep it up as long as I have to, because at some point you're going to realize the truth. You've got to, honey, and when you do, I'll be—"

"Peter!" Ashley's surprised exclamation interrupted Grant midsentence, and intense relief flooded through her as she watched, past Grant's left shoulder, the attractive attorney making his way through the crowded restaurant toward them. As Grant shot a glance over his shoulder in the direction of her gaze, loosening his hold on her hand, Ashley drew it back, standing up immediately when Peter reached their table. "Hello!" she breathed in urgent welcome.

"Hi," Peter returned. "I stopped by your office, and Ollie told me you'd come here. I was afraid you were lunching alone again," he said, casting an uncertain look at Grant. "But I see you're not, and that you haven't finished your lunch yet—"

"No, I was just leaving!" Ashley replied hastily, in anxiety that the unexpected means of escape might disappear without her, and she grabbed up her coat from the back of the chair, rooting around in her purse for her wallet. She found it, selected several bills, and laid them on the table. "This is for my lunch and drinks," she said quickly to Grant. "If you wouldn't mind paying the waitress for me? Peter is my attorney, and we have a number of things to talk about." And slipping her arm through Peter's she hurriedly left the table with him.

It took them minutes to make their way through the close arrangement of the tables out of the restaurant to the street, and Peter was smiling in pleasure when they reached it; he didn't know what had been going on back there with Ashley and her luncheon companion, if anything, but he didn't care. The upshot of it had been to his complete satisfaction. "How about dinner tonight?" he asked comfortably as they began to walk toward Park Avenue, where he would hail them a cab.

"Oh, I—yes, I . . . suppose so." Ashley hardly heard him at all; a loud ringing had come up in her ears, and she was seeing with vivid clarity what she'd just done—walked out on Grant with another man, right in the middle of his outpouring of feeling for her. *That was horrible, Ashley, and he won't take it,* the voice from somewhere deep inside whispered to her, and as she envisioned again the look on Grant's face when she'd left—his eyes dangerously narrowed—a gripping coldness of—what? fear?—seized her stomach.

". . . about Delmonico's? They have terrific steaks there," Peter was saying, then abruptly broke off as they turned the corner onto Park Avenue and he became aware that Ashley's eyes were scanning the storefront signs, distinct distress in them. "Ashley, is something wrong?" he asked worriedly.

Gone for good . . . Frantically, Ashley searched the row of stores, her hand at her throat. "I—Peter, I'll be right back," she said in a sudden rush, then left him and hurried across the sidewalk to the door of the small luncheonette she'd spotted. She pushed through, darting out of the way of several patrons strolling up toward the cash register as she half ran, half walked toward the door at the back marked "Ladies' Room." And once inside, she rushed to a cubicle and threw up her entire lunch.

At Templeton's Grant had watched Ashley disappear through the door with Peter, then had turned roughly back around in his chair. He stared unseeingly out the window, gritting his teeth, then abruptly got to his feet, shoving his chair back with his foot. He pulled out several dollars from his wallet and tossed them onto the money Ashley had left, then strode out of the restaurant.

Ashley and Peter were nowhere in sight when he reached the street, although it wouldn't have mattered to him if they had been. He didn't care where the hell they'd gone, he thought savagely, and headed up Madison Avenue on foot. He walked back toward his office with his eyes again on the ground, but they were flashing with anger this time and with the acrimony of his thoughts.

He'd had it with Ashley; he was sick to death of her perversities and constant backhanding, and nobody but nobody played him for a fool. Let her go with that guy anywhere, to hell and back if she wanted to. He didn't give a damn. A decision was made inside him, and he brushed by the pedestrians on the busy street, paying no attention to traffic lights as he returned to DuBrand's.

Reaching the banks of glass doors in front of the sleek building, he waited for several customers to exit, smiling

thinly at them, then went inside, the heels of his leather shoes
striking against the black marble steps as he trotted up the
wide main staircase, through the mirrored visitor's lobby,
oblivious to the people milling around the galleries as he went
directly to the offices. He passed through the door marked
"Private," walking by his own office down to Karen's. The
door was closed, and he knocked sharply. He heard her
muffled call to enter and walked in, closing the door behind
him.

"Oh, hi!" she said brightly. She was sitting behind her
walnut desk, the plate glass window at her back with its view
of a gracious old building across the street, and she laid down
the catalogue proof she was studying under the light of the
curved brass desk lamp sharply illuminating the glossy prints.
"How was lunch?" she asked.

"Fine," he said shortly, walking directly over and coming
to a standstill in front of her desk. "Did you get anything to
eat?" he asked.

She smiled at his concerned inquiry. He seemed in a
strange, intense mood, but at least he wasn't as preoccupied
as he had been when he'd left her in the cab, she thought as
she studied his handsome face, the sharp line of his jaw that
at the moment looked as if it had been chiseled out of granite.
"No, but I needed to get this work done anyway," she
answered.

"You work too hard," Grant remarked then and perched
down on the front edge of her desk; he was watching her
steadily, a half-smile on his face.

"Probably," she rejoined with a small laugh, then said
brightly, "Guess what I heard while you were out?" she
propped her elbows on the desk.

"Tell me later," he said brusquely, and resting a forearm
on his thigh, leaned toward her slightly. "Karen—"

"No!" she objected with a lilting laugh, "I want to tell
you now. It's *news*!" She paused dramatically. "Our friend,
Mr. Geary, is getting a divorce."

"Good for him," Grant dismissed. His eyes were roaming
her face, and he began again in a low voice, "Karen—"

"Good for him? That's all you can say?" she demanded
with a good-natured frown and absently tightened the scarf
around her ponytail. "I thought it was pretty important myself.
This is his third marriage. I—"

"Karen." She stopped talking finally at Grant's firm tone

and looked up at him inquiringly. When he had her full attention, he said intently, "What are you doing this weekend?"

Karen stared at him, then carefully put down the pen she was still holding. "This weekend?" she repeated slowly. At his nod, she shrugged to maintain a casual air. "Oh, well. Probably vacuuming carpets, dusting tables, and other exciting things of that sort," she said as lightly as she could. "Why?" she continued in a low voice.

Things aren't over between us, you can't convince me of that. His words to Ashley echoed somewhere, but he ignored them. He smiled at Karen. "Because I'm going home to Coconino," he said, as he reached over and stroked the side of her face. "And I'd like very much for you to come with me."

Chapter 33

". . . WAS MORE THAN a year ago that many people in the collecting world wondered just exactly where Galbraith Galleries would be going under the management of Ashley Galbraith. Her sale of a collection of bronze newel post statuettes was a spectacular disaster that set Galbraith's back considerably, but she has gone on to dispel the doubts anyone might have had about her ability to continue maintaining Galbraith's as one of the finest auction houses in the country. With only successes following her early failure, including her exceptional auction last month of artwork by the Old Masters, where a record price of 2.5 million for a single painting was set, she has regained Galbraith's high standing in the industry to the point where it is hard, at this point, to determine which of the two major auction houses, Galbraith's or DuBrand's, is the more prominent. . . ." Margaret's voice quoting the effusive article in *Antiques Update* trailed off as she looked over at Ashley; it was nearly the end of September, unusually chilly for that time of the year, and they were sitting in Ashley's cozy living room along with Ollie and Peter, she in a sophisticated outfit of tailored black slacks and satin blouse and Ashley in a striking long hostess gown of deep maroon.

"Well, I'm thoroughly impressed," she pronounced as she laid the magazine down on the couch beside her. "Such a paragon of achievement you are, Mrs. Galbraith! Opening an office in Los Angeles at the end of next month . . . record earnings just published." She sighed, though her eyes were shining with affectionate admiration. "I'll tell you, I think I've just decided that I'm out of my league in your company!"

Ashley laughed at her friend across the span of the coffee table, but her laughter was tinged with self-consciousness. "Will you stop, Margaret!" she admonished, then looked inquiringly around at her guests. Their dinner an hour before had been a last-minute affair Ashley had enthusiastically arranged to celebrate Margaret's totally unexpected visit—an offshoot of her two-day business trip to New York—and they'd reassembled in the living room after the meal for light conversation and drinks.

"Can I get anyone something more?" she offered. "Ollie, how about a refill on your brandy?"

He smiled and rose somewhat stiffly from the carved rocker by the marble-enclosed fireplace, checking the gold watch in the pocket of his vest as he set his empty glass on the coffee table. "No, thanks. It's nearly ten-thirty, and I've got to be on my way," he demurred, making his way through the small, intimate grouping of furniture around the hearth. He came to a standstill beside Ashley, who'd gotten up to escort him out, and smiled at Margaret. "It was a pleasure meeting you," he said sincerely. She nodded in return, and Ollie looked at Ashley then, taking her hands. "The dinner was lovely, my dear, as always. The perfect relaxation for the end of a long day."

"I'm glad you enjoyed it." Ashley kissed him on the cheek, then walked with him toward the living room doorway. "And don't forget now, Ollie," she reminded as they stopped for a minute in the threshold, a smile playing at the corners of her mouth, "tomorrow the *Times* will carry the story about our buyer's premiums. I got the press release to them this afternoon, and a reporter phoned later and mentioned the story would run tomorrow."

"Oh, I haven't forgotten," he answered darkly. "I'm braced."

She laughed. "I'm only teasing you," she confided, smiling at him fondly. "And will you stop being so nervous about it? It's going to work. We've all seen in the past year that Appleby's has been successful with the practice. It revolutionized the auction business in England, and it's time now to get the practice going over here."

"Just what I always wanted to be—a revolutionary," Ollie muttered, then grinned as Ashley shook her head in exasperation. "I'm a perennial pessimist, you know that." At her immediate nod, he laughed. "Well, you needn't agree quite so readily, you know. And by the way," he continued on a serious note, "are you seeing Leland Bartholomew on Monday or Tuesday? I want to be certain to be in the office when you get back from that meeting."

"My appointment is for Monday, at two o'clock," Ashley responded. "At long last!"

Ollie shared her look of heartfelt relief, and after bidding everyone a last good-bye, then retrieving his coat, left. Ashley returned from seeing him out and stopped again in the living room doorway, smiling at Peter. "Would you like another drink?" she inquired when she saw him sitting on the edge of the sofa next to Margaret, his expression morose as he stared at his empty highball glass; he glanced up at her question.

"No, thanks," he answered and got to his feet. "I'll be on my way, too. I know you and Margaret have a lot of talking to do, and since you've only got tonight, the sooner you get rid of your company, the better." His smile at Margaret was constrained. "I'm glad I finally got the chance to meet you," he said. "Ashley talks about you all the time."

She smiled, exchanging farewells with him, and he joined Ashley then in the living room doorway. They went out into the narrow entry hall, and when they reached the front door, he turned to her, frowning heavily. "Ashley, you didn't tell me you were planning to make this big move with buyer's premiums," he objected.

Ashley had been fully aware that something had been disturbing him and offered a smile of apology. "Well, Peter, I only made the decision to go ahead and take the plunge yesterday. I haven't talked to you in the meanwhile."

He wasn't mollified. "Ashley, I didn't even know you were seriously considering buyer's premiums for Galbraiths," he continued in a disgruntled tone. "Oh sure, I knew you've always been interested in the concept," he allowed, "and that you've been keeping a hawk's eye on the situation in England, but I thought that was as far as it went."

Ashley bit her lip; she knew what lay behind Peter's disconsolateness. They'd been having these tense conversations for nearly a year, and after glancing with troubled eyes to the tiled floor, she looked back up. "Peter, I—"

"Never mind. Forget it," he dismissed abruptly and strode over to the small hall closet to fetch his overcoat.

Ashley's failure to confide the important matter in him bothered him for the simple reason that it effectively left him out of her life. Not that he was really in it, not in any major way, he thought with a brooding frown into the closet jammed with Ashley's numerous coats. He'd assumed after that day in Templeton's restaurant that he and Ashley were finally on their way to the serious relationship he'd always wanted with her, but things hadn't quite worked out that way. Oh, yes, they'd dated over the past twelve months; they'd dined out, attended the theater, parties, and even some of Ashley's business functions as a couple, but only on a sometime basis, and there'd been no intimacy between them whatsoever, certainly no commitment. Ashley was the one who kept things that way, because of some emotional reserve in her that he'd never really been able to understand. He loved her and had even, for the first time in his contented bachelor's life, contemplated marriage because of her, but that was out of the question; he didn't even have to ask to know that. He sighed as he reflected that their private time together had become even more infrequent recently, but he forced himself to smile as he turned back to her.

"Look, I'm sorry I griped about this," he said as he opened the front door, trying to alleviate the tension between them. "It's been a long day, and I'm tired."

Ashley nodded, trying to smile, and after they'd exchanged a brief kiss, she remained watching in the doorway as he went out through the wrought iron gate to the darkened street, getting into his car. Her expression was pensive, but then as she remembered Margaret, she put away her disquiet over Peter and closed the door, going to join her friend again in the living room.

"Alone at last!" Margaret breathed, then grinned. "How's that for a grade-B movie line?"

Ashley shook her head as she laughed. "You never change, Margaret. Thank God!" she added feelingly. She tilted her head, contemplating her friend. "It's so wonderful to see you. You look terrific." She laughed again, ruefully this time. "When you just appeared the way you did in my office this afternoon, I think I was too stunned to really tell you how thrilled I am that you're here."

"You told me," Margaret assured her as she got up and crossed the room, "with this little spur-of-the-moment shindig that I'm sure was the very last thing you had time to worry with. I doubt seriously that just anyone who drops in on you unannounced gets a gourmet dinner with attendants," she added dryly.

"Oh, sure they do," Ashley dismissed blithely and linked her arm with Margaret's. "It's part of my regular routine." She chuckled at Margaret's undeceived expression, guiding her friend around into the hall. "Come on, let's go upstairs. You have to unpack your toothbrush and I've got to change out of this dress. It's time for me to turn back into a pumpkin. I have to get into my jeans with the holes in both knees."

"My God, you never change either!" Margaret exclaimed in mock horror, and dodging Ashley's laughing whack, she started up the stairs.

A short time later they were comfortably settled in Ashley's bedroom—Ashley in a big, roomy armchair, Margaret stretched out on the bed with pillows propped behind her back.

"You know, I really did mean what I said earlier, about being impressed," Margaret said quietly. "You've done such an outstanding job at Galbraith's."

Ashley's eyes shone with warm pleasure at the praise from her longtime friend. "Thanks, Margaret. It's been a long, hard year. Discouraging sometimes, tremendously uplifting others, but always exhilarating." Her expression flushed with the glow of inner satisfaction as she focused back on Margaret. "Thrilling! It really is, Margaret, the chase of suc—" She broke off abruptly, pressing her lips together as she glanced down at the floor with a small, flickering frown.

Margaret pumped up the pillow behind her head and laid back against it. "What?" she prompted.

"Oh, nothing," Ashley murmured as she brushed at some minute speck of lint on her jeans. "Just something that came to mind, that's all." She looked back up, smiling very firmly. "I'm simply trying to say that I love what I'm doing."

Margaret raised her eyebrows. "It sounded from your conversation with Ollie as if you've got more major things on the horizon with Galbraith's. Who's Leland Bartholomew, and is your meeting with him as important as it sounded?"

"Very." She got up and began picking up the clothing she'd merely stepped out of when she'd changed. "It's taken more than a year for Henry Maynard's widow to come to a decision about selling their Tarrytown property, but she's going to be getting rid of it—the property right along with the contents—and I assume, since Leland Bartholomew has finally agreed to see me, that they're not going to do it through private dealers as they'd talked about there for awhile." She paused, thoughtfully considering the apparent importance of the phone call from the Maynard executor that she'd received only yesterday. She opened her velvet jewelry case to put inside the small ring from Grif; she laid it in the narrow ring compartment, between an old keepsake silver band that had belonged to her mother and Ross's diamond wedding band, which she'd stopped wearing, almost unconsciously, months before. She reclosed the lid of the case and turned back to her friend. "Margaret, this is going to be a spectacular sale for whoever can land it, Grant or me, and believe me, I'm going to do everything in my power on Monday to talk Bartholomew into giving it to Galbraith's!"

Margaret studied her keenly for a moment. "And this other business of buyer's premiums? I gather Ollie is disturbed about your doing it. What does it mean, anyway?"

Ashley explained the concept. "Of course Ollie's worried about the risk you take when you break with the tried and true, but I'm not really nervous," she concluded confidently. "Buyers didn't balk in England, and they won't here either, I just know it. People will always buy at auction, and they'll go where they can find the best merchandise. And not only do I want Galbraith's to have the benefits of this kind of commission structuring, but I want it to be the first to take the step. I'm certain that this will become an industry standard here, just as it has in England, and the prestige of being the initiator of something like that is enormous!"

Margaret got up and crossed the room to fetch her cigarettes from her handbag. "Well, I'm sure you haven't gotten where you are now by being afraid to take risks," she observed, glancing into Ashley's enormous walk-in closet where her friend was hanging up the hostess gown she'd worn that evening. "And if Ollie—my God, Ashley!" Margaret's incredulous voice was full timbre again as she came to stand in the closet doorway. "This has got to be the most gorgeous gown I've ever laid eyes on!" she exclaimed. "Where did you get it?"

Ashley looked inquiringly at her. "Which one do you mean?"

"This one!" Margaret stepped into the closet and lifted a hanger.

At the sight of the red gown Margaret was holding, Ashley felt as if someone had just kicked her hard in the stomach. "I—Grant bought it for me. Once," Ashley answered in a constrained voice. She swept the gown from Margaret's hand and rehung it, farther back in the closet; she adjusted it carefully on the hanger, her fingertips lingering for the briefest moment on the soft fabric of the sleeve, before turning away. "He'd, uh, kept it at Coconino for awhile," she continued, giving Margaret a lifeless smile. "But then he sent it to me." With no note inside, no message, she added silently. It had arrived by parcel post, one week to the day after she'd walked out on him in Templeton's.

"Oh." Margaret leaned against the closet doorframe and watched as Ashley walked over to the bureau and busied herself with putting away a slip. "What is Grant's position on this business of buyer's premiums, do you know?" she asked after a moment.

Ashley didn't turn around. "Oh, I'm certain he's contemplating using them himself," she answered evenly. "I have no doubt he's been watching the situation in England as closely as I have. He never misses a trick."

"You know, I'm surprised to hear you speaking about Grant in such a mild tone," Margaret commented. "Once was the time when you were so indignant with him, you couldn't even say his name pleasantly." She paused, then added carefully, "Has that changed?"

Finally Ashley turned around to give Margaret an attempt at a smile. "Your specialty always *was* leading questions. I'd forgotten that," she said with a faint laugh.

Margaret grimaced affectionately. "I'm allowed. We're friends, remember? Or don't you want to answer?"

Ashley was silent for a time. "Maybe it's that I don't know exactly how to answer," she said then.

"I don't mind if you try." Margaret crossed back over to the bed and sat down on the edge, watching Ashley silently as she locked her hands around one knee.

Ashley didn't answer right away, but as she sat down again in the armchair, her expression grew deeply disturbed. How did she say it—that she could no longer condemn Grant for what had happened to Ross, hadn't been able to in a long time? Time passes, she thought, lessons get learned. . . .

"Yes, Margaret, once upon a time I was so indignant with Grant I couldn't even say his name pleasantly, but I can't feel that way any longer. I mean, I—" Her troubled eyes strayed to the window; she ought to get up and close the curtains against the black night. "I've experienced so many things in the past year, gone through a lot, and my contention that Grant should have been keeping Ross in mind all the time as he ran DuBrand's, that he should've backed off from his competition with him was . . . well, it was so naive," she added in a low voice and looked down at her hands. "You can't make the decisions that need to be made if you allow personal feelings to interfere with business judgment. If anything taught me that, it was that horror of a sale you read about in the paper." She cast a humorless smile toward Margaret, who was stretched out again on the bed. "It was a dreadful experience but painfully enlightening."

Margaret nodded sympathetically. "Well, that's what it takes sometimes to see things clearly—trial by fire," she said.

Yes, trial by fire—to see things clearly, Ashley thought and rubbed her shoulders in an attempt to relieve the tension that was holding them in a biting grip. She could see so much now. It hadn't been Grant at fault for Ross's failures, but Ross himself. Now that she'd run Galbraith's herself, with as much intelligence and objectivity as she could, she understood that, could look back and recognize so many things Ross should've done but didn't; he hadn't made any effort at all to keep his own company out of trouble when he was given some real competition. She'd been aware of that on some level at the time, just as she was aware now that she'd never processed that understanding into her thinking about Grant. *Why, Ashley, why? Why were you so quick to condemn Grant's behavior, so willing to condemn him?* The deeply unsettling inner questions that haunted her for months now rose up again, making her tremble.

"No, I can no longer blame Grant for simply running his company to the best of his ability no matter what other issues were involved," she said quietly. "And yet—" she frowned with a vestige of her old outrage over what had happened to Ross. "I can't vindicate Grant entirely. The fact remains that he did put the information about his success with the Van Holt sales in the newspaper in that heartless way," she said. "And Ross died because of it."

"Grant told you it was a mistake, didn't he?" Margaret replied, bringing to mind everything Ashley had told her in the long, emotional telephone conversation they'd had several days after Ross's funeral. "And hadn't he tried to get in touch with you, too?"

Ashley's troubled frown deepened. "It's true that he tried to contact me, and don't think I haven't spent sleepless nights wondering whether Ross would still be alive if I'd gotten to him with the news first—if he hadn't read it in the paper. But you see, the thing that hurt Ross most was the disloyalty of old friends and, I suppose, the public humiliation. I don't think I could have softened that blow much. And Grant *knew* how much that would hurt, Margaret—he knew! Maybe he did want to give me the news himself that morning, but I think that was just his conscience bothering him. I still can't believe he didn't engineer that article in the *Times*. Grant runs that company with an iron hand, and he wouldn't let something like that slip by him.''

"Well, things do slip past even the best of us every now and then," Margaret commented dryly. "So, you've stopped trying to ruin his company, huh?'' she finally said.

"I just found out I'm better off when I concentrate on what happens with my own," Ashley responded obliquely.

"I see," Margaret murmured. "I wonder how Grant would take the news that your viewpoints have changed so dramatically?''

"He wouldn't care in the least," Ashley answered tonelessly, then got up and walked over to her dressing table where she sat down and immediately picked up her brush, running it through her short hair. "That's been made quite clear." With the return of a dress he'd once adored, she thought. Really, though, she hadn't needed that eloquent gesture to know that her leaving with Peter that day at Templeton's had struck him deeply. She'd seen Grant several days after the episode at a cocktail party in the Riverside Drive penthouse of an art critic. He'd been there with Karen and had treated Ashley with only the coldest formality and indifference, confirming what some part of her had known as she'd left the restaurant: that she'd put an end to his love for her, the love that had remained steadfast through so much. And his attitude toward her hadn't changed since.

"He has another girlfriend now," she went on with ragged lightness. "Karen Ryland. She works with him. They're a very . . . passionate couple." Against her will, Ashley pictured Grant and Karen as they so often were when she saw them together everywhere, it seemed: standing close together and laughing in that private way people do when they're intimately involved, Grant's arm across the other woman's shoulder. A suffocating feeling closed around her throat, and she set her wood-handled brush down sharply on the dressing table, staring at it. "No, Grant's not interested in anything I might think, say, or do anymore," she repeated in a low voice.

"Does that matter?" Margaret asked softly from the bed.

Ashley pretended not to hear. "Enough about me," she said brightly as she swiveled around in her vanity chair. "We haven't talked about you at all! Tell me what you've been doing all these months. We've been so out of touch and—"

"Who are you avoiding by not answering the question, Ashley?" Margaret broke in. "Me or yourself?"

Ashley's smile dimmed. "Margaret, I'm—"

"Still in love with him. You have been all along, and you always will be, right?" Margaret finished.

Ashley stood up. "Drop it, okay?"

"Okay." Margaret paused. "On another subject, then, what's between you and Peter? And did I detect a bit of strain in the air when he left?"

The other subject, Peter. Ashley wasn't up to going into that one right now—the relationship she should never have let get started in the first place, that she knew she had to end, and would as soon as she could find the right words to let Peter down as gently as possible. She simply would never be able to return the depth of feeling he had for her, and was astonished he'd put up with her evasions for as long as he had. "Later, Margaret," she said with a long sigh, when Margaret interrupted in a somewhat nervous whisper.

"Ashley, I think there's someone on the fire escape."

Ashley heard the faint sounds of the window and grinned. "I know." She crossed to the far side of the room and after admitting Baker through the window, took up the big alley cat in her arms and walked back to the bed to introduce him to Margaret. "This is my little friend, Baker," she said, "who'll always be a third-story man." She chuckled as she continued to stroke the cat's head. "And if you plan on getting any sleep tonight, I suggest you keep your bedroom door closed," she advised. "Baker has a preference for pillows, and he'll curl up by your head and purr right into your ear. It sounds like a truck that needs a new muffler!"

"Wonderful," Margaret murmured, "Come on, let's go into the other room while I get changed, and I'll tell you all about my life. Though I warn you now, it's not going to be nearly so exciting as yours."

Ashley carried Baker along with her as she followed Margaret across the room, and though she'd resolved to resist, for at least a little while, her compulsive urge to get lost in thoughts about Galbraith's, as she went out the door, she couldn't help wondering how the art world was going to take her announcement that as of nine o'clock the following Monday morning everything that passed through Galbraith's sale room would be subject to an 8 percent buyer's premium.

Chapter 34

GRANT READ THE news over coffee at the dining room table. He was holding the Thursday morning edition of the *Times* in front of him, and as he stared at the headline, "Galbraith's to Institute Buyer's Premiums Next Week," he set his coffee cup sharply down on the table. "Well, I'll be damned!" he exclaimed. He skimmed the brief article, the muscles in his jaw tense; they tightened even more when he came to the line at the very end of the piece, and after rereading the final sentence, he slapped the paper angrily down onto the glass surface of his handsome table. He got up and, scowling heavily, strode back through the apartment to his spacious bedroom to finish getting dressed.

It was nine-thirty when he arrived at DuBrand's, and Karen was waiting for him at his office door. "Did you see the news about Galbraith's buyer's premiums in the paper this morning?" she demanded, a hand on her hip.

"I certainly did," he answered shortly and strode past her into the room, tossing his coat over the arm of a chair as he passed by; he went immediately to his desk, dropping his briefcase on top and picking up the telephone messages he'd already received that morning.

Karen moved from the doorway, and with a frown as heavy as Grant's she came over to stand by his side. "I was just so stunned when I saw the headline, I nearly fell over. And I simply can't believe that incredible line at the end of the article!" she added in high indignation.

Grant's eyes flashed as he continued to look down at the pink phone messages and envisioned once more the quote from Ashley.

Mrs. Galbraith is pleased to be the first to bring the new commission structure to this country and to see that Grant Copeland of DuBrand & Company seems to have been slower in appreciating the significance of what has been going on in England for almost a year.

290

So damn smug, and going public now with her dislike and her insults, he thought, and threw the pieces of paper down on the desk. "It's par for the course for her, where I'm concerned," he answered tightly.

Karen looked at him in bewilderment for a minute, then was gripped again by her angry dismay over what had happened. "She just can't do this, she can't be the first to start buyer's premiums in this country!" she objected. "You were supposed to be."

"Well, she'd doing it—has *done* it. I didn't move fast enough with my own announcement. Damn!" He glared down at the desktop, considering the important moment of prestige lost now to him and his firm.

Karen frowned sourly. "You know, that woman is getting to be a real thorn in our side," she complained. "I was so annoyed when she announced her new Los Angeles facility not even one day after you'd gone out with the publicity about ours in San Francisco.'"

Right with me all the way, pushing me, making me have to get down to shirt-sleeves to keep my company riding high, and now she's actually outgunned me. Grant calmed down a little as the thoughts about Ashley took hold of him, and without answering Karen, he left the desk and walked slowly across the room, slipping his hands in both trouser pockets as he stopped directly in front of the draped window and gazed out.

Karen crossed her arms and leaned against the desk, looking at his motionless back. "I'll tell you, a year ago, I'd never have predicted that Ashley Galbraith could do as well as she has done, much less that she'd have the wherewithal to preempt you on something as important as this," she confided. "Oh, yes, I'd always had a degree of respect for her professional talents, but after that Chilton fiasco, frankly, I'd decided she'd gotten in over her head after all." She frowned again. "I wonder what happened?"

A hell of a businesswoman. "Someone gave her some very good advice," Grant answered absently and narrowed his eyes down to the hotdog vendor setting up his umbrella stand on the street corner below.

"Well, whoever it was ought to be shot," Karen returned darkly.

Grant came to and cast a crooked smile at her over his shoulder. "Oh, I don't know about that," he commented mildly. His gaze drifted back to the window as his momentary amusement faded. "But all the advice in the world isn't worth a damn if you haven't got the capacity to put it into practice. And Ashley has that ability. In excess," he added.

Karen was hearing him with more than one ear now, and frowned quizzically. "Grant, what are you talking about?"

"Nothing. I'm just talking," he murmured.

"Well, so now what do we do?" she asked uncertainly.

Grant lightly jingled the change in his pockets as he remained with his back to her. "I'm going to follow suit, of course. I believe in buyer's premiums. But the thing is," he added ruminatively, "now I've got to decide whether to announce right away and look like I'm scurrying around to play follow the leader, or wait awhile for the dust to settle. Either way I'll *still* play follow the leader." Neatly upstaged no matter which way I turn, he thought. *She's got what it takes.*

Karen was watching his rugged profile, and when she saw his expression grow even more pensive, she pushed herself away from the desk and went to him; she slipped her arm through his, pressing it tightly against her as she studied him worriedly. "You're very upset by this, aren't you?" she asked.

He looked at her across his shoulder. "I'm not thrilled about it, no. But it's not the end of the world. There's nothing to be done about the prestige she'll gain simply by being first, but as far as actually losing business is concerned, I don't see that as a real threat. Pretty soon buyer's premiums are going to be standard practice here just as they are in England. Everybody will be jumping on the bandwagon." A faintly wry smile passed across his face. "I suppose this is really more of a shock to the system than anything else," he added. "Being outdrawn."

Karen was watching him with concern. "Then what *is* wrong?" she pressed. "Something's bothering you, very much."

Grant's eyes stayed on her a moment longer, then went back to the window. Yes, something was bothering him very much: that Ashley suddenly had such a lock-hold on his mind. Damnit, he'd written this kind of preoccupation with her out of his life a year ago; each time he ran into her—so often with her *friend*, Mr. Peter St. John, by her side—he was only reminded how glad he was to be shed of her. He fought against the feeling beginning to nag insistently at him—that he wanted to be alone, to find some solitary place where he could unwind from the tension that had come into him. But he had work to do, things to get busy with. . . .

"Grant?" Karen laid her cheek against his upper arm, smiling up at him imploringly. "Talk to me. Tell me what's on your mind."

He glanced at her, and for one stunning minute, in his vision, the eyes of the woman on his arm switched from brown to violet, the hair from brunette to raven black, the face from oval to one narrower, with chiseled but very soft features. Abruptly, he disengaged himself from Karen and turned to stride back over to his desk.

"Karen, I want you to take over here for the next few days," he instructed as he picked up the telephone and dialed. "Denise has a copy of my schedule. Please look it over and see to what you can."

Karen felt totally confused by Grant's precipitous departure from her, and more disturbed than ever by his enigmatic behavior. " But . . . why?"

Grant didn't respond but instead spoke to the voice that had just answered on the other end of the line, and when he'd completed his call to the upstate New York airport that sheltered *Silver Phoenix*, he replaced the telephone receiver and gave her his attention.

"Because you're going home." She answered her own question, and a leaden dejection swept down over her.

She'd never gone back with Grant to Coconino after that one time, a year before; he'd never asked her to. Yes, they'd had their relationship here in New York, of the nature that she wanted so very much, yet it wasn't really what she wanted. They saw each other exclusively, and there was sexuality between them—thrilling to her, electric—but he'd never once said, "I love you," and she was aware she'd never really *had* him; she could touch him emotionally only to a certain point, and beyond that discernible barrier, she knew, was where the real heart of him lay. She fought back the sudden sting of tears at the thought of his returning once more to his beloved home without her, and forced a smile.

"Coconino must be beautiful in the fall," she said in a light voice that quivered slightly.

Grant merely nodded as he opened his briefcase, checked the contents, then after adding several pieces of mail he hadn't yet attended to, closed it. Karen was still standing by the window, and as she watched him pull the briefcase from the desktop and move away, she said as brightly as she could, "You know, I'm worried about you, flying off like this in the middle of the week."

"Don't be," he answered as he headed for the door, and he grabbed up his overcoat from where he'd flung it onto the chair. "I just have some things on my mind, that's all. They need working out. And there's no better place for clear thinking than Coconino."

She nodded dully, and when Grant had reached the door, stopping there to look back, the businesswoman in her reemerged. "So, what are you going to do about our announcement of buyer's premiums?" she inquired.

"Worry about it when I get back," he answered, pulling open the door. "Rushing to announce right away doesn't get me a thing on the prestige factor, and a few days aren't going to make a critical difference as far as business lost to Galbraith's is concerned, which is the only thing I can try to combat anyway. Consignors aren't going to move that fast, not until they see which way the wind is blowing."

"And when will you be returning?"

"Sunday night. I've got to be back Monday for my appointment with Leland Bartholomew at eleven." He shifted his briefcase to his other hand, and as he started through the door, Karen called out to him quickly.

"At least say good-bye." She gave him a tentative smile as she walked across the room and stopped by his side. "I'll miss you," she said softly.

Grant smiled past his pressing need to be on his way. " 'Bye," he murmured, and after brushing his lips across hers, he was gone.

The ranch house at Coconino was bathed in midafternoon sunlight when the Bronco pulled up in front of it, Nick at the wheel, Grant beside him in his herringbone suit trousers and his flight jacket. Nick had been going over the events at Coconino since Grant's last return home, nearly a month before, as they'd driven from the airstrip back across the property, and after cutting the jeep's engine, he said, "And I took several heifers up to the cattle auction, too." He opened the door and began to slide out. "They brought pretty good prices."

Grant stepped out at the same time and slammed the door.

"I'll look over the sale sheets later," he said as the two men walked together toward the house.

"How long will you be here?" They'd stepped up onto the wooden porch that shaded them from the bright sun, and Nick pushed back his Stetson.

"Until Sunday. And while I'm here, I want to make a run up to Fremont and look at that quarter horse mare you've been talking about," he added. "Save time for that on Saturday."

Nick nodded, and they parted, Nick striding back off the porch, Grant entering the house. He stood briefly in the big living room, taking in the sight and feel of his home, then, after greeting the Redchiefs, he went up immediately to change his clothes. In minutes he was redressed in jeans, yellow plaid shirt, and boots, and settling his Stetson on his head, he strode back out of the house again.

He went directly to the barn, encountering Nick and several of the other ranch hands there. After a few minutes of friendly conversation with them, he headed off to Dakota's stall. Nick separated from the group of men and caught up with Grant at the doorway of the stable. "Going for a ride?" he asked.

Grant nodded, and when he reached Dakota's large box stall, he flipped up the bolt on the door and pulled it open.

"Like some company?" Nick went on.

Grant glanced over at his friend and smiled slightly. "Actually, no. Not this afternoon. I need a little time to myself."

Nick looked at him thoughtfully. "Everything okay?" he ventured after a moment.

Grant entered the dirt-floored enclosure. He hooked a lead shank on Dakota's halter, led him out onto the cement corridor floor, cross-tying him securely to both sides of the aisle, then quickly got down to the business of grooming. Taking up a curry comb from a small tool trunk against the wall, he began making short, brisk sweeps with it across the animal's back. "Yeah, everything's okay," he answered, shooting Nick a look over the horse's back. "I just have some thinking to do, that's all."

Nick could see he didn't want to be pressed, and with a nod, he left. Grant finished brushing down Dakota, tacked him up, and was finally mounted and heading out of the stable paddock toward the range. The sky was clear and cerulean blue, and though, out of habit, Grant eyed his property—the open ground stretching out on all sides, the

mesas in the distance—he was too preoccupied to really pay
attention to what he saw. He let his horse amble along for
awhile, then, feeling the coiled-spring tension still gripping
him, he kicked the animal out into a canter, pushing him
finally into a running gallop. He rode the horse hard until he
could feel him tiring beneath his legs, and bringing him back
down to a walk, continued riding on across the windy plain at
a steady gait.

It was nearly an hour and a half later when he returned to
the barn and stabled the horse again. The ride hadn't relaxed
him as he'd thought it would, and walking moodily across the
yard, he reentered the house through the back door. Michael
and Marina were both in the kitchen, working, and Timothy
was sitting on a tall stool next to the stove. At the sight of
Grant coming through the door, the young Indian boy slid
down off his perch and grinned brightly. "Hi!"

Grant always had a smile of genuine warmth for the engaging child. He stopped by the kitchen table. "Hi," he returned.
"Where were you earlier, when I got here?"

"Homework," Timothy muttered, as he stuck his thumbs
into his jeans pockets and sauntered over. "Been ridin'?"

Grant chuckled to himself at the boy's stance. "Yeah.
When are you going to learn how?" he inquired and cast a
glance up to Marina; she was quietly watching her son's
posturing as she dried a dish in her hand, and when Grant
caught her eye, she smiled.

"I already did," Timothy advised.

Grant propped a booted foot on the corner of the bench at
the table, resting his weight with one forearm on his thigh as
he gave Timothy an interested look. "You did?" he replied
in some surprise. "When?"

Timothy squared his shoulders, smiling with utmost com-
placency. "Yesterday."

"Oh." Grant did his best to keep from laughing outright.
"In one day, huh?"

"Yep."

"Well, I'm proud of you," Grant said earnestly. "I guess
that means you'll be going with Nick and me tomorrow when
we drive the cattle down to the lower pasture."

Timothy's shoulders fell visibly, and he shuffled his feet
for a moment. "Oh, well . . ."

Grant did laugh at that point and let the boy off the hook.
"Maybe next time I come home," he said.

"Sure." Timothy's beaming smile had reappeared, and he looked up at Grant hopefully. "And next time, is that lady coming home with you again, the one who taught me how to hook a halter?" he asked, his eyes glowing. "She was real nice. Pretty."

Grant's boot came off the bench and hit the linoleum floor sharply as he straightened. "Practice up on your riding," he said brusquely, giving Timothy's head a brief pat as he strode across the kitchen; Michael's voice stopped him in the doorway.

"What time would you like dinner, Mr. Copeland?"

"Whenever it's ready, I guess," he said indifferently.

"In an hour, then?"

Grant nodded. "Call me," he said shortly and went on through the house and up the last stairs to his bedroom. Inside, he took off his Stetson and sent it sailing across the room with a flip of his wrist; it landed on the low pine chest under the window.

Is that lady coming home with you again? Everywhere he went today someone had something to say about Ashley, even here in his own home, damnit. Her face rose up before his eyes, and then, seized again by the feeling of pressure in his chest, he slowly crossed over to his bureau, opening a slim drawer. Inside were various personal items, an old leather wallet he hadn't wanted to discard, a case for cuff links, and among an assortment of handkerchiefs, a small white jeweler's box. He stood perfectly still, just looking at it for a time, then finally reached for the box, bringing it out. He opened the lid and turned the container over, letting the objects inside fall into the palm of one hand.

They were the turquoise wedding bands he'd had made for Ashley and himself. The blue stone running all around the outside of each ring was set in silver. They'd been in that box, untouched, for almost two years now, since he'd brought them back from the craftsman on the Navajo reservation and put them away to wait for his and Ashley's wedding day. For some reason, he hadn't gotten rid of them, as he had the crimson gown that had enraged him when he'd seen it hanging in his closet that weekend he'd come home with Karen; he'd been alone in his bedroom, just about to change to honor Karen's request that he take her for a ride across his ranch, and when his eyes had fallen on the dress, he'd jerked it from its hanger, scribbling Ashley's name and address on a piece of paper at his bedroom desk before taking it and the dress downstairs and thrusting them at Michael, instructing the houseman to mail the gown.

He felt the constriction inside him grow more severe as he closed his fingers over the rings, holding them in the tight, possessive grip of his hand, and he looked off toward the narrow brick hearth. Was the problem that he'd never really gotten Ashley out of his system, despite his resolve a year ago that he would, could, and wanted to? Was that what this sudden feeling of being so unsettled, of finding himself totally absorbed with thoughts of her was all about: that deep down he was still in love with her? He opened his hand again, very slowly, looking at the rings, and then the memory of a line of newsprint intruded. . . . *pleased that he seems to have been slower in appreciating the significance of what has been happening in England.* Still love her? Christ. What was the matter with him? He had no love for her any longer. She'd done nothing but insult, hurt, or turn on him in one way or another since the very first moment he'd met her, and she was still at it, more openly than ever.

Angrily, he dropped the rings back into the box, tossing it again into the bureau and slamming the drawer on it. Ashley was one for the books all right, a real study in emotional inconstancy. His problem wasn't that she stirred some old feeling in him but simply that she aggravated him to the point of distraction.

He gazed restlessly out the window then, at the few maples he'd planted along the fence line that were blanketed now in the rusty gold colors of autumn, and he remembered Karen's comment about Coconino in the fall and considered again what a mistake it had been to bring her here, that time a year ago; he'd had a sense when she was here of everything being out of place, the serenity of his home somehow being disrupted the moment he'd ushered her through the door, and he'd known right then that she'd never be coming back.

He admitted to himself that the feeling that he needed to end his affair with Karen had been coming on him for a long time. He enjoyed her company, yes, but he'd never really been happy with her, and suddenly his discontent seemed doublefold. He caught sight of his face in the dresser mirror as he passed by on the way to the shower.

"You certainly seem to have a lot of that in your life at the moment, Copeland. Discontent, complications," he silently said to his reflection. "A heavy relationship you have to find some way of getting out of as painlessly as you can, and a jolt from Mrs. Galbraith you hadn't expected." His expression darkened. "Okay, Ashley. You've learned how to go after my business, but you're *not* going to get it."

He had to acknowledge, though, that she was handing him the stiffest competition he'd ever faced. And that thought didn't improve his mood at all.

Chapter 35

ASHLEY'S MEETING WITH Leland Bartholomew lasted precisely seventeen minutes. He was a very short man, in his fifties, dapper-looking in his snappy blue blazer, gray slacks, and pince-nez glasses, and he escorted Ashley into his spartan office and toward a chair, went around behind his desk to perch on the edge of his own seat and say what he had to say, then rose again to lead her out, in the same, almost remote-control way he'd brought her in: with a hand held a fraction of an inch behind her back, urging her forward. The only opportunity Ashley had to open her mouth was at the threshold of the door on the way out.

"But, Mr. Bartholomew——"

"I know you're disappointed, Mrs. Galbraith," he interrupted with a perfectly modulated smile of regret. "But Mrs. Maynard is firm in her position, as I told Mr. Copeland earlier today. She feels that the most auspicious and profitable disposal of her inheritance is through a sale conducted on the property with everything going at once under the management of a single firm, and unfortunately neither Galbraith's nor DuBrand's has full competence to do the job properly. We would prefer an auction, but under the circumstances, we have no choice but to give everything over to private dealers." He smiled carefully again, blinking twice.

And then she was out in the hall, Leland Bartholomew's door shut firmly behind her.

Dazed, breathless, and totally deflated, Ashley immediately left the midtown office building and returned to Galbraith's by cab, arriving at the bronze revolving doors on Park Avenue not even forty-five minutes after she'd passed through them on her way out to the meeting, brimming then with ebullient optimism. She went back through them now at a leaden gait, going in search of Ollie and locating him finally in the portal of the auction room where he stood watching as Francis Barclay conducted that afternoon's sale of jewelry. When he glanced absently across his shoulder and caught sight of Ashley walking slowly toward him down the carpeted hallway, her slim figure outfitted in the sophisticated black suit and white high-necked blouse she'd bought especially for the important occasion, he started visibly. "I didn't expect you for at least another hour," he said when she reached his side, then bloomed into an attitude of eagerness. "So, did we get it?" he inquired quickly.

Ashley smiled mechanically at two customers passing by on their way into the busy sale room, before turning a somber expression to Ollie. "No," she answered.

His face fell. "DuBrand's did."

"No."

He frowned in sharp puzzlement at that, and Ashley took his arm then, leading him away from the doorway and upstairs to the board room where they would have more privacy than in her office. Once inside, she slumped down into a chair at the side of the long table, and with her frustration and despondency openly showing, she proceeded to recount what Bartholomew had had to say: that although Galbraith's was a fine firm, able to masterfully supervise the selling of the furnishings and artwork in Mr. Maynard's estate, he was sure Ashley had no previous experience at auctioning real property, and that, though DuBrand's was a splendid organization with proven capabilities in sales of high-priced real estate and heirloom furniture, Mr. Copeland's auctions of paintings by the Old Masters such as the Rembrandts and Botticellis in Henry Maynard's collection just didn't do as well as Galbraith's, where record prices got set.

"That's the most absurd thing I've ever heard, that neither of the two top auction houses in the country is qualified to handle this sale!" Ollie exploded when Ashley had finished quoting everything the punctilious executor had told her, and he paced agitatedly back and forth alongside the table, his brow knit in a deep frown of disbelief. "Previous experience or not, we could pull off a sale of the house and grounds just fine, and Grant's artwork auctions aren't quite the disappointments Bartholomew and Mrs. Maynard would have them."

Ashley was sitting glumly with her elbow propped on the table, her chin cupped in her hand. "I know that and you know that, but try telling those two. Try telling them anything! Or Leland Bartholomew, anyway," she muttered in some annoyance at the high-handed treatment she'd been given. "After all these months of waiting, to find out it's no go for a reason like this! Oh, and Mr. Bartholomew told me he'd consented to see Grant and me, even though he and Mrs. Maynard had made up their minds to go with dealers, because we'd both 'pressed him so hard.' " She cast Ollie a nettled look. "I haven't yet figured out whether that was a compliment or a complaint."

"Surely there must be *something* we can do," Ollie insisted.

Ashley sighed again and stood up, wearily at this point. "No, there isn't. Mrs. Maynard stands firm in her opinion that neither Galbraith's nor DuBrand's makes the grade." She listlessly started for the door. "I've got some things to do," she said. "I don't feel like talking about this anymore right now. I'll be in my office."

"Oh, Ashley, one thing before you go." Ollie's voice was as dispirited as hers. "While you were out I interviewed a woman, Jenna Wainwright. She wants to work for us, in a sort of part-time public relations capacity. She's a socialite, some distant cousin of Ben Geary's, in fact, and she suggested that her contacts within wealthy circles might be useful to us." A trace of his customary buoyancy had returned as he talked. "It's an intriguing concept, actually, having a staff member on the inside track. And I liked her. Though she didn't pretend she's going to dedicate most of her time to a career, she seemed genuinely interested in doing this and gave the impression of a certain enthusiastic determination. Shall I give her a chance?"

"Sure. What can it hurt?" Ashley murmured, then forced a smile. "It's a good idea, Ollie." She left him then and walked across the hall to her office.

It had been completely redecorated in the preceding months, to her own simpler taste. Ashley had sent the Galbraith family antiques to the museum in Westchester, and the furniture in the room now consisted of traditional Sheraton chairs upholstered in muted tapestry-like fabrics, a stylish olive green suede couch with an oval table in front of it, and the draperies at the windows flanking her oak desk were wine-colored antique satin instead of gold brocade. Replacing the portrait of William Galbraith that had always hung on the wall above the couch was a small Renoir of two women feeding birds from a park bench. Ashley had just stepped behind her desk when Christine came in with several slips of paper in her hand.

"Telephone messages while you were gone, Mrs. Galbraith," she advised.

"Thanks, Chris."

Christine nodded and started to turn away. Stopping, she looked back around with a light smile. "Oh, Mrs. Galbraith, I was getting some of the filing out of the way in here while you were gone, and I didn't know if you wanted to keep that copy of Thursday's *Times* on your desk." She nodded toward the newspaper set beside the wooden in-box. "Shall I throw it out?"

Although Ashley had tensed the moment the paper was mentioned, she managed to give her secretary a smile of unconcern. "No, that's all right. I—I'll dispose of it."

Christine nodded again and headed for the door. Ashley remained standing behind her desk with every appearance of calm as she watched the young woman leave, and when at last Christine had disappeared into the outer office, she allowed herself to dissolve into distress, and sank down into her chair.

The newspaper. Was she saving it or simply unable to throw it away? Unable to throw it away, she thought as she looked at the paper containing the article about her buyer's premiums, at the end of which was her quoted comment about Grant. Quoted comment? It was nothing of the sort, but a horrendous case of words literally being put into her mouth! She'd never expressed about Grant the sentiments that had been attributed to her; what she'd done was be foolhardy enough to speak to that reporter when he'd called the previous Wednesday afternoon. He'd been an especially artful, cajoling newsman, and had obviously hoped to inject some color into his article by alluding to the rivalry between the two top auction firms. Surely she must be pleased, he'd suggested, that Grant Copeland, usually so innovative, had failed to act first. Wasn't it true that he'd left the way open for Galbraith's to gain the esteem that would naturally come to the auctioneer who originated a new commission structure in this country? Well, she'd said, she *was* pleased that Galbraith's had led the field, but as for the rest, that wasn't the way she would put it. But wasn't it fair to say, Mrs. Galbraith, that Grant Copeland had failed to pick up on Appleby's success with buyer's premiums? No, she'd insisted, if anything he'd simply been more cautious. Ah, I see. Well, Mrs. Galbraith, thank you very much. Good-bye.

"You were like a damn schoolgirl, led into every word," Ashley muttered to the mental replay of her ineffectual handling of the smooth newsman, and yet at the time she'd thought she'd answered him very firmly.

Her hands were trembling slightly as she picked up a long, typed memo to try to read it, but she dropped the paper almost immediately and simply stared at it. What everyone must have thought of her when they saw—*thought* they saw—that she would go out publicly with an insult like that about someone! What Grant must have thought when he read the line. Complacent . . . snide. Bitch. Her chin came up as a small cry involuntarily escaped her, and she smoothed the soft lock of hair across her forehead several times before looking at the telephone. She would call him, apologize, explain, that's what. As she'd done at least six times a day, every day since Thursday, she reached over and started to pick up the phone. And as she'd also done all those times, she imagined Grant's response to the announcement of her call.

Tell her to go to hell.

Her fingers slipped away from the phone, and with a stifled feeling rising in her chest, she propped her elbow on the desk blotter and put her head in her hands.

At his apartment, Grant was sitting on the couch staring at the coffee table, still dressed in the dark pinstriped suit and blue shirt he'd worn for his meeting with Leland Bartholomew that morning. He had returned to the office after his brief conference with the Maynard executor but had been completely unable to concentrate on anything with the aggravating appointment so much on his mind, and he'd finally given up and come home, tired, edgy, and disgusted.

He propped his elbows on his knees and moodily studied the issue of *Business Week* lying on the mahogany surface of the coffee table. The diminuitive man representing Cathleen Maynard had irked Grant no end with his prim, cavalier manner, which had offered Grant no opportunity whatsoever to speak for DuBrand's, but he'd put aside his annoyance at Bartholomew's personal demeanor. Save it for what the man had had to say, Grant, he told himself, and finally got up from the couch and went over to the bar to mix himself a stiff drink.

It was a ridiculous premise that he wouldn't be able to handle the artwork portion of the estate as well as Galbraith's, as ridiculous as it was to suggest that Galbraith's would fall down on the property end; Mrs. Maynard was just wearing blinders, bowled over by Ashley's fortuitous sale of a Rembrandt a month before, and putting too much emphasis on how much of a specialty real estate sales might be. Because of one woman's opinionated misconceptions, everyone was going to lose out on a monumental sale, he thought disagreeably, and moved away from the bar, raising his highball glass to his mouth.

"Cut Galbraith's and DuBrand's down the middle and stick the two halves together. Then maybe the woman would be satisfied."

Grant's glass stopped just short of his lips and he stood stock still as the echo of the flippant remark hung in the air. The import of it held him immobile for seconds, and then, completely unaware of what he was doing, he turned and began to wander around the living room.

Take half of DuBrand's, half of Galbraith's, and put them together. Then you'd have one auction house capable of meeting with Cathleen Maynard's full approval. It was unheard of, two rival companies working together on a single sale, but it certainly solved the problems.

It would mean that he'd have to work side by side with Ashley, every day, for the duration of what would probably be a month-long project.

"Not on your life!" His voice cut into the silence of the room, and Grant drained his drink in two swallows. Hell would freeze over before he'd subject himself to Ashley's full-time company; the alliance of the two firms was a sound idea from a practical point of view but totally out of the question because of Ashley. He went into the kitchen to scout around for some lunch, and moments later found himself chewing on a piece of cold chicken, with no memory of having taken it from the refrigerator.

Half of something or all of nothing, Grant, take your choice.

"I have no intention of hooking up with Ashley Galbraith in any way, shape, or form," Grant said aloud, and headed back to the living room to pour himself another drink.

Even if it means the loss to DuBrand's of hundreds of thousands of dollars? What kind of self-respecting businessman are you, anyway?

"Oh, hell," Grant muttered finally. He knew there was only one thing he could do.

Chapter 36

ASHLEY WAS DOWNSTAIRS in the supply room, conferring with Jeff Payson, when Christine came to tell her that Grant Copeland was here to see her. Ashley looked at the secretary in blank amazement for a moment, a stock clipboard held motionlessly in one hand, and then all of a sudden she went hot and cold simultaneously. The newspaper comment. Grant had been so incensed by it that he'd finally been moved to come and berate her face to face. Trepidation swept over Ashley, and a sudden nervous smile flickered across her face.

"Thank you, Chris," she answered, and handing the clipboard back to the stock manager, she excused herself quickly and hurried upstairs to the administrative offices, stopping just outside the door of the reception room. She stood there for a minute, brushing the hair back at her temples, pulling up the lacy ruffle at the neck of her blouse, and after running her hands down the sides of her skirt, trying to rid them of their clamminess, she raised her chin slightly and walked as calmly as she could through the door.

Grant was standing by the magazine table in the far corner of the narrow waiting area outside Ashley's office, flipping through a copy of *Omni*, and when he saw Ashley entering, he dropped the magazine immediately back on the stack of reading material; his face as he looked at her was devoid of all expression. "I'd like to talk to you if you have a minute," he said.

She nodded stiffly. "Yes. Come in." She went blindly past Christine's desk, and closed the door of her office behind them, standing for a minute with her back to him. Finally, she turned around, her hands clasped tightly at her waist. "Grant, I know why you're here," she said without preamble. "It's about that comment in the paper on Thursday."

"No, that isn't why I'm here," he answered curtly. "I want to discuss the Maynard estate with you."

Ashley was momentarily thrown off balance, but recovered and moved into the room, her expression intently earnest.

"Well, Grant, I'd like to talk about the newspaper article. You see—"

"Skip it," he interrupted. "I didn't come here to get into any kind of personal conversation with you. This is strictly business."

Ashley couldn't give up that easily. "Grant, I didn't make that comment," she persisted. "I would never publicly insult anyone like that, and what got printed was not something I'd ever said about you. It was a reporter's twisting of things."

"Ashley, leave it alone," Grant responded in sudden, sharp annoyance. "What was said, implied, or anything else is totally irrelevant."

"No, it isn't!" she insisted. "Grant, please listen to me," she entreated, and Grant looked at her face a moment longer, then abruptly turned to the window. "I want you to know what really happened," she went on and walked to the center of the room, stopping several feet back from him. "The reporter called here last Wednesday, and I did talk to him, but . . . it was an incredible conversation. He was the one who kept suggesting the derogatory statements, and I got led into answers that seemed to confirm the sentiments as my own. But they weren't."

Grant didn't say anything at all but simply stood like a statue, staring out the window overlooking Park Avenue. Ashley pressed her lips together for a moment, then tried again: "Grant, that is what happened," she pressed. "Words got put into my mouth, and I wasn't able to handle the man's slick manner the way I meant to," she admitted. "I hung up the phone knowing I'd denied all those insinuations, but the next morning I—" Ashley took a step nearer. "Grant, will you please say something?"

At that, he turned around slowly, slipping one hand into his trouser pocket as he regarded her blandly. "Can we go on now, to what I came here to discuss?"

"Grant! You don't believe me at all, do you? I'm trying to tell you exactly what happened, but you're not even listening! You don't *want* to. I'm being reasonable, but you're just standing there with a totally closed mind, stone deaf to me when I try to make you understand that this wasn't my doing but simply a—a *mistake*, for God's sake!"

There was a ringing silence in the room as Grant didn't move a muscle, and then he said finally, in a low, bitter voice, "How does it feel, Ashley?"

"I—" Ashley had already heard herself and stood stock still by the desk, hardly able even to see Grant anymore as the room spun around her. She was aware, however, when he abruptly strode away from the window and crossed the room in the direction of the door. Putting a dazed hand to her temple, the other on the desk behind her to steady herself, she said hazily, "Wait."

The muscles were working tensely in his jaw, and he put his hand on the doorknob, looking back over his shoulder at her. "We're through here, Ashley. Forget I came!" he answered harshly.

"No." She forced herself to think beyond her distress and extended a hand unconsciously. "What about the Maynard estate?" she asked. "I don't see what there could be to discuss."

Grant needed to get out, away from her, but he'd come here for an important reason. *Business, Grant; remember it.* He finally dropped his hand from the door, turning slowly to face her again. "I know you had an appointment with Leland Bartholomew today," he said in a monotone. "He told me you were coming. And I know you were advised of all the same things I was, that they won't give the sale to either of us."

She nodded mutely.

"We don't have to lose the sale," Grant stated.

Ashley became fully alert at that, and frowned at him in deep perplexity as she stepped away from the desk. "I don't see how you can say that," she answered slowly. "As far as Leland Bartholonew and Mrs. Maynard are concerned, neither Galbraith's nor DuBrand's could pull off a sale to their satisfaction."

Grant propped a hand on his hip, drawing back the flap of his suit jacket as he looked at her, the residue of an angry frown on his brow. "No, but DuBrand's *and* Galbraith's could."

She regarded him stupidly. "*And?*" she echoed.

"Look, Ashley," he said, resignation in his tone then, and he walked part way back into the room. "We can both get nothing from this sale or we can have at least part of the profits if we team up. A partnership would cover all the so-called deficiencies," he said. "I'm not anxious to lose out on this estate, and I can't believe you are either. I don't see how either of us can let it pass us by."

Ashley looked away, deep in thought. The concept stunned her, but it was a very intriguing idea, very sound. "What kind of split did you have in mind?" she asked, looking back at him.

"Fifty-fifty."

She nodded almost unconsciously. "On profits, expenses, advertising, everything," she murmured.

"That's right."

"I'm not sure Bartholomew would go for it. Or Cathleen Maynard, either," she said.

"There's only one way to find out." He walked over to Ashley's desk, putting his hand on the telephone. "Do I call him for a meeting of the three of us?"

He wasn't smiling at her or even speaking in hopeful inquiry; he was simply asking. Ashley studied him for another moment, then finally nodded. "Yes."

He picked up the phone, dialed the number from a small address book he pulled from his inside jacket pocket, and after a brief conversation with the Maynard executor, hung up. "All right. He'll hear us out," he advised, slipping the address book back into his jacket. "Tomorrow. At ten-thirty."

He was on his way back to the door, and Ashley looked at him as he passed by her. "Where shall I meet you?" she asked.

He pulled open the door. "There," he said, and walked out.

By the time Grant was gone, the gripping tension Ashley had been suppressing had exhausted her, and she went immediately to her desk, collected her purse, and left the office. She stopped at Christine's desk only long enough to advise the secretary she was leaving for the day, asking the young woman to relay the message to Ollie, and then she hurried out of the building. She caught a cab home, in the space of five minutes changing from her work clothes into jeans and a bulky fisherman's sweater, and she left the house again immediately, getting into her silver Jaguar and turning on her headlights against the early darkness as she pulled away from the curb.

It took her an hour to make the trip up to Westchester that she knew so well, and when she pulled into the gravel driveway of Shadow Knolls, night had fallen completely. The four aluminum buildings of Andrew's riding stable were lit up brightly, however, as Ashley had known they would be, and leaving her car in the lot, she quickly walked across the grounds in the direction of the farthest stable, where Sharif's stall was.

"Ashley!" Andrew called out to her as she was passing by the dusty indoor riding ring, open on both ends. Music was playing loudly as a team of eight dressage riders put their horses through the collected paces of the equestrian routines, and he ducked under the bar across the wide, open doorway and came toward her with an eager stride. "You're a pleasant and totally unexpected sight," he said, his smile wide as he came up to her. "I thought you might get up on the weekend, but I didn't expect you on a Monday evening. How about giving an old friend a hand with the dressage?" he invited.

Ashley's smile was strained. "Another time, Andrew. I . . . have things on my mind, and I came up here for a little by-myself time." Her smile asked for understanding.

"Sure, Ashley. Sharif's in his stall. He'll be glad to see you, too," he added before giving her shoulder a friendly pat and returning to the ring.

Ashley continued on, and when she reached the big box stall, it was as if Sharif had been expecting her; he was standing with his handsome black head out over the bottom half of the stall door, alertly watching the corridor, and he nickered when Ashley came up and laid a gentle hand on his neck.

"Hi, babe," she said softly as she unlatched the door, went in, then rehooked it behind her. She stood right by the horse's head for a time, crooning to him quietly as he sniffed her fingertips held out to stroke his downy muzzle, and then as the thoughts she'd been holding fragilely at bay until she could at last reach the solitude of her thinking place pressed in on her, she left Sharif's side and went over to hoist herself up onto the feed bin, a wooden shelf set into one corner of the stall. And she just sat there, her head resting back against the slatted wall, her hands quiet in her lap, her eyes closed.

I didn't do it. It was a mistake. Oh, how earnestly Grant had said those words more than a year and a half ago, and how deaf she'd been to them, just as he'd been today when she'd uttered the very same ones. She remembered what she'd said to Margaret, not even a week ago, and swallowed. *He runs that company with an iron hand. It couldn't have slipped by him.*

Pain was etched all over Ashley's face as she opened her eyes and put her face in her hands. There was nothing in all that Ross had suffered that Grant had been to blame for, not the losses, not the final blow. She had wronged him, misjudged him, denied him, condemned him.

She raised bleak eyes to Sharif standing off in the corner of the stall, nibbling audibly at his pile of alfalfa hay, and she knew that she'd finally come face to face with the moment she'd been avoiding for so long: that confrontation with herself as to just why she'd so readily and easily condemned Grant.

Your own damn guilt. A thundering quaking rose up within her as she heard the echo of Grant's voice raised in anger to her, and pressing her hand across her mouth, she slid down off the feed shelf, going over to Sharif. She was blinking rapidly, fear in her eyes as she stroked the horse's long, velvety neck several times, and then abruptly she threw herself against him, clinging tightly to his neck as if her hold on him might keep her from plunging down into the fire of self-acknowledgement.

Yes, her easy blaming of Grant—all of this—had been because of her own guilty feelings: that she'd never really loved Ross even after everything he'd done for her, that she'd fallen in love with the man who'd become his nemesis, slept with him, been with him when Ross had suffered the heart attack she might've contributed to—so many guilts, she'd almost lost count. And then there was the hurt. More of the angry altercation with Grant that day in his apartment so long ago raced through her mind—the insults he'd flung at her, the door he'd slammed.

"Hurt. Oh, Ashley you were *so* hurt." She spoke in a bitter, derisive voice as she stepped back from Sharif, dropping her hands from around his neck. "You were so wounded, even though you'd inspired Grant's retaliation, and you nursed your hurt, dwelled on it—so self-righteous about it, all the while you were never even looking at the hurt you kept handing out to him." Images of Grant in pain washed across her eyes as she walked back over to the feed bin, propping her elbows on the lipped surface to rest her head in both hands, and a shattering picture came to her: of Grant as he'd stood in front of her on those dreary, windy cemetery grounds, gripping her arms while he'd looked down into her eyes, asking, *begging* her to believe in him; he'd needed so much from her then but all she'd had for him had been the most unforgiving censure. She'd had a kind word, a gentle touch for everyone but Grant, and he was the one person in all the world she should've held uppermost in her heart, stood by, comforted. How he must have suffered when Ross had died because of an error he'd been connected with!

She laid her head down and cried. What kind of person was she that she was too weak to shoulder those difficult emotions herself but had to shift the burden of them to someone else? And that's what she did: threw them all onto Grant's back so that—what? She didn't have to be in the wrong or at least feel in the wrong? Oh, there was laudable compassion for another human being mixed in with it all, sweet sincerity of conviction, however foolish it might've been. There was some nobility to her, in all that contemptible weakness.

She sobbed for a long, long time; Sharif came over to her finally, curiously nudging at her neck, and at length, the creaking of the stall door as it opened, then closed again, whined into the chilly stillness.

"Ashley?" Andrew walked across the darkened enclosure to her, his eyes heavy with concern, and he laid a hand gently on her shoulder. "What's the matter?"

Ashley raised her head slowly, wiping the wetness away from her eyes with the cuff of her coat sleeve. "Grant at least always has a handkerchief to offer," she said with a jagged little laugh.

Andrew studied her tear-stained face worriedly. "Something happen?"

She looked down at the straw-littered dirt floor. "I don't like what I see when I look inside myself," she answered with a strained voice.

He smiled kindly. "I can't believe that." He cocked his head as if to look into her downcast face. "Want to talk about it?" he asked quietly.

Ashley's eyes were weary as they came back up to meet his. "It's a long, very complicated story," she sighed. "Suffice it to say that I've treated the man I love shamefully." The man I love. Oh, how easily it was said. And felt. Ashley had a vision of Margaret's sympathetic, knowing eyes and smiled with bittersweet sorrow. Yes, Margaret, she told her friend silently, I've been in love with him all along; I still am and always will be. He's my life, the rest of my soul.

Andrew was watching her. "We all do things we're not proud of sometimes," he offered in consolation.

"Yes, we do. And have to learn to live with them and go on," Ashley answered tiredly, thrusting her hands into the pockets of her jeans, and she turned to look down toward the cobwebbed corner of the stall.

Andrew nodded, then after a time said, "I don't know what you've done, or think you've done, but you know, you can always make things up to him."

Ashley laughed harshly as she raised her dismal eyes to him. "Make it up to him? I'm not sure I ever really could. But even if I wanted to try, it wouldn't be any use. He once loved me very deeply, but I—he doesn't anymore," she answered, swallowing the final words.

"Are you so certain of that? It takes an awful lot to kill real love, you know."

Ashley gave him a searching look. "Oh, Andrew, if only I could believe that maybe there *was* still some feeling in him for me, somewhere!" *Yours never died, even though you'd tried to make yourself believe it had, acted as if it had.* Hope fluttered inside her as she continued to study Andrew's face intently. "I just don't know, Andrew," she said uncertainly. "I've hurt him so many times, and he, uh, has another woman in his life now." The knife-thrust of jealousy cut into her, and she despised herself for the emotion. She had no right to feel it; she'd been the one who'd thrown Grant away. "I'd like to try to talk to him, to tell him that I understand now, that I want him back, but . . ." She pressed her lips together. "I'm not sure he'd accept any overtures I might make to him."

"Well, you'll never know until you try," Andrew rejoined.

"No, you don't understand, Andrew. He wouldn't give me any openings whatsoever."

"Well, then I guess you'll have to make your own openings," Andrew commented matter-of-factly as he lounged up against the stall door. At Ashley's expression of hesitancy, he cocked an eyebrow. "What's the matter, girl? You too good to take the lead?"

She let out a breath. "Andrew, taking the lead is one thing. What I'd have to do is more like . . . like . . . running after him!" she said in a fretful rush.

"Well?"

Ashley looked away, shifting uncomfortably.

"How much does it mean to you, Ashley, to have this man?" he asked gently.

"Everything," she whispered as her eyes went back to him intently.

"Then go after him."

Ashley held his look for another moment, then all of a sudden leaned forward and planted a kiss on his cheek, a shimmering smile appearing on her face. "Thank you," she said and began to fish in her pocket for her car keys.

"For what?" he inquired mildly, following slowly as Ashley hurriedly crossed the large stall to the door.

"For being so wise," she answered. "And for always being my friend," she added softly.

Chapter 37

"MR. COPELAND, MRS. GALBRAITH, I shall expect to hear from you within the next few days about the exact terms of your commission structures and how you will be proceeding with the sales," Leland Bartholomew said.

It was eleven-fifteen the next morning, and the three of them were standing in the threshold of Bartholomew's office door. Their meeting had been concluded, the proposal for joint participation by Galbraith's and DuBrand's in an auction of the Maynard property accepted, and as Bartholomew shared a final handshake with Grant, he looked at Ashley.

"I'm pleased that there has been a satisfactory way to settle this matter," he stated.

"So are we," Ashley returned with a warm smile. "And I know you won't be disappointed."

Grant and Ashley turned and walked side by side to the elevator. "Now we have to get organized," Grant commented as he reached out, hit the "down" button, then stepped back.

Ashley was tense as she stood next to him, one hand tightly holding the edge of her purse tucked under her arm; she'd gotten little if any sleep the night before, tossing and turning with the lingering drag of Peter's reaction to her breakup with him—she'd called him just after she'd returned home from Shadow Knolls, telling him, as gently as she could, that it was better if they didn't see each other anymore except about matters of Ross's estate—and with her contemplation of what lay ahead of her with Grant. She glanced at him nervously, wondering just how he was going to receive her overtures, and as she imagined them being met with nothing—or worse, open rebuffs—not only did her heart contract in anguish but her pride reasserted itself. Pride? she thought with a sharp frown of self-reproof. And just how, Ashley, can you possibly let the bruising of your pride be a worry? Grant had his share, too, but he'd certainly put his own behind him more than once, when he went on reaching out for you despite all the stinging rejection you kept giving back in return. Pain for the way she'd treated him for so long washed over her again in a harsh, debilitating wave, but she forced it away from her and steeled herself to look over at him with a light smile.

"We can go to my office," she offered.

The door on the elevator opened, and Grant let her precede him into the car. "It doesn't matter," he answered as they began their descent. "We could just as well go to mine."

Ashley laughed slightly. "Grant, we're going to have to establish some kind of routine here!" she said. "We can't forever be trying to decide where we'll meet. I don't know how you handle your on-site sales, but I usually establish a temporary office on the premises. It saves a lot of wasted time and energy."

"I was going to suggest we do that," he responded with a matter-of-fact look. "And we also have to choose the staff we're going to use for this project, as a first priority."

She nodded. "I'll make up a list when I get back to the office. You do the same. Who's your best cataloguer?" she inquired, despising the question as soon as it was out; she already knew the answer.

"Karen," he returned mildly.

Ashley studied the slate gray floor of the elevator for a brief minute, then with a smile very firmly in place looked up again. "Put her on the list," she said promptly. "I have several people. They're equally competent. I'll have to give some thought as to who'd work best on this sale."

They left the elevator and walked out the main door onto Fifth Avenue. It was a blustery day, with the promise of rain in the air, and cutting through the stream of pedestrians walking in both directions along the sidewalk, they went to the curb; Grant raised an arm to flag them a cab.

"I think we ought to get up to the house as soon as possible and take a look around." Ashley raised her voice above the noise of automobile horns and a jack hammer cutting into the pavement not far away, and as the wind gusted up, she closed her coat collar around her throat with one hand. "By the end of the week we should have everything set up to get started," she added.

Grant answered back across his shoulder as he kept his arm lifted. "I'd like to be settled in up there by Friday, at the latest," he concurred. "And are we meeting at your office or mine today?"

Ashley laughed again in frustration. "Grant, I don't care! All right," she declared pertly then. "I'll be decisive." Grant looked around to her at that, and meeting his eyes directly, she gave him a warm smile. "We'll go to mine."

A cab pulled over to Grant's signal just then, and dropping his arm, he reached over and opened the back door. He held it for her, motioning her inside, and still smiling, Ashley got in and slid over immediately to make room for him; he reclosed the door and leaned down to speak to her through the window. "I'll be at your office later, around three-thirty," he said, then straightened and walked away.

Henry Maynard's home in Tarrytown, New York, sat directly overlooking the Hudson River, just below the Tappan Zee Bridge. It was a huge, white colonial-style structure with twin brick chimneys jutting up on either side of the shingled roof, and a sweeping gravel drive cut through the manicured lawns, curving around by the pillared portico shading the double front doors. There was a magnificent view of the river beyond a line of trees just at the edge of the palisades, and acres of green meadowland surrounded the estate, broken up behind the house by a long stretch of formal English gardens, in the center of which had been placed a pool. By Friday, the combined staff of Galbraith's and DuBrand's was on the premises, busily at work getting started on the mammoth task of identifying, tagging, cataloguing, photographing, and appraising the multitude of priceless objects inside the house.

The temporary office had been located in the billiard room on the second floor. It was a bright, sunny room with windows on three sides, and everything needed for the preparation of the auctions had been brought there: typewriters, reference books, supplies of paper, pens, pencils, sundries of every description. All the valuables had been removed from the room, and the furniture had been replaced by two office desks and an old couch and chair from the attic. That Friday morning, the makeshift headquarters was the scene of constant activity, and Ashley and Grant were standing together in front of one of the desks as they went over a twelve-page list of things to do. They'd put it together during their meetings over the past several days, either at her office or his, also drawing up preliminary financial breakdowns and setting up staff assignments.

". . . and if we're going to pull this off in four weeks'

time the way Leland Bartholomew and Cathleen Maynard are pushing us to, we'll have to forgo a few of the things we'd talked about doing with the catalogues," Ashley was saying as she looked at Grant.

Like everyone else scattered throughout the house, they were dressed in casual clothing for the sometimes dusty physical work entailed in the project. Grant had one hand in the back pocket of his jeans as he took the list from Ashley, and he studied it with a contemplative frown. "I hate to do that," he answered.

"Yes, I know." Ashley sighed as she moved away and began pacing thoughtfully. "But I don't see what other choice we have," she went on. "I've been giving everything a lot of thought, and I think we were being a little over-optimistic about just what we could accomplish in so short a time." She turned and gave him a feeling look. "God knows, the picture-taking itself is going to require days, even with several photographers working!"

Grant conceded that with an incline of his head, tossing the list onto the desk. He sat down on the edge, folding his arms across his chest as he watched Ashley continue to move around the room, deeply absorbed with the matter. "So, what did you have in mind doing?" he inquired mildly.

"Well, I think we might have to skip the full write-up on Henry Maynard. And if we forget doing a separate catalogue for the silver and combine it with the porcelains brochure, that'll help too. It's not a lot, but it eases the burden, and I don't think those changes will make a big difference, do you?" she said with a quick glance back at him.

Grant mulled it over. "No, probably not," he agreed at length. "But I still want to keep everything full color."

"Yes, of course." Ashley smiled absently as she glanced through one of the windows out to the verdant lawns stretching down toward the wooded river's edge. Grant remained sitting on the desk, studying her in her low-heeled leather shoes that somehow made her seem all legs—gazelle-like—her crisply pressed jeans, the white knit shirt that lightly hugged the contours of her full breasts and dipped in with her slender waist. His eyes went then to her profile, a sharply defined silhouette against the bright outdoor light, and then catching himself suddenly in the lingering appraisal, he uncrossed his arms and abruptly got to his feet, glowering; turning around, he picked up the list, immersing himself in it immediately.

At the window, the ghost of a frown had come to Ashley's face also; she was unsure about the best way to lead into the matter very much on her mind, and finally deciding there was nothing to do but approach it head-on, she turned around. She hesitated briefly as she studied Grant's back, then said, "You know, Grant, we haven't yet addressed the subject of whether or not we're going to use buyer's premiums in this sale."

Grant's head rose slowly and he put the list down on the desk, but he didn't look around. "I know," he answered.

Ashley bit her lip at the unencouraging response, then waded on carefully. "It's standard procedure now for Galbraith's," she said, tilting her head as she smiled tentatively. "I'd hate very much to break it."

"I'm sure you would!" He turned around then and smiled grimly. "That would be interrupting your moment of glory, backing away from the pleasant one-up on the competition, wouldn't it?" he added silkily.

"Grant!" Ashley nearly rushed across the room to him, to throw her arms around him and tell him that the very last thing in the world she wanted to do anymore was hurt him professionally. It was true, however, that she and Galbraith's were gaining a great deal of favorable publicity from the move to buyer's premiums, and she doubted he would believe her protests. Besides, his angry antagonism was an effective barrier. "Grant, it doesn't really matter that much," she dismissed. "We don't have to use the buyer's premiums if you don't—"

"We'll use them." His manner had gone abruptly impersonal, and he left the desk to walk over to a pile of cartons set precariously one on top of another near the door; though the shadow of a frown remained on his face, his tone was unemotional as he began to restack the boxes and continued talking. "Eight percent. That's the figure you're using, and the one I'll be charging at DuBrand's first thing Monday morning. There's no reason for you not to know about it. It'll be all over the papers by tomorrow." His frown deepened just slightly as he tossed the last box into place and added, "I've been planning to use buyer's premiums for a long time and would've announced it soon even if you hadn't."

Ashley blinked, then suddenly understood: She'd preempted his own intention to begin the practice. And that had made him madder than hell with her. *Get off the subject, Ashley. Now.*

"Fine. Eight percent," she agreed with a brisk smile. "Grant, there's another thing that's been on my mind to discuss with you," she said. "I think you ought to be the one to take care of all the advertising."

He frowned questioningly. "Why?"

Ashley's eyes shifted away from him for only the briefest second before returning. "Because I think you'll do the best job of it, that's why," she answered softly. "DuBrand's ads always seem to have a touch more flair to them than Galbraith's."

Grant was perfectly silent for a moment, then slowly crossed his arms again and cocked an eyebrow. "Okay, Ashley," he said, "what's the kicker?"

She frowned uncomprehendingly. "Kicker?" she repeated.

His unpleasant smile returned. "Stroking like this from you can only mean I'm about to get a hard uppercut to the jaw," he replied.

Ashley's breath caught in her throat as she stared at him mutely for a moment, and then, swallowing hard, she looked immediately down at her hands. "There isn't any kicker, Grant," she answered in a low voice. "There wouldn't be."

Grant frowned in deep perplexity as he studied her standing before him quietly, looking hurt. Vulnerable. His arms began to uncross almost mechanically, and then he suddenly dropped them to his sides sharply and looked away from her, starting when he caught sight of Karen appearing in the doorway.

"Hi!" Her smile was bright as she came through the door, somewhat breathlessly, dressed in tan slacks and a green pullover sweater. She came directly over to Grant's side and laid the folders she was carrying down on the desk. "Sorry I'm so late," she apologized with a look of exasperation, and she paid no attention when Ashley abruptly walked over to the other side of the room, stopping by a small bookcase laden with reference materials. "I stopped by the office first before I came up and got involved in a couple of things I hadn't planned on, and then there was terrible traffic." Karen glanced to her watch, which read eleven-thirty, and shook her head impatiently. "It's nearly lunchtime!" she observed.

Grant smiled. "It doesn't matter if you're a little late today," he dismissed. "We're just getting things together here."

Ashley turned around at that. Her pressing need to get out of the room increased to insistence when she saw Grant and

Karen standing side by side near the desk, Grant's broad shoulder nearly touching Karen's, but she felt it was important to let Karen know immediately about the changes with the catalogues; she had been put in charge of their production. "Karen, Grant and I have been talking about pulling back slightly on what we'd originally planned with the catalogues," she advised, determined to keep her voice as friendly as possible.

Karen's eyes went over to her slowly, and she arched one eyebrow. "Oh?"

Ashley smiled, tilting her head sympathetically. "Yes. I'm afraid it just has to be."

Karen simply looked at her for a moment. Her dislike for Ross's widow had heightened significantly with the derogatory comment Ashley had made about Grant in the press, then had swelled to rivalrous proportions with the advent of this joint project. In the past few days that Grant and Ashley had been meeting to get the sale underway, they'd always done so privately; she'd never once been invited to attend their conferences, and she hated that. All of a sudden, she was no longer Grant's closest colleague and confidante—not on this matter anyway—but was just another employee who got told everything after the fact. Suddenly, she was no longer a lot of things, she thought unhappily, and cast a peripheral look at Grant then. Since his return from Coconino on Monday, there'd been a distinct change in his manner toward her. Oh, he was still friendly and readily talked business with her, but gone was the air of intimacy between them, on his part anyway; they hadn't lunched together or seen one another after work at all. She'd agonized about it all week, wondering what had happened, and it had been on the drive up today that she'd decided it was time to find out what was wrong, and fix it.

She smiled at Ashley thinly. "Catalogues are important," she said, resisting the cut into her territory. "Especially for a sale of this magnitude."

"Yes, I know," Ashley returned quickly, absently lifting the cover of a book on the shelf and flipping the pages. "But we're on a tight deadline here. And I don't think the changes we're talking about will hurt anything," she added consolingly.

Karen frowned again. "I just think—"

"Karen, it has to be." Grant broke in as he perched on the desk's edge. "Ashley's point is valid."

Karen was further piqued at Grant's backing up Ashley, and raised her chin as she gave him an arch look. "Well, since I'm the one who has to pull together what the two of you go around setting up, I'd at least like to know what you're talking about." She tempered her petulant tone immediately when she saw Grant raise an eyebrow warningly, and she shrugged, giving him a small smile of conciliation. "It was a long drive up," she offered in self-defense. "Look," she said lightly then, to Grant exclusively, "let's go get something to eat, and we can talk about it there. I saw a restaurant nearby. And anyway, there are a few other things I need to discuss with you," she added, her tone softening.

The book under Ashley's hand fell off the shelf, hitting the tile floor with a resounding smack that made Grant glance over sharply. He saw her quickly retrieve the textbook and place it back on the stack of other reference materials, and he watched her curiously as she became a picture of nervous energy, her slim figure tensed as she walked briskly over to the desk to reach around behind Karen for a pad of paper and pencil, then step back immediately.

"You two go on to lunch," she instructed with a luminous smile. "I've got things I want to get to immediately. I haven't even really taken a look at the paintings yet, and after all, I've got to put my mind very carefully to this business I'm supposed to be handling so well." The dry look she tossed at Grant hardly touched her face before disappearing. "I'll see you later," she added hastily, then walked hurriedly toward the door.

Grant's eyes followed her to the doorway. Just beyond it she was snagged by one of her employees and made to stop. Karen also watched Ashley's departure, but with satisfaction, then turned her full attention to Grant. "There really are some things I have to talk to you about privately, one of them being business." She smiled eagerly. "When I was in the office this morning, I found out that Ben Geary has got to sell off some of his collections to meet the terms of his divorce settlement."

Grant's intent gaze on Ashley outside the doorway shot over to Karen. "Are you serious?" he asked.

"Very." She nodded in emphasis. "And it's got to be done soon. This messy divorce of Ben's has been a long, drawn-out affair, but now that everything's been decided on, he's got to come up with a lot of cash."

A smile of genuine pleasure seeped into Grant's face. "Well, that's the best news I've heard in a long time," he said. "Right at the moment, DuBrand's could use a shot in the arm like this. What exactly does Ben want to liquidate? How much does he have to settle on Elizabeth?"

"I don't really know the full details," she said, feeling better than she had in days with Grant's smile on her, his eyes seeing nothing but her. "But I do know it's a sizable amount." She sat down on the desk beside him. "There was a premarital agreement, but there has been some contention about it. I'm sure Elizabeth isn't entitled to a full half of his property, but it might get pretty close to a quarter."

Grant's smile broadened even more, and he let out a rueful laugh then. "Gee, I hate to take so much pleasure in Ben's problems, but it certainly is going to do my business a lot of good. A quarter, huh?" he murmured, rubbing his chin. "Who knows what the man's full assets are worth, but Jesus!" He shook his head slowly, in complete satisfaction. "Whatever a quarter of his worth turns out to be, it will be astronomical," he said and laughed again. "And we thought this Maynard sale was a prize!" he exclaimed.

"I thought you'd be happy with the news," Karen said complacently, and she got up off the desk and went to him just as he turned around. She slipped her arm through his, looking up at him. "Let's go get some lunch now. There's something else I want to talk to you about. Us," she added with the smallest shadow flitting across her eyes.

Grant caught sight of Ashley still chatting with her staff member out in the hall as he glanced to Karen on his arm. "Yeah, us," he murmured with a sigh, and gently extricated himself, going over to the desk to pick up his wallet and slip it in the back pocket of his jeans. "Come on. Let's go. We do have some things to talk about."

Chapter 38

BY THE FRIDAY two weeks later, nearly all the hundreds of possessions in the stately home had been processed through the preparatory stages of on-site auctioning. Ashley and Grant had worked late nearly every day in those hectic two weeks, overseeing the work, reviewing their financial projections, the mountain of logistical details, and Grant himself had supervised publicity both in the U.S. and abroad, while Ashley had busily attended to the specifics of the artwork portion of the sale. Together they'd strolled through the lovely house time and time again, deliberating over the most impressive way to display everything for viewing. The question of which room to set up as the auction hall itself was ever present, and they were in a dilemma about it still; they'd made a tentative decision to go with the grand, forty-foot living room with its crystal chandeliers, but then had both wavered when they'd considered the huge music room at the far end of the house, wondering seriously if the oval-shaped room with the domed ceiling might not be a more inspiring backdrop for lively auctions; it had an elegant arched Palladian window facing directly out on the English gardens, lending a sunny, airy atmosphere. Ashley was once again caught up in the uncertainty of the whole matter that Friday morning as she stood alone in the middle of the music room, and she gazed around indecisively.

She was wearing black wool slacks and a heavy beige turtleneck sweater against the chill of that unseasonably cold October day, and as she tapped her pencil against her chin thoughtfully, she caught sight of a head popping through the door at the far side of the room. It was Barbara Taylor, one of her own people, and the young woman smiled. "Mrs. Galbraith, Mr. Willingham is on the phone for you," she advised.

"Oh! Thanks." Ashley stuck her pencil behind her ear and hurried out of the room, passing through two drawing rooms and the large center hall to reach the double-galleried staircase. She trotted up it, taking the left flight of stairs after the landing, and finally reached the billiard room at the far end of the upper hall. She went right over to the desk and picked up the telephone. "Well, Mr. Willingham," she greeted pertly. "I believe I vaguely remember who you are!"

His laugh from the other end of the line was clear through the connection. "Yes, I'm the one stuck back here while you're up there having all the fun."

"Fun?" she exclaimed. "Try hard work!" She laughed as she leaned back in the chair. "How's everything going? I know I've been remiss about checking in with you, but I'm just so swamped all the time."

"We've been busy," he said. "I just called about a few things, nothing urgent."

They talked about all the necessary issues, and finally Ollie remarked lightly, "By the way, I hear through the grapevine that Ben Geary is going to be putting a good portion of his things up for sale because of his divorce settlement. Had you heard?" he inquired.

"No," she replied and smiled dryly. "How would I have heard? I've been up here in Never-Never Land for two weeks!" she teased.

"Well, he is," Ollie stated, and Ashley pictured him flopping back in the wing chair behind his mahogany desk as he sighed audibly. "My, my, wouldn't it be nice for us to get our hands on *that* business! Oh, and something else! Bernadette told me she'd seen Geary here at Galbraith's the other day, wandering around the toy exhibition. She was sure that's who it was!"

Ashley's shoulders had stiffened. "Well, we won't get our hands on that business," she stated flatly. "Ben belongs to DuBrand's." And I wouldn't for a moment even consider going after him, she added with silent intensity; she could imagine the impact on DuBrand's if Ben were to leave them. "So, what else is going on?" Ashley redirected firmly.

"Nothing. Oh, except that Georgia called here this morning looking for you."

Ashley sat bolt upright, her knees cracking into the side of the metal desk; she rubbed it as she listened with consternation. "Is something wrong?" she asked worriedly.

"No, no!" Ollie's reassurance was immediate. "She said she just wanted to say hello."

Ashley relaxed. "Anything more?" At Ollie's negative response, she started to hang up, then hastily added after her good-bye, "Oh, Ollie!" When he came back on the line she smiled hopefully. "You are going to come to the sales here, aren't you?"

"Wouldn't miss them for the world," he assured.

"You'd better not!" she ordered fondly, and after bidding him a final farewell, she hung up. She left the office immediately, returning downstairs, but at a more leisurely pace this time, and as she wandered through the darkly paneled center hall, she smiled at her employees busily moving tables and chairs, attaching tags to faded portraits, and making notes. Grant's people were working right alongside them, and Ashley was able to call them all by name now.

Grant had an excellent staff, she thought as she strolled on out of the hall and back through the drawing rooms toward the music room. They were intelligent, completely knowledgeable in what they were here to do, with a marked energy about them and obvious interested in their jobs. A reflection of their boss, she thought silently, and a glow flushed her cheeks.

Grant was absolutely exhilarating to work with; his bright mind was always on the move, a step ahead of every issue at hand, and she admired the way he dealt with his staff: honestly, companionably, and fairly, though he wasn't a man to be crossed. To watch him handle himself professionally only sharpened her remorse that she'd ever judged him so severely, and working with him had made her feel more alive in her own work than she had at any time over the last year and a half. But then, he'd always made her feel that way, she thought as she reentered the music room, and all of a sudden her eyes lost their radiance; she crossed to the arched window and stopped there, lightly touching her fingertips to the glass as she studied the boxwood gardens beyond.

Yes, they'd worked well together, but that was all. There'd been nothing more between them. Ashley's hand fell from the cold glass, and she turned from the window, moving to stand listlessly by one of the two antique pianofortes in the room. No, there'd been nothing more between her and Grant than simply the relationship between two professionals working with shared enthusiasm on a common goal; he'd given no indication that he was at all moved by her sympathetic attitude, had made no response whatsoever to her gestures of friendliness, although he hadn't come back at her again with open hostility as he had that first difficult day here. What had hurt the most that day—more, even, than watching him stand arm in arm with Karen, then leave for an intimate lunch with her—was seeing just how hard Grant found it to have faith in her sincerity with him anymore; that he could think she'd turn right around from a display of caring warmth and strike out at him had been like a knife thrust into her.

But why shouldn't he think that? There had been so many times she gave her love to him, then took it away again. If he distrusted her, it was because she'd instilled that feeling in him herself.

Her thoughts were harsh with self-reproach, and her gaze grew despondent as she looked at the beautifully aged ivory keys beneath her fingers. She'd fallen so very far in Grant's eyes, and she wondered again as she stood there if there was really any use in continuing to try to get him back. *Don't give up, Ashley. Not yet.* The feeble inner voice of desperate encouragement came to her at the same time as she heard the footsteps she recognized instantly to be Grant's entering the room behind her. Quickly removing the somberness from her expression, she turned around smiling. "Hello," she greeted.

Grant was dressed in a steel gray suit and a crisp white shirt, his overcoat on his arm as he came across the room. His tanned face had the healthy flush of one just stepping in from the fresh outdoors, and he walked directly to her. "I was longer at the office than I thought I'd be. Sorry," he said, tossing his coat onto the piano. "Anything major come up?"

"Oh, only about a hundred things," she remarked. "What did you think, that a morning would go by without some kind of crisis arising?" He grinned, and she went over and sat down on the piano bench, crossing her legs. "There was a near calamity with the figurines in the dining room cabinet," she related. "One of the shelves fell when David and Pam were trying to fix it." At Grant's appalled expression, she raised her hand immediately, laughing slightly. "It's okay! Nothing broke," she assured him. "Although it was definitely a bad moment! And let's see, what else?" She put a fingertip to her lips. "Oh yes. Leland Bartholomew called and rattled off a list to me of about twenty-five or so people Cathleen Maynard wants us to send engraved invitations to for the sale."

"Oh, for God's sake!" Grant propped a hand on his hip as he frowned in annoyance. "Why can't the two of them just stay the hell out of it and let us run this thing?" he demanded. "All we need is another detail to get bogged down in, and I'm getting a little tired of Mrs. Maynard and her eccentric ideas."

"I know, I know," Ashley said placatingly. "I feel exactly the same way, and you can't imagine the self-restraint I had to use to keep from expressing that very sentiment to our friend, Mr. Bartholomew, on the phone. But the point is, Grant, we've got no choice," she said, spreading her hands palms up.

"All right," he acceded with a sigh, and leaned on the top of the piano. "Did you get the invitations into the works?" he asked. Ashley nodded, and he smiled. "Anything else?"

"Just one other thing." She began to frown and regarded him seriously. "I took home the estimate from the catering firm that's going to set up the concession stands for the sales, and examined it closely last night." She got up then, crossing her arms as she walked several paces away, then turned. "His numbers seemed a little high to me when I gave them careful thought. Would you take a look at them and tell me if you agree?"

Grant's eyes were steady on her. "If you think they're high, then I'm sure they probably are," he answered. "But I'll check them over." His gaze lingered on her a moment longer, and then he straightened. "By the way, I had a thought driving up here." Ashley smiled receptively, and he slipped his hands into his pockets. "I like the idea of throwing a party for the staff members who've helped put this whole thing together. They've been working like dogs and doing an incredible job."

Ashley's face lit up. "That's a wonderful idea!" she agreed. "But why limit it to just those who've worked on the sale directly?" she added then. "Let's go all the way and make it for the full staffs of both companies. I don't want anyone to feel excluded, and in their own ways, everyone has contributed."

He smiled. "You're right. We'll set it up for the evening of the final sale. I'll put Karen on the arrangements for it."

Ashley was suddenly compelled to move again, and she strolled over to a pedestal near the fireplace. On top of it sat a small bust of Mozart, and she carefully ran her fingertip over the alabaster piece, keeping her gaze trained on it. "Grant, was there some particular reason that you pulled Karen off the catalogues for this sale? Not that I minded bringing Nancy in to replace her!" she added with a hasty smile at him. "It's just that, well . . . I wondered, that's all," she finished rather lamely, looking back to the statuette.

"It wasn't my idea," he answered mildly. "Karen took herself off the project."

"Oh." Ashley glanced over again uncertainly, and feeling acutely uncomfortable under his direct look, she very quickly changed the subject. "We still have this decision to make about what room to use for the auction," she said, then asked for the dozenth time, "What do you think, Grant? This room or the living room?"

He walked slowly over to join her where she stood. "It's a toss-up. This one's got better lighting and atmosphere, but the living room has more actual space for seating."

Ashley had turned to look at him keenly, and on an impulse she simply couldn't resist, she suddenly asked, "Grant, do you have a quarter?"

He gave her an uncomprehending smile, then reached into his trouser pocket and brought out a handful of change; he handed her a quarter. A small light had come into Ashley's eyes and stepping away from him just slightly, she winked. "You and I are going to make a soundly based decision, my friend," she said. "But don't you dare ever tell a soul I did this or my professional reputation will be ruined for life!" Without further comment then, she flipped the coin into the air and smacked it down onto the back of her left hand. She turned to face him squarely. "Heads it's the living room, tails the music room," she called. She lifted her right hand, took a look at the coin, then extended her hand for him to see. "The music room it is," she pronounced, her eyes dancing as an impish smile played around her mouth. "And a *wise* choice, too, don't you think?" She tried to keep her expression solemn, but lost the battle and burst into ringing laughter.

The muscles were working tensely in Grant's jaw and his hands at his sides were balled into fists as he stood looking at her. "The music room it is," he agreed tersely, then abruptly turned and strode out of the room.

He went back through the house but once in the hall he didn't head up the stairs toward the office. Instead, he left the house entirely, his brisk pace never once letting up as he hit the gravel drive and crossed it to the lawns, and he continued on in the direction of the line of trees edging the river side of the property. He kept going until he reached it, and it was

only when he'd walked all the way into the sparse woods, to
the moss-covered riverbank dropping off in a sheer fall to the
Hudson, that he finally stopped, putting one hand straight out
against a tree. And he leaned there, head lowered, as he tried
to regain his breath.

He'd been just a single thread of restraint away from
grabbing Ashley after that nonsense with the coin and pulling
her into his arms hungrily. Her violet eyes alive with humor,
her lilting laughter, her playful smile lighting up her beautiful
face—they'd all hit him right in the center of his chest like a
physical blow, tearing away the last shreds of the emotional
barrier against her that for almost two weeks now he'd had to
consciously fight to keep in place.

He raised his head after a few minutes and dropped his
hand from the tree, shaken as he stood looking down at the
ground. He was still in love with Ashley; he could stop trying
to deny that to himself now. Inside him still was all the
profound need for her to be part of him, the intense physical
desire, the pleasure in her audacious nature so like his own,
and working with her over the past several weeks had only
been a spur to all those feelings. She was so quick, so
capable, had the same enthusiastic taste for the high rolls of
business that he did; she adored what she was doing, there
was no question about it, and if ever he'd wanted to know
just how exciting a partnership with her could be, he'd found
out as he'd joined her in taking hold of this project with both
hands.

He expelled an audible breath and walked to the very edge
of the precipice, oblivious to the cold river breeze ruffling his
hair, blowing back the flaps of his suit jacket as he thrust his
hands deeply into his trouser pockets and looked out across
the water. "All right, Grant. You've admitted it. She's still
got you. And so—what?"

His voice broke into the rustling quiet of the woods, and
his troubled eyes watched two sailboats drifting along the
blue water, their tall masts glinting silver now and again as
the wind rocked them in and out of the sunlight.

He didn't know what was going on with Ashley. She
wasn't simply being sweet and friendly, she was *trying* to be;
he recognized that. And he didn't know exactly what that
meant, any more than he knew what her jealousy with Karen—
he could swear that was what her tension around Karen
amounted to—really signified. Or her reaction, that first day

on the premises, when he'd unintentionally let his anger at her show; he'd expected a sharp comeback, not a look of hurt. And what about Ross, that central issue in all this? He was aware that she no longer wore his wedding ring, always such a visible symbol of her feelings. Was she trying to say with her new attitude toward him that she'd finally seen she'd been wrong about everything, and that she loved him again, or had she simply, for whatever reason, decided to let bygones be bygones and allow herself to be affable with him now?

He turned around and looked off through the trees, to the house just visible beyond them; Ashley was somewhere inside. He envisioned again her dancing smile at him, the light laughter, brief touches, quick compliments she always had for him, and his troubled frown deepened. He *wanted* to believe they were signs of renewed love, but he just didn't know.

He looked at the house a moment longer, then thrusting his hands down into his pockets, started walking slowly back up toward the lawns.

Chapter 39

THE MAYNARD AUCTION was a spectacular success. Under the balm of glorious weather—powder-puff clouds in the cerulean sky, the sun bright and warming the chill November air—the Maynard house and grounds were the scene of high excitement and activity for three days. Two concession stands with kelly green striped awnings sat out on the front lawn serving refreshments to the masses of people who streamed in and out of the house and, for the nine sessions of auctions themselves, filled the music room to such capacity that several times the Palladian door at the back had to be thrown open to accommodate the overflowing audience. At the instruction of Mrs. Maynard, a red carpet had been rolled from the double front doors down the front steps and as far as it would extend along the brick sidewalk. Everybody came: collectors from all over the world, representatives from all the most important museums, and among the throng of interested spectators and participants each day were Leland Bartholomew and Cathleen Maynard herself, Ollie, Karen, and numerous other Galbraith and DuBrand's employees eager to watch the production billed in the press after only the first day as "superbly professional."

The auction podium shared jointly by Galbraith's and DuBrand's was alternately presided over by Francis Barclay and Grant's able auctioneer, Trevor Simon. Grant and Ashley themselves were whirlwinds of constant activity throughout the entire event, seeing to last-minute rearrangements and midstream foul-ups, greeting, circulating, and though they hardly had a minute to call their own, now and then they were able to snatch a moment together where they could stand sandwiched in among the crush of people in the back of the music room, watching in shared elation the results of their long weeks of labor.

The last session ended at four o'clock in the afternoon. The paintings had been sold that morning in a rousing auction that brought final prices all in the high hundred thousands and two each over the million mark, and the final portion of Henry Maynard's estate to be sold was the house and property itself. Ashley was elegantly dressed that day in a turquoise jacketed dress with a simple gold chain adorning the bodice, and she squeezed herself in with the standing audience by the door to watch the last moments of the event. Grant himself had taken the microphone to enumerate the salient features of the beautiful home and its surrounding grounds, and when he'd finished he turned the proceedings over to Trevor with a motion of his hand, then stepped to the back of the podium to listen as the auction began.

The bidding was enthusiastically rapid, and when it was all over, the house and grounds had gone for $3.4 million, and though the figures for the rest of the sale were still in the hands of the recorder and hadn't been officially tallied yet, Ashley had roughly calculated the gross proceeds of the three-day auctions to be somewhere near $50 million, an astonishing figure. She felt a thrill of pride race through her when the audience stood up and applauded, and she moved back from the doorway then as the crowd began to break up, milling past her to file for the last time out of the music room. She was besieged by congratulatory handshakes, and when at long last the entire audience had trickled out of the room and dispersed, she turned to see Grant coming down the aisle between the rows of now-empty chairs, his leather heels striking sharply on the polished floor and echoing eerily around the room; she moved into the room to meet him at the end of the aisle, wearing the same wide smile of heady pleasure he was.

"Well, that's it," he said as he stopped beside her. "We've pulled in close to fifty million dollars. Not bad for three days' work, is it?" he added with a crooked grin.

Her eyes sparkled as they mirrored his intense satisfaction. "I'd say not! I wonder how long it will take to come up with the exact figure."

"That should be worked up in a few days."

She nodded, and her gaze swept the room. "It seems so hollow now, doesn't it? It's hard to believe it's really all over," she murmured, touched for a moment by the melancholy letdown of a long engrossing effort finally completed. She looked back to him with a small smile. "Now all we have to do is see to the hundred and one details of wrapping everything up!"

"We'll worry about all that in the next few days," he dismissed. "It's getting late now, and we've both got to get back to the city if we're going to be on time for the party. The host and hostess can't be late. Come on." He took her arm briefly, then walked with her from the room.

They went through the house and into the center hall, as vacant now as the music room and with the same clanging, hollow feel to it. There were muffled voices audible from upstairs as the last of the staff members collected their things, and there was still a small scattering of people out on the lawn, including the representatives of the catering firm who were already beginning to dismantle the concession stands. For the most part, however, the premises were all but deserted, and Grant and Ashley crossed the hall to come to a standstill by the open front doors. Ashley had retrieved her coat from a downstairs closet and stood with it draped over her arm.

"Grant, I can stay to see that everything gets closed up properly for the night," she offered.

"No, I'll do it. You go on."

She let him take the responsibility, and as she stood looking at him, wrapped in the intoxicating glow of their smashing achievement, she said impulsively, "Grant, you did an absolutely magnificent job with the property this afternoon! You really ought to be a professional public speaker."

A veil dropped visibly over Grant's eyes, and he glanced once at the floor before looking slowly back at her. "Thank you," he said, his smile brief.

The constraint of his response was palpable in the air, and Ashley become a sudden flurry of movement as she made to leave. "Well, I've got to be on my way!" she said, flashing him a light smile as she quickly got into her coat, then searched in her purse for her car keys. She found them, and when she glanced back at Grant, seeing that his easy expression had dissolved altogether as he stood watching her with some intense, unreadable look, she gave him her bright smile one more time and stepped out the door. "I'll see you later," she said. "Don't stay here too long, or the traffic will be terrible." Grant merely nodded silently, and she turned and hurried down the front steps.

She went across the gravel drive in the direction of her car with a consciously light gait and kept the fixed smile on her face the whole distance. It even remained as she got into her silver Jaguar, started it up and backed out of the spot on the grassy lawn, and with all the seeming unconcern in the world, she headed the automobile down the long, winding drive and onto the main road. Then she pulled the car over to the curb, out of the stream of suburban traffic, and after she'd shut off the engine, she rested her head against the steering wheel. A low moan she couldn't suppress escaped from her.

It is really over, isn't it? she thought desolately. Things could never be the same between her and Grant no matter how hard she tried, because he no longer wanted her. For him the spark had truly died.

Her anguished eyes closed tight as she finally gave in consciously to what she'd really known in her heart for two weeks, since the moment Grant had turned on his heel away from her caprice with the coin: that, as a woman, she no longer appealed to him, even in the playfulness he'd once found so alluring, but was actually repellent to him. She'd run from that torturing acceptance, fleeing mentally, praying she was wrong, but there was no longer any way she could keep resisting the truth. It was screaming at her, and she finally had to hear it.

"I love you, Grant," she whispered, and as she saw again his strained tension at any sign of affection from her, her tears finally came; they overflowed from her eyes, and she let them slide unchecked down her cheeks. She remained for a long time with her forehead against the steering wheel, her tears at last expending themselves, and she finally raised her head leadenly, aware that if she stayed here much longer, Grant might drive by and see her; that thought compelled her to start up the car immediately, and when she had the engine running, she set her shoulders with frail resolution.

"Well, Ashley, you've got Galbraith's," she said to the yawning emptiness in her. "That's something at least. Hold on to it and enjoy it." Her eyes in the rearview mirror held bleak consolation for herself, and she put the car into gear and drove away.

By the time she reached home, it was six-fifteen. She went slowly into the house, mechanically flipping on the overhead light in the wallpapered hall, then the small table lamp near the door in the living room as she tossed her coat on the couch. She went into the small kitchen, mixed herself a drink, returned with her Scotch and water that was more liquor than water, and eased down into the rocker by the fireplace. Though she should've been on her way upstairs to begin changing if she wanted to be on time for the staff party at eight, she didn't get up again; she simply continued to sit in the darkened room, quietly rocking back and forth as, every now and then, she sipped her drink.

She wasn't going to the party; she'd made that decision on the long drive home from the upstate New York suburb. She simply could no longer be with Grant, could no longer smile past the pain of his dispassion, and she'd made the decision, too, that she was going to have Ollie handle Galbraith's share of the wrap-up details for the Maynard sale. *You're shirking your responsibilities, Ashley.*

"I can't help it," she answered dully.

After a time, the almost silent padding of small feet was audible coming across the parquet floor of the living room, and in another few seconds, Baker jumped up into her lap. "Hi," she said softly and held her hand out to let the cat rub his head against it. "It's just you and me, Baker," she told him. She looked around the shadowy, attractive room she'd put together with so much pleasure; she felt joyless in it suddenly, thinking of the years ahead she would spend here. Alone. She'd come full circle, she thought, back to the point where she'd been when this whole complex, unhappy part of her life had begun. Though it wasn't all unhappy, she admitted, tears pooling in her eyes again. She knew Grant, and she had had him. For a time.

A sob shook her, and she continued to simply sit, the rocker creaking rhythmically into the dead stillness of the room as she intermittently sipped her drink. At length, as she sat staring at the tall, narrow window across the way, the bright spotlight of the streetlight visible through the gossamer sash curtain, a frown crept into her brow. "I don't want to go tonight, Baker, with all my heart I don't want to go," she said as she glanced down to the cat now curled contentedly in her lap, "but I suppose I really should." *Guilt, Ashley. Haven't you had enough of that in your life?* Yes, but this time it was appropriate. Just because it hurt her so to be around Grant didn't mean she didn't owe it to her staff to be there. Downing the last of her drink, she set the empty glass on the small table nearby, set Baker down on the floor, and rose resignedly to go on upstairs and get dressed.

By seven-thirty, she was showered, had her hair washed and dried and her makeup in place. In her long white silk slip and strapless lace bra, she padded over to her closet to choose something to wear, stepping into the walk-in enclosure after she'd flipped on the light. Her clothing was arranged in an orderly fashion—slacks and casual blouses together, business suits and dresses all in one section, her formal riding habit behind that—and all along the left side were her numerous evening gowns. She studied them listlessly, letting her eyes run over the black strapless, then the gold lamé; she could wear the violet dress with its dramatic haute couture flair, or the simple white silk. Uninterestedly, her gaze continued on down the line of garments, finally reaching the last dress in her wardrobe, the one at the back on a padded hanger.

She stood staring at it, choked despair welling up in her all over again as she looked at Grant's red velvet gown. Unbidden, the memory of the night she'd worn it for him rose up before her, the look that had been in his face for her then: the truest love, the most ardent desire for her openly written in the slow smile that had come to his lips each time he'd taken in her appearance. She put a hand across her mouth, crying out through her fingers, and she turned spasmodically back to her other gowns, going through them again, this time with a sort of panic as she tried to detach every part of herself from the crimson gown hanging to her right; her mind wouldn't obey her commands, however, and like a magnet she was drawn to the gown.

He loved you in that dress, and it has very special meaning. It speaks to both of you. Ashley shut her eyes tightly at her thoughts, knowing where they were trying to lead her, and she crushed together the sleeve of the gown she was holding in her hand as a whisper wrenched from her. "I could never wear it!"

But it would tell him loud and clear what you've wanted to have him know all these weeks. "I could never wear it!" Her eyes flew open, and frantically, she rummaged through her dresses, finally yanking the black strapless from its hanger and rushing with it out of the closet; she slipped it on hurriedly, her movements jerky as she shimmied it down over her head, and when she'd zipped it up the back, she went to stand in front of the cheval glass in one corner of the room, studying her reflection intently.

*It might just get to him. He adored you in that dress,
Ashley. He did.* Ashley expelled a breath and spun away from
her image in the black gown, desperation in her eyes as she
stood in the middle of the room, and sought to still the
singsong voice in her mind. "He can't be reached! I already
know that. There's nothing there!" she exclaimed. *Are you
really sure, Ashley? You would know for certain if you wore
his dress for him. His reaction to it would tell you.*

Ashley continued to stare blankly in front of her. Why was
she doing this to herself, letting hope spring up again to
torment her this way when she already knew that Grant was
lost to her? Because it was just so tormenting a prospect, to
live the rest of her life without him—without the thrill of his
love, without ever being able to give him hers again—that
was why, she answered silently. The broken-hearted would
clutch at anything that offered even the whisper of a suggestion
that there might still be something to do.

Ashley's shoulders slumped, and she went over and sank
down on the blue comforter thrown across the four-poster
bed, putting her face in her hands. All right, yes. She wanted
to grasp at straws, she *would* grasp at them, but this one?
She'd be baring her very soul to him if she wore that dress,
swallowing every ounce of pride she had ever had in her life.
Wearing Grant's dress at this point would be more even than
chasing him; it would be . . . begging him!

The horrifying thought propelled her up off the bed again.
She was imagining it, appearing in the threshold of DuBrand's
downstairs gallery room where the formal party was going to
take place, her heart literally on her sleeve for Grant to see.
What would he do? There was blankness before her eyes, and
into her vision came a recollection—of Grant turning away
from her in the sharpest displeasure when she'd laughingly
held out a coin for him to see.

"I can't do it!" she cried, clutching at the bodice of her
black dress. She thrust the mental visions away from her and
turned to glance at the clock; it was seven forty-five. She took
several deep breaths, calming herself, then with a firm resolution to go to the party just as she was already dressed, she
walked briskly back into the closet to select a pair of shoes
and be on her way. She studied the boxes lined up along the
shelf, deliberating, then choosing finally the black silk pumps.
She reached up, and as she put her hand on the box, against

her will, her eyes slid to the splash of bright crimson color that beckoned irresistibly.

How much does it mean to you, Ashley, to have this man?

Her hand stayed motionlessly on the box for another moment, then, as a plaintive cry of dread escaped from her, it slowly came down to pull Grant's dress off the hanger.

Chapter 40

THE PARTY WAS in full swing when Ashley arrived at eight-twenty. All the displays and exhibitions in the black-marble-floored auction hall had been removed, and in their places were four linen-draped tables, two placed end to end on each side of the long, low-ceilinged room, and on each of them trays of fancy hors d'oeuvres, cheeses, and platters of hot and cold entrées had been set out. An open bar had been placed next to one of the four marble pillars, and an eight-piece orchestra played to the dancers in the open area set aside at the back of the room. The strains of the popular tune the band had struck up were all but drowned out in the noise of voices raised in festivity as the full staffs of both Galbraith's and DuBrand's—just over 200 combined—celebrated the May-nard sales.

Ashley remained standing tensely outside the entryway to the gallery for a moment when she reached it. A uniformed doorman had let her in through the glass front doors, and with every step she'd taken through the hallway toward the sounds of the gay party, the tightness across her shoulders had increased until it was a vicious ache all across her back.

The beautiful red gown fit her just as perfectly as it had the day Grant had bought it for her; the full skirt whispered just above the floor, the sleeves and waist were tightly form-fitting, and the bodice with its low, revealing vee gently caressed the rise of her breasts. She touched trembling fingers to the scalloped edges, smoothing them down, and after drawing one final, deep breath, she moved into the very center of the wide doorway.

A sea of faces was below her, three steps down, and she forced herself to smile with warm nonchalance as greetings met her from all around. Grant wasn't in sight, although she knew he was here; she'd seen his gold Maserati in the parking lot when she'd driven in and parked her own car. Ollie, however, stood right at the forefront of the mass of milling people, all with drinks in hand, and when he saw her, he broke off his conversation with a young woman in a gold brocade gown and smiled at her.

"Ashley. My heavens!" he exclaimed, extending his hand as she descended the stairs and came directly to him, he was wearing a tuxedo, and when she latched onto his hand, he gave her an admiring once-over. "You, my dear, are absolutely gorgeous!" he said.

Ashley realized that she was clinging to his hand, but she didn't let go as she stood right by his side, feeling somehow secure there. "Thank you," she said with a shaky laugh. "I'm sorry I'm late. I . . . well, I couldn't find the right purse," she explained lamely.

He was still studying her appearance. "It wouldn't matter what purse you carried," he remarked, then smiled into her eyes. "I'm sorry I didn't get a chance to speak to you today at the sale."

Ashley's return smile was absent as her eyes fearfully scanned the room. "I'm the one who's sorry," she answered without looking at him. "I saw you several times, but frankly I was so busy with things to do, I just couldn't come over to say hello."

"No matter," he dismissed. "And Ashley, it was a magnificent production," he continued, his smile broad. "I've been waiting to tell you that. You and Grant did a superb job."

At that, Ashley looked at him. "I—is Grant anywhere around?" she asked nervously. "I don't see him."

Ollie frowned slightly as he looked out through the crowd. "He was here just a few moments ago." He continued to scan the room, then gave up and turned his attention back to her. "He's around somewhere," he remarked, then raised his eyebrows. "You know, I wonder if we've set a precedent with this joint sale," he said thoughtfully. "It's getting tremendous coverage in the press. Did you know they're calling you and Grant the perfect team?"

She managed a smile. "It came off really well," she answered. She knew that the time had come when she had to begin mingling, and she finally let go of Ollie's hand just as he'd begun to look at her quizzically. "I think I'll start circulating," she said.

"How about a drink?" he offered as she started to move away.

"Thanks, but I can get my own," she replied, touching him once on the arm before at last leaving his side.

She wended her way through the crowd, going from group to group, laughing, talking, an icy tension inside her the whole while. Caterers wandered through with trays of champagne, but Ashley declined and finally reached the bar. After ordering her Scotch and water—"strong, please," she'd added with a thin smile—she watched the uniformed bartender mix her drink, then accepted the glass. Turning with it in hand then, to study the noisy crowd, she looked toward her left, and it was then that she saw Grant.

He was not far away, standing with Karen and a group of other people, but the two of them were talking alone. Like Ollie, he was dressed in a black tuxedo, the jacket stretching tautly across his shoulders, and he was watching Karen with a half-smile as she tilted her head prettily and laughed at something he'd just said. Karen looked lovely in her strapless long yellow gown, the top edge of the bodice generously ruffled, and her long brown hair had been swept up in a sophisticated coiffeur that was particularly flattering to her oval face.

Ashley knew she had to get away from there before Grant saw her; she knew she had to leave this party entirely. It was difficult enough for her to have appeared in Grant's dress at all, but she could not, *would* not go through with it when he was standing contentedly in the company of his new girlfriend. Panicked, she set down her glass on the table behind her, her frantic eyes searching for an avenue of escape; she knew it was suddenly too late, however, when one of her employees loudly called her name in greeting, and all she could do then was stand rooted in fear, her arms at her sides.

Grant immediately broke off his conversation with Karen and looked around for Ashley, finally spotting her. And when he did, his breath locked in his throat, and he stared at her, transfixed by the sight of her in the crimson gown.

Ashley couldn't look away from him either. With each second that ticked by without Grant's shocked expression altering, she died a little more inside; finally, embarrassed to the very depths of her soul, she began to turn, to rush away, when all of a sudden Grant's expression came to life. He began to smile, in a very slow, comfortable way that curved one side of his mouth, and excusing himself from Karen, he started to walk over.

Relief hit Ashley in the backs of her knees, and with her eyes still widened fearfully as she hardly dared to believe what she was seeing in Grant's expression, she watched him approach; her whole body had begun to tremble uncontrollably, and she wondered if she was even going to be able to continue standing as Grant finally came to a standstill right in front of her.

"Mrs. Galbraith, you look ravishing," he said in a low voice, and his eyes made a slow trip down the length of her. They rose back up to hers finally, locking there. "But then," he added, his eyes darkening, "you always did in that dress. That's why I had to have it for you."

Never in her life, Ashley knew, would she get over feeling a thrill of electric excitement race down her spine when Grant Copeland looked at her that way. Her skin tingled everywhere, as she answered demurely, "Thank you."

A brooding intensity suddenly entered Grant's expression as he continued to look into her face. "Where is your friend, Mr. St. John?" he inquired. "I figured you'd be coming with him tonight."

Exultation had already begun to displace relief in Ashley, and at the jealousy written clearly in Grant's eyes now, it flooded over her completely. She'd been wrong; he did still love her after all! "I wouldn't have come with Peter," she told him, looking right into his eyes. "I'm not seeing him anymore. And it was never a really . . . involved relationship."

He looked briefly puzzled, then abruptly put his hand under her elbow. "Come on, Ashley. We can't talk here." Guiding her through the crush of people, he took them across the long room and all the way out of it, leading her upstairs to his office. When they reached it, he flipped on a lamp just inside and closed the door behind them. Then he gently pushed Ashley against the door. He moved in very close to her, resting his weight on his arm against the door, just above her head. Completely alone with her now, he let his gaze move down over her again, his appraisal this time completely open as he studied her body so beautifully sheathed in the crimson velvet. When at length his eyes drifted back up to her face, they were intent.

"Ashley, why are you wearing my dress?" he asked.

She was smiling, and she raised her hand to his face, laying her palm against his cheek. "Don't you know?" she answered softly.

Her passionate touch raced all the way through him, and he put his own hand over hers, pressing it to his face. "I need very much for you to tell me in words, Ashley," he replied huskily.

"Because I love you," she whispered. "I've been trying to get that across to you for weeks."

Grant's breathing intensified, and he brought her hand down from his cheek to hold it possessively against his chest. "That's a change of heart," he murmured as his eyes roamed her face. "The last time I heard, you couldn't stand the sight of me. What happened?"

Ashley's fingers entwined more tightly with his, and she tilted her head against his arm on the wall above her. "No, it's not a change of heart," she answered, "just a remembrance of something that never went away. And you haven't really talked to me for awhile." Her soft laughter died away as heavy emotions swelled over her, and the pain she felt for everything she'd done reflected in her eyes. "Grant, a lot has happened, and there are so very many things I have to tell you. In words," she said, her voice constrained with emotion. "I've hurt you so much, and I need to try to find some way to make up for all that."

His arm dropped from the wall to her shoulders, and sliding it all the way around them, he pulled her tightly against him; easing his other hand from hers, he lifted her face toward his. "I can think of any number of ways," he answered languidly.

She locked her hands around the back of his neck, molding herself to him. "Actually, so can I," she breathed.

A low groan escaped involuntarily from Grant, and their lips joined at last in a kiss that answered any doubts that might have lingered. When their mouths broke apart, his hand went to the side of her throat, and as they stood there embracing, he caressed her neck, then ran his hand hungrily down to her shoulder, along the length of it to the very point, beneath the fabric of her gown; it slipped from her shoulder slightly under the demanding stroking of his palm. "I've missed you, Ashley," he whispered raggedly, his eyes heavy-lidded as they roamed her face. "Do you know how much?"

"Yes," she whispered, feeling slightly dizzy with the urgency of her own desire rising in her. "There are a lot of things I know about you," she added suggestively. Grant's hand moved back to her neck and traveled down, his fingers edging under the scallops on one side of her dress bodice, and he drifted them along her chest slowly, finally reaching the point of the vee. Without stopping, they moved over beneath the dress, to her breast, and he traced the line of it sensually. Familiarly. "Grant!" Ashley's forehead fell against his shoulder as she spoke his name in a soft moan.

He removed his hand and took her suddenly into a full embrace again, crushing her against him as he looked up toward the ceiling, closing his eyes in desire about to break away from all restraint. Abruptly, he pushed her back with his hands on her shoulders, readjusting her dress. "Not now. Not here, Ashley," he said with difficulty, letting his hands slide away from her completely as he stepped back a pace. "Later, at my place. Or yours." His eyes caressed her, and then a grin abruptly began to tug at one corner of his mouth. "Or should we flip for where we go to finally get this mess between us straightened out?"

Ashley bit her bottom lip, able for a moment only to shake her head at him lovingly. "I don't really care," she said with a soft laugh, then couldn't help but ask right then, "Grant, why did you walk away from me like you did that day in the Maynards' music room, when I tossed the coin?"

He saw the shadow of hurt pass across her eyes. "Why did you think I did?" he asked.

Ashley couldn't look at him and kept her eyes on her hands. "Because you found me so . . . unattractive," she answered in a low voice.

Grant was silent for a long moment. "You and I do have a lot to talk about," he said finally as he expelled another breath. "But not now. After the party. Come on," he said then, taking her by the hand and opening the door. "The host and hostess have no business being locked away from everyone else, much as they might prefer to be." He flipped off the light as they went out, walking Ashley back downstairs, and when they stood again in the threshold of the gallery, the noise of the lively party an ear-pounding din around them, he smiled at her. "We're supposed to be circulating," he said. "You go one way, I'll go the other, and I'll meet you back here later," he instructed. Ashley smiled up in quiet agreement as they entered the room, and as she continued on past him into the center of activity, he suddenly tightened his grip on her elbow, pulling back on it and drawing her to a startled standstill directly in front of him. "But though this isn't the time or place to straighten out issues between us, I want you to know one thing right now, honey," he whispered into her ear. "I walked away from you like I did that day at the Maynards' because if I hadn't, I would have picked you up and taken you to the nearest available bedroom. Pronto." And with a kiss to her hair, he slipped one hand in his trouser pocket and nonchalantly walked away.

Ashley stared after him, then covered her mouth with one hand to hide her sudden smile. She moved back into the party then, lighter than air as she began socializing with genuine enthusiasm, and as the evening wore on, she caught sight of Grant now and again, sharing a momentary private smile with him above the heads of the other people each time he caught her eye. Sometime around ten-fifteen, she spied Ollie talking with a striking blond woman she'd never seen before, and noticed Karen, just behind the twosome, standing in the attitude of an intent listener. Though Ashley had intended to go over to join her colleague, she was instead drawn into the conversation around her, then swept on to another discussion.

It was ten-thirty when Grant stopped by the bar for a refill of bourbon, and while he stood waiting for the hired attendant to return his glass, he caught a glimpse of Ashley over near the orchestra, her statuesque figure appearing and disappearing like a beautiful apparition behind the continuous flow of people milling in the foreground. He accepted his drink from the bartender with a nod of thanks, then simply stood where he was for a moment, studying Ashley over the rim of his glass. An unconscious smile drifted onto his lips, and in his total absorption with her—and inner serenity that the situation between them was finally about to be resolved—it was with surprise that he realized someone close by was speaking to him. He glanced quickly across his shoulder; Karen stood by his side, wearing an expression of distinct distress.

"Grant, I have to talk to you, right away," she commanded.

Grant lifted his glass to his mouth and took a light sip of his drink. "Okay," he said mildly.

Karen hated his pleasant but impersonal smile; she hated everything that had happened between them—beginning with his ending their affair over lunch that day in Tarrytown. In angry hurt, she'd flatly refused to go on working on the Maynard sale, and so many times in the ensuing weeks she'd nearly quit her job at DuBrand's entirely. But she'd always stopped just short of submitting her resignation to Grant because she honestly enjoyed her work and because, once the initial shock of Grant's gentle but firm withdrawal from her had worn off, she'd harbored the hope that maybe, somehow, they could get back together again. She'd lived on that hope tenuously, growing more and more confident in it, until tonight. She cast a narrow, venomous look in Ashley's direction. She knew now the reason that Grant had broken off with her; it seemed that in just the short space of a few weeks, he'd become captivated by the lovely Mrs. Galbraith. The recollection of the two people as she'd seen them earlier—talking privately, Grant's eyes holding clear masculine appreciation as he'd looked down at Ashley, then leaving the party together for a time—stung her again, and she drew her eyes away from Ashley roughly, looking back at Grant, her chin coming up. Well, she would see just how entrancing Grant found the competition to be once he'd heard what she had to tell him.

"Come over here," she instructed, taking his arm peremptorily and leading him to a spot by one of the marble pillars where there was seclusion for the moment. When they reached it, she dropped her arm and faced him. "Grant, I have to tell you something," she stated.

He cocked his head inquiringly. "What?"

Her eyes began to flash in indignant anger. "I overheard a conversation earlier that was, to say the least, very interesting," she told him, one eyebrow arching. "It was between Ollie Willingham and a woman named Jenna Wainwright."

For the briefest moment, before Karen had clarified her statement, Grant had been afraid she was referring to his exchange with Ashley prior to their going up to his office; she hadn't taken their breakup well at all, and a jealous scene right here in the middle of the party wasn't totally out of character for her. Breathing a quiet sigh of relief, he smiled relaxedly. "What was it about?"

"Ben Geary," she snapped.

Grant's glass raised to his lips as he started to take another sip of his drink came back down slowly. "Oh?" he responded in new attentiveness.

"Yes." She crossed her arms huffily, looking him right in the eye. "Jenna Wainwright, it seems, is some sort of cousin of Ben's, and she's one of Galbraith's employees.'' She arched an eyebrow slightly. ''Nice in, huh?''

Grant shook his head confusedly, frowning slightly. ''Karen, I'm not following you,'' he answered. ''What's the point?''

''The point *is*,'' she delivered crisply, ''that you can cross the Geary divorce settlement sales right off your calendar because DuBrand's won't be having them. Galbraith's will be. *Ashley* will be,'' she added malevolently.

Grant didn't move at all. ''Karen, what are you talking about?'' he asked in a flat voice.

''What I'm talking about, Grant, is that Ashley has swiped Ben's sales right out from under you. And this isn't just hearsay,'' she went on in the face of his now-dead silence, putting what she'd overheard into her own words. ''Nor, as far as I can see, is it something that's just popped up. Ashley's apparently been working on Ben about this for a long time now and not only just to get his divorce sales but all of his business in the future.''

Grant was staring at her, his jaw rigid as he stood riveted by the blow that had just been dealt to his company, and then, slowly, his eyes left her and traveled over her head, going across the room to settle on Ashley. She was still standing near the orchestra, her head thrown back in gay, carefree laughter—Ashley who'd been so sweet, so loving, so totally devoted all over again, the whole time knowing just exactly what she had in store for him. . . .

Rage engulfed Grant in a tidal wave. He slammed his plastic glass down onto the food table beside him, sloshing bourbon out over the rim and onto the white cloth, and without another word to Karen, he began to make his way over to Ashley.

She was just concluding her laughing comment to Jack Rosen, DuBrand's treasurer, when Ashley felt the hand clamp down on her upper arm. Startled, she shot a look across her shoulder, relaxing immediately when she saw that it was Grant.

''Hi,'' she greeted softly, but her smile of welcome faded in the next instant when she registered the fact that Grant's eyes were seething and became aware that his hand still had her in a viselike grip. ''What . . . ?'' she began in perplexity, tilting her head as she studied him.

''Mrs. Galbraith, I need to speak to you for a moment,'' he broke in curtly and gave his colleague a tight smile. ''If you'll excuse us, Jack,'' he added in strained cordiality, then without another word, he turned Ashley around by her shoulders and moved her away.

''Grant, what—?'' she began again in growing bemusement, but she got no answer from him as he put a hand at her back and literally propelled her before him then through the crush of people. She had no choice but to go along and flashed apologetic and somewhat embarrassed smiles at the people they jostled in passing. When finally they'd made their way across the room, Grant kept her moving, on up the three steps and all the way out the door.

''Let's go,'' he snapped when they were beyond the room, and he took her arm again in that painful grip to drag her with him. He let go when she complied, going on down the deserted halls of DuBrand's premises at a clip, Ashley all but running beside him to try to keep up with his long strides; the whole time, she kept glancing at his granite-like profile, deep worry in her eyes.

''Grant, what's the matter?'' she demanded, following him as he went up a shallow flight of stairs in the lobby, and she lifted the hem of her crimson gown to keep from tripping. He said nothing but simply strode on into a small exhibition gallery divided into partitions. The only illumination in the room was provided by the lights attached to each partition at the top, brightly spotlighting the portraits hanging below and throwing the rest of the area into ghostly shadow, and Grant finally came to a stop on the far side of one of the dividers, wheeling around; Ashley was just behind him, her eyes searching him in consternation.

''Grant—''

''You know, Ashley, you're almost too much to be believed!'' he said, his voice low with fury.

''Grant!'' Ashley was confused and shaken by both his statement and his wrathful manner. ''What's happened?'' she implored, moving closer to him as she looked at him with entreaty.

''What's happened,'' he answered in a deadly tone, ''is that I've found out about Ben Geary, Ashley. And Jenna Wainwright. Ben's divorce auctions. All of which, of course, you've known about for a long, long time. Karen overheard this Wainwright woman talking to Ollie about it.'' His entire body was rigid as he faced her, his hands clenched at his sides, his strong features sharpened by the bright halo of light

on the paintings in the background, and he cast a bitter look
down the length of her. "That's what this was all really for
tonight, wasn't it, Ashley—the dress, the display of passion?
Tell the man you love him. Get him to relax. Make sure
Grant is good and softened up so the blow really connects!"
He jerked his chin up. "And were you planning to go ahead
and sleep with me, Ashley? Were you going to go as far as
that?" His eyes raged at her, and then suddenly he looked up
to the ceiling, his teeth gritted. "Christ, I should've known! I
should've *known* you never meant it!"

Ashley had no idea what he was talking about but fully
understood that he was as hurt as he was angry—once more
because of her. "Grant!" she cried as she reached out for
him, to hold him tightly, but when she put her hands on the
sides of his tuxedo shoulders, he irately dislodged them by
throwing both arms out, sending her reeling backwards.

"It won't work anymore, Ashley!" he roared. "Save your
sweet, loving touch for someone else, someone who's a
bigger fool than I am. If there is one," he added derisively,
and his fury overtaking him completely, he stormed away.

The room was swimming around Ashley as she steadied
herself with a hand against the partition. She finally came to
from the shock of Grant's violent anger and, looking in the
direction he'd disappeared, hiked up her skirt and ran after
him. She could hear the fading sounds of his staccato footsteps on the marble floors as she raced across the room and
followed them out of the gallery. When she reached the head
of the stairs, she saw him below in the lobby, striding not
back down the hall toward the party but out the front doors.

"Grant!" He didn't stop at her frenzied call, and Ashley
hurried down the stairs, her red gown flowing down the steps
behind her like a train, and when she reached the lobby, she
rushed to the doors. Fifth Avenue as far as she could see out
was deserted, Grant nowhere in sight, and Ashley spun around,
her frantic eyes darting across the floor as her thoughts spun
wildly. Abruptly, she looked up in the direction of the gallery
where the party was still going strong, the noise of music and
laughter just barely audible. Ollie. Karen had overheard Ollie
talking to this Jenna Wainwright, and Ollie could tell her
what in the world was going on.

She literally ran down the hall, stopping with chest heaving
in the threshold of the doorway as she scanned the room. She
spotted Ollie in the ocean of people finally, and threaded her

way to him, grasping his arm, to his complete surprise, the same way Grant had grabbed her. "Ollie, I have to talk to you!" she exclaimed, casting a tight smile at the people around them as she pulled him away. She had him by the hand and led him back through the doorway, stopping them in the hall just beyond it. She turned around to face him directly. "Ollie, what's all this about Jenna Wainwright?" she demanded, out of breath.

Ollie was frowning at her in consternation. "Ashley, what's the matter?" he asked, putting his hand on her shoulder.

"Never mind," she dismissed, her eyes locked on his face as she clutched her hands together tightly. "Ollie, just please tell me what this woman's done, and what Ben Geary and his divorce settlement have to do with Galbriath's."

Ollie's shoulders relaxed and he smiled, although he was still confused by Ashley's obvious distress. "Oh, so she's talked to you, has she?" he commented.

"No. I—someone else told me." She tried to make a show of calm, dropping her hands to her sides, but her fingers kept gripping the velvet of her gown repeatedly. "Ollie, I scarcely remember who Jenna Wainwright is. I know you were thinking of hiring a socialite who's a cousin of Ben Geary's, but I haven't heard another word about her since."

"Well, I'd kind of forgotten about her myself," he admitted with a rueful laugh, then seeing the frustrated insistence heighten in Ashley's expression, got on with his explanation. "All right. I was waiting to give you the good news at the end of the evening, to top off your day. Or rather, let Jenna give it to you," he confided. "But it seems we've both been preempted." His eyes shifted abruptly to the scene of the party in the room below them, and he frowned intently as he scanned the crowds. "You really must meet Jenna as soon as possible, Ashley. I think she's going to be very good for us, more so than I'd ever suspected. Though this is just an incidental bit of employment for her, she's obviously taking it very seriously. She mentioned several other people besides Ben that she's been working on steadily, and they seem very receptive to her persuasion."

"Ollie!" Ashley breathed in uncontrollable impatience, and she put her hands on his arms, actually shaking him. "Just tell me about Ben!"

"Okay! Jenna has been talking to Ben, ever since we took her on, about switching from DuBrand's to us. Which, I'm happy to say, has happened. Ashley, we've gotten the Geary divorce sales, and maybe even Ben's business from now on!'' he announced, his face aglow with excitement as he clapped a hand on her shoulder again, this time in professional comradeship. ''He advised Jenna this morning when she called him again that he'd made the decision to change over to Galbraith's. And not simply because of Jenna's pressuring him.'' He smiled slightly. ''She admitted that. Ben told her what really convinced him to come to Galbraith's was you yourself—your daring to begin buyer's premiums at Galbraith's. What he likes more than anything in the world are aggressive professionals who aren't afraid to take risks, and you impressed him greatly with your nerve to start the buyer's fees. He was surprised that Grant hadn't done it himself, and a little disappointed in him for it, I gather. Jenna knew how thrilled we'd be and came to the party tonight specifically so she could be the first to break the news to us, before Ben had a chance to call. She said she'd— Ashley!''

Ashley didn't need to hear anymore and was already ten steps away from him, flying back down the hall in the direction of the lobby, her dress billowing out behind her as she ran to find Grant again. She knew exactly what Grant thought, and oblivious to Ollie's repeated calls of her name growing fainter by the minute and caring nothing for what he might be wondering about her peculiar behavior, she finally reached the glass front doors and went through them with both hands outstretched.

''Grant!'' The cold night air hit her bare chest as she screamed his name, and she wrapped her arms tightly across her body as she came to a standstill just outside the door, her eyes combing Fifth Avenue for some sign of Grant. He was nowhere in sight on the dark street, and rushing to the corner then, she scanned the cross street, shivering in the biting wind; there were only two late-night strollers on the city avenue, walking in different directions, and neither of them was Grant. Keeping one arm protectively across her chest, she picked up her skirt again with the other hand and raced down the side street, along the edge of the DuBrand's building, flying around the corner into the lighted parking lot in back. She stopped again, out of breath as her eyes scoured the parking lot jammed with automobiles, but Grant wasn't there either. An audible breath of frustration escaped from her, and she whirled around to run back into the building and search for Grant there, to tell him she hadn't known about this all along, that she hadn't turned on him again, when a clutching thought struck her. She whirled around again, her eyes on the reserved parking place near the back door where Grant's gold Maserati had stood when she'd arrived.

It was gone.

Chapter 41

AT EIGHT FORTY-FIVE the next morning, Ashley was perched tensely on the edge of her living room couch, clad in dark brown slcks and a cream-colored turtleneck sweater. There was a steaming mug of coffee sitting in front of her on the drop-leaf table, and after glancing over to the square clock on the mantel again, she sighed restlessly and picked up the mug, sipping coffee absently as her foot tapped sharply against the floor.

The sunlit room was disordered; the big, comfortable throw pillows on the blue velvet couch were strewn about, out of place because Ashley had slept there the night before—when she'd slept at all, that was, still dressed in her long, red evening gown—and the handsome coffee table was all but hidden under a litter of papers from her weeks of returning home from long days at the Maynard estate, then sitting right down to go over even more matters of business for the project. Her eyes roamed over the messy surface of the table, usually so straight and neat, but she saw nothing; her mind was only on Grant. And on the ticking clock on the mantel.

She'd tried repeatedly to call Grant the night before, all the way up till three o'clock in the morning. After she'd left DuBrand's, on the heels of her disheartening discovery that he'd gone, she toyed with the thought of driving directly to his apartment on Central Park South, then discarded the idea, knowing that there'd be no way for her to get past the uniformed security guard without Grant's permission and knowing, with the same heavy heart, that Grant wouldn't give it. She'd come straight home and begun trying to call him, hanging up the phone in furious frustration each time it had simply rung and rung with no answer. She'd drunk coffee until she was blearily wide-eyed, roaming around and around the small living room in agonized tension, and when by three in the morning there was still no answer to her calls, she'd finally forced herself to give up for the night and had stretched out restively on the couch; she'd gotten perhaps two, maybe three hours of honest sleep before she'd risen like a jack-in-the-box with the first light of dawn and finally gone upstairs to get out of her rumpled evening dress.

She set down her cup on a clear edge of the coffee table and sat staring at the telephone sitting squarely in the center of the disarray of paperwork, biting at her lip when she looked over and eyed the clock again. Eight fifty-two. What she was waiting for, on pins and needles, was for nine o'clock to come, when the switchboard of DuBrand's would open and she could finally try to reach Grant there; she'd already called his home three times since seven-thirty this morning. And still there'd been no answer.

Prove it . . . prove it . . . prove it. . . . The urgent refrain that had played relentlessly through Ashley's mind all night long picked up again and propelled her up to pace back behind the couch, wringing her hands. Oh, yes, she knew now that Grant still loved her with all the old passion and intensity, but unless she could find some way to remove his distrust of her sincerity, his loving her would count for nothing. They would be lost to each other.

Despair was pulling at her again and could overtake her if she let it, because she didn't know what more she could do or say.

But I won't let it get me, she thought. I'll find the right words, somehow. I *will* make him believe me! But in the meantime, I have to get him just to *talk* to me!

She sat on the very edge of the couch, with only two minutes left to wait, and her restless eyes moved to the coffee table, where they rested on a copy of the principal Maynard catalogue, with its twin emblems of the two companies that had allied as one to solve all the problems. Ashley's gaze moved on, then suddenly flicked back to the catalogue, and she stared at it. Two companies that, when made into one, solved all the problems . . . *prove that you mean what you say.*

Ashley's hand flew out and was already on the phone when the mantel clock began its resonant chiming of the hour. In a jangle of tension to speak to Grant that was suddenly more urgent than ever, she could hardly hit the push button numbers fast enough. When she finally got through to DuBrand's switchboard, she asked for Grant's office, getting his secretary after two rings.

"Denise?" Ashley was sitting at the very edge of the

couch, her free hand at the small of her back pressing against the ache there. "This is Ashley Galbraith," she said quickly. "Is—may I speak to Mr. Copeland, please?"

"Oh, hello, Mrs. Galbraith," Denise responded pleasantly. "I'm sorry, but Mr. Copeland isn't in."

Ashley's knuckles had gone white around the telephone receiver, and she forced herself to speak evenly. "Do you know where I can reach him?" she inquired. "It's very important that I speak to him immediately."

"Well . . ."

Ashley nearly screamed at the hesitation and stood up abruptly, picking up the phone console as she walked around the edge of the coffee table. "Denise," she went on in a constrained voice, "this is quite urgent. It's—something has come up about the Maynard sales," she improvised on a sudden inspiration to break through the wall of secretarial discretion.

"Well, in that case, Mrs. Galbraith, and since it *is* you," Denise relented reluctantly, "I guess I can tell you. Mr. Copeland has gone out of town," she advised. "He flew home last night to his ranch in Arizona. He left word with the answering service that he'd gone and that he wasn't to be contacted except in the case of emergency. He'll be gone for a few days. Mrs. Galbraith, this *is* an emergency, isn't it?" she added hastily.

"It's an emergency all right," Ashley assured. "Thank you."

Ashley hung up, still holding the telephone in her hand. She thought of what faced her now if she wanted to see Grant right away, as she simply had to: following him all the way across country, into the sanctity of his very private refuge. Her eyes closed in horror at the prospect of doing that, and then she finally opened them again and sat down to make another call. This time she would phone the airlines to find out what was the first available flight she could catch to Flagstaff.

It was three-thirty that afternoon when Ashley turned her rented blue Oldsmobile into the lane leading to Coconino. The tall ponderosa pines lining the dusty drive were perfectly still in the breezeless November air, and there were dingy gray clouds in the sky above. After rounding the bend in the lane, Ashley could finally see, directly ahead, the long, sandy-

colored ranch house with its low columned porch, the surrounding grass a dusty brown with the onset of winter, the big
barn, stables, and weathered post-and-rail fences in the background, and the sight sent a sharp pang of bittersweet happiness through her. She parked the car under the leafless maple
tree directly across from the house, and after simply sitting
for a moment, she finally got out.

She was still wearing her dark slacks and heavy turtleneck
sweater, and as she stood briefly by the car door, she brushed
nervously at the lapels of her navy pea jacket, patting her
hair, then straightening the high collar of her sweater around
her neck. Drawing a deep breath, she started across the front
yard toward the house and was halfway there when she heard
a call off to her right. Glancing over, she saw Timothy
Redchief coming in her direction at an enthusiastic lope, and
despite her acute tension, she smiled. Timothy came right up
to her with a sliding halt, his face beaming, his knit cap
askew, his unzipped coat hanging slightly crooked on his
shoulders.

"Boy, you did come back after all!" he exclaimed happily.

Ashley was intensely warmed by the glowing welcome,
and she leaned down to kiss him on the cheek. "Hello,
Timothy," she said as she straightened again, and her smile
faded as her anxiety returned. "Timothy, have you—do you
know where I might find Mr. Copeland?" she asked.

"Yep. He's there." Timothy's arm shot out in the direction of the paddock. "He's been working Dakota. You know,
ropin'," he added nonchalantly and stuck both hands in his
back pockets, looking at her again. "I can ride now," he
added in the very next minute.

Ashley gave him her most approving smile. "And with the
best of them, too, I'll bet." Her eyes were drawn back to
the riding enclosure, and after touching Timothy lightly on the
shoulder, she said, "I'll see you later." She gathered herself
and began walking toward the paddock.

Off in the distance, the red-rock canyon mesas were visible, and Ashley could see Grant finally as she neared the
paddock. He was standing in the center with his back to her,
wearing boots, jeans, his tan sheepskin coat, and Stetson, and
Dakota was standing quietly in front of him as Grant worked
at the saddle. Nick was by the horse's head, one arm slung
over Dakota's neck while he talked to Grant, and Ashley
stopped for a minute on the far side of the paddock gate,

which stood slightly ajar. She went on through at length, the soft creak of the gate as she pushed it open a little farther making Nick look over.

"Hello, Nick," she said quietly, continuing to approach until she was several yards away from the two men; she stopped there, clasping her hands in front of her.

At the sound of her voice, Grant shot a glance first at Nick, then looked back over his shoulder sharply. When he saw her, he turned roughly back to his chore with the saddle, jerking up on the girth under his hand so hard that Dakota's head bobbed up and he sidestepped nervously.

Ashley looked over at Nick, now engrossed in an intensive study of the ground. "Nick, would you mind leaving us alone for a bit?" she inquired.

He gave Grant one fast look, then nodded to her with a smile, and he strode past her on his way to the gate. Grant paid Nick's departure no attention whatsoever, remaining with his back to Ashley as he continued working briskly with Dakota's saddle, and finally alone with him, Ashley took a step nearer. "Grant, may I talk to you?" she said.

He didn't respond immediately as he took the heavy wooden stirrup thrown back over the seat of the saddle and dropped it back into place, slapping the leather panel down over it afterward. "You're here," he finally answered in a monotone. "I imagine that's what you intend to do."

Ashley studied his broad back, biting her lip. She didn't really know where to begin and at last settled on saying quietly, "Grant, I didn't know anything about Ben Geary giving his business to Galbraith's until last night at the party. Until you told me about it, and then Ollie later explained everything fully."

At that, Grant turned to look at her. The fiery anger of the night before was gone, and his handsome face held no expression at all as he regarded her matter-of-factly. "Look, Ashley," he said, "you've wasted your time and airfare coming out here. I know what's going on with you and I don't want to talk about it." His eyes narrowed abruptly. "And just how did you find out where I was anyway? I left specific instructions that I wasn't to be bothered."

"Denise told me, but it wasn't her fault," she answered. "Don't be angry with her. I pulled the information from her. And Grant, you're wrong about this Ben Geary thing."

Grant watched impassively as Ashley walked right up to

him then and stood at his side, her hand going out to rest lightly against Dakota's neck. He said nothing, and she went on earnestly. "Grant, I didn't engineer this with Ben. I wouldn't have. It's something that simply happened, that I knew nothing about."

Grant frowned sharply in annoyance then. "Oh, come off it, Ashley," he answered in heavy disgust. "Don't insult my intelligence by trying to hand me a line like this—that Galbraith's chief executive didn't know about something of this magnitude. Sweetheart, if there's one thing I've learned about you over the past month, it's that you know every last thing about your company and then some." His scowl deepened as his chin came up. "Don't give me this——"

"Grant." Ashley silenced him with a hand on his arm, and her eyes were intense. "I know exactly what you think, that all the while I was telling you I loved you, I'd been working right along to hurt you, and that my motive was entirely vindictive. But it simply isn't true!"

Before he could come back sharply again, Ashley rapidly explained the circumstances of Jenna Wainwright's hiring, relating everything Ollie had told her the night before. "And Grant," she went on intently when she'd finished, letting her hand slide down and away from his suede coat-sleeve, "Jenna came to the party last night so she could be the first one to break the news to us. I hadn't the faintest inkling that this was coming, that Ben had been so impressed about that business with the buyer's premiums. And if he knew the reality of the situation, he wouldn't have switched his loyalty. You had the same confidence about taking that risk."

"Reality is the way the cards fall on the table for everyone to see, Ashley," Grant answered shortly, "not what goes on in the shuffle. You ought to know that by now. And in this case, they fell to you. Only because of a simple matter of fortuitous timing," he added, one eyebrow arching slightly.

"Yes," Ashley responded immediately. "And that's what this is really all about, not that I went after Ben myself. I didn't! And if I'd known that anyone associated with my company was trying to convince him to switch over, I'd have put a stop to it immediately."

"I don't believe you for a minute, Ashley, but if it's really so, then it looks like you've had extraordinary good fortune all around with those buyer's premiums, doesn't it?" Grant's smile barely touched his lips, and reaching past her, he took

Dakota's reins and threw them back over the horse's head. He looped them around the saddle horn, putting his hand on top as he prepared to mount up, and he looked for a moment at Ashley across his shoulder.

"But whether it's just good fortune or careful planning, Ashley, you're finally getting what you've always wanted," he said. "Ben's leaving DuBrand's knocks a major hole in my company."

"No, Grant, you're wrong! I meant everything I said to you last night. I don't ever want to hurt you again, in any way!" A light gust of wind picked up strands of Ashley's hair as she grabbed his arm, and she forced him finally to take his foot from the stirrup and lower it back to the ground. She went on quickly then. "Grant, there are things I want you to hear me say." His eyebrow cocked in an expression of irritated impatience, and she let go of him, dropping her eyes to the dirt and standing in sudden diffident tension before him, her hands meeting in a tight grip. Finally, she raised her eyes up again to meet his directly.

"Grant, I . . . I was so wrong about you and Ross," she said in a constrained voice. "You were never to blame for anything that happened to him. You were perfectly right to manage your company as well and as aggressively as you could, regardless of me and Ross, and you were never being inconsiderate or insensitive by doing that. I understand that now and that it was my . . . own feelings of guilt that made me look at things the way I did, made me *need* to." She wet her lips once with the tip of her tongue. "You always understood what was motivating me. You even told me, but I . . . wouldn't hear you.

"And you'd hurt my feelings," she went on, raising her chin a bit in the face of his deafening silence. She wanted to glance down to the ground, to avoid his gaze, but made herself look him straight in the eye. "I lived on my hurt, and it made it that much easier for me to think harshly of you, easier for me to . . . transfer to you the guilt I couldn't deal with myself," she said with difficulty. "You understood I was doing that, too." She pressed her lips together hard. "I'm ashamed of my weakness, Grant—that I had to pass off onto another person emotions that were too hard for me to handle myself. I suffered from that understanding about myself more than you could ever know."

She needed a respite for a moment, and in her silence,

Grant spoke at last. "So, I've finally been vindicated," he said unemotionally. "Thank you. I deserved to be." His eyes were cold, and he grabbed the back of the saddle as he again began to mount his horse. "I've got things to do, Ashley—"

"I'm not finished." Once more Ashley reached out to his arm and made him stop his movements. "I know how much I hurt you with Peter that day in the restaurant when you came to talk to me about the Chilton sale, and I want you to know what that was all about," she said.

His eyebrow raised slowly as he eyed her. "You are confessing it all, aren't you?"

"Yes." Her voice was a whisper under his biting tone, and she steadied herself again with a hand against Dakota's neck. "I needed to get away from you that day, desperately. I felt so completely humiliated sitting there with you after what I'd done with those awful bronzes. You knew exactly what had happened, had told me so, and also told me to my face how you'd had better sense than I had. I . . . couldn't cope with that, and when you wouldn't let me go, it only made matters worse." She glanced down, smiling with difficulty toward the dusty ground. "I didn't walk out with Peter to hurt you purposely. He was simply my means of escape. And for whatever this may be worth to you, Grant," she said, her eyes lifting to his tenderly, "there is no one else in this world who could've made me feel as ridiculous that day as you did, because there's no one else in the world I respect and admire as a professional more than I do you. I've always felt that way and I always will."

Grant studied her another moment, and then putting his boot back into the stirrup, swung all the way up this time. Ashley was forced to move back, out of the way of the sidestepping horse, and Grant settled himself in the saddle as he gathered the reins on his horse, adjusted his Stetson, then looked down at her dispassionately. "Thank you for the vote of confidence," he said formally. "Now go on back to New York, Ashley. You've gotten it all off your chest. There's nothing more you and I have to say to each other, except for what has to be done to tie up the loose ends of the Maynard estate, which we'll do just as quickly and painlessly as possible. I'll call you about it when I get back into the office."

Although Ashley had known in her heart that her sincere words of affection and apology probably wouldn't make an impression on him, still, when confronted with the reality of his refusal to be touched, she nearly cried out. Her heart was suddenly in her throat as she watched Grant about to ride away from her, and though every part of her wanted to rush over and grab onto his boot, holding him there, clinging to him, she didn't. She forced herself to stand her ground in the center of the riding ring, lifting her chin and thrusting her hands down into her coat pockets as she made her final play.

"There's one more thing I want to talk to you about," she called up to him as she saw him put his heels to his horse, to urge Dakota away. "It's about merging Galbraith's and DuBrand's. Legally. Permanently."

Dakota snorted and tossed his head belligerently as Grant abruptly countermanded the signal to move forward with a sharp pull back on the reins. He sat his prancing horse, his eyes narrowed as he looked at Ashley, standing below him. "Why would you want to talk about something like that?" he asked finally.

"Because I don't want Ben Geary's business." Ashley's fingernails were digging into the palms of her hands as she clenched them tightly, and she had to turn her head to one side briefly to escape the dust rising up from Dakota's hooves as he pranced about. Grant finally got his horse to stand still, and when Ashley looked back at him, her eyes were an open mirror of her heart. "Grant, I don't want to ruin your business!" she cried. "I don't! We can merge the two companies, it would work beautifully!"

He looked at her for a long moment in silence. "That's an absurd thing for you to do, Ashley," he said finally. "You've got absolute success right at your fingertips."

"I know," she responded immediately, "but I don't want it. Not if it has to be at your expense."

Grant was resting his weight with one hand on his thigh, and he gauged her a moment longer, then straightened, tightening up the reins once more. "Ashley, I thought you'd learned a long time ago to keep your personal feelings out of your business," he commented.

Ashley stared at him, dumbfounded, and then all of a sudden she absolutely exploded. "Personal feelings . . . !" she echoed incredulously, and her eyes widened even more as her hands came out of her pockets. "I'm standing down here handing over my company to you, doing everything I can to prove to you how much I mean it when I say I love you, and all you can do is give me a damn *lecture* on professional conduct!'' she exclaimed, totally incensed as she flung out a hand. She stared at him a moment longer, then abruptly spun in agitation, marching several yards away before pacing back to the same spot, her breath coming in audible pants as she glared up at him sitting motionlessly astride Dakota, just watching her now.

"I want to tell you a few things, Grant Copeland!" she stormed, her hand going to her hip as her chin snapped up. "I've been wrong. I've done things to you that were terrible. I've been irrational and stupid and in my way as cruel as I once accused you of being. I admit that. I *have* admitted that in the most straightforward and painfully open manner I know how. I've swallowed every bit of pride I ever had trying to tell you how I feel. Wearing that dress last night and not knowing how you'd react to it was the hardest thing I've ever done in my life, and following you all the way out here today was no easy thing either, but that's all right!" she allowed with a sharp dip of her head. "I had it coming to me. I deserved to suffer everything I have in my efforts to try and make up to you. I deserved what I had to go through to come to my senses in the first place. I even deserve some measure of censure and mistrust from you, but *not* to the degree you're giving it and *not* for the rest of my life!"

A flush had come into her face as she stood confronting him from the ground, her eyes glittering, her hair blowing lightly about her face. "I'm not the kind of person you're making me out to be—hopelessly untrustworthy, malicious!" she defended with a deep frown. "I'm just a person who went through a difficult time in her life and didn't always handle herself as well as she should have. Who made mistakes and who, yes, was once very weak. But I *don't* deserve to be judged by that for the rest of my life or to carry the burden of my mistakes in your eyes forever! ·

"And don't sit up there being so critical and self-righteously detached! You're not so perfect either!" she rampaged on, her distressed anger fueled all the more by the sight of Grant slowly pushing his Stetson up from his forehead as he eased back in the saddle. As he watched her, one corner of his mouth had begun to twitch.

"You blow your stack out of all proportion to reason sometimes, with me anyway!" she told him hotly. "And you haven't been right all the way down the line in this. You said things to me that day in your apartment you didn't have to say, that were just as cutting as some of the things I said to you. Jesus, Grant, you kicked a door shut right in my face!" she cried. "You were horrible! And look at you now!" she commanded, sweeping a hand up toward him. "You're doing just the same thing to me I did to you. I know you love me just as much as I love you, but you're not going to let yourself feel it because you're all hurt and won't let go of it. You don't let me explain a thing. You won't give me the least shred of the benefit of the doubt about anything. You didn't for one *second* last night offer me the chance to speak in my own behalf before you hauled off and threw a fit!" Both hands came to her hips. "You're so damn sure you know exactly what I'm doing when you don't know at all! I never insulted you in the paper and I never set you up with Ben. But you'll just be damned if you'll believe any of it! You'd rather just go on being unfair and unreasonable and pig-headed . . . !"

She stopped. Her anger was beginning to diffuse as exhaustion and frustration took hold, and she bit her lip when she saw Grant raise his eyebrows inquiringly at her pause. With an unhappy scowl, she tried to go on, brushing once in vexation at the lock of her dark hair falling down on one side of her forehead, but she got only so far as to mutter, "You're just as bad as I am," before breaking off entirely. Her indignation had suddenly turned to despair. It was no use; Grant was sitting as implacably as ever in that arms-folded position astride his horse, but even if she might have had some chance finally to reach him, she'd blown it now. What she'd wanted only to be a quiet, loving appeal had turned into a tirade against him, and as tears welled up in her eyes, she turned away abruptly; she wasn't going to let him see her cry. Not this time.

"Good-bye, Grant," she said in a choked voice back over her shoulder and walked briskly across the paddock to the gate, hurrying through it and back across the grassy lawn of Coconino that she was seeing for the last time. Putting one hand hard against her mouth to keep from openly sobbing until she could at least reach the car and get in to drive out of sight, she'd just come in line with the majestic pine shading one side of the ranch house when she was slowed abruptly by a hand on the back of her shoulder and then, in the very next instant—to her heart-stopping fright—swept right up off her feet. Hardly missing a beat, Grant kept on walking, Ashley now carried easily in his arms.

"My God!" Ashley had a hand to her pounding breast, her other arm encircling Grant's neck, and she looked up at him in wide-eyed shock. "Grant, you scared the living hell out of me!" she breathed.

"Nothing scares you, Ashley Welles," Grant said comfortably as he smiled caressingly down into her eyes. "Least of all me in my—what was it?—'self-righteous detachment'? And why did you quit?" he inquired mildly as he continued to walk with her in the direction of the house. "You were going so strong. I've never known you to stop right in the middle of telling someone off."

"Grant . . ." Ashley's eyes had grown suddenly uncertain and were searching his face; he lifted his eyebrows at her expression.

"What's the matter, you think I can't shape up, too?" he remarked. They'd reached the house by that time, and he took her right up onto the porch, setting her down there. He pulled her to him, holding her by the shoulders, and as she looked up with eyes imploring him to explain, her palms against his chest, he smiled quietly. "What I'm doing, Ashley, is saying that I'm sorry, too. That I've been wrong, too. Unfair, unreasonable, judging you harshly because I was letting my hurt rule me, too. I deserved every word you said to me, although"— he tried to frown, not having a great deal of success at it as a smile kept tugging at one side of his mouth—"pigheaded? I don't know about that one," he objected with a slow shake of his head.

Ashley's laughter started in her shoulders, then rose to her lips as her head fell back slightly. Her eyes were shimmering with tears of relief and happiness, and she put her hand up to his cheek. "Oh, Grant, I didn't really mean that!" she apologized lovingly. "I was just mad——"

"Sure you meant it," he countered with laughing eyes, and they stood looking at one another a moment longer, then suddenly fell into a tight embrace. She buried her face in his shoulder as he hugged her to him, and they simply held each other close for minutes, needing the physical release at the resolution. Finally, Grant's lips found hers, and they kissed deeply for a very long time. Grant was the one to finally break them apart, and as he eased his head up slightly, he rubbed her cheek with his.

"Did I forget to tell you last night that I love you?" he asked in a husky voice. Ashley nodded absently as she moved both hands up the sides of his neck and into his hair, her eyes caressing his face, and he pulled her up against him even more closely. "Well, I do," he murmured. They kissed again, and then pushing her away gently, Grant put his hands on the back of her shoulders and turned her toward the door. "Now come on, lady, get on into your house," he directed comfortably and began propelling her forward. "There are too many things to do around here to be fooling around out on the porch like this, and you and I have a business deal to discuss."

Epilogue

ASHLEY PUSHED OPEN the bedroom door with her elbow, then closed it behind her again with her bare foot as she came in carrying two long-stemmed glasses of wine, one in each hand. The loft room at Coconino was shadowy and warm, the light of the crackling fire in the small hearth across from the bed dancing around the rough-hewn paneled walls, and in the flowing blue satin dressing gown that was all she was wearing, she padded over to the bedside, handing one glass of wine to Grant. He was stretched out on the bed, resting with his back against the headboard, still wearing the trousers of his black evening suit, his white silk dress shirt unbuttoned all the way and falling open to bare his muscular chest, and as he accepted the glass with one hand, he took Ashley's hand with the other and drew her down beside him.

"It's cold down there with the fire out!" she said, shivering as she snuggled up against him, and she settled herself in the warm circle of his arm, smiling up at him. "The Redchiefs have gone to bed," she advised.

Grant sipped his wine and lowered the crystal glass to his leg as he kissed her lightly. "Michael said they were on their way when we came in," he answered, and after studying her face brightly illuminated on one side by the fire, he smiled in deep contentment. "Mrs. Copeland, did I tell you that you're a marvelous dancer?" he inquired.

"Several times tonight, but it's all right if you want to tell me again." She smiled sweetly, then kissed him.

"You're a marvelous dancer," he murmured.

"Thank you, but it's all in the lead." She shifted again, lying on her back beside him, and her eyes strayed up toward the ceiling. "And that has such a nice ring to it, you know?" she said serenely.

"What?"

"*Mrs.* Copeland," Ashley answered softly, and she was conscious of the simple turquoise band on her ring finger; Grant was wearing its mate on his left hand, where she'd placed it with the deepest love and quiet tenderness three weeks before. Grant said nothing, but simply let his eyes roam down the length of her stretched out gracefully along the beige coverlet, and after a moment, a small laugh escaped her.

"What's funny?" he asked.

"Oh, I was just thinking about the shock waves our wedding sent through Galbraith's and DuBrand's," she answered, reaching over to set her wineglass down on the pine bedside table. She smiled as she got comfortable again, her head on his shoulder, and she pictured Ollie's expression when she and Grant had quietly walked into his office and announced that they were married; he'd been stunned, and she'd let him go on thinking she'd fallen head over heels in love with Grant in a few weeks' time. He'd been too close to Ross for her to have ever felt comfortable telling him the whole story.

The wedding had been a simple civil ceremony in Flagstaff, taking place four days after she'd come to Coconino to talk to Grant, and only the two of them had attended, along with the necessary witnesses; they hadn't wanted anyone else there, for it had been a very private thing, their marriage—the righting of a wrong that had gone on for too long.

"Yes, we sent shock waves through the companies, and the whole damn industry," Grant agreed with a reflective smile of his own, and he leaned across her to set down his glass also, then began gently tracing the line of her forehead with one fingertip.

"Hmmm, we did," she murmured, and a flicker of regret passed across her face as she looked up at him. "You know, I'm sorry Karen felt she had to leave the company," she said. "She was a valuable employee, and I know she liked her work."

"It was inevitable. And better," Grant responded, the languorous look that had drifted into his face disappearing briefly as he eyed her. "You see, she doesn't have your capacity to be totally unbothered about the other women in my life," he commented.

Ashley tilted her head slightly, eyeing him back. "No, I guess she couldn't rise above something like that, the way I can," she answered and slipped her hand under the fabric of his open shirt, running it erotically across his bare chest. "And like you can." She sighed lightly as she gave him a guileless look.

Their teasing looks vanished as Ashley began to slide his shirt back over his shoulders. "I gather you're not planning on talking much longer," he commented.

Her glance up from her hands working at his shirt was sultry. "You looked uncomfortable, that's all." When Grant's shirt was all the way off, he settled back against her and began unknotting the sash of her dressing gown.

"There's one thing, though," he said as he got her belt undone and slid it from around her waist, dropping it over the side of the bed onto the floor. "You've got to see Tom Jenkins next week about signing over Ross's estate. He called while we were out tonight. Michael gave me the message when we got home. Apparently the papers are ready." His hand on her side rested there motionlessly as he grew momentarily serious. "Honey, you don't have to do this with Ross's money, you know. It doesn't really matter, in the whole scheme of things."

"It matters to me," she answered, looking off across the dim room as she laid her head in the crook of his shoulder and neck. "You know that, Grant. I want that chapter of my life closed completely. I don't want anything left tying me to it. And I like to think that Ross would have wanted to make a donation to cancer research," she added with a wistful sigh.

"This is one hell of a donation, the residue of the Galbraith estate," he remarked dryly.

Ashley moved back slightly to look quietly up to his face. "It's needed, Grant," she said intently. "And it's important to me, for Grif. It's the best thing I know to do with money I don't want for myself, and the facilities that are to be built will all be in Ross's name." She felt momentarily somber, but the brief melancholy left her as the love of her life again took hold of all her thoughts; she cuddled back to him closer, giving him a sudden smile. "Besides," she said, "I don't want to deprive you of the opportunity to be my sole provider. It'll be good for your ego," she added.

He drew his head back slightly to look at her, laughing. "My ego? What the hell does that have to do with anything?"

Ashley kept her eyes on her hand moving in a small, caressing circle near the triangle of bones in his throat. "Well, it's just that it got so badly trounced there for awhile when your ladylove nearly rousted you, that's all. I thought it might need a little soothing," she said sweetly, her eyes moving up to meet his slowly; though she pressed her lips together, her smile finally escaped.

He was fighting his own smile as he narrowed his eyes darkly on her. "You think that's funny, do you?" he inquired.

"It just infuriated you that I was the one who came close to finally doing in Grant Copeland," she answered comfortably and slipped her arms around his neck, looking impishly into his face. "That's what really had you so mad, wasn't it?"

His eyes were roaming her face. "What had me so mad was nearly being done in period, lady. Don't be so damn smug about it," he answered, and running his hand up into her hair, he gripped it gently and pulled her head back away from him. "And if you ever do something like that to me again . . ." He let the threat trail off, then kissed her hard. When he brought his lips from hers finally, he left his mouth just a breath away from hers. "You're one hell of a woman," he murmured. "And you know what had me really going? That you were working against me, not with me." His smile caressed her as she touched a loving fingertip to the scar on his cheek, and then he raised his head a little more, eyeing her again. "And I'm not sure I can afford to keep you, not in the manner to which you seem to have become accustomed. You've already got me spending a fortune building hunt fences all over my property, cluttering up my range just so you can work that animal you call a real horse."

Ashley laughed. Sharif had already been trucked out to Coconino and now occupied a remodeled box stall next to Dakota, his name, like Dakota's, inscribed on a bronze plaque attached to the door. "My horse *is* a real horse, not just some cow pony," she scoffed. "And I didn't demand that you build those fences all over your property, Grant Copeland. You started doing it all by yourself."

"Well, hell," he said, "I knew you were going to ask anyway!"

'Oh, that's not it at all!" Ashley dismissed, bringing her hands from around his neck to begin running them over his chest. "It's just your total adoration for me showing. *Admit* it!" she teased.

Grant's eyes darkened suddenly, and he cupped her chin, raising her face directly up to his. "I admit it," he said in a low voice.

A thrill of the deepest kind went all the way through Ashley at the emotion in Grant's expression, and she sud-

denly pulled herself against him, hugging him again tightly.
"I love you, Grant," she whispered into his shoulder. He
didn't answer with words, but put his lips to her neck, and
Ashley arched it toward him, letting her hands drift down to
his back. He kissed her lightly, pushing the robe back from
her shoulders, and after a time, Ashley smiled absently, her
eyes closed. "How do you suppose the world is going to take
the next Copeland announcement?" she mused in a murmur.

Grant didn't raise his lips from her as he shifted the two of
them down further on the bed, away from the headboard, and
he pushed the robe down over the point of her shoulder,
kissing her smooth skin there. "I imagine everyone will be
just as stunned when we tell them we're selling the company
as they were over our marriage and the merger."

"Hmmm." Ashley trailed her fingernails down Grant's
back, smiling in pleasure when she felt the shudder run
through him, and as his kisses on her throat became more
urgent, she strained against him reflexively. "Do you think
we ought to tell them why we're doing it?" she asked absently. Grant didn't answer, and she smiled again. "No, you're
right. It isn't anyone's business but our own. They probably
wouldn't understand anyway," she added and thought about
what she and Grant, as a professional couple, were about to
do: sell their now-massive auction empire because it no longer
offered them the challenge that it had. It was time for them to
move on. Challenge, Ashley thought; she would chase it with
Grant Copeland for as long as she lived, loving it as he did,
loving him as he did her. She felt his lips leaving her body
and opened her eyes to look up at him.

"And so, my darling," she said softly, raising her hand up
to his face, "just what do you think the Copelands are going
to go on to next?"

"Nothing for awhile. Professionally, that is. They're going
to be honeymooning on the ranch." His eyes had grown
heavy with desire, and he ran one finger along the edge of her
robe, ever so slightly touching her breast. Abruptly, he slid
his entire hand beneath the fabric, and in one long motion
down her side, he swept the robe back from her, baring her
entire body to him.

Ashley's breath left her; her own desire flooded over her,
and as she saw Grant's smile of ardent pleasure at the sight of
her, her hands went to the clasp of his trousers. He helped her
with it, then to remove them, and when he was again lying

beside her on the bed, his hard, masculine body naked against hers, she slipped all the way out of her robe. ''Love me,'' she breathed, reaching for him. He moved onto her as her arms slid hungrily around his neck, his passionate eyes holding hers beneath him, and he put both hands at the sides of her head and gripped her hair.

''I'll always love you,'' he answered, by the low light of the crackling fire, in the room that was theirs to share for the rest of their lives.

Chasing Rainbows

A novel of love, enduring courage and soaring triumph!

BY
ESTHER SAGER

They grew up on a lush estate in Virginia—Winna, the selfish blonde beauty, and Libby, the lovable auburn-haired lass. Then, at ten, an accident left Libby to face life against towering odds. Yet Libby is a survivor, and it is she who captures the heart of sophisticated Adam Bainbridge.

Suddenly Winna invades their perfect world—with malice and betrayal in her heart. Libby and Adam must learn that love is, like a rainbow, so very hard to catch and keep.

————— 05849-1 CHASING RAINBOWS $2.95

Available at your local bookstore or return this form to:

JOVE/BOOK MAILING SERVICE
P.O. Box 690, Rockville Center, N.Y. 11570

Please enclose 75¢ for postage and handling for one book, 25¢ each add'l. book ($1.50 max.). No cash, CODs or stamps. Total amount enclosed: $ _____ in check or money order.

NAME _____

ADDRESS _____

CITY _____ STATE/ZIP _____

Allow six weeks for delivery.   SK-15

Bestselling Books
for Today's Reader —
From Jove!

___**THE AMERICANS**   05432-1/$2.95
John Jakes
___**BURIED BLOSSOMS**   05153-5/$2.95
Stephen Lewis
___**FIFTH JADE OF HEAVEN**   04628-0/$2.95
Marilyn Granbeck
___**HAND-ME-DOWNS**   06425-4/$2.95
Rhea Kohan
___**NIGHTWING**   06241-7/$2.95
Martin Cruz Smith
___**SHIKE: TIME OF THE DRAGONS**   06586-2/$3.25
(Book 1) Robert Shea
___**SHIKE: LAST OF THE ZINJA**   06587-0/$3.25
(Book 2) Robert Shea
___**A SHARE OF EARTH AND GLORY** 04756-2/$3.50
Katherine Giles
___**THE WOMEN'S ROOM**   05933-1/$3.50
Marilyn French
___**YELLOW ROSE**   05557-3/$3.50
Shana Carrol

Available at your local bookstore or return this form to:

J **JOVE/BOOK MAILING SERVICE**
P.O. Box 690, Rockville Center, N.Y. 11570

Please enclose 75¢ for postage and handling for one book, 25¢ each
add'l. book ($1.50 max.). No cash, CODs or stamps. Total amount
enclosed: $ _____ in check or money order.

NAME _____

ADDRESS _____

CITY _____ STATE/ZIP _____
Allow six weeks for delivery.   SK 23